Colony's Dawn

Book One of the New Europa Trilogy

N Joseph Glass

Monocle Books, N. Joseph Glass

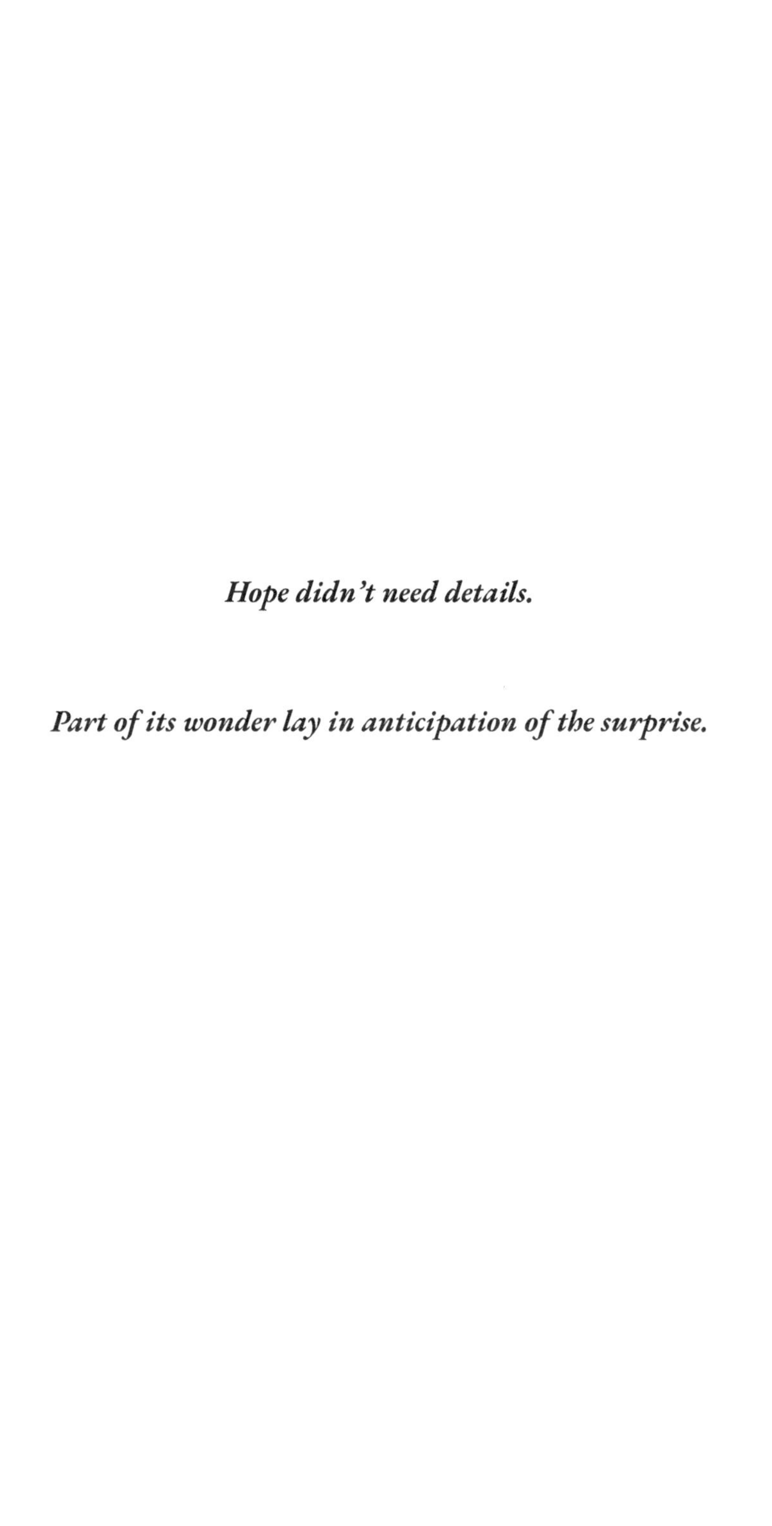

Hope didn't need details.

Part of its wonder lay in anticipation of the surprise.

| RAFFAELLA |

The woman in the mirror lied to Gift. Raff didn't love that she did it, but she didn't wish to divulge the nature of her evening—a covert rendezvous with persons unknown, grouped together with intentions she couldn't begin to guess. Baffled as to how she'd reached this point, she stared into her reflection, searching for clarity.

Dressed but unsure she was ready to go, Raff's mind drifted through memories of the last few weeks in search of answers...

As a data operator, Raffaella had been performing her duties examining data packet logs. Anomalies had been seen in the data flow that looked to be residual code to be discarded, yet she couldn't shake the *feeling* this was unlike anything else she had seen. Few could have caught it, and it was not likely Raff's bench-mate did. Claudia wrote excellent code but gave less focus to the monitoring tasks. The clarity of data ordinarily flowed as a stream reflected in Raff's jade green eyes, but this became a challenge to decode. Unsure what she had found, Raff kept it from her colleague, letting Claudia ramble on about some song she liked which Raff considered *noise*.

Pieces of chatter in the data stream, she pondered. If those bits could be compiled, they'd resemble an outdated form of... *Chat!* Encrypted text chat fragments sent in the data stream, nearly impossible to detect. No reason why independent text-based chat code would be hidden in plain sight came to her. To investigate away from Claudia's curiosity, Raff took home a hand terminal. Determined to find answers, she pored over the logs, letting the hours pass in search of an idea. Unable to decode the encrypted data, she could append a tiny information string onto one of the packets—her terminal ID. Her joy deflated in the realization she had been replaying old streams long after the data stopped. For the plan to work, she'd have to catch live chat data.

The next day while performing her usual tasks, Raff's device found the code and appended her terminal ID to one of the chat packets. Then came the hard part: waiting. The *nothing* that happened for two days was excruciating. No more chat noise. Plausibly, the chatters got spooked at being found out and she would never know. Something worse than waiting.

The corner of her eye noticed a small red dot on her device vying for her attention. When her biometrics unlocked it, the screen filled with an archaic looking app. A message in block letters appeared on the top half of an otherwise empty white box.

- R: Who are you?

With a sly smirk on her face, Raff replied, "Don't you know?" When nothing happened, she considered the keyboard filling the lower half of the screen below the text. *How quaint*, she thought. It took a few tries to enter letters on the tiny qwerty keyboard with two thumbs—she found it most inefficient.

- \>Don't you know?

- R: Hello Raffaella.

The device shook in her hand as she raised it from the floor, all but dropping it a second time. Soon she realized *they* were more than one. It was a group chat, but the nature of the group remained a mystery. Then the questions came.

> - B: Have you seen anything odd?
>
> - R: What do you think about the rations?
>
> - S: How many water recyclers supply the colony?

With no suitable replies, she decided to press her luck.

> - >Can we meet? I have so many questions.
>
> - B: Tomorrow 18:45. Piazza San Marco. Alone!

Raff pulled herself from the memory and apprehensive legs shakily carried her to Piazza San Marco. Amid a sea of residents, she stood alone in the center of Citadome Three. A hand from behind grabbed her elbow and warm breath on her ear said, "Don't turn, walk."

In a narrow alleyway she found four nameless faces standing before her with invasive looks. The hand and warm breath came from a tall, plump, middle-aged fellow with thinning black hair and a scraggly beard. Beside him stood a redheaded slender woman around thirty, Raff suspected, with a pointy nose separating stunning eyes a deeper green than her own. On Red's left, the skinny kid looked sixteen at most. Last was a short, gruff man with thick graying hair, scowling as he spoke. "How did you find the chat?"

"I analyze the data stream." After a pause, Raff added, "It's my job."

"It's hidden," the aged man barked.

"I'm good."

The redhead lifted her heels. "Untraceable. Impossible to assemble or decrypt. No one is *that* good."

Must be the chat program code writer, Raff deduced. "*Vero*. I didn't say I traced it or assembled it. And I didn't even try to decrypt it."

"How'd you know to tag your device ID on a packet then?"

"I knew it was some type of basic chat code."

"*Basic*?" The coder scowled under the red bangs, obviously insulted by the remark.

"*Elegantly* basic, I mean. Chat using no voice or video to identify its users. Very smart. Encrypted text in random chatter packets in the data. Brilliant, Red. Hidden in plain sight."

"But *you* found it." The skinny boy drew a glare from the older guy, suggesting the kid was there to observe.

"Yes. She. Did." Red spoke with hints of admiration lacing her words.

The gray-headed man said, "Tell her."

An information dump spewed suspicions on various aspects of colony life they believed to be fabrications. '*All lies*,' they repeated after each supposed revelation of a concealed truth.

"We know nothing about the other colonies."

"Rationing is messed up, it's overly strict."

"They're manipulating us though medical injections."

"Our whole lives are being controlled."

Then the big one came, a theory to end all others: "It's safe to go outside and has been for years." That one resonated with Raff since the terraforming project was fifty years from Phase One Livability. She wondered, *Are these folks on to something or just flat-out nuts?* She needed answers.

"What now? What do we do about any of it?"

Answers varied, but none brought her to a good place.

"Time to take action."

"Get the truth out there."

"Sabotage. We need to prove it."

That last one tightened in Raff's intestines, and her throat went dry. She didn't want to be there any longer, and these people started to scare her. "*Allora...*" she stretched the word on the O and held her chin. "This is a lot. Let me process everything you've told me."

"*Sure,*" the pudgy guy said with slight condescension. "Take a few days. Just don't tell anyone about us."

Red hoisted her eyebrows. "Um, or the chat. No one learns about the chat."

The older man tugged the corner of his eye with a thumb and Raff got the significance: *We're watching you.*

*****

As Raff walked home lost in wonder, old history lessons popped like flashbulbs in her head for the first time in ages. When the so-called Doomsday Clock was set to 90 seconds to midnight, the scientific community had all but given up on Earth. Within a decade they considered its environment too far gone. That was the final catalyst for political leaders to push forward the colonization project that brought man from the blue and green jewel to a red rock. She wasn't sure what meaning she hoped to find in two hundred fifty-year-old events thought forgotten. Colony life was all she and everyone else ever knew, ever would. In childhood Raff had learned of the project's beginning and its glorious goal of forging the red planet into their new paradise home. It was expected the *maintenance period* would be the most challenging phase on Earth's progeny.

She thought of the First Ones, who finished colony construction. They had survived, migrated across the stars, and forged a new destiny for humanity. The final generation in the colony would live under the bright light of shining hope for stepping outside and starting life on the surface. But for those in between, life was the colony and nothing else, from birth to departure. The solidity of the domes and walls meant they would never see the sky. For the first time, Raff learned not everyone was content to fill that role.

1 | DAY ONE

"Buongiorno." Her eyes squinted under bright overhead lighting as Gift offered her standard morning greeting entering the sizable open workspace that included her bench. A high hand wave joined a glance to her left, only to realize Raff hadn't arrived. Her cheeks flushed red. Likely everyone saw through her attempt to act like it was a general, *good morning*, to all the benches. Her bench-mate Mike arrived shortly after her, putting a smile on her lips.

"How are you, sweetie?"

"Same old. You?"

"Wonderful." The word reflected her relentless enthusiasm for the everyday. "Had a great evening. I finally got with Mom, been a while. She made Egusi soup, and the aroma filled the corridor. I'm not sure all her neighbors enjoyed that bit."

"For sure. Many don't appreciate Nigerian food."

"I remember your face when you tried some of Mom's Jollof." Gift giggled. "That's much tamer than her soup. You provided quite a bit of laughter for us. And poor you, spent most of the night in the toilet box. Last time I gave you anything *spicy*."

Much of the day brought mundane maintenance tasks. A matter of finding the damaged part and replacing it. Gift had a knack for it and enjoyed her work as an engineer. Completing such repairs scratched a life-long itch to put things right and align them. Routine tasks meant doing that, so they were fine. Keeping two-hundred-year-old equipment in working order was vital to their survival and filling that role gave Gift a sense of purpose.

New Europa's six huge concrete and metal domes and the passageways connecting them made up Gift's whole world. Her eyes often fixated on the celestial curve of its domed ceilings. Painted pale blue with dull yellow trim, they were open and spacious. Well-lit in the daytime and slightly dimmed in the evening, she had been taught it promoted mental health by mimicking the natural light exposure of living on Earth. On occasion, the onset of 'claustrophobic madness' resulting from living in such a finite space overcame a resident. Like a child in her mother's arms, Gift found comforting security in the constraints that outlined her life.

Too many times she had heard Mike's conspiracy theories, that to others, colony life felt like wearing a straitjacket. Some yearned to *live*, to have a freedom they could only imagine. A freedom he said they didn't have, insisting the Management of the colony had been keeping substantial secrets from the residents, controlling their lives. More than once, Mike warned social unrest was building. Gift tried her best to dismiss it.

Their years on the bench brought them close despite Mike's annoying tendencies. The caddy beside his terminal display, always a mess of tools, had spare parts tossed in such a way Gift marveled at how he could find anything. Hers were all lined up, exactly in their proper places. Working as close as they did, often too close as he took more than his one-meter half of the gray bench's surface, they'd become best mates.

"That's it," Mike said in victory. "Look at this one."

"Whatcha got there?"

Pointing with narrow-end pliers to the circuit board he'd been tinkering on, his face oozed with excitement. *"That."*

Gift leaned over for a closer look. "Burned-out chip. Seemed a struggle to find it, hidden right there in the center, nothing over it and all." A snort escaped as she tried not to laugh at her own wit. "And it's still there, so… nice work?"

"*Exactly*." His gesture inadvertently brought the pliers too close for comfort, jerking Gift's head back. "Sorry… But watch this."

As he inserted a low volt connector to the module's rear port and switched it on, Gift meant to say *Don't* but went speechless when the sparks she expected hadn't ignited. Relieved ears welcomed the familiar low hum of a functioning circuit panel. "But how?" Beyond that question, Gift wondered, *What's that chip I've never seen, and how'd it get there in the first place?* In the recesses of her mind, she squashed notions of foul play.

Over crossed arms, Mike raised his chin. "It's a dummy redundant chip."

"You made that up. What the heck even is a dummy redundant chip? If it's dummy, there's no redundancy. If it's redundant, then it's not dummy." With a widened smile she added, "Also too, there's no dummy chips. *Dummy*."

"Have a look." Sliding off his stool Mike held his open palm toward the module.

"Dang, Mike, you're right. This chip shouldn't even be on this board. It's only getting weak current to justify its existence. Bravo." A congratulatory slap landed on his back.

"So, what do I do about it?"

"Swap out the chip and send it back. Log it."

"Way to take all the *umph* out of my triumph." He often lost her in his expressions.

***

When Raffaella joined the lunch table in the Dome Four workers cafeteria, Tina had started eating and Mike and Gift shared a laugh at something between themselves, as they often did. Charlie played with his *Pasta in Brodo*. Recently joined in Union, he had pulled away a little from the group as Sakura occupied much of his free time, which Gift considered proper for a new Union, so it was fine.

"*Pasta in Brodo*, Charlie?" With a smile Raff added, "Nice choice."

"Yeah, it's not bad."

"What'd I miss?" While Raff spoke to the table, her eyes found Gift and Mike. No secret to Gift, Raff watched their friendship with concern for signs of it morphing into romance. Mike was much too young, and Gift had a couple of years to go, so she dismissed it. Romantic notions didn't begin before G.M. She tried to see Raff's concern as protective care and love, though at times, it felt a tad smothering.

"*Ciao Bella*," Gift said from a smile. "Nothing much. Just remembering when he started trying to grow the boy-beard."

"Who could forget that?" The lightness in Raff's tone didn't match the stiff green eyes still fixed on the pair.

Though she'd come to appreciate it on him, Gift never stopped teasing Mike about his beard. It had grown slowly and uneven, making his already round babyface resemble a boy who hadn't yet had his first shave. Once it had filled in—always kept short and well-trimmed—Gift found it gave him a mature stature.

"How's Sakura, Charlie?" Raff asked what Gift had been thinking. They hadn't seen Charlie's partner in weeks.

"Good, yeah. Same. Busy as ever in Medical. She asks about you lot all the time. We'll pitch up at the next dinner, hopefully."

The first of Gift's friends to join in Union, Charlie did it young, at thirty-two. It made Gift grateful Raff, six years Charlie's senior, hadn't. Selfish for their time together, Gift basked in the warmth and security of

Raff not rushing her transition. It felt like how Gift imagined having a big sister.

"Who's for noodles this evening?" Tina had missed several dinners as well.

"Sorry. Dinner with my parents."

Puzzled by the way Raff's hasty reply lowered her head, Gift collected everyone's plates as she did almost every day unless Mike beat her to it. He often tried. For Gift, she couldn't have the empty containers, forks, and napkins strewn over the table. The sight made the back of her head just above the base of the skull hurt—quelled by the restoration of symmetry.

Towering over Mike and Gift, Tina hissed, "So, no one for Noodles then?"

"What, no *mystery* man this evening?"

"Shut it, Mikey." An obvious irritant, Mike's question pulled Tina's shoulders back. She kept her relationship a closely guarded secret, not even sharing his name with the group. Sensing an oncoming argument, Gift confirmed on their behalf. He didn't object. Tina relaxed her shoulders, easing Gift's anxiety. "Perfect. Nineteen thirty. See you kids there."

2

Tuesday was a shower day for Gift, one of only two per week. Strick water rationing safeguarded such a precious resource on a planet with none to offer. Everyone had two water showers a week and an extra, for any reason, cost ten rations.

Gift had one additional shower in her adult life when her first bench-mate, Luca, spilled nano resin on her. The middle-aged man offered more attention to her coverall hugging her backside each time she leaned forward for a tool than he had ever given to his work. The paper-thin disposable she had to wear the rest of that workday didn't help dissuade his eyes. A young girl in her first years of independence, an innocent sixteen, ogled daily. A decade later, the memory still brought her chills.

All six pale gray square meters of Box B34 were Gift's. She had chosen to accent it in blue and had one sad little green plant on the shelf by her faux window. A foldout bed wall opposite a video wall, both with storage bins, ran front to back. The small kitchenet in the rear had a sonic sink, food warmer, hob, and cabinets. It was cozy, it was home, and standard issue for everyone when they got their work assignment at sixteen. Unless she pulled her bed down to have dinner while watching a vid, Gift lifted the table and unfolded the chairs from under the vid screen to eat. Countless episodes of MSS Banzai had been rewatched over her dinner plate. Set in the future where humankind lived on the terraformed surface and explored the galaxy in the implausible spacecraft bearing the titular name—a spaceship capable of faster-than-light speed and artificial gravity—Gift found it enjoyably foolish.

"*Ciao Gift,*" came from the slim opening of Marco's shy smirk. The boy from Box B36, directly beside hers, arrived home about when Gift headed for the shower in her robe. Gift suspected he tried to make the happenstance happen often. The young man moved in a few months back when Mister Norbert reached ninety-eight. His awkwardness, Gift assumed, sprang from inexperience talking with adult women.

Union was forbidden until thirty, when GnRH-M—commonly known as Gen-Maturity and called by most G.M.—typically occurred, give or take. Social dating before thirty was discouraged and growing up in the colony meant very few children of the same age group to help each other hone their social skills. Some young men showed premature curiosity and gawked at a pretty woman here or there—not typical in pre-G.M., but not unheard of either. Marco's attention never creeped Gift, but often brought her back into a memory...

There were five in their adolescent group. The juvenile boys gave an occasional look over their female friends, but nothing beyond idle curiosity. While Aimée seemed to enjoy the attention, Gift did not. It had been years since they all left for their work assignments, their contributions to the colony. At sixteen, Aimée was the oldest and the first to go. Gift next, a few months past her fifteenth with Sammy approaching his. Tomas at thirteen with little Matteo so close to twelve he'd already started saying it. Gift met up with Aimée often for dinner and long *catch-up* chats. Though she didn't see Sammy or Tomas, Matteo got with her when their schedules allowed, and Gift cherished their annual tradition of an evening watching vids together in his Box.

Kind greetings floated to and from familiar faces along the way to the shower box. As she passed the clothes hopper, Gift discreetly deposited her dirty underwear to be cleaned and packaged and made ready for pick up at the Laundry Service in her block's passageway. No rations were deducted for standard laundry.

Ahead of Gift, a nameless man of nearly two meters chatted up the giggly woman second in line, Sara. When he turned to her—chiseled jawline, blue eyes, lush blond hair—Gift thought, *Who are you, gorgeous?*

"Max."

Gift's cheeks reddened. *Please tell me I didn't say that out loud.*

"We haven't met, I'm Max."

"Oh. *Ciao...* Gift, I'm Gift."

"I'm sure *you* are." The obvious and overused pun on her name came with a devilish smile and gleaming eyes that panned down her standard issue yellow robe. "Nice robe." His gaze flooded her with memories of Luca.

"Oh, um. *Oh?* It's just, just... like everyone's."

His head shook slowly. "No. You are *not* like everyone."

Ogling and flirtation felt misplaced on her, discomforting. It was not fine. She couldn't know why, but she felt uneasy around this guy she'd never seen in the queue previously. There had been only one change of the eight assigned to this shower slot when Meredith reached ninety-eight and Stanley replaced her two years back. Who was this guy and why was she so unsettled by him? The shower box door opened, releasing eight nameless and freshly cleaned fellow residents.

"Anyway, nice meeting you, Gift." In one fluid move he turned and wrapped his arms around Sara from behind and followed her to the shower box's door until she pushed him away playfully. Only then did Gift realize he wasn't in a shower robe. He stood in the queue to be with Sara. *In Union? Did Sara get joined? Did she not notice his blatant flirtation?*

When the door sealed behind them, booths filling the left and right walls with eight bodies to eight shower stalls in the shower box was perfectly symmetrical. Gift loved the clean feeling begotten by the freshly sanitized slightly blue frosted glass, but not as much as the modesty panels that allowed her out of and back into her robe unashamed. Waiting for the spray of suds, Gift couldn't understand why negative thoughts of Sara occupied her mind. Other Unions, like Charlie's with Sakura, never brought such musings. Why would Sara's Union with Max be bad, causing such an adverse reaction in her?

Back in her Box, she plucked the coverall from the sonic sink. The fabric cycle had it dry and odorless, ready for the next day. Folded neatly, Gift put it away in the tilt-out bin on the wall. "What to wear?" The question asked to no one always had the same reply. The temperature hovered about two degrees too high for her, so Gift strolled into the spoke between Citadomes Two and Three in her standard shorts and tee-shirt. Most residents called the wide passageways connecting domes *spokes*. The earliest memories of New Europa were a near-perfect match for the ones made that day, and Gift found comfort in its permanence. She walked by the same habitat blocks and resident service centers and shops as in every spoke. Passing a small commissary, which allowed the purchase of basic food items with rations, reminded Gift of the colony's fair economic system where, no matter the work assignment, all colonists got the same monthly stipend.

Having arrived first, Mike picked a square table with four seats and sat there in the open piazza with a goofy grin. Tina hadn't arrived. They'd sit in an imbalanced configuration. After taking a seat on a small round table with three chairs, Gift waved him over. "Right. Sorry." He knew better but sometimes forgot. A soft smile offered Gift's forgiveness.

Tina arrived and stood between them, a palm on each of their heads. "Let's get food." She never hesitated with food. At the noodle stand, patterned after street vendors of old Japan, a broad German man named Gunther made the noodles in two options: soup bowl or stir-fry. Tina ordered first. "One of each, please. No protein in the soup, double in the stir-fry."

Gunther's eyebrows crawled up his forehead. "That's eight extra rations, you know?" She nodded with a wide smile as she paid with biometrics. Mike ordered a stir-fry while Gift opted for soup, and each paid in the same manner. With behavioral biometrics no ID or physical currency were needed in the colony.

"Splurging a bit, eh Tina?"

Tina sucked in the wad of noodles draped over her chin. "I got it covered, Mikey. I'm taking two night shifts this week and each gets me twenty bonus rations."

A slow eater, Gift often took lukewarm last bites. Watching Tina inhale her soup and finish sucking down the stir-fry noodles caused Gift to wonder if she ever savored the taste of a meal. It didn't seem likely, though satisfaction shone from Tina's face whenever she downed her last.

Looking at her friend, Gift considered how G.M. came on the early side of average for Tina. Navigating the unfamiliar territory of her first courtship, Tina may have been unsure and scared of new feelings. Each of them had reached physical maturity years ago, but hormonally, Gift and Mike were like preadolescent children and couldn't relate. When the slow eater sucked her last noodle and sipped the last of the broth, she asked Mike to take their stuff to the recyclers and find them an espresso. Though Tina was rich in rations, he didn't object. With the coffee bar located across the dome, Gift had time alone with Tina. Even if overbearing at times, she would have preferred Raff's sage advice, but Tina had nearly three years more experience than herself and was there.

"Tina, may I ask you something?"

"You just did. Now you may ask me something else." Tina overused that joke and snickered each time.

Hesitation stalled Gift and fear of the topic clasped her tongue. The implications overwhelmed her. She leaned in with an open mouth, but no words came. A second attempt found words but struggled to string them together. "How old were you? When... when you started? I mean. *Allora*. When, when you—"

"When I started getting the hots for guys?"

Gift's cheeks flushed red. "Well, yeah. I mean... *Hots...*? Gen-Maturity, it's called. G.M."

"Earlier this year, just before my thirtieth. *So...*? Who is it? *Oh*. Oh, please not Mike, tell me it's not."

Pumping her palms, Gift pushed the assumption away. "No, there's no one."

"Whew. Okay then, go on."

"But... how? What did? I mean?" Unable to form coherent thoughts, Gift found the uselessness of her brain unfamiliar.

"My dear Gift, it will just happen when it happens. Don't overanalyze it. *Look who I'm talking to.* Don't try to rationalize everything. You can't out-think feelings and new emotions, line them up all neat and make sense of 'em. Just go with it."

"Just go with what?" Mike's voice arrived ahead of the espresso's aroma.

"Niente. Tina was telling me about the new spicy sauce for the noodles." Gift didn't like how easily that lie came to mind and slipped through her lips but didn't want Mike joining the topic.

"Too hot for me. Anyway, an espresso for you both."

Did Tina's words help clarify the matter? Gift was nearly three years younger than Tina had been when she reached G.M. and exceptions before twenty-nine were unheard of. *Twenty-six? It's way too early for me.* She tried suppressing it, reducing her reaction to this Max guy to nothing more than adolescent curiosity like Tomas, Sammy, cute little Matteo, and now Marco. That thought brought comfort, so she accepted it.

"Ping-pong?"

"Sure, Mikey. I'll embarrass you. Come on, boy."

Gift raised her hand and named herself *Ref*.

When Tina declared victory, Mike shrugged it off. Of course, he didn't mind winning either. "Gift, take the loser?"

Grabbing the tiny paddle from Tina's hand—now significantly larger in her own—Gift said, "Sure." In no time, Mike had a commanding lead.

"Twenty-one, twelve." Mike announced victory gently. Gift enjoyed the game and didn't mind losing, the fun of play remained.

Occupation of her thoughts with pleasant distractions ended with the game, as if relinquishing the paddle gave her mind permission to resume its former course. Why could she not stop the thoughts of Max? And how had Sara become an enemy? Gift never had an enemy. She thought she should talk to Raff or her mom. *Maybe James Müller?* Clarity evaded her, and the randomness of her reflections hurt that spot in the brain where disorder and chaos often struck.

It was not fine.

3

Dinner and ping-pong brought them to an hour from Lights-Out. Gift imagined everyone appreciated the guidelines. Those running New Europa taught its founding tenets well—inculcated in little minds eager to learn—primary of those being, *For the good of the Colony*. Never considering Lights-Out a curfew, the restriction hardly felt oppressive or suffocating to Gift. Turning off dome and spoke lights saved resources, allowed a good night's sleep, and contributed to the best efforts on their work duties the next day.

Tina offered a cordial *goodnight* and departed toward Dome Six and Mike walked Gift home. As they entered Gift's passageway, Mike's sudden stop stopped her. His lowered eyes directed her attention to a service kiosk with *All Lies* scribbled over its screen. The plant-based fluorescent ink message, invisible in the daytime, glowed when the display switched to evening mode backlighting. *"See?"*

"Yep, seen bunches lately." Her head swiveled emphatically from side to side as Gift tried rubbing the ink from the kiosk with the end of her tee shirt. It seemed determined to stay there. A deliberate nod accompanied Mike's lips saying, *Exactly,* without the audible word escaping. He grabbed her hand, stopping its futile action. "A little vague, no?" Gift said, pulling her hand away. It didn't return to the work of wiping the ink—too tedious. "All lies? What lies? Not exactly specific. Seems pointless to me."

"The whole thing, everything. Our lives. It's *all* a lie."

"Conspiracy nonsense. Don't start with that again. Stuff like that? It would have left us to die on Earth two hundred years ago. You know, lots of poor souls *stayed?* Sought shelter in caves and old government bunkers. Listened to those stupid idiots. Likely died a few months after we left them. You're not buying into this crap, are you?"

Colonial history taught children about natural disasters, rising sea levels, climate crisis, and the global economic collapse. Governments failed and those who took over completed the colonization project with unprecedented international cooperation. From prototypes constructed on Earth, as Gift had learned, five colonies were built on Mars. Transport ships had carted 'coffins' of near-dead humans in stasis across the void to their new home. First Ones, those who did the finishing work the auto-construct machines couldn't do, became the first residents, pioneers of the new frontier. The tutors were less vocal about those left behind.

Mike put a finger over Gift's lips in a hush gesture. "Not so loud. Talk like this makes people *disappear*. You'll see."

"What do you imagine we'll see? I don't—"

The sight of two approaching black uniforms truncated her words. Gift thought their pants were cool—so many pockets. Typically, kiosks and moss panels were more notable than administration guard personnel but these two were running toward them. Never had she seen them doing much beyond strolling by, keeping the peace—a peace that needed little keeping in the tranquil colony. From the corner of his closed mouth, Mike said, "Now you've done it."

Both froze as the guards approached and ran by. In unison, they spun around. What could have called them to action in the cool pants and clumsy vests? Cautiously Mike and Gift held several meters back when the guards reached the arch to habitat blocks Nine through Twelve. "In there," a female voice said. Both black-clad guards ran into the block. Helpless to the novelty, the two observers moved to the archway. Despite the temptation to go into the block, trepidation overpowered Gift's curiosity.

"What the heck?" Gift whispered with the tremble of anxious excitement. "You think it could be... black market?"

"As good a guess as any. Been rumors about water and food supplements. Or those euphoric drops—they're big now too. Supposed to calm 'claustrophobic panic.' Not sure I buy that."

"I didn't think those were real. Water, sure, cost half the rations." Gift didn't like that she knew that and frowned at the memory of benefiting from it once. Matteo had confessed a source for water and insisted she take a bag home. Along with the water came guilt as she felt *she* had done the wrong, that accepting it condoned the unlawful deed. She drank the water—better than wasting it.

"It's real. But who knows what's in that crap."

"Also too, our meds have all the chemicals we need."

"This is wild. I told you. What're they doing up there?"

"I've heard the rumors." Unsettling as they were, Gift dismissed them. People allegedly going missing, guards detaining innocent people. "Never seen guards move so fast or like... at all."

"Shh. I think they're coming."

Footsteps loudened. One set of feet clambered intermittently with erratic noises that reminded Gift of scrubbing the floor of her Box in long sweeping motions. An idea moved her hand to wave Mike over to her side of the archway and wrap her arms around him, moving her hands in wide circles over his back—it was mechanical, robotic.

"What the heck?"

"Play along... So they don't think we're here just to see what they're doing."

The clever ploy worked as intended, though the guards were so occupied the deception wasn't needed. They emerged from the corridor dragging a young woman whose legs came along despite their best efforts to flail in every other direction. Her angry grunts formed themselves into words of protest. "Let me go. You have no right. I didn't do anything."

"Shut it."

Ignoring the gruff male guard, she added volume to her outburst. "Let. Me. *Go.*"

"You have been inciting people and spreading lies. It's criminal activity."

"*Criminal?*" Their captive objected to the woman's word choice. "I scribbled on a few kiosks. That you react like *this* only proves the point."

The giant male captor raised the hand he had under the girl's arm, lifting her toward his face. "The only lies are the ones you're spreading."

His partner reached inside a pocket on her security vest, withdrawing what resembled a medical hypo-stick, and placed it against the young woman's neck. She went limp.

"Bout time, thanks. Getting annoying, that."

"Way too much voice. She can save it for the admins."

The brawny guy lifted the petite, pendulous body over one shoulder and wrapped his thick arm around her legs, ending the scene as they walked away leaving the onlookers locked in an awkward embrace, carrying on the unnecessary charade. In unison they let go and observed the vandal's frizzy black hair bouncing as the large man strode, the girl's arms swaying side to side with each step.

Beyond puzzled, Gift asked, "What *was* that?"

"Exactly what I told you. I told you you'd see, now you saw. People get *disappeared* when they speak against the authority in this colony."

"They were taking her for questioning by the admins, not *disappearing* her. What does that even mean?"

"Don't be so naïve, Gift," he hissed. "She wrote those *All Lies* messages and got caught. They don't tolerate challenging the status quo. It's rebellion to them."

Seeking to find words to make sense of it all, Gift paused. "But... I mean, if it riles people up? It disrupts normalcy. Life is good. I mean, it's fine, the same as it's been for two centuries. This nonsense they're spreading... only causes problems. Why are they trying to ruin it for the rest of us?"

Mike exhaled a long sigh. "Ruin what, Gift? If they're keeping stuff from us? Like, suppose they built our way of life on secrets and lies. We have a right to know."

"What lies could they be talking about? Our life is good, I mean, for us, we have a *good* life here. The Founders who started it gave us that. But that's not enough for these people. Why isn't it enough?"

"Because we deserve the truth." If his matter-of-fact delivery aimed to make his words irrefutable, it didn't. "It isn't about the past. Oh, and those people who stayed behind? They didn't make a *choice*. It wasn't from falling for conspiracy theories. Grow up, Gift. No more than fifty-one thousand per colony—there wasn't *room* for everyone. We're here now and this... this is about now... How they control us. Lights-Out, rations, work assignments. Every aspect of our lives is being dictated at every step. *That affects us*."

"Mike, the truth is our life is what it is and it's fine. I love my life. And these people are only trying to mess it up for us. Please, let's just drop this and go home."

A wedge formed between them for the first time, and the knot in Gift's stomach warned her of its potential danger. This exceeded mere disagreements about what music to play at the workbench. The dread something horrible had just happened between them overwhelmed her. When they said goodnight, Gift worried Mike saw the tears in her eyes.

4 | Day Six

Sunday morning at the workbench settled Gift's mind; the wedge between her and Mike had departed when the emotions of the moment surrendered to the passing days.

The air handler controller board in Gift's queue had been switching its fans on and off for no logical reason. No one knew those modules better. No equipment had greater importance than life-sustaining systems, so Mike watched over her shoulder as an eager apprentice. Three detailed diagnostics pointed to a software issue, but no decent hardware engineer would blame the coders by default. Some played that blame-game. Data operators faulted the hardware because their code was 'perfection.' Hardware grunts passed it back with less than complimentary observations on said code. Occasionally, Gift and Raff did it in jest, but Gift had to rule out every hardware issue before going that route.

"*Crap.* There's nothing wrong with the hardware. It's all fine." Gift wanted to solve this one without help. "I'll ask Raff to look at it for me."

After placing the module board on Raff's bench, Gift recounted everything she had done to troubleshoot and assess the fault. Silent, and with healthy amusement at the passion on display, Raff listened attentively to the detailed story being told. "I hate to bother you, really. I tried everything."

"*Clearly.*" Raff chuckled the word out. "No worries." After attaching two terminal connectors to the board, she voiced commands to her display.

They were in Raff's world now, the data operator processing the results on the screen. Deep concentration obscured the conscious part of Gift's brain to Claudia's existence until she noted the attention Raff's bench-mate gave to her partner's performance, ignoring her own work. Pointing to a section of the gibberish on her display, Raff said, "There's your problem, see?"

"I see... why I'm in hardware. Not brilliant like you."

Raff made a small but satisfied noise. "*Ciao,* it's just my thing. I didn't get any of that stuff you told me. No one gets the hardware on these units like you. Here it logged a control system upgrade. Seems ordinary enough."

"Ordinary doesn't explain how it's been behaving."

"*Esatto.* But it was a *rollback* of a failed upgrade, not an OS update push. You get it?" The confused look on Gift's face supplied the answer. "No Operating System updates were released recently, and the OS build date in this unit is from over three years ago. The unit started acting wonky when, about eighteen hours ago?"

"About then."

"That matches. It looks like the auto-monitoring agent saw a version mismatch and tried to reverse the control system upgrade. But none were pushed. So, something got royally hosed in it, or else someone mistakenly sent this unit the wrong OS update."

"I can note that in my log. Should justify all the time I wasted on it."

"No time wasted. Due diligence is time well spent. Besides, if you'd have come right to me... I'd have blamed the hardware." The last few words pulled the pair into a hearty giggle. "I'm reloading a clean control OS now. When they put it back, it will work perfectly."

"Great work Raff. Thanks so much."

"*Niente.*" Her way of saying *you're welcome.*

***

A burst of the Ramen's intense aroma saturated her nostrils as Charlie and Sakura's door slid open. Gift felt the saliva flooding her mouth. Soon, the entire gang was there when Tina arrived last, as expected. With the center bed wall splitting the double Box, the small group crowded the space.

Tina had slurped her way through her bowl and waited to be offered seconds—accepted with a smile full of teeth when the offer came. Mike did alright with the chopsticks. He'd been observing Sakura's masterful use of her own and trying to copy, learning the trick of getting a small bit of noodle onto the spoon, avoiding the splattering of his slurp.

"Outstanding, Sakura," Mike said.

Tina nodded as she inhaled a thick bunch of noodles, happy to share her broth with the rest of the table. Slowly sucking hers in without splashing a drop, Gift made sure no food was in her mouth before speaking.

"Mm, mm, mm. I'm with Mike. *Outstanding*. No one tells my mom. She thinks I only get this way about *her* cooking."

"Yes, dear, outstanding is the definitive verdict. Thank you." Charlie's peck on his lovely partner's cheek reddened it.

"Thank you, all of you. We are so glad you could come for dinner. I am so sorry we missed you all on Friday, I really wanted to join you."

Everyone had assumed Sakura kept Charlie away, condemning her with accusations unsaid. Sometimes said by Mike. Could it have been *Charlie* pulling away, and they wrongly placed the blame on Sakura? Raff had cautioned the group not to jump to erroneous conclusions—advice that stopped thoughts from vocalizing, not from occurring.

"Yeah... I'm sorry guys, it's my fault." Charlie's head hung low as Sakura collected the bowls, forcing Gift to stop doing it.

"What do you mean, Charlie?" Raff asked.

"Yeah, the thing of it is... I've been trying to balance our time since we were joined. It's important for a new Union, you know?"

"We understand." From the corner seat, Gift's arm failed its attempt to grab his hand, so she slid it along the table in his direction.

"Sakura, she's been on me about not getting with you lot. She wanted to come on Friday, but I asked her to stay home. Try to build this right."

"None of us blamed your dear Sakura." Tina's gaze shifted to Mike. "You've got no reason to apologize to us."

"Yeah, well, I wanted to come clean... It's great you all could come tonight, and sorry it's so cramped in here."

Sakura nodded. "Me being a medic, you might assume we would get a flat. I hope Charlie did not think he would get an upgrade when we joined."

"He most definitely upgraded. Not the Box. *You.*" Everyone chuckled at Tina's outburst. Charlie often said Sakura was out of his league, which Gift figured drove him to work so hard to get the Union started right.

"Sakura, how are things in Medical? What do you do?" For the first time, Gift realized they had no details of her work assignment. She felt herself an awful friend for it.

"My specialty is working with medical anomalies, so I don't work in a clinic. I have an office in Pronto Soccorso in Citadome One."

"That's fascinating." Excitement brightened Mike's face.

"No, not really. Medical anomalies are quite rare. Most of my days are research and routine patch-ups when someone hurts themselves on the job."

Mike leaned forward. "Come on Sakura, you must have seen some crazy stuff."

Returning from the kitchen space, Sakura sat beside Charlie, every eye trained on her. "Well, I have been seeing an unusual increase in C.I.D. cases lately. And I have noticed—" Gift raised her hand as a schoolchild and waited to be called before speaking. "Gift?"

"I'm sorry, slow to catch up. C I D?"

"It is called Chemical Imbalance Disorder and usually pronounced *sid*. It is extremely rare, with one case every few years, mostly *Delayed* CID. We have seen seven cases in the last two months, all young women, all of them with *Early* CID. Odd... *Gift*?"

"So, this CID. What is it? How do you get it? What does it do to you?"

Without condescension Sakura said, "As the name implies, it is an imbalance in the chemical makeup of the body. Some of us have reached Gen-Maturity, Mike and Gift are getting there. It is when the human body's chemical reactions begin maturing to match the physical development that started as an early teen."

No one spoke, hungry ears waiting for more.

"With Chemical Imbalance Disorder, that process goes wrong. Delayed, or D.CID, is easily treatable. We look for it when someone reaches thirty-two years without G.M. In rare cases where it occurs early, it often misfires. The body and the brain are not ready for it. We have seen it in as young as twenty, *Early* CID. Again, it was rare, almost nonexistent. This many cases at once, all E.CID? Very strange."

Gift speculated a connection between her encounter with Max and the discomforting feelings she still couldn't understand. *I'm too young for G.M., could it be this?* Desperate for answers, she tried to muster the courage to ask when Raff lifted the pressure.

"And what are the symptoms of Early CID? I'm guessing not like the normal process of G.M?"

"Correct. Unlike healthy G.M., E.CID symptoms include aggression, anger, poor sleep habits, loss of mental focus, declining work ethic, and social difficulties. Left untreated, it could escalate to violence. The earlier it starts, the more amplified the symptoms." Sakura looked concerned by her own explanation.

"Fascinating," Mike said. "What's the treatment?"

"We have special drug compounds, but they proved less effective in these patients. Normally, treatments work to keep aggression and anger subdued. It is hard to catch as it does not show in weekly checkups. Our patients have either come in reporting symptoms or were brought in after an outburst of anger or other subversive behavior."

"Did you get a new patient, a short, thin girl with frizzy hair, a few days ago? Probably brought in for subversive behavior after being tranquilized?"

"*What?*" Sakura stood up, visibly uneasy with Mike's questions. "How? How... can you know that?"

"I saw her. We saw her... me and Gift. Two guards hunted her down after she wrote *All Lies*. They got her and knocked her out cold. And now where is she? What are they doing to her?"

"You mean what am *I doing* to her? I am trying to help the poor girl. She is barely twenty-one and E.CID is destroying her life."

Mike raised his hands in apology. "No, please Sakura. I know *you* are trying to help these folks, but people above you, *they* have another agenda. What happens when someone doesn't respond to treatment?"

"They get put into an induced comatose state and we monitor them, administer treatments, and continue to test their blood. Hopefully they will respond and rejoin society. That is the goal." Sakura sat back in her chair, put her elbows on her knees, and buried her face in her palms.

"How many are in induced comas?"

"Over this last year we have placed twenty-three young women into a comatose state."

"And how many successfully treated and released?"

"None."

Sakura excused herself for a toilet break but seemed to need a break from Mike's relentless questions. Charlie walked his distressed partner to the toilet box.

"*Ragazzi.*" Raff took charge. "We need to get off this topic. It has even overshadowed that amazing meal."

Smiling mischievously, Tina said, "I can do that. Mike, tell us a joke." His jokes were long stories.

As the door slid open, Mike expounded the story, Tina giggling long before the punchline. For reasons no one else got, she loved his tasteless jokes. "...and their work was sloppy. They hadn't logged a single completed task all morning, yet their bench was covered in parts. You know? The supervisor just couldn't work it out. So... she looks back at the two with the straightest face. She says to them, 'Last time I let bench-mates get promised in Union.'"

Tina burst into a roaring laugh with the others laughing more at her than at the juvenile punchline. The plan worked; Sakura smiled.

"People think that is how Charlie and I met."

"You're saying it's not?" Charlie chuckled at himself.

"None of us were there," Gift answered. "But we *do* remember when we first met the lovely Sakura."

"Please, Gift. Not this one again."

With a playful wink, Sakura said, "Well... I have never heard the whole story—only his version. So, I would very much like to hear yours."

Having a fondness for storytelling, Gift took the floor. "So, we never heard of you for the first three months..." As she continued in exhaustive detail, Sakura offered her full attention. "...and there you were, standing next to this clown. Our jaws dropped. No way he's with her—you. We had only one concern about you."

"She's crazy," Tina exclaimed. "She needs to have her head examined. No way *she* goes for Charlie. No offense bro, love you. But *really*?"

He smiled in agreement then asked Tina, "What about your mystery man? When do we meet him?"

"Oh, no. This ain't about me, Chuckles. Keep to your bench."

"Fair question," Raff said. "We love you, too, and know nothing about this guy. Not even a name."

"And that's how it will stay, for now. I told these kids…" Tina waved a finger back and forth at Mike and Gift. "I told them I'd do like Charlie, let you vet him, but only after I… *If or when* I decide he's even worthy. Looking good, but there's room for it to swing, so let's give it that room. Deal?"

"Fair enough." Raff tucked her big sister persona away.

"And we're so glad you all could come." A sign from Charlie the evening had concluded.

5

Walking from Charlie and Sakura's Box into the passageway, the topic of the E.CID patients sat front and center in their minds. Unsurprisingly, Mike gave voice to his thoughts first. "That Early CID? Interesting stuff. Such an increase. And comas. What do you make of it?"

"Sakura said they've put twenty-three people in comas. Young women, all of them. No cure. How sad." Gift's words were dampened in melancholy.

"Um, no. She never said no cure." A scrunched face matched the adamance of Tina's tongue. "She said treatments work most of the time."

Mike rebutted, "Sakura didn't seem *that* optimistic to me. Not one of these women has yet to make it out of the coma."

"*Infatti*," Raff agreed. "It makes you wonder about those rumors of people going missing. 'Reassigned' is the official word."

To posture himself, Mike lifted his heels. "*Official* word. But now we know different."

"Differently," Raff corrected. "But how sad for those poor people. What will become of them?"

Wearing the face of a tutor during a boring lesson monologue they considered of great value—forgotten before reaching its conclusion—Mike said, "And let's not forget this, it's important... That girl Gift and me saw the other night—" when Raff slid in another correction he flashed her a harsh look "—was brought to Pronto Soccorso. Just twenty-one, right? And now she's there, in treatment." He put air quotes around *treatment*. "She's likely next in a coma. Heck, maybe it's already been done to her."

"Wait." Gift squashed a mental image of that. "No one said she was in a coma. You don't know that."

"But it is *possible*. And for what? All she's done is what? Scribbled *All Lies* around the colony. Now they've labeled her as aggressive, subversive, and violent. Complaining against the admins is now a symptom of some kind of... of a sickness—giving them an excuse to lock these people away for nothing more than questioning them. It's all part of them controlling us."

Raffaella raised two hands. "Okay, Mike, everyone. We got a bit of new information this eve—"

"*Facts.*"

"Sure, Mike. Facts. Understand that we saw *a piece* of a much bigger picture. *Ma*, we don't have *all* the facts and we don't know more than what we do. So, please, no rash conclusions. Agreed?"

"Okay, *Mom*." He gave a less-than-convincing shrug.

"It will be Lights-Out soon. Off to your Boxes." Grabbing Gift by the elbow, Raff waved off Tina and Mike. "You two go, I need this one."

"Okay Raff, what's up?"

Raff gave the others time to clear earshot. "You know how for years now Mike's had his head up his behind with his theories?"

"I'd not put it *quite* that way, but sure."

"I think he may not be entirely wrong on this." Raff's face blanked in disbelief as if someone else had said it.

"*Seriously?* You agree with Mike?"

"*Ciao*, I said not *entirely* wrong... *on this*. He's wrong about most everything else, sure. All those crazy ideas of his... makes it hard to separate any truth from all the nuts, *vero*?"

"I suppose so, yeah." Under closed lips, Gift licked her front teeth but couldn't wipe away the uneasiness.

Dragging her by the elbow, Raff showed her another *All Lies* message on a kiosk by a Resident Services office, and placed her finger on Gift's lips as Mike had done those days ago when discussing the same subject. "That's what this is all about."

"What? You sound like Mike. I need you to be… *you*." Pushing the words around Raff's finger, Gift ignored its intent.

"No theories or wild assumptions. Something you and I saw that I think is connected to those messages and the people behind them."

"What did we see? I'm lost."

"Remember how sure you were the controller for that air handler, your priority task this morning, was a hardware issue? Why were you so sure? Why didn't you blame the software code?"

"Cause I'm stubborn. Wanted to solve it without help."

"No, you're not stubborn. Well, sometimes. *Ma*, why did it *have to be* a hardware issue?"

"A software issue made no sense. The failures, the *way* it was failing, screamed hardware malfunction."

"*Esatto*. It looked exactly like a hardware failure, the kind of thing you see and fix routinely, *vero*?"

"You… yeah, you said no updates were pushed. There was no reason for anyone to check the code. It was obviously faulty hardware, except… except it wasn't."

"And what if that module stayed running?"

"All that on and off and the vibration of the unbalanced fans; the unit would have failed." Gift saw the pieces coming together but the picture remained incomplete. "I don't see what this has to do with those… those *maledetti* kiosk messages."

"Language, Gift." Raff interlocked her fingers over her chest. "What if someone used a deliberate code corruption to mimic a hardware failure, to make it look like a typical maintenance issue? Would that explain what we saw today?"

Worried palms hid Gift's face and her elbows tucked themselves into her gut, hunching her back. She began rocking. The chaos consumed her, she needed to find order.

"Someone sabotaged that unit, meant it to fail, but didn't bypass the redundancies. They wanted it to pass for a typical hardware fault. The *All Lies* people believe our resources are more abundant than we're told—they say rationing is overly strict, part of the control over us. Some even called for sabotage to prove it. I think we may have caught *that* today."

Gift raised her head. "Raff? How could *you* know any of that?"

"Rumors. But more credible than what Mike hears. I had dismissed them until this evening, *ma,* it fits with the *All Lies* messages and the sabotaged module you found."

"But the illness... Where does that fit in to any of this?"

"You're good at patterns. What's the connection?"

Saucer eyes brightened Gift's face. "So, those *All Lies* people keep writing that message everywhere—so vague, no one knows what it even means. Now they escalated to sabotage. This... E.CID, may have caused the subversive behavior, so they get treated or put in a coma... Or worse—plausible, hope not—they *blame* E.CID for it, and the poor women get *disappeared.* Some twisted form of justice for... opposition to the admins. They get put in comas instead of jail cells."

"Looks that way."

The two stood with no more words, with no rational way to comprehend the enormous weight of the moment. Two spokes away from Gift's habitat, a flickering signaled the last call before Lights-Out. Without a goodnight kiss, she turned and started toward Dome Four as the lights reduced to seventy-five percent. A harsh, audible thump came when the circuits switched off. Picking up the pace into Dome Three, Gift scampered through its piazza as the thud of another light reduction shuddered her shoulders. At fifty percent, the jog became a sprint into her spoke with the archway to her habitat block in sight. Thud. Lights reduced to twenty-five percent. Passing another defaced kiosk slowed her pace. "Gonna make it." She was wrong.

Halfway up the staircase at the center of the block's corridor the lights in the spoke went dark with the loudest thud yet as remaining circuits cut off in the domes and passageways. Illumination in the housing block corridors reduced to twenty percent for night mode. While permitted to traverse the halls for toilet use after, residents had to be in their Boxes by Lights-Out. When the door panel outside her Box identified her, a message appeared.

> Lights-out tardy. Loss of 15 rations.
>
> Report to Resident Services 18:30.

6 | Day Seven

Nervously walking to her passageway but not toward home, she dreaded the outcome. Gift would never be careless enough to receive a Tardy—except she had been, nine years back. Her mom had given her Jollof rice, which she shared with old man Norbert in his Box. (The one Marco now occupied.) He told anecdotes from his youth; he always had funny stories. So wrapped up were they in delightful conversation, neither had noticed the warning of the Lights-Out deadline. At seventeen, she thought they had gone easy on her for the tender age and the innocent nature of the Tardy. This time she had no excuse.

Not the Resident Services main office with its pleasantly bright and welcoming open reception space, the faint gray waiting area begged for a fresh coat of paint and the place had all the charm of a recycler's waste collector. When the display beside the door read 18:30, Gift expected to hear her name called and was confused when she didn't. Not to be presumptuous, she waited two minutes before approaching the display. When she did, it read, Gift Ojo. Room 3. The door slid open to a narrow hall of faint-gray walls with accents in blue. After stepping through, the door to room three sealed her inside.

The two-meter-square room had a steel-gray table or desk in the center with one chair. Gift stood alone in the soft-white room. As minutes passed, the emptiness intensified her anxiety, dripping as sweat on the small of her back where the coverall hung loose over the waistband. The room didn't respond to her *Hello*. A camera's status light warned of someone watching. Feeling trapped, her uneasiness matured into fear.

After standing in isolation for what felt like an hour, a distinguished man of seventy some odd years entered. His white-with-blue-hue hair intrigued her, and she considered if the diffused lighting painted the color in it. Taking a position behind the chair, he stood with his hands on its back, casting a judgmental look over her. Shivers hurried down Gift's spine and her arms hung awkwardly at her sides, so she brought them in front and wrapped one hand around her wrist. The nameless man sharing the room sat in the chair while Gift stood motionless, anxious. A display tilted up from the desk illuminating his pale face.

"Twenty-six."

"Yes."

"Why the Tardy?" From under a raised brow, he studied her.

"Well, we were at my friend Charlie's for dinner. He's in a recent Union and—"

A raised hand signaled stop. "*Relevant* details, Miss Ojo, please. Passageway?"

"Five-Six."

"When did you leave Mister Atkinson's home?"

"Um, about twenty-three twenty, I think."

"Mm-hm. So, it took you forty minutes to reach your home in Passageway Two-Three. Do you suffer from an unregistered health issue? Got a bum leg or something?"

"No. See…" Trembling nerves started her rocking. "We talked a bit in the Passageway, walked, paused again to talk. I lost track of time."

"Lost track of time, eh?" The blue-haired man kept his eyes glued to the display and sharpened his tone. "Nine years ago, you had the same excuse for another Tardy. Lose track of time often, then?"

"No. I mean… that was nine years ago. *Often…?* And I was just in the Box next to mine. I was—"

"You were seventeen. We went easy on you, didn't we?" Gift nodded. "This is different, you're an adult. Who were you with and what were you discussing when you should have been walking home?"

"Sorry, sir, if I may? That's… invasive. I was with my friend, and… we always talk about personal and *private* things. I don't think you have the right to ask me that." Having spoken up for herself, Gift crossed her arms in a defensive posture. If he had pressed, she would have complied.

The interrogator scowled at the new posture. "How are you feeling?"

"How do you mean?" The sudden change in his line of questioning threw her.

"How do you *feel?* The easiest question yet, I think."

"Um… *fine?*"

"You don't seem so sure. Sleeping well?"

Gift didn't consider the truth in her favor. "Yeah… Good."

"We have deducted fifteen rations from your account."

"I see. May I… go then?"

"No. You must understand how important maintaining order is in our controlled environment. We must carry on if we are to reach our destiny and establish ourselves on this planet. What we are doing is building that future." As she nodded agreement, the man stood. His stepping toward her moved her back, bumping the wall behind her. "We'll need to do a simple test."

Discomfort grew into a wave of anxiety sweeping over her. "But, why?"

"We have reasons to be concerned over your recent behavior. We'll run a preliminary scan to check for connections between your recent behavior and potential health issues. It is just to make sure you are healthy."

"This is something you do for a Tardy?"

"Not always, and not just for Tardy. It has more to do with… patterns."

"I fit some pattern, then?"

"That's just it my dear, you don't. That's what concerns me and why we want to be sure you're okay... Stand here." With a gentle touch on her shoulders, he guided her into place. "Keep still, arms loose, down at your sides. It will take a few seconds and then you may go."

As she walked home, Gift couldn't suppress thoughts that, considering recent events and the information Sakura had shared, she'd been tested for E.CID. *Patterns, the man said. I don't fit any patterns.*

In the system now, suspected of Early Chemical Imbalance Disorder, Gift could have been next in line for treatment or ended up in a coma. And if they found out what any of them were discussing, they could *disappear* her and her friends, as Mike called it. As she was getting changed to meet Aimée, her brain made a connection. *Aimée works in Resident Services. Maybe she can help.*

7

Her earliest memory of Aimée was as a five-year-old with Gift just over four. They drew pictures in Mom's Box and had been sharing crayons amicably until both wanted the same one to color the sky. With neither willing to give, they each pulled against the other until it broke. Gift wailed her forced cry while Aimée rolled on the floor engulfed in laughter. Passing years brought appreciation for their differences in character. It kept their relationship lively and spontaneous, sometimes a little unpredictable, and always fun.

The two came up the closest of friends. Gift's mother raised her as a solo while Aimée had Union parents, as all other children did. A tenet of New Europa Gift knew well stated that Unions produced stable, grounded adults. Stability in a strictly controlled microenvironment—isolated physically, atmospherically, economically, and socially—was paramount. Rarely had Gift pondered her mother's unique circumstance.

Walking to her friend's place, Gift recalled how, at just fourteen, Aimée entered Resident Services training then an apprenticeship mere weeks after turning sixteen. At only twenty-seven, she managed the office in her passageway. The colony's corporate-modeled framework had no ladder. Resident Services and Medical Care were the only ones to offer the rare chance for class advancement. While her dear companion was on that track, Gift never would be.

When the door slid open, a t-shirt and underwear immodestly covered her childhood friend. *"So hot in here,"* she said as she stepped back and waved Gift in. Her jet-black hair hung straight, trimmed short with bangs touching an eyebrow. Aimée wrapped her arms around Gift.

"It *is* hot in here. Whatcha making?"

"For you my dear, I've been slaving over this hob *all day*."

"You've not been home an hour and a half."

"Okay, so not *all* day." A meager snort-laugh escaped.

"It smells amazing, what is it?" Gift's mouth watered in expectation.

"Dad's French Lentils with Dijon Vinaigrette. I call it *yum*."

Gift sat and watched the jovial cook bring two steaming bowls to the table. Whatever Aimée did became the most fantastic thing ever, a trait Gift envied since that memory where her world had ended over a single broken crayon while Aimée soaked every millimeter of joy from the same experience. Not to disrupt the light dinner conversation, Gift tried to be in the moment. She always loved the *what have you been up to since...* question-and-answer sessions they shared.

"... and then I grabbed the mic and shouted, 'Vive la France.' And I don't even get what it means. I know what the *words* mean, I mean the significance. But it seemed the right thing for a little French girl like me to yell into an open mic."

"I'm sorry, I didn't get it. *Why'd* you shout in the mic?"

"The guy's voice was rubbish. He couldn't sing worth a ration—flat and off key." Gift smiled as far as her lips would stretch. "Hey, how's Raffa? It's been a while. Now *that's* a voice."

"Yeah." Gift's distraction unhid itself.

"Something wrong, Love?"

Gift paused. *Don't drag her into this.*

"You there, Love? Something's bothering you. Wait, I got it. Gather your thoughts, get them organized and lined up as you do. Then we'll talk."

***

Visibly shocked, Aimée didn't interrupt Gift as she recounted the events of the last days from the frizzy-haired girl to the damaged air handler board to her bizarre encounter with the blue-haired man in the little white office. Nestled beside her friend on the bed, Aimée listened lovingly.

"I almost forgot… they made me take a scan of some kind. Weird, a medical scan in Resident Services."

"Not as weird as you might think. They started about five, six months ago doing that. They're looking for anything serious, some medical link to odd behavior. Sounds like they added the video to your file and let you go. So, you must be fine."

"Wait, they recorded the video?"

"Cameras are *always* on and recording."

"Sometimes the status lights go out. Like in Medical."

"Meaningless. They're always on."

"Oh mamma."

"Please, Gift, you can't say anything. I have no clue what they'd do with me if they knew I told you that."

Gift swiveled on her bum and crossed her legs to face Aimée. "Maybe… you can help me?"

"Anything. What can I do?"

"Could you, I mean… do you have access to my file? Could you… remove the part about the scan?"

"I'm not sure I can access files outside my office. I'll try of course. But Love, why that? What's the problem with the scan?"

"Remember what Sakura said about the E.CID? I think that's what they're looking for. Find I have it, or just say I do, and they could disappear me like the frizzy-haired girl. I'm... scared."

"Okay my sweet Gift, I'll take care of it for you. Don't you worry."

"But, what if you, can't... My file from, Two-Three?"

"Do you think Raffa is up for a bit of side work? I'm free tomorrow if she's game."

***

Relief battled anxious concern for dominance as Gift walked home from her dear Aimée's Box. Comfort came in the listening ear of a compassionate friend—someone able to help—but she had to drag Raff into it, as Aimée couldn't do it without a data operator. *Raff is the reason I'm in trouble... Don't blame her, wasn't her fault.*

Waiting in the queue for a toilet booth, she greeted Sara exiting and resisted the temptation to ask about Max. To satisfy curiosity, Gift's eyes followed her to Box C16, her same solo Box. "So not in Union?" A smile found reason to accompany the words, but her mind did not approve.

"Sorry?" A nameless man behind her in queue surprised her by speaking.

"No, sorry, I talk to myself. A little crazy, me."

"My partner does the same. Eight years now and I still reply every time."

"That's sweet." She didn't think so, imagining having a partner that responded every time she spoke to the air. *His poor partner.*

"Not really. Causes lots of fights over nothing." His laugh came from the back of his throat like an annoying crackle. "Your turn, Miss."

During the bedtime routine of cleaning her teeth and using the body pad as she did on non-shower days, her world froze in the mirror's reflection. The upper-right corner of the bed stuck out from the wall, not resting flush. Gift pushed in on it only to have it pop out a full centimeter. Three repeated bangs each came with a word. "You. Stupid. *Thing*." In defeat, she lowered the bed.

***

Gift lay in a case fitted just large enough for her body. Over a small glass panel above her eyes, Sakura's face slid into view, but she spoke to someone else. Not able to hear the words, Gift developed the ability to read lips.

'Patient coma stable... Yes, we'll up her nose then.' *Maybe she said dose*, a sleeping Gift reasoned. 'Nothing worked. So aggressive this one. Dragged her in here after they found her in a small grass field in Dome Three screaming *Max*. She has E.CID for sure.'

Roused hot and damp, every millimeter of her skin dripped. For the second time short of a week, Gift grabbed a cleaning wipe and cleaned the bed, then herself with a body pad. "Stupid Max."

Dreams replayed as she searched for patterns. Gift believed there was a hidden truth related to E.CID. Barely two minutes late and defaulted for the scan, which she knew was for the disorder. *This is a bigger problem than they thought*, she reasoned. *Those comas are most definitely an excuse to* disappear *those poor people*. "Me next."

Big questions remained. Was E.CID the big lie advertised by those fanatics? Or could it have been causing their behavior? The treatments and comas for the common good? The loyalist in Gift desperately sought to accept that as true. *What will they do to* me *with that scan in my file?*

8 | Day Eight

A knock echoed through the door, which opened to Raff in her deep-blue dress, reflecting light in subtle tones. Raff often wore one of her two issued dresses and had saved rations to buy this one. She had three pizza boxes in her hands and a dainty bag over her shoulder.

"Sleepover then?" Eyeing the lowered bed, she leaned in to kiss Gift on both cheeks. "Aimée?"

"Coming. Not the best for punctual, that one."

A thump on the door came as the words finished. With her face shining as always around her perpetual smile, Aimée entered the Box. "Ooh, a sleep-over."

After eating most of her pizza, Gift placed the box beside her on the bed cushion and crossed her legs and caught Raff up on her Tardy interview.

"But Gift, a Tardy? That means a visit to a Resident Services agent, disciplinary action, loss of rations... *Oh*. Don't worry about the pizza, I got it. But why do you think they suspect you of E.CID for a Tardy?"

"That's where you come in, Raffa." Aimée's face beamed with excitement. "I need you to help me jump from my office to the one here so we can see what happened in her interrogation."

"I think I may have had a preliminary exam for it. Why we need to check."

When she finished her last slice, Raff widened her eyes as she looked at Aimée, who reverted into a giddy teenager with a spark of mischievous excitement. A quick twist of the device to Aimée along with verbal authorization got Raff into her account. It took seconds for her to hack into a trusted identity database and put Aimée into the admin's group for the office in Gift's passageway.

In Gift's file were four folders: *Housing*, *Work*, *Medical*, and *History*. Another icon cryptically named *EXP142* had a lock glyph on it. When Aimée sent the handheld's output to the vid screen, she and Raff moved to either side of Gift on the bed.

"Nothing medical here. It logs your Tardy and the visit but no details. Let's check the Medical folder... Ah ha. A full E.CID exam is on your next visit, so... delete. Go to Folder History, sort by most recent... Play newest vid file." It began with Gift entering the office and played through to the medical scan.

"I can edit out that last part." Aimée accomplished that with scrub-editing controls. "Now the transcript." She removed the incriminating text. "Finally, the agent's notes. There, where he says 'a high suspicion of E.CI D' he recommended you for a follow-up and prescribed that exam. *Deleted.* Let me just double-check a couple things." She handed the terminal back to Raff to clean up. "All done. Nothing to worry about now, Love."

"But he wrote, *high suspicion* of E.CID. They think I have it. It ruins your life."

Raff rested a hand on the trepidatious young woman's shoulder. "They may also be blaming normal behavior on E.CID. It doesn't mean you have it."

"But... I *do* have symptoms."

"Like what, Love?"

"Anger. I've gotten angry a few times, snapped at people. Trouble sleeping. Woke up hot, covered in sweat."

"You're always warm," Raff said.

"True. Well, no… it's Max." The silence of confusion told Gift to elaborate. "I saw this guy, Max. I think he's in Union with Sara, only it doesn't seem like it because she's in her solo Box from—. Sorry, short version: Max. Blond hair, blue eyes, and gorgeous. I've been dreaming about him."

With widened eyes, Raff exclaimed, "Oh mamma."

"You're twenty-six, Love. You may be starting a little early. Doesn't mean Early CID, just early G.M. *Normal*, healthy G.M. Sometimes starts early."

"No one gets it at twenty-six."

Aimée twisted Gift to face her. "I may have hit it some time ago. Maybe… since I was fifteen. I felt anger all the time. Lots of sleepless nights. You remember how I was in school, and I had dreams of boys even then. Never figured there was anything wrong with me."

Raff's chin dropped. "Is that true, sweetheart?"

"Yep. Gift, you remember how I was as a teenager. Always loved the attention when the boys looked at us. Still do. What I'm trying to say is that these feelings of yours coming at twenty-six, not twenty-nine or thirty? Seems perfectly normal to me."

"Cara, the worst is over, your record is clear." Raff rubbed Gift's back. "No one will test you now, we took care of that. Now… I do want to hear more about this Max. Tell us everything."

"Absolutely," Aimée said with a glowing smile.

9 | Day Twelve

As always, Gift arrived on time. Well, as usual. Entering her passageway's medical office, fern fronds waved a welcome from artfully placed planters in the reception area. Up at the counter, a warm, familiar smile awaited. Agnus had been there for all of Gift's ten years of visits. Nearing ninety-eight, she would soon be replaced. Agnus set her thinning hair of black and gray in a comb-back in what couldn't rightly be called a style. Her character made her beautiful to Gift.

Exam room two brought a yawn to Gift's jaw with its pale-yellow surfaces accented in shades of blue. A few plants reached downward from wall sconces and Gift imagined them climbing up from the floor. She sat on the exam table when Martha, a medic of light-pink complexion with freckles dotting her skin, entered. After she checked Gift's vision, hearing, lungs, and heart rate, she left.

When Gift woke from a light sleep with her face nestled in the massage table, fingers caressed her scalp. After her muffled *Ciao* she didn't recognize the returned *Hello*. Strong hands moved along her neck and shoulders, gently relaxing the muscles. She breathed out a long, satisfied sigh as the tension melted.

"Okay, rest the muscles for a minute, then flip onto your back."

To catch a glimpse, she twisted her neck and saw his back as he exited. *Not Robert's buzz-cut black hair, a blond.* A familiar voice, but Gift couldn't place it. "Oh mamma... *Max?*" she said to the air. That frightening possibility coagulated in her muscles. "Please, no." Who Max was or where he worked, she had no clue. *He had his hands on me.* Frozen in anxious dread, her eyelids joined when he entered.

"Hello again," Maybe-Max said.

"Good morning." An unknown voice. Gift allowed her eyes to discover an adorable round-faced young lady with a light brown complexion and a cute nose, if a bit wide. A smile drew itself on Gift's face and relief settled over her skin as Not-Max leaned into sight. The new girl, Naa, took away the stress from every muscle down to her toes.

Alone, Gift noticed the camera and felt the eyes behind them slither over her skin. In strolled a graceful woman in her mid-to-late sixties, Maria, tall and fit. She and her partner had a son called Ralf in his second year in Resident Services who worked with Aimée.

"Good morning, Gift. Everything okay?"

"Ciao. No complaints, same as always."

"Good. Let's get you ready for this exam."

"I know I'm not to talk about my exams. And I don't. But... I know how it is for everyone—the women, I mean. At sixteen I had my first exam, then once a year since, like everyone. Now you've been taking my blood and running tests on me every week. I don't—" No other words came, only her lingering doubt.

"I know, sweetheart. According to your file, they have categorized you as *EXP One forty-two.* Says you are the only one in the colony."

"But... what does that even *mean?* Is there something wrong with me?" Regrets came over her, bringing a mistake to mind she'd not be able to correct. She should have opened that file labeled *EXP142* in her medical folder. *Why didn't I open that file?*

"Honestly, I don't know. But I *do* know there's nothing wrong with you, you always check out healthy. I expect it means you're... special, in a way."

Gift rolled her eyes. "And it means we do the full workup on you, scans and drawing fluids, every time. It doesn't take long."

Special? Gift wondered how.

The remaining exams were routine, the same for all residents, male or female. Gift assumed the bone density scan measured the effects of being in lower than one G. Her thoughts countered the conclusion with the notion that by then, the gravity of Mars was the new one G for them—all they had known for two centuries.

Cathy found Gift waiting in a room with a treadmill and various exercise equipment and guided her through a series of stress tests before giving her the standard injections.

"Thanks, Cathy... Oh, wait. Could you tell me what's in all these injections we get? I mean, they're all chemical compounds, right? But what's in them?"

"Medicines. Nutrient supplements."

"Yeah, but what exactly? I get seven a week. What do they do?"

From a sneer, she said, "I'm a cardio-physical therapist, not a nutritional scientist. All I know is the treatments balance our health and supplement our nutritional intake. Others help balance our digestive tract. For us women, one helps to regulate our cycles. Without these, women used to have it much worse, painful cramps and bleeding every month. Can you imagine? Beyond that, I can't really say. I just give the injections."

"Do you think they influence our emotional development? Are they related to G.M? Like, could they affect our moods... feelings?"

"Not that I know. Dear... I wouldn't ask such things."

"How do you mean?"

"Some might deem it... not in the best interests of the colony."

"I see."

Gift entered the next small white room and removed her shoes, leaving them in the cubby. The recliner sofa cradled her body in its soft gel-foam cushion. She floated in comfort as the silent minutes alone were enough for her to doze—worry had robbed her of a good night's sleep. The sound of the door woke her and in walked James Müller, a man of almost fifty or he could have been sixty. At two meters tall, his white robe hung shorter on him than everyone else's. He administered the last part with Gift weekly. He'd always been kind and friendly.

"Gift, lovely to receive you again."

"Hello, Mister Müller. How are you today?"

"Good, thanks. But we're here to discuss you." She smiled but said nothing in reply. "So, how are you?" He grabbed her wrist and pressed a small round monitor pad onto the skin.

Desperate for understanding, Gift considered relating everything about her emotions and private feelings. She thought she should ask him about early G.M. or E.CID and tell him of her sleepless nights and dreams. *Fine* seemed the safest response, so she went with that.

"Okay, now let's try for more. How are you getting on with Raff, Mike, Charlie, and Tina?" He placed two monitors on either side of the base of her neck.

"Good. Oh, Charlie came to dinner yesterday, so that was nice."

He held her wrist, pressing gently on the radial artery and asked, "Is Raffaella seeing anyone?"

"Her? No, I don't think so. I'm sure she'd tell me."

"Has she given any unsolicited advice about you and Mike recently?"

"No. *Raff*...? I mean... not really." Even though the controlling nature of her mature friend's personality felt a bit too forceful at times, Gift considered it a sign of Raff's love and made herself okay with it.

It felt strange how intimately this stranger knew her life as if he'd been a part of it. Talking with James Müller was easy, as natural as chatting with a trusted friend. Perhaps that was the idea, to lower her guard, her inhibitions, to expose her soul, her deepest thoughts and feelings. What did that change? A ten-year rapport developed between them. Even with it being one-way, Gift thought it was fine.

"Tell me what comes to mind when I say... *Max*."

"*Huh*...? Nothing. I mean... I met him is all. I don't *know* him. He sees Sara, in my Box—no, I mean, in my block... I think." For reasons she couldn't yet understand, the sharpness of her tone could cut steel. *Is he looking to find an emotional or physical reaction? How does he even know about Max?*

"Just some passing guy, I see." He stood up and moved to the foot of the couch. Taking each of her heels in his hands, he lifted her legs, straightening them at the knees until they were at about a forty-five-degree angle. Gift couldn't guess the reason for such posturing.

"Sleeping well?"

"Yes sir." The guilt of the lie left a sour taste on her tongue.

"Anything you want to express? Questions you'd like to ask me? I'm here to listen and to help."

How'd you know about Max? she thought but dared not ask. "No, nothing."

"Okay. That's it for me."

***

An espresso and brioche quieted Gift's rumbling stomach before returning to her Box to freshen up and dress for work. After picking up her clean coveralls, a couple of sets of underwear, and a t-shirt from her spoke's laundry service, she returned home with a single thought bouncing in her head, cloudy and terribly unnerving.

How'd he know about Max?

A question she would wrestle with for some time.

10 | Day Thirteen

Blaring alarm sounds screamed at Gift and Mike. The unfamiliar signal came with confusion and panic equal to the piercing noise. Their displays turned solid red, flashing words in bold white text appearing over a background that made Gift think of blood.

> Emergency Alert: Critical fault found in primary air handler 11. You are dispatched immediately for repairs.

Blank stares. Neither had seen such an alert nor ever been called on site for an emergency repair job. Mike asked where air handler eleven was and lifted shoulders said Gift had no idea.

Noticing their supervisor, Jane White, out of her office, they raced over to her. Her typical facial expression of mild disinterest vanished, replaced with a sense of urgency in the crease of flesh over her chin and the steely gaze fallen over her eyes.

"Gift, full diagnostic kit and handheld. Mike, repair kit and handheld. Gift, yours has diagnostic data, review that while Mike leads. Mike, yours has directions."

"Copy that." The women's gazes showed confusion. "It means okay."

"Go. *Quickly.*"

After minutes at jogging speed, they climbed narrow, poorly lit stairs. The vibration of dull clanking from the thin metal reverberated with their footsteps. Gift hadn't been anywhere like this in her life. A second flight up found them at a low passageway of a hundred meters, maybe more.

"Where are we? You sure this is right?" Gift questioned the unknown more than Mike's navigational skills, but his bravado said he heard it differently.

"Yes. I have the directions in front of me. We're over a housing block for the cultivators, on the inner side of spoke Four-Five by the farm dome."

Mike crouched through, waddling as a duck Gift had seen in history vids. *Or was it a penguin?* They ascended a ladder and climbed through a hatch onto a narrow metal-grated walkway with no handrails. Realization of their absence instinctively caused Gift to squat, unbalancing her. Once she steadied herself, she stood back up slowly. "There should be handrails."

Barely discernible conduits peered through the black of darkness to their backs, a breathtaking vista before them. They overlooked the massive farm. Mike identified corn and wheat fields then fruit groves and vegetable patches forming a perimeter with hydroponic gardens hanging suspended over the ground-level crops. *The life of the New Europa colony*, Gift contemplated. Deep breaths of farm air tasted fresher, crisper, and cleaner than any prior.

"There." Mike pointed forward and up. "We need to climb up there. It's in that box."

"*Woah.*" Gift assessed the rectangular metal enclosure to be about the size of a solo habitat Box. Evaluating the ladder rising to the machine a newfound fear crawled over her skin. "We have to climb *that*?"

Mike spoke tremulous words Gift didn't wish to hear. "Looks that way."

"Oh mamma."

At the ladder's base, relief shook off a touch of fear as they found four tethered harnesses. In an unexpected display of courage Gift found reassuring, Mike grabbed the highest rung he could reach and ascended over the *nothing* between himself and the ground below. The tether failed to convince her of the safety it promised, and all the muscles in Gift's body stiffened, refusing to move. Mike climbed onto the air handler's narrow platform. To Gift, the climb of three meters seemed unreachably high.

"Come on. Climb up here."

"No." Her reply lacked power to fend off the acoustical barrage from the alarms and rattling air handler.

"Look at me. Just focus on me and climb, one step at a time. You got this."

Before she realized it, Gift had nearly reached the top. Mike grabbed her arm to pull her up with a grip that sent a wave of confidence through her flesh. The parapet rail around the platform helped bolster her as well. Mike held Gift's arms tight and said, "You good?"

Three steps left had her facing an access panel to the main controller module. Gift hastened loose the wingnut fasteners, pulled firmly on the handle, and set the panel at her feet. "Okay. Let's see what we've got." After she pulled the primary board outward, her diagnostic kit fed actionable data to her handheld. Five alerts appeared.

1. Negative result: Aux transistor 12a.3c in open circuit

2. Negative result: Redundant proxy-flow overload

3. Positive result: Aux transistors in closed circuit

4. Negative result: No redundancy circuits found

5. Positive result: Two redundancy circuits operational

"This makes no sense at all."

"What doesn't? What does it say is wrong?" Mike shouted over the noise saturation.

"I see a burned transistor yet the thing's still running."

"The redundant circuit's active then?"

"That's just it. One second, they're offline. The next, fine. It's like the data flowing through this module is... it's somehow disconnected from the physical elements. I'm running a full diagnostic now." Gift attached three cables from her kit to data ports on the module. "Meantime, let me see if I can turn off this alarm, it's deafening."

A *near-fi* connection from her handheld to the auxiliary input brought up a command line interface. The unit screamed aggravated beeps at her mistyped commands. Four tries failed before Gift found the correct syntax to silence the alarm.

"I think we'll need a data operator." To the device in her hand Gift said, "VidChat Raffaella Di Gaetano." The soft lines of Raff's face replaced the CLI on the display.

"Where in the heck are you, Gift? What's going on?"

"Air handler eleven." The glow of the handheld palely lit Gift's face with the darkness of deep shadow as its backdrop. She summarized the issue and Raff tried but failed to connect remotely.

"Could you come here? Mike, send her the directions."

Anticipating the need, Mike descended the ladder before Gift could ask him to meet Raff in the corridor. Down looked more frightening than up, but she'd consider that later.

"What else can I check?" As if the unit spoke a reply, a visual inspection reminded the young engineer how critical units had redundant redundancies for each component, all laid in triplicate with live intermediaries connecting them as hot-swappable. What was happening never happened, by skillful and pragmatic design.

Massive rotating fans hummed with consistent harmonics—a rhythm which ended in a clamorous rattle. A sour coppery odor reeked of plastic and heated metal. Turbines coughed and sputtered until Gift heard them screech to full stop. The air handler was no longer handling air. She failed the repair job, and the unit went offline. What would that mean for the colony?

With the first board slid back in, Gift pulled the second toward her, joined her test kit to it, and received the same diagnostic alerts. On to the third with the same results. As if the Artificial Intelligence coprocessor jumped off the board onto the tip of her nose demanding recognition, she saw the problem. Only, diagnostics didn't show it as an A.I. chip or as being present at all. "It's a dummy redundant chip!" Though serving no purpose on the board, it had caused the entire module to fail. *Shoddy design?* No. Hesitantly, Gift suspected foul play. A chip where it belonged, repurposed into the dummy redundant one Mike discovered, influenced the module when it had no right to do so. Her head leaned in for a closer inspection.

A touch on Gift's back jerked her upright, the motion stopped only by the top of the panel inset greeting her head with a solid bang. "Sorry. I thought you heard me call you."

Dizzied eyes found Raff. "Lost in focus here."

"What've we got?"

"So this is really bizarre. Like all environmental systems, this unit's in a stacked three-tier redundancy. Any single component goes out, and its match is instantly live on another. It's flawless design. They never fail, never stop running. This one failed, stopped, for no reason. Mike found this dummy redundant chip on another module that crashed the thing. I found the same dummies on each of these boards, but the only physical damage is this one burned transistor on the primary. I replaced it before you got here but no change, the unit died and won't restart."

"Now you want to blame the code?" Raff winked.

"No. Well, yes, I guess so. Like the other day... when you found the update that wasn't an update. Maybe that?" Gift's ineloquent words matched the chaotic state of the thoughts that created them.

Gift stepped back as Raff worked. Expletives and grunts from the data operator proved unsettling in Gift's belly until Raff found something. "You were right, sort of. This *is* like the other one, but also it isn't."

"What does that even mean?"

"I'm convinced this is sabotage. No doubt."

"*What*? What sabotage? What other thing?" Mike hadn't been privy to Raff's speculative musings on the previous module failure. "Wait. You've seen this before?"

"Yes. Well, not exactly. I think what Gift and I saw last time was... a beta test. Someone wanted to see if they could push an unauthorized update, if they'd get caught, and how it might disrupt the module. We caught it, and all it did was fault a single redundancy with zero operational impact."

"This time it killed it, the handler I mean. It's offline and I can't get it going or anything. I even swapped out parts. Nothing." Frustration dripped from Gift's words.

Mike added, "And it locked Raff out."

"Not just me. The system isolated itself completely from the data stream. After the garbled initial log dump, it went dark. I couldn't see it from my station. That does *not* happen. This was a complete overhaul of the control OS, built on entirely new code."

A hint of admiration told Gift the skill behind the hack impressed Raff. The mental construct of that idea brought a ghostly chill over her, raising the hairs at the base of her neck. Gift shivered.

"What do we do? This unit is critical, it can't be offline. I mean, I think. What does it actually do?" Gift realized she didn't know the purpose of many critical systems she repaired beyond their names. An air handler handled air, water recyclers recycled water, and water reclamation units, they did something too.

Reading from his device, Mike explained, "This handler mixes natural air from the farm with recycled air from a unit below, then pumps the mix back into Dome Five. It's the area's primary delivery of clean oxygen."

"So, bad. It being offline is *really* bad." Like a headache, Gift felt the pressure of that realization.

"Really bad, yes. By now the air in Dome Five is impure and will continue to worsen exponentially. That will add strain on the adjoining corridors, then adjacent domes, and so on. It could overload the entire system!"

"*Basta*." Raff dropped the word hard. "We need less *we're doomed* and more *this is how we fix it*. You have one field kit. I assume there are replacement parts, beyond what Gift already used?"

Both nodded. Gift said, "*Ma*... we have few basic parts. Could be enough to repair *one* board. Not three. Not even two. One, if we're lucky."

"Even if we did get one patched up, and that's a big if, it'd still be off the data stream and running a hosed-up version of some crappy code."

"Right, Mike, but I'm here. My device is online, and I can get a clean controller OS. A format and reload with your spare parts should get the one module going, and one is all it needs to run the unit."

"Yeah, until that one fails and has zero redundancy." Pessimism hung like a shadow over him.

"She's right." Gift rifled through the repair kit taking inventory. "We have enough to patch up one, that's all we need. We'll race back to our bench and repair the other two and stick'em back in long before anything else blows up."

"You had to say *blows up*." Mike found his softer voice.

The engineers replaced parts on the primary board with the speed and skill of years of experience, then Raff wiped the corrupted OS and loaded the new software in seconds. "That was the base system, like firmware. Now I will push the OS install and that may take a few minutes."

Eighty-five percent, two minutes remaining. Eighty-six, four minutes... Ninety-nine percent. The 'Three seconds remaining...' message taunted them longer than promised. *Why always that* mal'd *ninety-nine percent? Zero to ninety-nine in two seconds, the last one percent always takes forever.* "*Dai...*" Gift broke the intolerable silence. "Finish."

"Patience. Almost—" success chirp "—there. Now give it time to load and let's see if it will start this unit up."

None of them had ever seen an air handler start, few ever had. They always ran... normally. The low-pitched whirring of fans coming off full stop followed optimistic beeps from the controller. The sound increased with the rattle and hum of the housing encasing the gigantic machine, sending rhythmic vibration up their legs through the metal grate below their shoes. The mechanical beast came back to life.

"It's working. We *actually* did it." Delight glimmered in Gift's hazel eyes from speckles of the artificial sunlight latticed in the ribs of the dome's support structure—an imagined experience of being under the light and warmth of the Sun. She lifted her face to the distant star and basked in its warmth. How it must have invigorated humans on Earth before its rays began to burn through skin and radiate the flesh beneath.

"We did it." Mike's cheer landed blissfully on Gift's ears as a refreshing departure from the pessimistic dread.

With the panel cover in place the trio scarily took careful steps down the ladder and back across the safety-rail-deficient catwalk. They descended the dim narrow stairs and entered the corridor to be stopped in their tracks by a *wall* of four large admin guards. A tall woman and an older man in coveralls beside them relieved the three of their modules, toolkits, and handhelds. From his square face, the largest of the guards said, "Come with us."

11

The procession took them through Marienplatz, the piazza at the center of Citadome One, with its showpiece of a four-and-a-half-meter statue of five homogeneous figures called The Founders. Unnamed, they were known only as the ones who reshaped the governments of Earth into a corporate structure and pioneered the colonies project, leading the mass migration of the remnants of humankind. Anonymous saviors said to have been among the most elite of the super wealthy from the United States and United Kingdom.

New Europa's corporate structure provided well for the needs of its inhabitants and had held the colony together for two centuries, offering more than mere survival of refugees from a dying planet. They were living, thriving, the legacy of The Founders, as Gift saw it.

A voice crackled over the comm panel at the Admin building. "Four Twenty-one, escort our guests to waiting room one." As the transmitted voice ended, the double glass doors opened to an unwelcoming space having two sconces with green plants and a double door opposite the entrance.

The seven squeezed into the tiny lobby, waiting for the inner door to open while the outer one closed in airlock style. Pressing in on each other increased the response from Gift's sweat glands, exacerbating the extra two degrees. Swooping curls tickled her nose as Raff's shoulder touched Gift's chin and, with one breast pressed against Mike's shoulder blade, Gift could feel a myriad of items pushing on her back from the security guard's vest. *Torch? Taser? Hypo-stick?* Had the inner doors delayed another second, she would have screamed. Perhaps psychosomatic, the rush of air over her face as the doors slid open lifted fainting's nearness from Gift's body.

Alone in a pale gray room a little larger than Charlie and Sakura's double Box, they stood. A table covered in a soft taupe laminate occupied the center, with four chairs to one side and two opposite them.

"Relax." Raff's stern confidence barely peeled off the first thin layer of Gift's fear. "We did a good job. We were up against a masterfully executed attack on that air handler, and we fixed it. This sort of failure never happens, only it happened, and they need to learn why, prevent it from happening again."

Unable to draw up words, Gift nodded complacently.

"This feels wrong. It won't end well. They herded us in here like criminals."

"They never said that, Mike. Only asked that we come and escorted us."

"If not criminals, suspects. We were not *asked* to come. They *made* us come. I don't remember being given a choice. They sent us there to fix the air handler. Why us? They need scapegoats. That's what we are, scapegoats." His finger wagged at Raff. "You watch, we'll be arrested. *Disappeared.* They probably just heard all that too. I don't care." Looking at a camera he repeated in a deafening shout, "I. Don't. *Care.*"

By the end of Mike's tirade, Gift's emotional vigor failed to conquer a foreboding rush of panic overwhelming her. Suddenly on her feet, she darted to the door. Jerking her head left, right, up, and down, showed her a red circle on the biometric scanner panel and no door handle. *Trapped!* Pounding on the door her only recourse—the fight-or-flight auto-human reaction triggered flight—she needed to get out of there.

Raff stepped beside her, but no consoling words or shoulder rubs equaled the unbridled hysteria, so she clutched Gift's arms and pulled her from the door. With Gift's emotional and physical exhaustion pushed well beyond her tolerable limit, Raff helped her to a seat. "Water. She *needs* water."

When the door slid open a hard-faced man entered, tall and lean. He had a prominent chin with a deep cleft and held a device about twice the size of Gift's book reader with two hands. He had no water. Saying nothing, he cast a judgmental look over Gift—not fully recovered from her panic attack. Her glazed-over eyes met his briefly.

"Water?" Raff demanded.

A full-figured older woman entered with a bun atop her hair reaching the man's shoulder. She had kind eyes and a cup of water. Raff took it and helped Gift sip it slowly.

"Now, if we could all please have a seat, we can begin." A statement so bland, the expression so empty, he could have been working at a coffee bar and taking their order.

Mike took the last seat on the side with four chairs, while Raff's chair screeched in complaint as she dragged it next to Gift and put her arm around the trepidatious young woman. The tall, lean man sat across from Gift, while the lady with the kind eyes sat facing the empty chair between Raff and Mike.

"What exactly are we—" A raised hand from the woman stopped Mike cold, its palm toward his face. She said nothing.

"As I said, we can begin." Deadpan in facial expression and monotone in words, he said, "Mister Russo, you and Miss Ojo are bench-mates. How long have you been together now?"

"Seven years."

"And almost four months," Gift added in a whimper.

"Good." The guy shifted his eyes from Mike to Gift. "You're with us now. So, seven years and nearly four months on the same bench. You must be close." His statement hung in the air like a question.

"Yeah, sure." Gift added, "We're friends." Dim light from the harsh man's handheld cast a ghostly glow over him. He maintained eye contact with Gift.

"I see. Tell us about him, then."

"Huh? *Mike?* Tell you what about Mike?"

"Yeah. What do you want to know about me? I'm right here, you know." A stern look accompanied another stop sign from the silent one, hunching Mike into a submissive posture.

"Miss Ojo, my dear." Placation slid the words off his tongue. "Please tell us about him."

She looked up from between raised shoulders. "We're friends, like I said. He's an excellent technician, did good work."

"Sure, he did, you all did. But is he a complainer? Does Mister Russo have problems with the way we manage the colony? Has he ever spoken against Administration or the Board of Directors?"

Chills ran down her back as Gift contemplated the line of questions. *He's digging for problems. Could Mike have been right?* "I... I don't know what you mean."

"What I mean, young lady..." Hardness made the term derogatory. If meant to put her in her place and assert his dominant position, it succeeded. "When Mike complains about colony management. When he says you are being told lies. There is a grand conspiracy. Do *you* agree?"

With glossy eyes opened wider than seemed possible, incapable of blinking, Gift's chin dropped just enough to separate her lips. "I. I. Um. I..."

"Che *diavolo*." Uncharacteristic language from Raff. "What is this about? We just saved the colony from a major catastrophe. You should thank us, Mike too. He was invaluable in getting that air handler back up and running. And this is what we get?"

Surprisingly, the woman offered no stop gesture to Raff, allowing her to finish her thought uninterrupted while the wide-chinned guy stayed locked onto Gift's eyes. "Jean?" he said.

"Something impossible happened today and we need to understand how. We received your field record and the automated logs from your handhelds, which gave us an overall view of what you found. The thing of it is... The knowledge to carry out what happened, that would take a team, say, of someone with a proficient understanding of the hardware, plus someone brilliant enough, a highly skilled data operator, to write and deploy the malicious code, the corrupted OS, you called it."

"Esatto." A horizontal raised palm emphasized Raff's word. "That's exactly what we concluded, and it will be in our full report. So why—"

"Because, Miss Di Gaetano," the woman, Jean, said. "Because we are looking at such a team *here*, aren't we?"

The thought landed hard, punching Gift in the gut, bringing a bitter taste to the back of her throat. Raff sat speechless with her mouth wide open.

"Why... Why would we? I mean... why would we break it and, and then go fix it? Why would *anyone* do that?" Like cards across the table, Gift dealt out the words, putting them in play.

The man squinted at Gift. "Why indeed. Maybe you had no choice. Didn't expect to get called to fix it. Conceivably, you just wanted to prove you could do it. Perhaps you thought an hour offline was enough to prove your point. You tell us."

"We climbed up there, risked our necks. This is crazy. You people—"

"Miss Ojo performed the diagnostics. Did you observe her, Mister Russo? From your vantage, could you see what she was doing?" Questions and accusations floated from him to Mike with eye contact never breaking from Gift.

"Wait. No. You... just wait." Mike jabbed a finger at the nameless man as if poking him to make his point stick. He got the hand signal from Jean again and, for an inexplicable reason, he obeyed. Gift considered the little woman's power over him, not sure how it worked even if she also fell under its spell.

"Could be one of you." The man waved his hand over Gift and Mike, then pointed at Raff, reaching near to her nose from across the table. "But you. You'd only need one of them to do what you wanted. Would you use your gullible young friend who would likely do anything you asked? Or would you have used the wild talk and conspiracy theorizing of Mister Russo? An easy sway to do your bidding. All you'd have to do is listen to him and agree with his theories. You probably even got him to think the whole thing was his idea."

Raff leaned back from the accusatory finger, crossed her arms, and wore a cold steel face Gift had never seen. It didn't suit her. A single tear rolled down Gift's cheek as Raff shook her head deliberately, exhaling deeply. The man's hand returned to the device, but his rapt focus stayed on Gift. What was it about Gift? Did she seem the most vulnerable?

Whatever the aim, the results reached the desired effect: Gift dissolved into a mess of nerves, like loose wires—their shielding melted and peeled back, twisted in knots. Such unrelenting pressure filled her with a compulsion to comply, to submit and obey, do whatever they ask and accept any consequence for the good of the colony. But they were the heroes in this story, Captain Arcadia and his gallant crew, not the monstrous purple alien trying to destroy the MSS Banzai. They had saved the day, and it wasn't enough.

A steely gaze exposed Raff's disgust at the proceedings. "This is what you want? You treat us like criminals, make wild, unfounded accusations."

The man looked deep into Raff's eyes, his stare cold and unnerving, Raff a prisoner to it. "The code, it impressed you, didn't it? You admire it. But how many people do you honestly think could have written it?"

Raff paused with eyes squinted in contemplation.

The echo of a blaring alarm saturated the space as a klaxon sounded a high-pitched tone that started deep and rose in volume, settled back to nothing, started again, rose, and settled. Deafening, but not coming from a display or device. This surrounded them, rattling their bones. The man's face became paler than the tabletop laminate, and his colleague leaned over to see his display. What it showed her opened her eyes like Ping-Pong balls.

"*Explosion.*"

12

Explosion! What could that have meant? The two rose instantly to their feet and pushed their chairs back in haste—the man's tilted and let out a hollow pop when it met the concrete floor. "Which water recycler?" the woman asked as they fled. The tall, lean man's scowl told her she'd said too much in front of their *guests*. Once again, the three were alone, still trapped in the small room and even more confused. They would have thought that impossible three seconds earlier.

"We weren't meant to hear that." Mike stated the obvious and Gift found hearing it aloud gave it a sense of realism.

"She said explosion. Was anyone hurt?"

Shrugging off Gift's question, Mike said, "These nuts are targeting key environmental systems in the colony. Air. Water. They're making their point way more forceful than the *All Lies* messages."

"But... an explosion?" Gift's words trembled. "People may have been hurt, or..."

"Cara, we don't know. But water recyclers aren't in public areas, so it's likely no one would have been near it. We just don't know, so we can hope for the best."

Mike paced along the short wall in the back of the room. Three steps, turn, again, then stopped. "Don't forget they've been accusing us of breaking the thing we just repaired. They accused us of sabotage. Now a water recycler on the same day? They're going to lock us up, maybe disappear us for good. They think we're *terrorists*. And if they hurt anyone...?"

"*Allora*..." The pop of Raff's palm smacking the table filled the room. "There's nothing we can do about it, so let's not spend our waiting conjuring up every horrific outcome or possibility. It'll only make us anxious, worrying about what won't happen. It isn't healthy, not productive."

With no assurances in Mike's nod, Gift stretched her arm over the table and laid her head down. A cough came more from nervousness than any need in her lungs or throat. Raff moved beside Mike and placed her nose against his ear's soft flesh. "You need to stop with the negativity. You're making Gift upset. If you don't stop this—"

Jerking his head away, he mouthed *Okay* as he raised his palms and pushed them toward her in a sign of compliant surrender. The silence of time passing cooled the moment. Since their inquisitors abruptly detached, they were left with no idea what happened, and no one bothered to check on them.

Mike looked up at the camera. "Hey. Someone must be there. Watching. Listening. You know we're all starving here, right? Must be hours past lunch and you leave us in here with no food or water. No one even asked if we needed to use the toilet. This is unacceptable. Hello?" A voice raised in frustration was the limit of his power. The replied silence was maddening.

Another fifteen or twenty minutes pulled against the last strings of patience any of them had left—it could have been longer. At the sound of a door sliding, six eyes fixed themselves on the open space. The second it took for a figure to appear dragged as the last hour of a morning shift when a waft of air from the cafeteria carried in lunch's aroma. A silhouette became the form of a petite young woman with hair buzzed short on the sides and piled high on the top. She said nothing as she placed a tray holding three sandwiches and three cups of water on the table.

"Thank you," Raff said.

The girl nodded. "This door will remain open. To the right is a restroom. We ask you to stay here until someone comes for you." She turned back to the door and got a foot out when Gift's words stopped her.

"Wait, please. We know there was an explosion. Can you just tell us what happened? We're worried someone may have been hurt."

"There was an overload of a noncritical system near Citadome Four." She stepped out hurriedly before being stopped by more words or inquiries. She'd done her job, answering their questions clearly not part of it. Gift wondered if she may have gotten the poor girl in trouble.

None of them would have described the sandwiches as good—passable, at best. But they gave their bodies needed nourishment and settled the roaring beasts that had been pulling their bellies tight. Hopes lifted that with fuller stomachs and much-needed water, clarity of thought may return—after using the toilet.

Returned from the restroom, the women were more at ease until they noticed Mike's delay and Gift's face paled. "What's he doing?"

"He's probably trying every door, looking for a vent to crawl through, any way out. Knowing him—" Raff stopped herself as the reason for his delay became obvious, swirling in the air around them. Mike needed to do more than urinate. Gift coughed and Raff waved her hand in front of her nose. For the first time in hours, they both smiled. Spit sprinkled through Gift's closed lips, unable to restrain the outburst of a chuckle. When Mike returned, they were demure.

Mike had to react to the girl's report. "Overload of a noncritical system? I mean, can you believe that? You saw the panic in what's-his-name's face. And that woman said '*explosion,*' not overload. And a water recycler, that's not exactly noncritical."

"You think she lied?" It bothered Gift to think negatively of anyone, so she never did—except for Sara. That she could think so poorly of Sara, who'd done nothing deserving, disturbed her deeply. She would not allow that for the petite young lady who'd brought them much-needed food and water.

"No, I don't think so. She told the truth… about what *she* heard. That's the official story for the colony."

"Now I guess you finally believe me. You laughed and called my ideas *crazy conspiracy theories*. Now you see." Mike made no attempt to hide the smugness in his pontification. "I told you they built the colony on deception. This is what those *All Lies* messages are all about."

"But you understand how these things sounded. *And* most of it is utter nonsense. All that's happening now doesn't make all the other crazy theories true. So, let's not blow this out of proportion."

While Mike shrugged once again, Gift wholeheartedly agreed.

Another hour passed, or longer, until the unmistakable sound of an opening door spilled in from the corridor and captured the trio's attention. In unison, their heads turned to see Jean followed by the tall man with no name. Gift had been interviewed—interrogated—twice by nameless men. She saw the tactic in anonymity, flooding her with an unnerving trepidation, her heart pounding each time. Its return with the man was unwelcome, sinking her deeper into her seat.

The little round woman with the kind eyes, which lost their compassion during the pause, spoke first. "We are sorry to have left you here for so long. How is everyone?"

How is everyone? What kind of question is that? Gift's thoughts were best left unsaid, find a nicer opening. "How is everyone? What kind of question is that?" came out as her opening just the same.

"Let's settle. We are almost done here, but I wanted to apologize for keeping you so long. I will let Fred explain the rest."

The cold, calculated harshness of the interrogator waned with the anonymity removed. He was Fred, that changed things. At least Gift thought it did.

Fred said, "We left abruptly due to an incident which demanded our full attention. Everything is fine with the malfunctioning unit—noncritical and working again. So back to you lot."

Scowling, Mike barked, "*Noncritical*? Are you serious? A water recycler explosion? We deserve the truth after what you put us through."

"What we put you through, Mister Russo? You are being investigated for two system malfunctions today. One confirmed sabotage. And you heard incorrectly. The second incident was a hydroponics regulator overload."

Perhaps Fred having a name improved nothing, his harshness undiminishable, just as forceful and intimidating as when he was nameless. Although Gift reckoned that made him good at his job, she couldn't admire that about him. If Mike were a turtle, he could have hidden himself inside his shell. Unsure it was called turtle, Gift marveled at how its head and neck completely disappeared into the safety of its own shell when frightened. In that moment, she wished Mike were a turtle. Left defenseless without an outer shell, his only recourse was to withdraw into himself.

"Miss Di Gaetano, Miss Ojo." Fred's cadence returned to its default monotone. "Please follow my colleague."

"What, what about Mike?" The question inadequately expressed Gift's rambling thoughts. *Where are we going? Why are you separating us? What will happen to us? To Mike? Why'd you say Mike was the subject of your open investigation?*

"Don't worry about Mister Russo. The two of you are excused... for now."

They followed Jean out of the room and down the hall with Gift's mind racing through every possible fate Mike may experience next, however improbable. At the end of the corridor, they traversed a proper reception area with inviting chairs that were single-person sofas in a room cheerfully outfitted in soft yellow and shades of orange. Plants hung from the walls and a tree stood in the center. Its precise positioning pleased Gift but only momentarily distracted her anxiety as they entered another hallway.

"We must confiscate all your clothes as evidence. There are disposable coveralls and shoes for you both." In the narrow corridor Jean's words ended at the door labeled *Locker Room*.

Obediently, Gift stepped into the room. "I don't understand. Our clothes are evidence?"

"That's what they said. I need all your clothes and shoes in that bin. Undergarments too. You have two minutes to change."

When Jean stepped back through the open door, the two shared a look that said, *let's get this over with*, then shed their clothes. The coverall was the same as what Gift had to wear after her workplace shower years ago. Its discomfort felt familiar but at least creepy Luca was not there. Jean returned as promised.

"What about our clothes and shoes for tomorrow?" Gift wondered the same before Raff asked.

"Retrieve them from your passageway laundry station before work. Toss those disposables in the bin."

"What about Mike?" Anxiety cracked Gift's voice.

"Probably taken to change."

When the confused friends reached Gift's Box, Raff took her hand. "Gift. Do you want me to stay? I'm worried about you."

"No... I'll be fine. I just wanna rest. I'll check on Mike later. See you in the morning."

13

Wrapped in the paper coverall, Gift sat in silence on her bed and drifted into sleep—thirty minutes not nearly enough. In frustration she ripped the disposable garment from her body and tossed it in the rubbish bin. Devoid of mental clarity, Gift stood beside herself in silence. Unknown minutes faded into the past before she addressed the vid screen. "On. VidChat Michael Russo."

Clarity struck like a forehead smack when the camera showed her unclothed self on the display and her pale-yellow shower robe made its way over her shame in haste. A pleasant animation took the center of the screen in a splash of various blues swirling like a digital waltz. A No Reply notice replaced the happy graphic, taking its feeling with it. *Try not to worry. Raff said not to worry until there was something to worry about.* The thoughts failed to bring comfort. Five minutes later, another attempt found an identical result. Another five minutes yielded the same. "Perhaps now it's okay to worry."

An echo of three taps penetrated the door and Gift jumped up and ordered the door to open, her cry of Mike's name falling upon Marco's ears. He may have noticed the disappointment in her stare. It wasn't for him—not his fault, not being Mike. He held a food container. "This was at your door. I thought maybe it came after you got home and didn't want to leave it." The smirk he may have thought to be a smile froze on him, awaiting a reply.

"Sorry Marco. Come in." The surprise of her invitation showed on his face. The boy in her home, she in her robe. It didn't seem to faze him in the slightest, or her—each concept equally intriguing. The recognizable food container, Mom's Jollof Rice. As if she'd known, the way mothers just knew things, that Gift needed comfort food more than ever and lacked all desire to go get herself anything to eat. Grateful hands took the container from him and placed it on the counter. His head tilted toward the lowered bed, filling his brow with an unspoken question.

"It refuses to go flush. I... I just can't look at it like that. So, I leave it down. It's silly."

"I get it. Not silly. You logged a maintenance request?"

"Yeah, couple days ago. They said eighteen days in queue. Not a top priority. Not even a problem for anyone else, I guess."

"Let me take a look."

Gift knew the boy worked in housing maintenance, but she'd never have imposed. "Just don't fuss about it. Non fa niente." He took that for a yes and inspected the bed, gave it a few pushes as Gift had done, and got the same result.

"Did you bang this repeatedly the other night?" She nodded, embarrassed he'd heard. "I can fix this for you."

"Oh no, I don't want to put you out. Maintenance will be around soon enough."

"I can fix it in five minutes. I mean, if... you're not going out or doing anything, I can take care of this right now."

Marco's energetic eagerness swept a flow of easiness over her, so she allowed his assistance, and he left to retrieve a toolbox. Another three raps on the door, she let him back in with toolkit in hand. Gift made her way past Marco and considered her robe as she knelt carefully on the floor beneath the faux window beside the door.

After the last minor adjustments, Marco packed his tools systematically. Gift leaned in to see the order, the neatness, and found it soothing. Never had she imagined she and her young neighbor would share that in common. He stood and invited her to have a look. A hand swirling over the corner of the bed found it flush in the inset. "Marco, thank you so much." The gentle peck she placed on his cheek turned it bright red.

"You're welcome. Glad I could help. I know the backlog of requests we have right now."

"You're an angel, really. Grazie mille."

"My pleasure. Any time you need something, please, tell *me* before you open a maintenance request."

"You're sweet. And this is the longest conversation we've ever had... Hey, you like spicy foods?"

"Yeah, sure. Why?"

"You said no plans, me either. The container? Mom's Jollof rice. It's *amazing*, my absolute favorite. There's enough to share... if you want."

"Um... Sure."

With the boy gone to put his toolkit away and wash up, Gift put on proper clothes and tried to reach Mike again. Same no reply. Nothing she could do, waiting would be the hardest part. When Marco entered, he didn't seem to know what to do with his arms or the hands attached, as if he had never stood before, uncomfortable with the bones and muscles under his own skin. Gift imagined she must have looked the same at her Resident Services interview. This was different, and she thought it was cute how she made him nervous. They sat to eat.

"So, Jollof rice?"

"Mom's specialty. A recipe passed mother to daughter since we left Nigeria so many generations back."

"Nigeria, that was in... Africa, right?" Tutors didn't bother teaching Earth geography.

"Yep. My First Ones were an Italian man and a Nigerian woman who came to work on the project from its initial stages on Earth. Twenty years they lived here while it was unfinished, helping to build what we have today. They gave all those workers residency in the colony." That last part *was* taught to students.

Marco finished long before Gift and amused her with stories of funny things he'd seen on his maintenance job. One older woman in her senior work assignment didn't trust the laundry service. Marco would enter the Box and she'd have strings run overhead with all her underwear hanging to dry even though the sonic sink she cleaned them in used no water. When called to repair her food warmer, he asked about how it broke.

"She said... She said, *'I cleaned my blouse and pants in the sink, and I wanted to dry press them, so I put them in the food warmer on reheat.'* Clothes in a food warmer to dry press them. Real bag of nuts."

The *old lady* voice invoked more laughter than the tale. "You're funny."

Marco rose and grabbed the bowls and spoons from the table before Gift could protest. He cleaned them, and Gift allowed it, though she would redo them later when he left. "Thanks again, Gift. I really, really enjoyed it." His gratitude seemed excessive for a meal and company, causing guilt to flutter in her stomach for selfishly using his companionship. But Gift enjoyed the evening too, finding Marco to be sweet, funny, and kind.

Alone again, her thoughts shifted to Mike, bringing a painful guilt that stabbed like a knife in the gut from enjoying herself while Mike could have been who-knew-where, having who-knew-what done to him. How could she have enjoyed herself? Another failed vidChat request.

Enveloped in the darkness around her bed, Gift tossed and turned, wrestling with clothes unwilling to adapt to her contortions. She jerked at her shirt in anger, as if it were the source of everything bad that had happened. At 03:42, her display asked for confirmation before connecting her vidChat request. Groggy eyes followed the dancing graphic, waiting for the No Reply message. Instead, a head's silhouette distinguished itself from the surrounding darkness, the screen's glow its only illumination. "Mike?"

"Huh? Gift?" The palms of his hands pressed into his eyes, and he rubbed deeply.

"Yeah sweetie, it's me."

Mike blinked hard. "Oh, hey. I was asleep."

"Yeah, sorry. Tried calling so many times. I was worried when you didn't answer."

"I'm fine. They escorted me home about O-one thirty. I climbed into bed and died. Too late to call you. Sorry."

"I'm just glad you're okay. Go back to sleep, I'll see you in the morning. Love you."

14 | Day Fourteen

The collision would have tossed Gift to the floor beside her workbench if not for Raff's arms surrounding and supporting her. "*Come stai*? Did you sleep? Did you hear from Mike? Are you okay?"

"Buongiorno, Raff. Yeah, I'm fine. I finally reached him, late. He said they brought him home after O-one thirty."

"He's okay then?" The concern almost surprised Gift as she had a hunch Raff only tolerated the young man for her.

"Yeah, I was such a mess. I woke him, but he was okay."

"I'm so glad. I tried him as well..." Raff looked at the empty space beside Gift. "*Ma*, where is he?"

"Making up his medical. He missed it yesterday."

"*Vero*. He goes on Sunday after lunch." Gift nodded. "It felt wrong to leave you, I wanted to stay."

"No, I told you. Thought I needed to lay on my bed and cry 'til I fell asleep. Then Mom left Jollof at my door. Marco and I ate. Mom gave me a lot."

"Marco? The boy next door? The one who barely talks to you and likes to gawk at you? *That* Marco?"

"He's not like that. Not creepy or anything. *Actually*? Turns out he's real sweet. He fixed my bed, it's flush now."

"You spent the whole evening with the boy?"

"Look. He found the rice at my door and brought it in and asked why the bed was lowered. He didn't even think it was silly. He insisted on fixing it for me, took him no time. Then I offered to share the Jollof. It was nice."

"Gift, he's ten years younger. He's a child."

"He-did-me-a-favor. Was-being-nice. We-ate-together. All-of-a-sudden, you think everything-has some… *romantic* undertone. Mike. Marco. I'm *twenty-six*, remember?"

"*Mi dispiace*. No need to get upset."

Get upset? Raff's words told Gift her tone was harsh. She felt anger. Raff was just being her usual big sister persona, so why did Gift get angry? "No, I'm sorry. Really, I shouldn't've snapped. It's…"

"I know, *Cara*. Mike is fine, that's the important thing."

Gift nodded and sniffled.

***

"What happened to Mike?" Tina asked when Mike wasn't at the lunch table.

"He's fine." Raff spared Gift the emotion needed for the explanation. "With that emergency yesterday, he missed his medical visit, so he made it up this morning."

"Good. I got a little nervous something may have happened." Charlie avoided pointing out the emotional storm reddening Gift's eyes.

His thoughtfulness took Gift back to when Luca had been part of the weekly dinner group. Charlie couldn't understand why Gift refused each time he and Raff tried to include her. Over lunchtime chats with the young Gift, Raff had asked her why she never joined. After repeated prodding, Gift told her of Luca's obsession with her backside and how it made her feel uncomfortable and dirty. The idea of being in a social setting with him—and in anything less than a coverall—horrified her. Raff told her to report it. After three weeks of Gift not doing so, Raff told Charlie and the next day Luca was reassigned. Charlie must have told someone on her behalf. With Luca ousted from the group, Gift happily joined. How they looked out for each other filled Gift with a sense of security.

***

When 14:00 arrived without Mike, Gift's workbench display activated. If her screen danced across the bench, it wouldn't have been enough to grab her attention. With no conscious decision, she pressed *Start* for her first task of the afternoon. A hopeful glance to Raff met a gaze of concern offering no answers. Also, there was Claudia, with no concern in her eyes. To be fair, Gift didn't know Claudia well, so had no read on her expression. It could have been anything from curiosity to trying to hold back flatulence.

Gift did the work, but it felt surreal, like watching someone else do it in a vid playing in the background and giving it little interest. More than once, she caught herself and rechecked her work. One board would have malfunctioned because she replaced a working part, leaving the damaged one in place. She didn't recall ever being so sloppy, so careless at her work. Raff's message lifted Gift's mental fog. It said, *Charlie's directly after work.*

***

It was time for Tina and Charlie to get the complete story. Raff told them everything, with Gift following as if hearing it for the first time. It helped her line everything up and organize the events and details in order, making sense of it, from the frizzy-haired girl to the air handler. When Raff mentioned Claudia, Gift's ears perked up.

"I don't know about her. She was keen on following what Gift and Mike were doing even before I left to join them. She watched over my shoulder as I tried to access the unit from my station. There's *something* about her... I just don't trust. She asked me so many questions, wanted to understand how the code worked, how it damaged the unit. Endless questions about how I stopped it. And not a single question about us, or Mike. I found it strange. I wonder..."

***

In the corridor the walk's silence broke when Raff asked Tina about her mystery man. The way Mom knew when Gift needed Jollof, Raff knew when her mind needed to come down, to be occupied with something trivial. The blankness in Tina's round face could have meant anything. Then it soured.

"Seriously? After all that, this is what you wanna talk about? We still know nothing about what happened to Mike, we have saboteurs in the colony, and you want to talk about me and Massimo?"

There it was. She let the name slip past her lips.

"So, we have a name." Raff offered a playful smile.

Gift became giddy. "We have a name... we may as well meet him."

"A name is all you get. *Raff?* You sly little fox, you."

"*So...?* Still potential in him, then?"

"Potential. Decent chance, actually."

An unfamiliar glitter sparkled in Tina's eyes in contemplation of Massimo. Of possibilities. Its radiance led Gift's musings to wonder, *Might they announce a Union. What about Raff? What will become of group dinners?* Dread followed that contemplation. She might have had her last dinner with Mike, but not known it. Would it have been any different if she'd known?

"Tina?" Gift hadn't noticed that Tina said goodbye and left them. When she saw a kiosk in the spoke, not sure which they were in, she ran toward it. "VidChat Michael Russo." Those familiar swirls in shades of blue were hateful again. When they reached Gift's Box, Raff held two pizzas Gift didn't recall stopping to pick up. Too worried to eat, Gift barely touched hers. She tried Mike again. Those dreaded blue swirls started their dance but this time an image dissolved into view. "Mike?"

"Hey Gift. Just got home. Sorry I missed you at work. More questioning today after my medical visit."

"You okay, sweetie?"

"Fine. Nothing more for you? Oh, hey Raff."

"Ciao." Raff waved at the screen. "We were home by eighteen hundred and that was it. I keep thinking it isn't, but for—"

"Did you eat? I have a pizza here and I can't eat it."

"I'm really beat but no, haven't eaten. I may just fall out in bed. I'm too tired to come all that way. Thanks though."

"I'll bring it to you, you should eat. I need to see you."

Gift heard the pleading in her expression and didn't care. She offered to appease herself as much as—more than—to feed him.

"I'll be right over... End... Sorry Raff, I need to see him. I need to know he's okay."

"We just saw that. He's exhausted, you could tell. Let him go to sleep."

It angered gift that Raff's words were logical. She had no room for logic. "I've gotta see him. I have to." Already on her feet, Gift unzipped her coverall. No stopping her. With shorts and a t-shirt on, she opened her door. "Stay, finish your pizza. I'll see you tomorrow."

"Gift...?"

"Don't Raff. Don't say anything. I'm going."

"Forgetting something?" She handed the pizza box to Gift. "Give Mike my best."

15

Mike picked at half of the pizza, insisting Gift take a slice, and piled all the salame on her piece—too spicy for him. She took a bite and swallowed. "Tell me, sweetie, if you want. What's happened since they dismissed Raff and me yesterday. What do they want from you?"

"Yesterday? Well, they hurled accusations, speculations for what felt like hours. All these scenarios they dreamed up. Like they were trying to bait me into giving up some version of a truth they'd accept because they didn't like the one we told. They pushed me to give up Raff, let her take the blame. You? Me? We might have been duped into doing the physical stuff."

"So, they really think it was Raff. That's crazy."

"They wanted me to say that it was *you* and Raff. I was in the wrong place at the wrong time, you know? I tell them it was you two, and I go free. When I refused, the big-chin guy said they'd look more closely at you and Raff, and they let me go."

"And today? After your medical, they came for you?"

"Something like that. That same woman came in and started with more questions about you and Raff, but mostly you. She wanted so much detail about me and you. How close we are, how often we see each other outside of work, how I feel about you? She even asked about us hugging. If I thought you were pretty."

"And... how did you answer *that*?" Gift planted an elbow in his gut with a playful smirk. Mike's brow furled, making a vertical crease above the bridge of his nose. His classic, *Please, you should know better* look.

"She asked if we kissed or have been intimate? I had to remind her we are *both* pre-G.M."

"E.CID. They keep looking for it. To blame our behavior on it."

"Guess so. I mean, I never figured that. As Sakura said, it's more an issue for women. But I don't have those thoughts or desires yet. Oh Gift, truly, I never... *never* think of you like that. You gotta believe me."

"I know, sweetie. I know."

"Oh, this was weird. I mean, the whole thing was weird. They took me back to that same room in the admin building, gave me another gross sandwich, and asked me about Claudia. I told them I barely knew her. They wanted to know if I noticed anything odd or suspicious about her. If I'd ever seen her and Raff talking about something in secret. Like I'd have any way to tell if they spent time together out of work or were conspiring or something. Each time, I told them I didn't know anything. Then they asked me how often *you* talked with Claudia, if you two were close."

Gift's eyebrows raised to the logic in the investigation.

"Flat out, I said, 'No. They don't talk or spend any time together.' But... sneaky woman, she asked if I was with you every moment so I could say for certain that you and Claudia were never together? She made it more than it was. To say that my not being able to confirm your every movement was the same as saying you and Claudia *were* spending time together. It was all so... twisted. Gift, I'm sorry. I hoped they'd stop looking at you and Raff if they were looking at Claudia."

"You did your best, Mike." He shrugged a less than convincing shrug to say, *I hear you*, while not surrendering agreement on the subject. "*Claudia.*" Gift's face shone as if a lightbulb switched on above her head. Dots started connecting. "Raff just told us she doesn't trust Claudia. Raff didn't say—I guess I just inferred—she suspects her bench-mate was curious how to *bypass* it being found and stopped. Maybe she just meant that Claudia wanted to learn how to do what Raff did, you know? To advance her career. Or maybe she meant that she's the saboteur. I'm speculating now. Am I? *Speculating?* You think?"

"What else can we do? We know so little, besides what we know. Someone sabotaged an air handler. Likely the same one caused that explosion. Oh, wait a minute. It took out an *entire* water recycler. There should be serious ration cutbacks by now. Have you heard anything?"

"No."

Both felt the weight of the word.

"The colony can run without an air handler for an hour. But one of the water recyclers? As strict as they ration. I mean, we have sonic sinks for Pete's sake." Unsure how Mike's friend Peter fit into it, Gift followed Mike's reasoning. One of the colony's most precious resources, any inequality in water reserves would disrupt the balance of life. "Two showers a week, Gift. And we get what, mist. Not even a flow of water. If it's that tight, and there are only six recyclers, far as I know—we have one per section. So how can we be fine with a fifth of our supply gone? An explosion. That recycler and water reservoir are gone. Where are the ration reductions?"

"Oh mamma. What if the rations don't need to be so strict? Also too, one recycler down would be one-sixth. If there's six, I mean. Not a fifth." The correction scrunched Mike's face in confusion. "Is this some form of control over us? Or... could this mean maybe the terraforming *has* been more successful than they tell us? Might it be cooperation from one of the colonies? We know so little about them. I'm speculating again. Am I? Sorry."

"No, you're right. Honestly, it could be so many things."

Gift overlaid her countenance of gloom with optimism. "It may be nothing... Wouldn't it make sense, I mean, it would be prudent if the rationing's intentionally stricter than needed. Think about it... If, if we absolutely needed *all six* recyclers to have the bare minimum of water, with tight rationing, and we lost one? You'd expect an immediate reduction—have to be. That would be poor planning, risking the life of the colony. And on two-hundred-year-old equipment we're constantly repairing and maintaining. It makes more sense, it would be a much better plan if... say, we can make it fine on five, maybe on four recyclers, and the rationing allows for a reserve."

"Okay... We can make it fine on five, maybe four recyclers, and the rationing allows for a re—"

"Stop that. Why are you repeating what I just said?"

"You told me to. You said, '*Say,* we can make it fine—'"

The slap to his chest may have hurt Gift's hand more than him. Mike's sense of what he called humor sometimes got under her skin. *"Anyway.* If we lose one, or even two... and we survive. I mean, I never thought about this. Never really had to, I guess. But if *you* were planning this colony, wouldn't that make sense? More than using every bit of resource and being one failure away from total catastrophe?"

Mike's deep exhale made his objection loud and clear. He wouldn't agree. To him, his conspiracy was no longer a theory. Gift knew to leave it at that or risk heightening emotions that would have only one potential effect—driving a wedge between them. One nearly split them over the frizzy-haired girl, and she had determined never to let that happen again.

Walking home with the puzzle pieces swirling around her, fitting them together, the picture took on a new form. What came into view, despite a few gaps awaiting pieces yet unfound, formed the face of Claudia. *Might she be the center of the whole thing? If not, perhaps a key player?*

Now Gift had two enemies, one of which may have been justified.

16 | Week Three

S olace floated like clouds in a sky Gift had never seen, never would. It came from the knowledge that the colony had reserves, planned well by *The Founders*. The vandals, saboteurs, were wrong. And if Claudia had been involved, the focus of those hard-nosed inquisitors would be on her.

She gets what's coming.

A morning such as this could only have been elevated if actual sunlight shone upon her. Radiation-protective solid walls and domes meant no one knew what the current state of terraforming made of the sky beyond. As with prior generations, the artificial was all Gift had known. Yet the hope burned brighter in her than in most. By her senior years, the surface would be semi-livable and she would spend evenings outside, inhaling air that hadn't passed through a handler. In truth, no one had realistic expectations of what life would be like outside the colony. How close would it be to memories of Earth? Hope didn't need details. Part of its wonder lay in anticipation of the surprise.

From across the open workspace, the corner of Gift's eye met Claudia taking her seat at her bench. No, at Raff's bench. A new yet familiar tension in Gift's muscles stiffened her back and squinted her eyes. She'd learned to recognize it, but for the first time she welcomed it. Looking at Claudia, anger didn't feel out of place. Sara's felt different, wrong. Not this. Claudia's actions exceeded equipment failures which put people in danger and risked the colony. She was the reason Gift and her friends were suspects, interrogated as criminals, and humiliated. The anxious worry, the loss of sleep, the panic, the draining of raw emotion, it was all Claudia. Anger found its place, it belonged there.

A feeling of normalcy settled in, and Gift desperately wanted the day to be mundane, but the day had another idea. A new task popped on the display, priority job, urgent, pushing all other tasks to the back of the queue. It wasn't on *her* screen. Besides the insult of getting snuffed on the task, she had to finish the board Mike started. The *why* demanded time on the brain, which Gift's brain readily apportioned it. The senior tech always got the priority task. The *why* hung over the bench like a branch reaching out from the tree in her childhood group's spot, its shadow casting darkness on what had been a bright and cheerful day.

Two admin guards set a cart beside the bench on Mike's side and left. From the cart's basket he pulled a control board about the size of a pizza box, but a narrower rectangle. Mike removed a small box containing various parts from chip arrays to transistors to crystal diodes, and laid everything on his side of the bench. Gift looked over it with fascinated curiosity. "Something tells me this is related to that explosion," he said in a whisper only Gift would hear.

While the board had the same design language of modules for various devices from shower booth injector controllers to regulator modules on tropospheric ozone reactors, her keen eye noted the one difference on this board that unmistakably put it on a water recycler. Only they had H_2O purification filters that required a secondary microprocessor to run its algorithms. She said nothing. After learning from past mistakes, Gift gave him room, not holding a senior position over him or offering suggestions he'd scowl at her for making. Acting as an assistant, hopeful he'd see it that way, she reached for the circuit flow monitor, the next step in the diagnostic process. His reach for it with a short nod told her he'd accepted the help as such.

To initiate step three, he jacked cables from the board into his terminal to run full system diagnostics, but Gift wondered if he was making connections yet. Initial instincts having been spot on, had Mike deduced which part he held? He removed the remaining items from the basket, which Gift couldn't see earlier without looking like she was trying to look. "What the...?" she said. Mike studied it silently, processing, trying to figure it out. *Don't take over. Give him space,* she reminded herself.

Mike set the box on the bench. "Not sure. It looks like shards of something, or what *was* something." He held one of the larger pieces—jagged, rough, with burn marks on the edges. "Not an electrical burn. See the edges here?" She did. She noted the same and guessed the conclusion he was about to make. Lowering to a whisper, he continued, "I guess it was part of that explosion. Something violently ripped it off. I'd say, the casing of that recyc—*hydroponics regulator* that overloaded."

Why trust Mike with this? she couldn't help wondering. His getting this task didn't sit right in Gift's mind and unsettled her stomach. *If they think I'm working with Claudia, is this a trap for me?*

More of what looked like shrapnel spilled to Gift's side of the bench. She had been craning her neck longer than she realized. As she straightened up and tilted her head back to relax the muscle, she became aware of the cameras and made a logical assumption. *They're watching me right now.* Shivers chased the chill Gift's pondering brought. *They're watching to observe my interest. Would they assume I'm trying to protect myself? Keep Mike from discovering the truth?*

To think in such dubious terms, getting into the mindset of a saboteur, hurt Gift's brain. It took being wrongfully accused of a heinous act to start her mind on such a path. Corrupted by the implication of corruption. Her head became heavy holding the profound wrongness of that.

***

Raff and Charlie had already started eating, Claudia sitting with them. *Curious. Today of all days?* Mike and Gift grabbed their lunch from the self-service dispensers. Grilled veggies and tofu for Gift, protein burger for Mike. The unusual quiet hanging over the table didn't seem to serve Claudia's interests.

"So… It looks like you've got an interesting job today, Mike. I noticed those guards bring it in. Strange. Must be something important." A question clearly implied.

"Not really. I'm finding a fault, like most other tasks we get. Hardware stuff. You'd find it boring."

Gift swelled with pride for his deflection, even if insufficient to stifle the woman.

"No, no. We'd be nothing without hardware. We can't write controller code with nothing to control." A brief half chuckle escaped with the words, but no one joined her in it. "I think that must be a module from that failed regulator, eh? Seems a lot of fuss over it."

"We're just trying to identify the fault, like any piece they give us." The abrasiveness of Gift's condescending tone scratched her throat. "They don't always provide detail on what device or unit they come from." She chomped her teeth at a piece of tofu on her fork to punctuate the thought.

"But sometimes you need us to check something, and you've been at it a while. Last week, *Gift*, you needed our help." Claudia dropped her own pomposity. "If you want, Mike, bring it by my bench. I'd be happy to do an OS diagnostic for you."

From Raff, that would sound sincere. From Claudia, not so much. Again, there was the *why*. Of all the question words, that one always got under Gift's skin. Why was Claudia so interested in this?

***

A task update greeted Mike. A question posed by the admin taking the lead on the case, Frederick Williams. *Jean referred to her fellow inquisitor as Fred.* Mike read silently with Gift reading over his shoulder, mindful of the eyes behind the cameras. It made her forget how to stand and where to put her arms and hands. She was Marco standing in her Box, the difference in the source of the indecision. Gift's mind had no room to consider the faint amber dot glowing in the top right corner of Mike's display.

When Mike stared at the message longer than Gift's patience tolerated, she read the question aloud. "'Are your findings conclusive with a surge buildup of pressure caused by an overload in the module under your diagnostic investigation…?' They just want you to agree."

"Mm hm."

"What do *you* think?"

"Actually… It could be as they suggest. If the overload had built pressure, and if the casing was airtight, then yes, possible. *Conclusive?* I don't think I'd go that far."

He said it was possible, she thought. To desperately cling to optimistic and rational explanations, Gift paused to consider if what Jean blurted was wrong. Findings of initial datasets often lacked context or clarity; she could easily have been mistaken. Even if it was a recycler, the truth stretched, saying a hydroponics regulator was damaged could have been to allay undue panic, to sustain the peaceful calm. It was in the realm of possibility this was in the colony's best interests. Besides, if they had upgraded a hydroponics regulator to include an H$_2$O purification filter, no one had to tell Gift. It was also in the scope of reason they told the truth. That one detail didn't make this part of a larger conspiracy either way. She chose to believe in the mantra so deeply ingrained: *For the good of the colony.*

Another *why* stood on the bench, taunting her. Why did it fail? To accept an overload as suggested, something caused it. Every piece of equipment Gift had ever worked on was designed never to fail. The time needed for enough pressure to build in a unit to generate an explosion would be significant. Redundancies bypassed, monitors missed alerts, nothing in the logs, and none of the automated diagnostics noticed the problem. A highly unlikely coincidence. *Units failing like this could never happen,* Gift considered. *The last stop-gap failsafe on such units is shutdown. So why did this safety module, one of three redundant boards, let its unit explode?*

"I get *what* happened, but I have no idea *why* it happened. Gift?" Permission to interject.

"Hardware-wise, I see the result, but no reason this did what it did. This fault had to trick the sensors, bypass safeties. I think, like the one I had last week, we need to check if the software code is corrupted."

"Like the air handler. But how do I ask Raff? I mean, that annoying Claudia, they're right next to each other."

Without answering him, Gift marched directly over to Raff and said, "I need you." Raff followed her but Claudia didn't react, disappointing Gift, who looked to get a rise out of her, make her feel the burn. Gift wore her skin like a garment that didn't fit well, baggy in places and tight in others. She didn't care for the person she saw herself becoming. *Time to rein this in and gain control, stop giving in to emotions. Stupid Claudia!*

Connecting the module to Mike's display, Raff noticed what Gift had disregarded, knowing the faint amber dot meant someone had accessed his terminal remotely. As if aware of her realization, the dot blinked off, closing the connection. At once, Raff pulled up a command line window and typed faster than Gift had ever seen fingers move. With so much done by voice command, only a data operator needed to be so proficient on a holographic keyboard. Gift noted Claudia also fanatically pecking at her own keys, hunched over with elbows bouncing as Raff's were. It was a duel and Gift's skin tingled with excitement.

Raff banged two fists on the bench in frustration as Claudia stood up straight, wearing a perverse smugness all over her. Giving Gift a friendly wink, Raff hinted she hadn't been beaten. No, she'd outdone Claudia, the frustration a ruse enacted to give the vile woman a false sense of confidence. Gift didn't fully follow, but if Claudia had been able to access Mike's diagnostic data and notes, she would have gotten nothing from Raff. She had not gotten the all-important *why*.

"Allora. Let's see what's up with this module then, shall we... More sophisticated this time." Raff's words came with glints of awe. It was wrong, vandalistic, but Gift saw she admired the skill.

"Same creator or someone else?"

"To me, it's the same coder. That first one you and I found? Good as it was, the redundancies and monitors worked. It got isolated on one module, that's why they were able to bring you the one board. So, while that code caused a fault, it didn't affect the unit's operation. I wonder..." She paused, eyes bouncing as if reading something on a vid screen no one else could see. Gift had observed her process many times and taught herself to use it. "Did you guys get what happened before?" Raff's eyes left to find Claudia and returned quickly.

Although lost, Gift nodded. Mike looked as confused as she felt.

Raff continued, "I wonder if *someone* used what we found to improve the code. The one in the air handler had bypassed the securities and safety protocols and didn't get caught by sensors or monitors. It was much more elegant. Like the coder learned from the beta version we found and stopped last week."

"And this one?" Mike asked.

"I think they were loaded in advance, days before the units failed. I'm certain it runs an Artificial Intelligence algorithm. The A.I. can run for days, weeks, or longer, learning. Once enabled, it can fool monitors, fake log entries, then write itself into the redundant modules and execute. They coded the air handler to fail, but this one was coded to overload and let that build undetected for some time. I'd say it worked as designed, to cause an explosive reaction. They meant this to be noticed."

Raising a finger toward Raff, Mike blinked slowly. "But did it work as designed? From my diagnostics on it... I'm not sure it was enough to take the entire thing down. I mean, it did, but I think the recycler itself is repairable. The damage was mostly in the outer casing."

"Yeah, that's true. Maybe they hoped for a larger explosion. But we don't know, really, if this was a water recycler or a hydroponics regulator, like they said."

"But Gift, what sense would there be in damaging a regulator? The recycler is the better target, I mean more impactful."

"All I know is that whoever did this was good. And what I haven't found yet, what is really bothering me, I don't know who is doing this or how to stop them." Again, Raff's eyes pointed to Claudia and returned. "I can't identify the software in the data stream soon enough to block it. That needs to be my focus."

In her report, Raff attached a sample of the rogue software code safely isolated in a secure data package and included the captured logs exposing Claudia's spying on Mike's terminal, Raff's real victory over her in their dueling keyboards row. She gathered the evidence before Claudia could purge it, while making her believe she had failed. With the report sent, the trio felt they had done well. They were a considerable step further in efforts to protect life in the colony. They had giant steps ahead.

17

Warm suds foamed over her, and the mist rinsed her cares off with the dirt and grime, down the drain and carried away. Where didn't matter, that they were away did. Gift had fully committed herself to letting the conspiracies go. Raff would stop the sabotage. She caught Claudia spying and sent incriminating evidence to Administration. The hot air was exhilarating. Well, nice. It mostly dried her.

Life in New Europa was good again.

With the bin pulled open to select her t-shirt, she paused. The evening needed to be ordinary to keep her mind settled, yet it also needed to be special. Tingles ran through her abdomen, and she felt light on her feet. The weight of worry lifted; its dread washed down the drain. *A victory to be celebrated*, she told herself when she reached for her red dress. Or was she embracing new and dangerous passions? She wore the anger well, finding the occasion for it like the perfect tool for an engineering task. Now the red dress for tacos with friends. The Gift looking back at herself from the mirror had thoughts not of victory over anxiety or catching Claudia, not on ending the sabotage. She looked good. And for a reason foreign to her, that made her *feel* great.

Ambling to the taco stand, Gift's mind drifted, and she smiled over memories of Nonna, who called walking somewhere, *going by leg*—an expression Gift found cute. Most people went by leg. When she arrived at the piazza, she found Mike at a table, round and with three seats. He didn't seem to notice the red dress and Gift couldn't understand why that bothered her. It wasn't as if he'd ever noticed or commented on her attire. Why would he? Still, why didn't he? When Raff arrived, she gave Gift a once-over. She noticed. Of course, Raff was also in a dress, her black one. She always came to dinner in a dress. Unusually crowded for a Tuesday, Mike offered to hold their place while the ladies went first for their food.

"Ciao, Sonia." A warm greeting to the friendly taco lady.

"Buonasera, Gift. Looking lovely dear."

"Grazie mille."

One of Gift's goals was to be familiar with the people with whom she repeatedly interacted—Sonia, Gunther at the noodle stand, Agnus in Medical, and Samantha at the pizza station. Sonia's solid white hair was magnificently piled in sweeping curls.

"Protein or Vegg?" A choice of textural preference. Straight vegetables or a compound mixture of vegetables and legumes in various consistencies depending on the protein it tried to imitate. For tacos, it was small bits held loosely together in a viscous sauce.

Raff ordered first. "Vegg, per favore. With spicy sauce."

Sonia and Gift said together, "One of each," which is what she always ordered—with extra splashes of spicy sauce. Waiting for their meals, Raff again considered Gift and her red dress.

"*Cara*, why the dress? A bit much for tacos, no?"

A deliberately forced exhale proceeded Gift's words. "Raff, please don't. It's just a stupid dress. I felt like it, that's it. Why do you have to make a big deal out of everything? Can't I just wear what I want for no reason?"

"*Mi dispiace*."

"Besides, *you* wear dresses all the time."

The two were grateful when Sonia announced the tacos were ready. She handed two veggie tacos to Raff. Behavioral biometrics reduced the rations in her account, and she grabbed some napkins to head to the table.

"One of each for you, dear."

"Grazie, Sonia." Gift offered biometrical payment for her meal and turned to walk away then stopped herself. "Oh, I almost forgot, two of the same for Mike please. No hot sauce."

Taking her first bite, Gift noticed Raff hadn't touched hers. She stared at her lap. *She's not sulking over our little tiff, is she?* That wasn't like her. Mike came back with his dinner. "No hot sauce, thanks for remembering."

"Who could forget?" Gift chuckled over her reply.

One taco down, Mike stood to address the table. "Beer?"

"No thanks, sweetie."

"Raff?" She looked confused by his existence. "Beer?"

"No grazie, a wine gal. Nothing for me, thanks."

"Water?"

Gift found his way of insisting when being generous an endearing trait. It would have been rude not to accept. "Okay, a small cup. Thanks."

As Mike walked away, Gift had to break the silence. "Raff, what's the matter? It's not like you to be so quiet. Was it... earlier? I... I snapped. I shouldn't have, I'm sorry."

"Ma no. *I'm sorry.* You were right, it's just a dress. You look absolutely lovely. *Bellissima.*"

"Still, I did. I snapped. I shouldn't have... And grazie. You really think so?"

"*Certo.* Beautiful."

"What are you doing? Is that a handheld?"

"Sì. Um... I... need to start on that cha—, um, project... looking for that code. I figured I can start a couple of routines running and let them go overnight." The shakiness in her voice didn't belong. Even under the most intense pressure, Raff had been steady and confident. This felt off, her being careful about her words, but Gift couldn't imagine why.

"Beer for me and water for you." Setting the water in front of Gift Mike noticed the red dress for the first time. "Nice dress."

"Grazie."

"What did I miss?" He looked left, then right, and the elegantly dressed ladies leaned into his whisper. "Anything more about... the incidents? Any idea how to catch these people?"

"Raff's just getting started with a handheld."

"Good. Once we catch them, all this stops. But I want to know who they are. Raff, tell me when you find them."

"I must report it, so we catch them. Stop this madness."

"Yes of course. But what about these cover-ups, the secrets and lies? If these people get disappeared... I want to speak to them first. Just give me a head start, that's all."

If not so annoying, Mike's enthusiasm might have been refreshing. He wouldn't let this go and Gift couldn't stomach it crawling back out of the drain, back up her legs, slinking its way over her skin, and seeping into her every pore. Like her discarded shower water, she needed to be done with it and leave it gone. "Please, sweetie, can't we just let it go? Raff will stop these crazy people. We were released, and they trusted you with that diagnostic. These are all wins. No one is against us except these terrorists."

"Hold on, that's a strong word. They're protesters, truth seekers, and they've hurt no one."

Raff lifted her head. "As far as we know. What they've done could have hurt someone. Maybe it did, and they don't want to tell us."

"*Exactly.*" Mike's sweeping hand gesture tipped his cup, spilling beer over the table. "What else are they hiding?" He used a napkin in a futile effort to sop up the beer.

Moved as much by instinct as conscious choice, Gift ran to get more. She returned with a kitchen cleaning cloth borrowed from Sonia and wiped the table dry in no time. After returning the towel to Sonia's dirties bin, she fell back down into her seat in a relaxed slouch. The hurried movements moistened her skin and left her winded. "Whew, that was fun."

Raff looked at Mike then Gift. "I'll say. Looks like it took *a lot out* of you too." Green eyes led Gift's gaze downward to the fold of her red dress, unfolded a bit from the rigorous activity and slouched posture. Mesmerized, Mike's eyes lay nestled in the exposed cleavage. Gift adjusted the fabric discreetly, snapping him out of his trance and, for the first time, she shared a hint of Raff's concern over the nature of their relationship.

Curiosity, she concluded. Like Marco and the childish friends of her youth, and doubtlessly fueled by Jean's strange questioning which caused Mike to consider Gift physically against his nature. *Something beautiful enters your field of vision—you look. Like a piece of fine art. That's what this was.* It was nothing because that's what she needed it to be.

"Oh, Tina's guy? Guess what, we got a name," Gift said, giddy.

"*No way*. She's a vault. How'd you do that?"

"She slipped."

"Really? *So*... his name?"

"Massimo."

"Max." The weight of that word, he couldn't grasp.

"Wuh... Why'd you say *Max*?"

"You know, Massimo... the nickname for it is Max, short and simple. Her man's name is Max."

Turned to Raff, Gift's jaw hung low, forming her mouth into an O. *Could it be the same Max? Poor Tina if it was. Best not to pursue this in front of Mike*, she thought. "Could it be the same Max?" she said. Mike had no reaction to the words lacking context. He disappeared.

"Fifty thousand plus in the colony. He doesn't seem like a guy Tina would go for. It must not be him," Raff said.

"I hope you're right. You're probably right. I hope so."

Mike pursed his lips, then said, "I'm confused. You know the guy?"

"No. I know *a* Max. Not really *know*. I met him once. He's with my neighbor, Sara. Courting, I guess."

"Well, if he's with someone, then not Tina's Massimo. Still, we have a name."

Gift tried not to assume *her* Max was Tina's Massimo. And why did her mind use the possessive? *My Max? That creep?* What if he was the same guy? Concern for Tina tightened in her throat and dried her mouth. She finished her water in a single gulp—anxiety left no room for sipping.

After almost finishing her tacos, Raff left Mike and Gift in each other's company.

"Guess it's just you and me, Gift. So, ping-pong?"

"Let's just walk the long way home and call it a night."

As they traversed Dome Six in silence, Gift began humming one of Mike's songs. The words never made sense, something about a subdivided culture and casting people out of subterranean bars. She remembered the band came from Canada, which she felt almost certain was one of the fifty United States. The details were fuzzy, but she was sure there were fifty. The quick and powerful pacing made the song enjoyable. Mike smiled and hummed along, playing air drums. Was he off-key or was it her? It didn't matter, the sensation of friendship was there.

"I don't get one thing in the lyrics. Actually, I don't get most of it. But why were they racing against rats? Weren't those small loathsome creatures?"

Mike expounded on the hectic pace of economically driven lives of people long since gone on a planet left far behind. When he finished by telling her the lifestyle was called 'the rat race,' she nodded unconvincingly. The pair shared a chortle when she realized he saw through her pretense—she still didn't get it.

"Here's your corridor. Guess I'll see you tomorrow."

"If you have time, there's something I want to show you." The words trailed around the back of Gift's head as she pulled him along by the arm.

"Where we going?"

"Come on... but don't get too excited." She led him into Dome Three, through the piazza, and down a narrow alley between a building of flats and a closed shoe shop, where a small plot of grass tucked out of the way revealed itself. Only someone who knew where to look could find this tiny patch of green with one uninspiring little tree. The spot wasn't especially beautiful or impressive looking. "See?" Childish joy and wonder filled her.

"Wow." Sarcasm dripped from the word. "Amazing. So... green." That got him an elbow in the gut and they both laughed.

"It isn't much, I know. This is where Aimée and I spent lots of time as kids. Even our group—we claimed this spot. It's... nostalgic. I come sometimes just for its tranquility. More the memories, I think, than the strip of grass."

"I get that. Nice."

They sat for a while, talking about lighter subjects until Gift became drowsy. After saying their goodnights, each headed home.

Something in her corridor caught the corner of her eye, Max and Sara outside Sara's Box. Sound waves from their hearty chuckles reached her but the conversation had less depth of range. Her gaze glued itself on the couple as Max pulled Sara in for a long kiss. Gift chuckled under her breath, remembering how Aimée used to call kissing *sucking each other's faces*. When Max saw her, he smiled. *Creep. That better not be Tina's Massimo.*

18

Wednesday passed as any day, common tasks came and got done. It was strange looking over and seeing Raff alone all day at her bench. Claudia hadn't returned since the guards collected her from her station first thing that morning. Raff didn't seem to mind, smiling and humming Pavarotti songs all day.

That evening, Gift went to her mom's for dinner. Aimée joined and jovial reminiscing filled much of the evening. The three of them in Mom's Box transported Gift back eleven years. The mention of seeing her neighbor *sucking face* nearly dropped Aimée to the floor with contagious laughter. Gift could bask in the glow radiating from her mother's face at having them in her home, as in bygone times.

Strolling home with her best friend, Gift spoke of her concern about Max being Tina's Massimo. Aimée broke it to her gently that some in G.M. saw multiple people at the same time. In a show of her disapproval, Gift wore a sour face.

"What about you?" Gift assumed her friend would have told her these things but only recently she learned sweet little Aimée, with the perfect little heart-shaped face and thin nose, may have reached G.M. years ago. Maybe she had E.CID and didn't care. At twenty-seven she was still on the exceptionally long curve for G.M.

"No one *now*." The words carried a devilish slyness.

"So, wait. There *has been* someone then, at your age?"

Aimée scrunched her face. "Not at my age. Over a year ago."

"Whoa."

"Yep. He was thirty-one at the time. Thought I was thirty, so I let him go right on thinking that. He may have freaked out to know I was barely approaching twenty-seven then. It was fun. He was nice. We kept it casual until it seemed he was looking for a partner. No way I was considering a Union—wouldn't even have been allowed. And if I did, wouldn't be with him. We're still friends, well *friendly* anyway."

"You never cease to surprise me."

"And you love that about me." They shared the laughs that truth brought.

The chill of eyes crawling over Gift's skin came ahead of seeing them. "Sweetie, you've noticed more admin guards around the colony recently?"

"Sure, Love. They started just after that hydro-whatever thing popped the other day."

"Popped?"

"They said on the news vids. You must have heard."

"Yeah. But you're the first person I've heard use the word *popped*."

"I heard it, massively loud, a huge *pop*. I was relieved to hear what it was, I assumed it had been something much worse."

"Maybe it was."

Gift updated her trusted friend about the sabotage of at least three devices. The air handler incident amazed Aimée, she could hardly believe Gift's bravery in climbing the farm dome, proud of her for it. It seemed Gift could surprise her too. While she maintained her optimistic view the good of the colony was their priority, Gift left the possibility open to some lies being told. She asked Aimée to be on the lookout for anything out of the ordinary, especially if she saw anything on adjustments to water rationing.

Approaching Gift's corridor, Aimée paused. "It's all just a little bit crazy. That frizzy-haired menace writing on the kiosks... my kind of girl. And your E.CID scare—that one worried me, Love. Now sabotage. I'm so sorry you've had to bear it all. How are you holding up?"

"You know me." With a forced smile her words told the entire story. Outwardly, Gift put up her usual good front—always positive. But inside, a mess of new emotions tugged at her intestines and tightened her chest. A mental struggle, she tried to understand the connection her emotional fluctuations had on her physical self, having assumed these to be separate aspects of her being.

"Look, I know you've got *the good of the colony* stuff embedded in your every fiber. Don't lose that. I'm no true believer like you. You of all people know how independent I can be." Gift smiled in agreement. "But I'm telling you, what I see, how Admin works, my Resident Services office. I believe it *is good*. I don't see any layers of corruption or any overarching plot against us. This colony's been going strong for two centuries. *The Founders* got a lot right. You don't lose your beautiful optimism, you hear me?"

Full of appreciation for the affirmation she wasn't being naïve or gullible, Gift nodded. With no mal-intent, Mike had made her feel small—a child desperate to see and accept only the positive. Aimée may not have realized the full impact of her words, or just how needed they had been.

19 | Day Seventeen

Previously blended into the meaningless background, they were everywhere, in twos. It used to be she was aware of them the way she was aware of a tree in the park or a table in the piazza. An uncommon chill came over her skin not from the temperature. To see all those guards on her morning fitness run was strange, yet the safety of it touched her. They were doing their part to stop further acts of sabotage.

Unsure if she should greet them, Gift looked away as if making direct eye contact was wrong. Full gazes greeted the set of guards in Dome Three. One sent her a smile, they were human. A *Ciao* offered to the next pair in dome four received a *Mornin'* in return. Their existence may have been unusual, but the people were normal enough. As she jogged, Gift greeted everyone from the guards to nameless colonists to cleaning persons. Warm tones of community radiated on her skin.

***

After lunch they found a new nameless person at Claudia's post. A large man, tall, with wide shoulders. Not overly muscular, but strong looking with short hair that stood in place like soldiers at attention. Sporting a big smile, his stare traced Raff's approach. Gift followed curiously.

"Ciao. I'm Raffaella."

"Hans Fuchs. I've been assigned here. That makes us bench-mates."

"Guess so. Welcome."

Hans Fuchs leaned around Raff. "And you are?"

"Gift."

"Pleasure Gift. What a lovely name. You must be a very good friend of Raff's, here to make sure I was okay." His smile shone friendly and sincere. She couldn't say why, but she instantly liked him.

Playfully, Gift waved her tiny fist at the man more than twice her bulk. "Yep, and I've got my eye on you. I'm mad protective."

"Noted." Hans Fuchs raised his hands in surrender.

For the rest of the day, Gift shared the attention her tasks requested with Raff's bench, one eye repeatedly glancing her way to see if she was comfortable with this Hans Fuchs character. "He seems alright," she thought aloud. "Got assigned quickly. Wasn't it quick? And he's sent here to work with Raff while she's on that special task. Suspicious. Is it... suspicious?"

"For sure, that's why he's here. The mission to stop the attacks will push other tasks to the side with no one to take the slack."

"What do you suppose happened to her?"

"Claudia? Most likely she's still being investigated, interrogated. They must like her for the saboteur. Seems to have the skills, and being beside Raff, she was in the perfect place for what she needed. I guess she must have taken advantage, but she got caught."

"She did. I can't help thinking she wasn't working alone. Notice the increase in the guards? They're everywhere." Gift waved her hand in a wide circle.

"Can't hardly miss'em. It's like they *want to* be seen."

"*Right?*"

"I just hope Raff lets me know who these *All Lies* folks are. I really need to know what they know before they're disappeared."

"You really suppose they're the ones behind this?"

"We can't tell who to trust. Keep an eye on that guy." Mike's head leaned toward Raff's bench. He obviously meant Hans Fuchs. "Carefully. Who knows who he really is?"

"*All Lies,* you think?"

"I doubt they have the pull to get someone in here. Probably a coincidence, Claudia getting on the bench with Raff. Or... maybe *that's why* they recruited her. Yeah, that must be it. Right place, right time, and all. Now that guy? He's a plant from Administration... spying on Raff."

"Oh mamma, this is all too much."

"Even so, she's not done anything wrong, and she's helping them. That's all he'll see."

"Also too, they really seem chummy. More than ever with Claudia. Hans Fuchs only just arrived... and *look* at them. Like they've been bench-mates long as us."

Squinting one eye widened his other. "I hope that's a good sign."

"It is. Raff is an excellent judge of character."

***

After Gift finished cleaning and organizing her bench, she reached the exit at the same time as Raff. "Hans Fuchs seems real nice."

"*Certo.*" Under a raised eyebrow Raff added, "Let's see though. He's friendly, easy to talk to. Reminds me of my psycho-physical examiner, like he's *supposed* to be that way. I need to be cautious."

"Mike says he's from Admin, sent to check on you."

"Spy on me, likely how Mike put it." Gift breathed out a chuckle in agreement. "I thought of that. Then I figured, so what? I'm trying my best to find more bits of that malicious software code. We're helping them, and I'm sure that means we are no longer suspects. Let him watch me."

"That's exactly what we said. *Ma*, is he watching you, or *watching you*?"

"*Cara*." Raff gave the implication a smile. "Do you want to stay together this evening? You seem better, but I worry."

"Really, as I told Mike—and I appreciate it—I just want to spend time with my book this evening. I'm alright, honest."

***

Everything ceased in an instant. Shock stiffened Gift in place and her muscles became stone as two guards stared back at her from inside her home. Her mouth went dry, and she became aware of her teeth as if they'd just grown in place, too big for her mouth as her tongue pressed into them. A noise from the back of her throat squeezed out through clenched teeth, but she had no words. Strangers looked at her forever, as if surprised by the audacity of her daring to enter her Box.

"Miss Ojo." Gift needed a second to process it. Soft, feminine. "Miss Ojo?" Her name was now a question. Why was her name a question? Who else would have opened her Box? She was Miss Ojo, but that wasn't the question. What was the question?

"Take a breath, Miss Ojo, it's alright." The woman in Gift's home grabbed her arm to steady her.

The Box tilted slightly to the left the way the bridge on the Banzai did when something hit the ship. Tilting the camera created the effect, so what made her home tilt? The second guard folded open a chair and the soft voice aided her to a seated position. The room returned to level and Gift's breaths were deep and forced.

"Miss Ojo, breathe normally."

Her face looked small, like a child's face, like Matteo, only more womanlike in the features, with higher cheekbones and a thin pointy nose. The eyebrows were wrong. Her hair pulled so tightly back the skin of her face was taut.

"Miss Ojo, you are all right... You're home..."

Her home, but not her home. Her things were scattered everywhere. Clothes piled on the floor, the bed cushion leaned against the wall, shelves and bins emptied. This was wrong, someone else's Box. "I'm sorry, I must be in the wrong... I, I... I'll go now. I'm sorry. I'll go home now."

"No Miss Ojo, you *are* home." The pale face darkened.

Slowly, the blackness behind the woman shaped itself into an outline and spoke. "We are conducting a search, routine."

Gift found her voice. "Routine? Look... My stuff."

"I'll be outside." Paleness returned to the young woman's face and the door slid closed when the darkness departed.

"Please, can you tell me your name?"

"Oh, of course. I'm Beth. With me is Albert."

"Thank you. I'm Gift."

"Yes, we are aware."

"You called me Miss Ojo. That's my mom."

"Right. So... why are we here, searching your home?"

"You think I'm a terrorist."

"That was rhetorical, I'm about to tell you. You are a person of interest in the ongoing investigation into at least three acts of sabotage. The third and worst has many unanswered questions, so we came here ahead of you this evening to examine all your things thoroughly. We have one last thing to check."

"*Me...*"

"My colleague left as I need to examine your clothes. Please remove them and put on your robe, okay?"

Okay? Like I have a choice. Beth faced the door and Gift put on her robe after stripping out of her clothes.

"Is that all?"

"Miss Ojo, you are a person of interest. Whoever is doing these things? They probably believe it's in the best interest of the colony. And of all our persons of interest, *you're* the zealot. You know what zealots are capable of, for their cause?" Gift shook her head. *"Anything.* Even killing an innocent bystander to make their point."

Gift stared deep into Beth's eyes as if to see the thoughts that revealed how anyone could consider her as a suspect in this. Why her more than Mike or Raff? "They killed someone?"

Stony silence. She had said, 'capable of killing.' Had someone been killed, or did she speak to the possibility? Now Gift understood the Admins had no idea what was happening, and it terrified them. Considering their response thus far—harassing her, ripping her home apart, and tossing wild allegations around with her things—tightened Gift's chest, pressing her into the wall. *They have no idea who's doing this or how to stop it. There will be more attacks.*

"We're finished here. Nothing has been taken or damaged."

When her door slid open, Marco was with Albert. Wild images fluttered through Gift's mind of Marco spying on her for the guards. No, he was arguing with Albert. *What are you doing to her?* she thought he said. "Let me go. Let me see her." Yes, that was clear.

Beth barely raised her hand in a wave. "Let him go." She outranked that hulk of a male guard when Gift thought it the other way around.

When Albert released his forearm, the young neighbor stepped into the Box to kneel before Gift. Like a classic film scene transition, the sliding door wiped the guards from sight. Marco reached for Gift's hands then withdrew as she interlocked her fingers, resting them on her lap. She said nothing. The line on her cheek was the remnant of the one tear she allowed to fall for the thought of someone being hurt or killed.

A cocktail of heightened new sensations swirled in her stomach. Embarrassment, frustration, anger, dread. She gagged as they rose to the back of her throat, ready to be spewed out. Only, she couldn't vomit. Still as a photo, the moment was only an image of her, an idea of her home, her things, herself. Intense pain in the back of her head the only clue she wasn't in a nightmare.

20

"**G**ift, are you okay? What have they done?" Someone new in her Box. No longer her home, it had become a space shared with strangers.

"Marco, ciao." He wasn't there, then he was.

"Ciao?" Air caressed her skin as he waved his hand in front of her face. "Gift, are you okay?"

"Yeah. Shiny." Her own calmness felt out of place and unexpected. "I'm fine. Guess I should be used to this by now."

"Used to this... *This*?" He swung his hand in a circle. "This happened to you before?"

"Yeah... Not exactly. The wrecked home is new. But this isn't the first time they've questioned me, treated me like I was a suspect, a criminal... And for nothing."

"What could they possibly think you've done?"

"Some light treason, terrorism, and sabotage... Maybe killing someone."

Marco raised an eyebrow at the incompatibility of her blasé manner to the situation. "You're not making any sense, Gift. What's this about?"

Pensively she put her head to the side and looked him dead in the face. "What do you know about me? My friends? What I do evenings? You can't be sure all those things are *not* me. You've no idea who I really am. How well do we know anyone?" The boy seemed bothered by the concept. "No,

I'm not any of those things. But as much as *you* can't really know that... *they* can't either. So, until I'm not those things, I *am*... or I could be."

Marco ran his hand through his hair, piling it higher, thicker. "How can you be so calm about it? Why aren't you upset?"

"They're scared. It's not about me, my things tossed on the floor. They're desperately trying to keep us safe, keep our resources protected... And they have no idea who is breaking things or how to stop them."

"Breaking things? You said terrorism, sabotage. What do they think you did?"

After outlining the highlights of her last two weeks, Gift looked over her small home in complete disarray. To take in the sight rang inside the headache like an angry klaxon. Standing too quickly caused slight light-headedness which increased the throbbing. Gift hadn't seen anything this chaotic, messy, and devoid of order. The pain reached deeper in her brain filling the grooves engraved in its soft tissue until every millimeter hurt.

Starting with her shoes she said, "Front to back."

"What's that?" Unfamiliar with Gift's mannerisms, he assumed she spoke to him. Wanting to help, Marco reached for the clothes pile and picked up the first item his hand found on top. As if he'd lifted a hot pot from the hob with his bare hand, a girlish yap bellowed as he dropped her bra so fast the reaction brought Gift a hearty chuckle. The boy's returned smile connected two blushed cheeks.

"Sweetie, I appreciate you want to help me. Truly, I do. But you've got no idea how particular I am. Anything you do, I will just redo. I'd do it with anyone. Just one of the idiosyncrasies I've gotta live with, is all. So please, don't worry. This won't take long, really. I need to do this myself. Thanks for everything."

Marco hesitated. "If you need anything..."

"I know, thank you. Please don't worry, I'll be fine."

As she looked at the pile of her clothes, she saw those guards. *They touched them, dropped them on the floor.* They all needed to be cleaned, so Gift did a quick inventory on her mental display and added the last date each item was washed. She would get ration deductions for cleaning certain items too often. Two piles grew on the floor and most clothes ended up on the hopper pile, the rest for the sonic sink.

Thinking of Marco's story of the old woman who cleaned all her clothes in the sink gave her a smile. It was the first time Gift did anything other than her coverall in the sonic, and she couldn't imagine doing that often. It was tedious and less effective than using the laundry service. In no time it was coming together, looking manageable. When she considered the things from her kitchen, she saw the need to clean her plates, cups, and utensils. Not that there were many, but they couldn't go in the cupboards until they were cleaned. *The cupboards and clothes bins.* "Oh mamma." Gift had to clean them all and wasn't nearly as close to done as she imagined.

When she had nearly finished, the sink signaled the underwear and t-shirts were done. Realizing intrusive hands had touched the robe draped over her bare skin, she put it in the sonic and slipped into underwear bottoms and a tee. Growls came from her stomach, the pinch of hunger demanding satiation. Just as Gift had begun to clean her personal-care items cabinet, she heard three taps on the door. The youngster from the next Box stood beyond the doorway holding a bag of takeaway noodles and two beers. Gift's shoulders dropped, releasing a weight she held so long her muscles trembled. "Bless you, sweet Marco. My tummy was growling." He remained at the doorway, awaiting permission. "Come in, please."

Slowly he entered and locked his eyes on the ceiling. "I can just... leave yours... if..."

"Don't be silly. Look how much I've already done. I'm almost finished."

"I can come back... if... so... if you want to get dressed."

She had forgotten that since her inquisitors' hands had contaminated her shorts, they had been tossed on the hopper pile. The shirt and underwear were enough, modest-*ish*, as Mike would say. Gift hadn't mastered using the *ish* suffix but didn't let that stop her from trying. "Nah, I'm always warm anyway. Let's eat, I'm starved." She grabbed the noodles and beer. "Thank you so much for this."

"The least I can do. But really... if you prefer to be alone? I just wanted you to eat dinner. I didn't mean to impose, or that you should have me in to eat with you."

"No, really. I'm glad for the company. Now that most everything is away and the clothes are ready for the hopper, my headache is almost gone." Pointing to the pile, she made a sour face. "I can't wear those. They had their hands on them. I'm doing a couple of things in the sonic—just what'll take rations to wash. I'll toss the rest in the hopper. This t-shirt just finished before you knocked, and my undies. Or I'd be sitting here naked." Blood rushed to fill Marco's face and its weight lowered his chin as if her shame would have been his. "I wouldn't've opened the door, silly. Come on, let's eat. Did you remember the chopsticks?"

The noodles hit the spot, but Marco was much quieter than on their last shared evening. "You're quiet, what is it?"

He pointlessly moved the noodles in circles with the chopsticks before raising his eyes from the cooling broth to meet hers. "Do you have any idea who did what they accused you of doing?"

"Not a clue, but we suspect the people writing those messages on the kiosks. You've seen them, *All Lies*, they say. Only visible when the kiosks switch to evening mode. They get removed pretty quick."

"You think it could be them, really?"

"You know, I was told I'm a person of interest because of my zeal for the colony. Can you believe it? That's why they say I'd do anything, even kill. *Kill.* Maybe... these people have risen to that level of zeal."

Looking at Gift through his eyelids Marco said, "Wow. I thought they were just a nuisance."

"My friend is working hard to find them. She's good, the best. She'll find who's responsible... Oh, let me credit you the rations for the food and beer."

He raised an emphatic palm. "No, absolutely not. What kind of neighbor would I be if I took that? I'd say you deserve a meal after all you've had to endure these last few days. Much more, really. Please, my treat."

She acquiesced with a nod and a smile.

When Marco left, sleep came quickly, deep and sound.

21

Excellent judge of character—that's how Gift described Raff to Mike. With his charm and charisma, Gift instantly trusted Hans Fuchs when only an introduction had been shared between them. Seeing how Raff interacted with him had layered blocks on that foundation, a wall of trust being built when years failed to do so with Claudia. *Or was it a façade?*

"He's very good." That's what Raff said to the lunch table after supplying detailed exposition on a troublesome bug they tracked down together that morning.

"So, is he joining us for dinner this evening?"

Tina's question plastered a grimace on Mike's face. "Hold on. No one gets to dinner this soon. We have no idea about this guy and can't be guarding every word over dinner. Even you. Took weeks before we let you in."

Charlie leaned back, interlocking his fingers behind his head. "Aye, Mike, don't be a wee scunner. I'm sure Tina was jokin der. We all of us, ken she was an easier in than yersel. A good skelping we gave Gift about inviting you in, we did." Laughter pushed its way out of Charlie's forced Scottish accent. That, more than his attempt at humor, spread giggles through the group.

When Mike sulked, Gift thought it best to change the subject. "On to more important topics. Who's in for Tacos this evening?"

"*Ma*, didn't we just have tacos?" Raff complained.

Tina pouted. "I didn't"

"Blame Max, not us."

Gift didn't like Mike calling Tina's man Max. Hearing that empowered the thought it was the same Max in her dreams, the one very much with Sara. Unsure, she said nothing to Tina.

Charlie said, "Don't blame anyone. Obviously, Tina is saying she's joining this evening."

"How about we do Augustiner Bräu? It's a great beer garden and we haven't been there together in... forever."

"Ottimo, Tina." Raff seemed happy with anything but tacos.

All agreed. Even Charlie said he'd be there.

***

Gift's watchful eye resumed scrutinization of Hans Fuchs. Not that she didn't trust Raff—that was a constant. Romanticism couldn't be trusted. Unwanted advances that left her feeling dirty as a child barely blossoming into her adult life soured her own pitiful taste of it. Later, more mature—not completely—she felt cheapened, reduced to nothing more than her physical features. An object. Worse still, it was reciprocal. She had returned Max's attention with her own covetous desires, without understanding what those were or how they'd be satisfied. No, such feelings were not to be trusted, even in the more mature. Perhaps less so.

It troubled Gift to think of people in terms of physical characteristics. Yet, impressive to her was how a person's physical beauty was enhanced or diminished by the revelation of their inner character. Gift thought of Agnus. Then of the butterflies in an Earth nature vid she once watched. She marveled at how an ugly caterpillar transformed into a creature of such delicate beauty. Humans could do the same, once their personality dared to emerge from its chrysalis. Physical perception of a person could morph from caterpillar to butterfly merely by letting someone get emotionally close enough to see who they really were. Outwardly ordinary people became something comelier, even exquisite in beauty, by their revealed character. The secret, Gift considered, to why some people seemed to only get more attractive with age.

Mike noticed Gift's lack of focus. "Where are you?"

"Sorry. Just keeping an eye on Raff and Hans Fuchs."

"You told me she knows to be cautious. 'She's an excellent judge of character,' you said."

One part of Mike's personality that did not particularly appeal to Gift was how good his memory could be when he wanted to rub something she had said back in her face. Utterly useless for remembering important things, he'd recite verbatim something she said then later tried to walk back. Typically, when the moment settled back to nothing, she'd reason it kept her honest. This moment hadn't yet settled. She blew out a forceful exhale in a show of frustration, which Mike seemed to interpret properly, not pushing the point.

Gift resumed her task of scrutinizing the body language between Raff and Hans Fuchs. *This is how Raff looks at me and Mike,* she concluded. Hans Fuchs smiled at her a few times while she checked him out throughout the day, and she made a connection. The admin guards said *she* was a person of interest. If Hans Fuchs worked for them, he may not only have been there for Raff. All those times he'd caught her gaze, *he* was looking at *her*, observing her. *Person of interest.*

The only ones left in the workspace, Hans Fuchs and Gift sauntered out together. The day prior, he went right while she went left. They'd part. Good, she feared her nervousness may have started to show.

"Buonasera." When she turned left, he turned with her.

"I need to go this way as well."

Crap.

"Raffaella is a pretty special lady, isn't she?"

"She's the best."

"I mean more than as a data operator. She's fetching... and smart... and funny... and kind. She's a very special lady."

Gift wore an expression of concern like an obvious mask. He paused, but did he expect a reply? She heard no question in his words. *Just keep walking, Gift,* she told herself. That was the right choice—inexplicably not the one she made. "And?" Steps halted and she craned her neck to look at him. "Seems like maybe a question was in that."

When he turned to her, his eyes expressed an apologetic longing. Then a hopeful glee put itself in his smile. "I know we've only just met. I'm not rushing or assuming anything, but... is she... *with* anyone?"

"Oh mamma." Imagining she'd only thought it, the sound of her words surprised her. "I don't..." She stopped there, unsure how to reply. What was and was not her place? The situation entered new ground and everything she thought to say or do was wrong.

"Sorry if that made you uncomfortable. It's just that if she is, I'll drop it here and now. No trouble."

As she considered the pattern the floor buffers laid over the concrete, Gift thought long and hard. Saying yes, telling him Raff was with someone, would make him stop the pursuit. He'd be less charming, causing Raff to lose interest if she thought he did. And he handed her the opportunity to end it before it began, to send Hans Fuchs on his way.

Overwhelmed by one consuming thought, her heart beat hard, its rhythmic thumping rattling her ribcage. *This is not my place. Raff deserves to make her own choices.* And Mike, with his selective memory, feeding her words back to her, was right. Which meant *Gift* was right when she said

Raff was an excellent judge of character, and she could trust that. She owed her friend that much.

"No one I know of," she said in a simple, neutral reply.

22

Sara and Gift stepped out of the shower box to find a childish grin decorating Max's face. Sara's Max—hopefully not Tina's—was to Gift a person of interest. Love for Tina made her something new and terribly important—a spy. The mental processing of her unfamiliar role smacked her in the head as thoughts met contemplation of the previous evening's harrowing ordeal. The guards became hard-nosed jerks and put her under suspicion, violated her privacy, and stripped her of her dignity, for the good of the colony. She'd said it enough to nearly convince herself, but only in comparison to what *she* had to become regarding Max did the idea finally take root and sprout.

"Hey, Gift. It's lovely to see you again." Max's sultry voice creeped her out a little, bringing the same wince Luca's stare on her backside did those years ago. *Sara's directly behind me. Why's he greeting me?* she wondered as she considered her robe's immodesty—an immodesty which only manifested around Max.

"Ciao."

Sara smiled as she swooped by Gift and threw her arms around Max's waist. "You two know each other?"

Seriously? Did you really not notice him creeping on me last week in the shower queue? was what Gift wanted to say. She waited to see how Max would answer.

"Hey babe. *Know* each other? Not really. We met last week when I wait-ed with you for your shower. Gift is such an unusual name, I remembered it."

Do you also remember staring me up and down? Creep!

"It is. A lovely name." Sara eyed Gift. "Very beautiful too, isn't she?" Gift perceived Sara may have been less oblivious than she'd given her credit.

"Gorgeous."

Gift judged his enthusiasm inappropriate. Sara chuckled and playfully slapped his cheek, a mock gesture that raised Gift's eyebrow. When Max leaned in for a long kiss, his gaze reached around Sara's cocked head to watch Gift watching them. The chill that crawled up her spine didn't come from the temperature change from stepping out of the hot shower. She understood nothing that was happening.

By the time the couple finished sucking face, Gift had crafted a clever plan. If Max was so loose with his... *appreciation* of another woman in front of Sara, and Sara seemed okay with it, he'd be the wastewater scum that would two-time on her with Tina. Unlike Sara, Gift's brawny mate would doubtless square one off in his face. No black eye or broken nose meant Tina had no idea. Tina's Massimo—now a person of interest—guilty until proven so in Gift's mind. For her friend, Gift vested herself in the case.

"Any plans for this evening?"

"*Yes.* Max is making dinner. Just the two of us for a romantic evening. It's our three-month anniversary." She gave Max a modest peck, and Gift noted he was busy that evening. Perhaps not so coincidentally, Tina was free for their group's Friday dinner. *And he cooks?*

Max wiggled around Sara. That's the only way Gift could describe his unusual movements. He slithered? No, he wiggled around her.

"Nice. Well, enjoy." Gift paused; the couple too caught up in themselves to ask about her evening. "I'm having dinner with friends, kind of a Friday tradition. I'm excited because my friend *Tina* is joining. *Tina* misses a lot because she's seeing some guy. Like last Friday. *Tina's* free this evening, her man must have plans."

Say it. Say his name is Massimo and ask him if Max is short for Massimo. She left it there. Enough to get him thinking, make him aware of Gift's detective skills, get him to slip up. Did Sara pick up on it? Was their thing so casual it wouldn't matter?

***

It overjoyed Gift when she saw Charlie and Sakura at the Augustiner Bräu beer garden.

"You actually came." The three shared a delightfully tight hug.

"Gift, looking lovely as always."

"No, Sakura. *You* are gorgeous. I'm so glad you guys came."

"Yeah." Charlie's typical unenthusiastic manner didn't mean anything. "I didn't take a table yet. Didn't know who's all coming and... you know, I wasn't sure how to arrange the seating."

He had never once teased her. Mike did, a few times making jokes about her idiosyncrasies. Thoughts of Charlie being a good man, a great friend, glazed Gift's eyes. And he was there with Sakura. The evening was a smashing success by the time Raff and Mike arrived together. Mike quickened the pace on the last three steps and grinned to himself in victory.

"Tina?" Charlie asked. "Said she's coming, right? Can't be sure until she shows. Been about as dependable as me lately."

The heavy paw that gripped his narrow collarbone nearly made his eyes pop. Their stout friend had stepped up behind him to hear his last comments and he seemed unsure of her reaction, too frightened to look. The burst of laughter from Mike and Gift softened his face, and Tina patted his shoulder.

"Always good to see you too, Chuckles."

Charlie chose a table, a large round one with six chairs, sure to satisfy Gift's almost insatiable need for symmetry.

Augustiner Bräu was nothing more than a food counter and dining tables. Special to this establishment, it had a menu terminal on the table, giving it a touch of sophistication. They chose from a variety of vegetable- and legume-based proteins standing in for meats none of them had tasted or ever would. They, like everyone in the colony, came for the beer selection—the only place serving German and Belgian beers on tap. Even Raff conceded her beloved red wine didn't pair as well with the menu as a nice crisp beer.

Jovial conversation flowed over the food. Gift let the mood of a near-perfect moment surround her, dissolving into it like a scene in a dream—one from which she wished never to wake. The beer tasted excellent, too. She'd chosen a Belgian brew that went down smooth with a reddish-brown hue and balanced but assertive acidity. It smelled of yeast and left notes of genuine oak from forests long gone lingering on her tongue, followed by a pleasant aftertaste.

Raff spoiled the moment. She had her face in her lap through most of the meal, picking so slowly at her food Gift nearly finished before her. A handheld greedily captured the better share of her attention. "Sakura, I don't wish to disturb you. Just a question. Have you received any new CID patients lately, particularly any with Delayed CID?"

Sakura looked around as if expecting someone to be eavesdropping. The increased guard presence had everyone on edge and the cautious pause made Gift aware of the pair in the courtyard's corner. "I am not supposed to say." The soft words were barely audible over the din.

"Just nod if you've seen someone, mid-thirties, close to Tina's complexion?"

Sakura's head dipped and Gift realized Raff meant Claudia. She felt stupid for not picking that up immediately.

"You all noticed the guards everywhere? Didn't know there were so many." Charlie's observation may have been a subject change, protecting his partner. Gift valued the effort as she desperately hoped the couple would be present for more dinners.

"Yes, of course. Since all the *malfunctions*," Mike put air quotes around the word, "in the most critical systems. They have us working on it, Raff trying to find'em. But I'm not convinced those stupid guards have dropped us as suspects. I mean, we're helping them. But I'm sure they're still watching us under a microscope."

"*Infatti*." Gift offered more accentuation than she wanted.

"What do you mean?" Mike asked.

Raff's overprotective side emerged. "Has something happened?"

"No, nothing. It's... nothing. It's just..." Gift searched her vocabulary. She found words, missing were the thoughts to articulate, to find a way to finish the sentence. It hung there incomplete, leading to more unwanted questions.

Raff reached across the table, taking Gift's hand. "*Cara*, tell us what happened."

All eyes on her, Gift could feel them peeling back layers of her skin, desperate to see inside, to learn what troubled her. It was compassion. It was love. It was too much. Her belly became an oak barrel with fermenting barley and yeast bubbling, building pressure like the pangs of an oncoming bowel movement. Without reaching the decision, she ran toward the toilets outside the courtyard.

In the toilet booth, it became apparent the knot twisting her insides wasn't pushing waste through her intestines. A physical sensation caused not by the body. When it manifested, its movement took another direction, folding her at the waist, bringing her knees to the floor with her head over the toilet basin.

Violent emesis, the lurching left her throat sore. A nasty hint of bitterness in her mouth soured. Gift needed water but couldn't get up, her energy faded from her like an unplugged fan. With nothing left to haul up from her gut, the vomiting ceased, leaving her on the floor, one arm tossed over the toilet.

Overtaking every emotion, anger raged as a fire inside her. She made peace with the home intrusion, and the role the guards had to play. A person of interest, Gift thought she had accepted that. She hadn't. One word triggered her friends' alarm and caught her completely unawares. Now she wanted nothing more than to stay on that floor, hugging a toilet.

Gentle taps on the door loudened into knocks. "Gift. Gift, are you okay?" Muffled vibrations pushed through the door—Raff's voice. "*Cara*, please, open the door." Raff found her on the tile floor, hair tossed to one side in a way Gift didn't remember doing.

"Oh mamma." The tiny booth reeked of butyric acid and old yeasty beer until Raff flushed the toilet, casting the putrescence away. She helped raise Gift to her feet.

Strength slowly returned. "I'm okay... I need the sink." Combining the sonic basin and a wipe, Gift put herself back together, ready as could be to head back to the table. "I don't wanna talk about this, not now."

"I'll take care of it. *Ma*, you *will* need to explain this to me. You know how I worry."

Conversation carried on without her, about her. To be fair, she hadn't heard a word over the ambient noise from the sea of surrounding nameless people. Dreading the questions and all the *are you alright's*, she approached. Thankfully, Raff did as she promised. "Seems her beer hit harder than expected. The Belgian ones have a much higher alcohol content than her little frame can handle. She'll be fine."

"Glad to hear it." Charlie gently rubbed his palm on Gift's shoulder blade. "Yeah, if you're not ready for it, they can get you. Fine beers they are."

Raff said, "What I couldn't say at lunch, about Hans, is I'm certain they sent him to check on me."

"*Check you out*, I think." Mike's chuckle perked Tina up.

"What's that? He's sweet on Raff already?"

"Seems so. And... I think it's reciprocal."

"*Whoa*. I knew it. About time, Raff. I need to meet this guy. I bet he's a looker, too." Gift nodded a 'yes' to Tina.

"*Ciao*, I hardly know the guy... And he's spying on me, don't forget." Raff's objection seemed forced, leading Gift to wonder how smitten she'd become.

Gift added, "He asked if you were seeing anyone."

"That's it. She's done you guys. Raff's finally got herself a man."

"Alright, Tina. Everyone. The first impression is good, some potential, but that's it. I'm talking about this sabotage. I'm sure Claudia is part of this. I think Hans was watching *her* on the data stream, then got assigned next to me when they took her. Sakura, that's why I asked about D.CID earlier."

"She is not in Pronto Soccorso."

"Yeah, we knew about her. What we need to know is if her code's still running out there and what it might do next." Mike was always good for pointing out the obvious.

Charlie cupped his chin. "Wait a second. From what I know... I'm not directly in your area, so it might be I've got it wrong. You're saying her software, this code, is out there... and may be about to do something else?"

"Almost definitely," Raff said.

"How do you go from defacing kiosks with magic ink to this?" Tina offered anger and spit with the words.

"It's not them, not those *All Lies* people. They talked of escalation, possibly damaging a key system they believe to be not as critical as everyone thinks. But it was squashed." Raff's eyes cautiously scanned nearby tables. "They've got a good coder, a Junior Data Operator. *Ma*, this level of sophistication? The access needed? I doubt very much she could have done it. And Claudia wasn't in their group. We have a second group, one that is much more aggressive and violent."

Tina pointed at Raff. "Hold on, you know that they have a data operator, and you said '*she*.' How do you know about a coder in their group?"

"Yeah, I was thinking the same." The others nodded in agreement with Charlie. Gift recalled how days ago—which felt like a lifetime ago—Raff gave a hint she'd heard something of this group. Now her familiarity extended to members and details.

"I'm in their chat group." Raff raised a finger to her lips.

"*What?*" Mike missed the *shh* signal. The outburst brought the guards' eyes to their table.

"Yeah," Charlie barked. "German beers *are* better than Belgian. That's a *fact*."

Confusion peaked Mike's brow until he saw the guards resume their conversation, ignoring them and the rest of the diners' existence.

"Bravo, Charlie," Raff whispered.

Tina winked. "Nice save. Now everyone shut up. Raff?"

Raff related how she'd found that chatter code and eventually met the infamous *All Lies* group. "They are terrified. They think people will do what we did—assume it's them doing the sabotage. The data operator is a good coder, but she says she hasn't the first clue how any of the hacked equipment works, and I think she's telling the truth. Only a handful of data operators have access, and she's not one of us. Claudia was."

Gift looked at her fellow accused, her friends. "Guys, they took Claudia out of play. If something else happens... we're right back in the admin building."

Mike pointed to the ceiling. "Not if we stop 'em."

"That's where Hans comes in." Looks of surprise replied to Raff's words. "The software's out there and could be running code on any of hundreds of units. I need his help. We'll start with the most critical systems and go from there."

"May I make a suggestion?" Mike didn't wait for permission. "We should talk to the *All Lies* group, find out what they know, make sure they're not involved. You met four. Maybe there's more. Maybe Claudia *was* with them. I mean, you met them, and they told you stuff. But why would they trust you? There's no way they told you everything."

"He has a point," Gift agreed. "If they let you in, we should try to talk with them."

23 | Day Nineteen

James Müller was good. Systematically, he had been building bridges into Gift's psyche for over ten and a half years. With a few minutes every week, he gained Gift's trust and had gotten her innermost thoughts. He had the whole picture of her life, her deepest feelings, her emotional reactions, darkest fears, and brightest hopes. Only him. Realization that he knew her more intimately than anyone brought Gift a profound sadness. His ears received what no others dared, not her mom, Raff, Aimée. Her soul stood naked before him with no detail hidden. James Müller.

"Tell me the first thing to enter your mind when you saw those two guards in your Box."

The infiltration into her life ran deeper than Gift realized. Chills crawled over her skin. "What do you mean?"

"Thursday you enter your Box, only it wasn't your always pristine home—everything in its place, beyond clean and tidy. Two strangers in *your home*. They ransacked the place, stuff strewn about. What was the first emotion, your first thought?" Gift hesitated, unsure what to say. "First emotion. First thought." His demanding tone tightened her stomach.

"Um... fear? Confusion?"

"Which was it, fear, or confusion?"

"Confusion," she hissed. "I thought... I was in the wrong Box."

An odd noise approaching a cackle came from the back of James Müller's throat. "Is that even possible?"

"Well... I *guess* not."

"Of course not. You had an irrational idea that *your* biometrics opened someone else's Box. Why? Were you playing innocent?"

"Playing? I *am innocent*. I mean, I... didn't do anything."

"You are the main suspect in the biggest act of insurrection this colony has ever seen." He lost his usual compassion. "Innocent? Then how did you react to seeing complete strangers rummaging through all your belongings, touching your clothes, *underwear*, your personal items. And *you didn't do* anything. How. Did. That. Make. You. *Feel*?"

Faster than she could have thought to, Gift sat up straight. "Angry. Violated." She had no idea how much volume joined the words. Not enough. "I've done *nothing*, and they destroyed my home. Went through all my personal things like... like I was something less than human. Ripped my dignity from me. I was *angry*. And I... I had every right to be."

To Gift's surprise, the tear ducts were dry. It seemed crumbling under the weight of emotions didn't apply to the ones strong enough to stand up on their own. The silence nudged her anger to the side, making room for nervous anticipation. What would result from her outburst? Did such powerful emotions—she thought she may have said anger—mean she would be fast-tracked to a sure E.CID diagnosis? Did her slip up mean the end of her freedom as a colonial resident?

"Who is Gift Ojo?" His question yielded a blank stare of confusion. A second time he said, "Who is Gift Ojo?"

"Um, *me*? I'm Gift Ojo?"

"You don't seem so sure."

Gift's shoulders withdrew. "I don't... understand."

"Tell me who Gift Ojo really is. Describe yourself to me like I've never met you. Who are you? What defines you as a person?"

"Oh." Her pause lingered. "Okay... I'm Gift Ojo. I'm twenty-six. I work—"

"Wrong. The real you. Who is Gift Ojo?" Each time he repeated the peculiar question, the more bizarre it became. She needed to offer an answer he'd accept with no idea what that might be.

Two breaths settled her mind. "Okay. Gift Ojo. Me. A strong woman with warmth and love in my heart. I'm an optimistic and cheerful person—though people try to rob me of that." She gave him a stern look, hot enough to melt ice. "I'm an excellent engineer. I like music and good books. My favorite show is MSS Banzai. And I have great friends who love me, and I love them. I enjoy my time with them as well as a quiet evening alone in my Box. And I love this colony and live by the tenet, *For the Good of the Colony.* And I always, *always,* try to do that. I obey those in oversight and am a model resident and a good person."

She thought her words would make a decent departure eulogy. If this ordeal meant her end, it comforted her to contemplate the possibility they might use it in her ceremony.

"Okay. That's a wrap for me, but stay here, make yourself comfortable." With that ominous direction, he left. Anxiety flurried up into her stomach. *Now what do they want?*

When a guard arrived, Gift expected to be marked for E.CID. *They're taking me to see Sakura. Who better than her? Who worse than her? The painful guilt she'll experience from this isn't fair.* When they reached Pronto Soccorso, Gift inhaled long and deep—her last breath of freedom. A foolish gesture as she would breathe the same recycled air in the building. The action, purely symbolic, brought a finality to the dread.

Her first time in Pronto Soccorso presented her with the whitest place she'd ever seen, filled with waiting chairs and a long reception counter. In her experience, white rooms were soft, with thoughtfully added accents. What she saw here felt cold, stark, harsh. The last thing Gift would see before being put into a coma. An unexpected calmness cuddled her soul considering that prospect.

Sakura's office, a wide room with a desk and a typical exam table, resembled the ones in the medical clinic. Gift stood with Marco's uncertainty about how to do that.

"Please, Gift, sit... So, why are we here?"

"E.CID." Sakura's face told Gift it was rhetorical.

"Yes, you are a *potential* sufferer of Early Chemical Imbalance Disorder. The preliminaries are not conclusive. Expressed anger, poor work habits, romantic tendencies, and trouble sleeping. These are the symptoms you have manifested over the last several weeks. Do you have any questions?"

"Poor work habits?"

"I am reviewing your work logs. The air handler is a red flag in your file. According to the report, the repair could have been completed in less than fifteen minutes, yet it took you over sixty minutes from initial diagnosis. Analysis proposes the repairs should have been implemented while the system ran on redundancies and would have resulted in zero downtime of the critical unit." The raised eyes of the gentle physician conveyed apologetic softness. "Please, Gift. I am only reading the report." Gift replied with a somber nod. "It says due to your negligence, the unit went offline and could have had catastrophic consequences."

"I see."

"Other items listed are taking too long on routine tasks, redoing poorly done repairs, distractions on your bench. You may hear all of them... if you like."

"No... I think I get the general idea."

"Gift, if you wish to speak to any of these, it will really help. E.CID is not the only reason for any of these. It will be good for you to offer an explanation other than the sickness."

"Like what?"

"I cannot answer that. If you could supply any reason for this behavior…"

"The air handler was a mess. The redundancies had already failed by time we got there. There was no way to prevent its shutdown. And when they called… I mean when they sent us there. It was me and Mike. We needed Raff for the controller OS, and it was already offline by the time she arrived."

"That is helpful. But what about the daily tasks? You have been distracted, had to redo work, and replaced the wrong part on one just recently."

"We're looking for the saboteurs. That's been my focus."

Sakura typed each time Gift spoke. "I added those notes to your file. It will help. For the specifics on the other items…" Her tone carried the weight of guilt, as Gift feared.

"I don't know… I mean, *how?*"

"How what, sweetie?"

"Romantic tendencies? Trouble sleeping? How could they know any of those things?"

Sakura scrolled her display. "The reports do not say. Likely, much comes from the cameras. I assume they are more closely observing you."

"Observing me *sleeping?*" The possibility made her feel cold and naked.

"Of course not. Perhaps you appeared tired at work. Or you may have mentioned it to someone. Mister Müller?"

"No… At this point, it wouldn't surprise me if they had a camera in my Box. I've learned we have little to no privacy." Gift held up air quotes too early to put around, "For the good of the colony."

"I am sure that is *not* the case."

She shrugged in reply.

"In the write-up under romantic tendencies, I must ask you about some of these. The first is Matteo Leitner. It says here you often spend the night in his Box. I am to remind you physical intimacy and sexual relations in pre-G.M. persons are signs of Early CID. And... I am sorry Gift, I *must* ask. Do you and Matteo engage in intimacy or sexual activity of any kind when you spend the night in his Box?"

Gift closed her eyes and swallowed hard. "No."

"Then please tell me why you spend nights in his Box? What do you do together?" Inaudibly, her lips said, *Sorry.*

"Just watch vids. That's all. *Often...?* We do it, like, once a year. Anyway... we sorta grew up together and I took him for a little brother. We watch Banzai and talk until I fall asleep. He goes to work third shift, past Lights-Out, so I stay, *alone*, until morning and go to work."

"That is so sweet. Still under romantic tendencies, I must ask you about someone called Max."

"Again with Max? *Seriously?*" Her frustration expelled itself in an exhale. "I don't even *know* the guy. He greeted me in the shower queue. *Once.* And he creeped me out. Was looking me up and down—with Sara right beside him. That was it, our whole torrid relationship. *So* romantic." An uncomfortable sarcasm hit the trailing words hard.

"Then Gift, why were you afraid he was the one giving your massage last week?" Sakura's eyes begged for Gift's forgiveness.

How could she know that? "I don't know what you mean."

"Visit logs recorded you saying aloud on the massage table you did not want Max to be the one doing it."

There it was. Her habit of speaking to the air is what got her. She must have verbalized her thoughts aloud. Alone but not, always under the cameras. "I guess I thought out loud." Gift's shoulders rose and her face squinted. "I must do that a lot. Listen... I thought... for just a moment, that this guy Max, from the shower queue? I know absolutely zero about him. He could work anywhere. Because of how *he* looked at me, I thought *he* couldn't be professional rubbing his hands all over me. But I had no romantic tendencies toward him."

"Thank you, this helps. Last, for the anger. I do not need to ask you anything about it, we have your session with Mister Müller from earlier today. But I can give you the opportunity to speak to that if you like."

"You heard the whole thing? The guards in my Box?"

"I did."

"Then you know *that's* what it takes to bring me to anger. I think anyone would be justified in that, at any age or maturity, don't you?" Gift looked longingly for empathy. She found it in Sakura's eyes, the words evidently forbidden.

"I am not to give my opinions." Raised eyes quickly brought back reminded Gift the cameras were watching their interview.

"And now? You tell me I've got E.CID, and then what? Try to medicate me? Or do I just go straight to—"

"No Gift. Please do not think like that. This has not confirmed a diagnosis. The interview gives us a baseline. We need to do bloodwork, and the results take a few days before we know more. Let me draw your blood and get a urine sample, then you will be free to go." Sakura collected the needed samples—normal medical visit procedures. Whatever that questioning bit was, it was something altogether foreign. "I assume you have eaten nothing today?"

"No, for my Medical. What time even is it?"

"Twelve seventeen. We kept you much longer than usual. Please, join me for lunch before you go to work."

***

They both ordered soup from Gunther at the noodle stand, and Sakura insisted on paying. The side order of guilt that came with it was free.

"I am going to do my best to get a negative result on your tests. Even from your interview, all the so-called evidence, you do not seem like a sure candidate to me."

"No, please. I don't want you to get into any trouble, not on my account. If I'm negative, *va bene*. If not, I guess... I guess I will need whatever comes with it."

"No, that will not happen. I oversee the tests and will look out for you. Do not worry, I will not get into any trouble."

"Please Sakura, I'm begging you."

"There is something else I need to ask, Gift." Sakura set her chopsticks on the hashioki and put on a more serious face. "When I entered your blood and urine for testing in my report, I saw something I am not familiar with on the form. Does EXP One-forty-two mean anything to you?"

"I've seen that in my file but, no. I've no idea what it means. Well..." Gift hesitated. She was not to discuss her medical day visit with anyone, but was she having lunch with a friend or talking to a medic? She chose medic. "I'm not sure why... it means, whatever it is, it means... every week I have a full workup, blood and other... fluids. Extra tests."

"Interesting. For most of us that is every six months."

"They said it means I'm *special* in some way. I don't know how."

"If I can find out what that means, I will. Now, finish your noodles before they get cold."

24

The echo of a distant alarm rang, loud and intense. Its scream bounced through the open workspace pressing on her ears. Nothing on Gift's or Mike's screen. Raff stared at her display with an intensity that could burn through it. That the alert targeted her was curious and frightening, mostly frightening.

They feared more malicious A.I. code slept, learning, waiting—another attack sure to come. It had. What else could it be? Hans Fuchs pressed in tight against Raff's shoulder, something fixated him on her display. At once, Gift and Mike ran over to their bench.

"What is it?"

"Fire." Hans Fuchs' nonchalance to the circumstance puzzled her. Then Gift remembered she didn't know the guy.

Raff's, *Oh mamma,* addressed the display.

"It's the farm. My goodness, the farm." Experiencing Hans Fuchs' fear-voice heightened Gift's panic.

"It's out now." Raff addressed them while the screen held her gaze. "Suppression countermeasures did their job. A bit late. This *should not* have happened. Put out at the first spark—how they're designed. This shouldn't have happened."

"How'd-you-stop-it?" Removing the spaces between her words, Gift spit them out.

"I didn't. As I said, the automated systems engaged. Just, late. Hans, I'm throwing something to your terminal. I'll try to figure out what caused the fire, you're on why the suppression delayed."

"Gift. Start remote hardware diagnostics. I'm sending part numbers to your terminal. Mike, help her. Something tells me this is far from ov—" a second alarm sliced the word in two. "—ver. Gift. *Go.*"

When the bench-mates reached their displays, Gift gestured across hers to send half the part numbers to Mike.

The second alarm blared like swirling water around a drain, spreading its confusion through noise saturation. When it stopped, they saw Miss Jane running toward them. The panic in her eyes ran deep, full of every plausible scenario and outcome.

"I stopped that blasted alarm. I'm following Raff's system log; she asked you to be ready to go. I'll have your field kits and fire protective equipment. If you enter the farm dome, you'll need that. I'll be in my office getting yelled at." As quickly as she came, she scurried off.

Gift stayed on task. "I've got something. Initial diagnostics on the controller that regulates the filtration system on the hydroponics garden that burned... It's showing a faulty current flow monitor on its main board *and* redundancies. Mike, unless I'm wrong, I don't think any code did this."

"What are you saying?"

"Someone was in there. The parts? Someone physically replaced them. Look here." Mike craned over her shoulder to see her display as Gift pointed to a dot on a schematic. "What do you see there?" What he saw rounded Mike's eyes. "Your dummy redundant chip. Oh mamma! Mike, you may have found the key to this whole thing. These chips have no business being on any of these. And when a flow valve fails—because someone swapped it out for a crap one—your chip short circuits the whole board then..."

"*Fire.* Oh my—"

"Quick. Check all your parts numbers for these flow valves and monitors and the genuine parts swapped for your dummy redundant things."

They raced through every part to generate an inventory of the ones they'd need to replace in thirty-two units, then ran back to Raff. "We're ready to go."

"Good. You need to fix that hardware. We confirmed the suppression system has a corrupted OS, but it's not isolated. We got the system going and extinguished the second fire, but it took longer. It's like it... learned, improved, in just minutes. We need to stop new fires starting. Go now. And be careful."

Mike and Gift plucked up their field kits and made a hurried dash through the stockroom for the replacement parts. At the farm's main entrance in Dome Six, they found a cultivator waiting for them.

"When did the second fire stop?" Mike asked.

"Took the suppression unit eighty-six seconds to get going. We don't need more fires. You two do whatever it takes. Some of ours are in there. Let's not let 'em get burnt."

"Get us where we need quickly."

The man raised an eyebrow at Gift. She swallowed her pride, but the assumption Mike was on point left a bitter aftertaste. She recalled how she had done the same with Beth and Albert and let it pass. The nameless man pushed between them and moved to a ladder. Mike followed, climbing it like one of those funny-tailed creatures. *Monkey?* Gift contemplated the ladder as Mike became a tiny figure of a monkey-man.

"Suck it up." She threw her field kit strap over her shoulder and began her ascent. Gratitude for the railings filled her when she reached the catwalk and caught up to Mike.

"Here's the first ones, four of them together." The helpful guide knew the layout well.

"Thank you..." Her spinning hand implied, *What's your name?*

"Oh, Sal. Call me Sal."

"I'm Gift, he's Mike." Her calmness surprised Sal as much as herself. Her resolve to be strong—as she described *Gift Ojo* to James Müller—won the fight over what she had learned was acrophobia after she froze the last time she confronted a ladder. She accepted it as a *minor fear* of heights—not readily putting labels on herself or anyone. Gift figured any sane person should be troubled by the prospect of falling to their death.

The Electronics Engineers assessed the first unit and noted the process for replacing each part in their log. After swapping three parts with good ones, a reconfiguration of four of the modulation crystal chips completed the repair. Gift noted the six minutes the first unit demanded. "Four done, twenty-eight more to go." She logged the steps and noted the completed ones then asked Sal to lead them to the next units. Gift sought to balance speed and quality.

"We need to get closer to five minutes a unit. Two each, ten minutes for the cluster. We can stay ahead of it." The second cluster took just over eleven minutes. It missed Gift's goal, but a decent improvement. Sal led the way to the next set of controller units on a walkway branched off the main and farther from the dome's side, reaching into the massiveness of its open space.

"Sal, do you know Matteo?" Gift had to shout.

"You mean Matt? Matt Leitner?"

"Didn't know anyone called him that."

"Yeah, good kid." *Kid?* Squinting, she noticed the gray highlighting the black cropped hair. Perhaps to him, they were all kids.

"He's a great guy. A sweetheart. Known him most of my life."

The dome went dark. Brilliant flashes of light forced their eyes closed ahead of thunderous booms pressing in on them when the air's weight increased by an order of magnitude. Flames engulfed a set of controllers on a distant walkway. The suspended hydroponics garden below glowed orange as molten metal and wire intertwined with vines and branches falling onto a crop of some sort, working it into a fire. Instinct started her running toward the smoldering device. Sal's honed instinct caught her by the arm and held her in place.

"No. You stay on the ones not on fire, keep them from becoming so. We'll deal with those."

"Right. Mike let's split up. We'll be faster that way. Do a set and move quickly as we can, okay?"

He nodded while his lips said *okay*. Gift was unsure if he mouthed the word or if her ears missed it for their ringing.

"Sal." Gift yelled because she couldn't hear well. "The next two sets, please. We'll take one set each."

Hurried steps amplified the thinness of the metal under her feet. Its spongy give unsettled her. To look straight below made the decking vanish for the holes of its mesh design. Gift shoved it to the corner of her brain—no time, the garden and crops below hadn't been extinguished. Daunting as it was, they had to keep going. *No more fires.*

Before they separated, Mike said, "Maybe we should get a couple more techs up here and knock these out faster?"

"Yeah. Sent a request to Miss Jane. Help's on the way. We need to keep moving."

Sal pointed Mike toward a short walkway branched off the main catwalk, a set of four controllers at the end. Gift followed the guide's turn at a junction. Heat embraced her, increasing the dampness over her skin.

"You got fire gear in there, yeah?"

Gift nodded her understanding and removed the gray fire-retardant cowl from the bag, placing it over her head. The plex-shield, larger than her face, passed filtered air to her nostrils. Sal pointed forward, sending her gaze to meet the next set of modules suspended over an open flame. He waved his hand over his face and Gift inferred she'd go alone, Sal unable to join without fire protection.

"You can do this." Her words to the taunting walkway led her over the flames. Hard and deliberate steps became slower and shorter as the controllers neared. As she knelt beside the first module, she set the toolkit at her feet. With the fire's heat roasting her shins, Gift started the repairs. *Where's that mal'd suppression?*

With placement of the last part on the fourth unit, Gift aligned the crystals. It took her over five minutes and a half each, twenty-three for the cluster. *Not good.* She found Sal talking into his fist as she approached, then saw a small black square with rounded edges in his hand. A two-way radio. "Matt? Amanda?"

Fright in his voice reached Gift's bones, and she took it as her own. "Where's Matteo?" Sal pointed into the fire and Gift screamed his name at it.

Mike ran up in fire gear. "Let's go, next sets."

The guide grabbed Gift's arm and turned her from the spectacle of raging flames. "You gotta keep going, stop more fires starting."

Dropping her head to nod splashed a tear on the inside of her face shield. The handheld chirped, an orange light pulsating on the display. "They're here, the other team. I'll send them the bottom half of what we've got left. Sal, we need another you to lead them."

"Already on it, they'll be up the ladder in a minute. Now we need to get you to your next."

The three set off running farther into the expanse of the massive farm dome. Gift's handheld received an update. "Team two's in place. Sixteen left."

"One set each, then. Let's do it." Mike's shield muffled his voice. He followed the aim of the guide's finger along the walkway to his last set, and Gift trailed Sal to hers.

"Any news on Matteo?"

He shook his head. "He's got full fire protection."

At the cluster, Gift dropped her bag. Initial diagnostics taught her the specific order of parts replacement before a reconfiguration of the modulation crystals. One board, the next, the last piece on the third. "One more." A quick check of the handheld showed Mike's last was nearly completed and team two had started theirs.

A faint whimper of a crackling sound tickled Gift's ear. Raising her hand to the last unit proved futile. The heat wouldn't come until the pop of fire and light. Raising the shield, she leaned over the board to let in unfiltered air. It was only the stupidest thing she could have done after she'd done it. An acrid odor of burning plastic completely overtook her sense of smell—a module in overload. Pure instinct drove her muscles when her mind may have made different decisions, moving her hands before she realized she had a choice to make, even if she didn't.

With parts laid out, Gift considered her fire protection gloves. Knowing she'd not manage the parts replacement with their thickness, they kept their place in the bag. Current monitor first, verified to be seated properly. Flow valve next.

Her scream came out gruff, from the depth of her diaphragm, as signals from scorched flesh reached pain receptors. The intensity of the valve's heat peeled a layer of skin from the tips of the thumb, index, and middle fingers of Gift's right hand. Fragments of flesh clung onto the replacement valve as she verified its insertion on the board. Nothing to do but carry on until done.

Voltage regulator next—it was actively overloading. With no angle of approach with her left hand, Gift placed her throbbing fingers over the piece. Through the filters of her mask, the coppery charcoal stench assaulted her nose and caused a short, deep cough. *Burning flesh.*

A quick pull on the part produced magnificent sparks. Shadowed blotches filled her vision. She inserted a new regulator before pulling the thing Mike called a dummy redundant chip and putting a capacitor in its place. Pushing through the pain with diminished vision, barely able to focus, she managed the crystal alignment. Five minutes, seventeen seconds.

To lift the handheld from the grating took all her might. Gift considered the fingertips on the right hand—raw with throbbing pain. Pinhead dots of blood laced over them as they shifted out of focus. Everywhere she looked went dim, narrow. Her eyesight lost definition, and her right periphery emptied, cropping her vision. A shadowy contrast transformed the controllers into dark ghostly blobs over shades of murky black.

Total darkness.

An outline out of focus, Mike's face was a blur. "Gift. You fainted. Your hand's hurt bad." He spoke as if from behind a closed door. He and Sal from either side raised Gift to her feet.

"We need to go now. The failsafe is being activated." Sal spoke with a clearer voice.

"What failsafe?" Her voice sounded hollow, a distant echo, as her feet remembered how to walk.

"Last fire's not out. We've held it back some, but the suppression isn't working. The O2 is about to be sucked out." The urgency in Sal's shaky voice distracted Gift from realizing they were running. A word, a number, came from a distant monotone voice.

"What's that?"

"Countdown. We have seventeen seconds to get out."

"Or?"

"We suffocate."

Gift felt the turns, seeing only the back of Sal's head, her arm over Mike's shoulder. "There," Sal growled, pointing straight ahead at a hatch.

'Eleven... Ten...'

"Hurry." The desperation in Mike's word hit Gift like a shot of adrenaline.

'Seven... Six...'

Sal spun the lock-wheel in the center of the hatch, cracking the seal, and pulled it open—a piercing groan of metal on metal. They pulled Gift through as the door swung closed and the flat voice said, 'Two...'

Gasping to catch the breaths lost to the run, the men had hands on their knees. When Gift removed her mask, the ringing in her ears closed her eyes. "Team two?"

"Already out." Mike removed the facemask, no longer speaking in echoes.

"Matteo?"

Sal said, "Don't know. Can't raise anyone on the two-way." Gift's head dropped as anxious concern weakened the muscles in her neck. "Air is already pumping into the dome. When this..." Sal tapped a red light on the hatch panel. "...goes green, we can open it."

"Where are we?" An insufficient light exposed the gray dullness of the claustrophobic space and the walls pressed in on her.

"An emergency environmental hatch. Built for this purpose, hoped never to be needed. This may be its first time used. The failsafe deoxygenates the farm dome because without oxygen..."

"Fire can't burn."

"Exactly."

"So, the second fire? I mean third. It never went out? Raff didn't get the suppression system going? Could the code have been that good?"

"What's a raff? What code?" Sal had no context for Gift's words.

25

Sal considered Gift's hand. "Think you can make it down the ladder with that hand?"

"I'd rather not leave it up here." Her reach for humor drew a smile on Sal's face. Examining both hands, Gift saw her damaged fingers as if it were the first time. Blisters boiled over the raw flesh. "I... don't know."

"Okay, no worries. Mike, you take her bag with yours and go down first, I'll help her."

Once Mike began, Sal took to the ladder and extended his arms, pushing his torso away from it. "Okay, step on, holding firm with your left hand, and come between me and the ladder."

With careful movement, Gift placed her left foot on the rung by Sal's waist and grabbed four rungs higher with her left hand and committed her right foot to the ladder.

"Now... take your right wrist. Lay it on the rung and tilt your palm over it for grip, careful not to use your fingers." Cautiously she did as he said. "Now come down a rung. We keep this position, stepping down one rung at a time together. Ready?" When Gift nodded, they began their tandem descent. Eight meters up, give or take, Sal paused. "How we doing?"

Gift didn't call him on using *we*. "Fine. I'm fine."

"Keep it slow and steady. Ready?"

"Yeah."

One step.... Another... Another.

Her guttural scream filled the dome. Gift's right index finger writhed in agony when it banged against the side of the ladder. She missed connecting her wrist to the next rung and the imbalance shifted her center mass, causing her foot to slip its next step.

The jerk of her fall pressed Gift hard into Sal's chest and a yelp swirled up from her diaphragm. Her torso pitched hard to the side, folding her over his forearm and casting her gaze downward to the distant ground, summoning a shrieking squeal.

"It's okay, I've got you." She felt his arms press in from the side as he pulled himself closer to her, she closer to the ladder. Dangling from a still fatal height, reassurance came in warm, heavy breaths on her neck. The descent took hours condensed to just over ten minutes.

"I need to see Matteo." Gift's feet went flush with solid ground ahead of her manners. "Sorry, Sal. Thank you. I'd not've made it without your help."

"No worries. Let's see about Matt."

Sal led Gift to the farm office not twenty meters far. Mike followed as they entered to find four men sitting on the floor with two women seated on the only two chairs, all six wearing oxygen masks, all with the black of smoke peppering their coveralls. One of the oxygen-depleted men stood, pulling the mask from his face. "*Gift?*"

She ran into Matteo and wrapped her arms in a tight hug, careful of her fingers. "I saw you... in the fire... I was so worried."

"You saw me? How? What are you doing here?"

"I was up there." Gift pointed to the office ceiling. "We worked on the controllers, the ones that were overloading and setting the fires. I was right above you when the fire started."

Nostalgic tears from earlier dread resurfaced past the dread's expiration to mix with ones of joy, rolling streams over her cheeks. A droplet followed the jawline to her chin, and Matteo reached a finger to tenderly catch it. Holding up her right hand, she said, "I hurt my fingers."

"Ouch. You need to go get that treated ASAP."

"We're on that." A surprisingly assertive tone in Mike's words.

"Yeah. Had to make sure you were alright. I'm going. Hey… let's do our next vid night sooner than later, okay?"

"Definitely."

Stepping out of the office, they met Administration Guards standing tall to greet them—two this time, both women. Gift questioned why that surprised her. Perhaps she had associated large male guards with an intimidation tactic. She fully expected this next bit, and Mike's face told her he did as well. However, when Sal questioned their presence, the guards looked puzzled. "We need you to come with us."

Gift nodded at him to say, *Just cooperate*. Being less compliant, Sal didn't step when they began walking. "Sir, you need to follow us." Guard One seemed to be forcing a depth to her voice to lend it greater authority—an obvious pretense. The wrinkling of her brow squinted her eyes as her face attempted a show of strength beyond its ability.

"*No*. She needs immediate medical attention." Pointing to her hand Sal said, "Show them."

"My. We'll have to get you to Pronto Soccorso then."

Gift nodded appreciatively.

A short walk from Dome One, Gift barely had the physical or emotional stamina to move one foot past the other. The talking guard leaned into the ear of the other, sending her away. A minute later, Guard Two rolled up in a cart. Made for four, it struggled under the weight of five. Gift's bum was squeezed between the men's thighs on the bench behind the driver and Guard One. The traction of the soft rubber wheels over the smooth concrete of the floor created a constant hum. Their turns or slight steer corrections added frequent squealing to form a melody as uncomfortable on the ears as it was soothing. Gift found herself humming along to it until the cart jerked into a hard stop and her knees hit the back of the bench in front of them. Just before grabbing the top of the bench, her right hand retracted, sparing her additional agony.

Weary eyes found Sakura at the entrance standing behind a wheelchair. Sal and Mike each took an arm to help Gift up and onto the chair. She allowed their chivalry, though she believed it unnecessary as she had regained her strength. A soft look from Sakura's eyes thanked the men, then she turned Gift toward the doors and wheeled her into the now familiar sterile white of the reception lobby. Traversing the same corridor she had followed Sakura through just hours prior, they reached the office where she'd had her official E.CID interview. The purpose of this visit sat more soundly in mind.

"I told you three days." Sakura's soft voice was calming as she tended to Gift's damaged fingers.

The door slid open, and a slender young lady entered, pushing a white box the size of her head attached to a pole on wheels. The girl couldn't be more than in her first years, assumed by the smoothness of a brow lacking wrinkles of age or anxiety. Gift considered her hair, short and straight with blue highlights, cute. The effort needed to focus reminded Gift of her dim vision.

"Thank you, Holly."

After sharing a smile, the perky junior assistant turned and departed. Sakura put Gift's hand in the device and, faster than what Gift figured enough to get results, it beeped. The glow of Sakura's desktop display shrouded her in paleness.

"Good news."

"I could use a bit of good news."

Meaningless words explained Sakura's diagnosis. All Gift heard was that her skin would grow back, good as new, thanks to 3D-printed medicated bandages.

The door closed behind Sakura, leaving Gift alone. Gift's mind drifted to the young assistant. What if she never saw her again? A whole person, an entire life, only a glimpse in Gift's. Who were her parents? What sort of friends did she keep? Favorite foods? Favorite vids? Was she a loner who enjoyed solitude or a party-crazed youth seeking the next fleeting pleasure? What might she have been thinking at this very moment?

"So many people," she said to the room.

Waves of contemplation came for the lives of the over fifty thousand souls in her colony, New Europa. What of the other hundreds of thousands in the New Republic of China, The Russian Federation, United Africa, and the United Republic of Mars. The U.R.M. was said to be the largest of the colonies, easily over twice the size of New Europa, possibly more. How different that would be, floating through life passing by a hundred thousand souls, most nameless. Would it be any different?

Once the medical printer had applied the bandages to Gift's fingers, Sakura used an ocular scanner and returned to her desk to check the results. "Good news, there is no permanent damage. I will give you drops that will help. You will have to deal with your vision as is for a day or two and it will return to normal."

"And the bandages? Showering?"

"Showering is fine. Now, we will get you checked out so you can go home. I must finish here, so Holly will escort you out."

Holly stopped the chair in the lobby. "All done. Hope you feel well soon."

"Wait. A silly question if I may... What's your favorite food?"

Puzzled, the young lady paused then said, "My mom's mushroom risotto." One less nameless person in fifty thousand strode off.

Guard One had waited for her. "Everything okay?"

"My fingers will be okay, and my eyes... eventually."

"I'm glad. Now, if you'll come with me, please."

"If I'll come? Please? So... if I said I'm exhausted, hurt, had a long day saving the colony... I could go home now?"

Guard One's look bordered on apologetic and a semblance of a smile supplied the expected answer.

"Lead the way."

26

An unfamiliar room, much smaller than she remembered, had one chair facing a vid screen. The same gray looked duller, perhaps from her cloudy vision, or more likely from her current mood.

"Have a seat." Guard One left with the clank of the door lock. A prisoner once again, the minutes left her alone with her thoughts—a tactic designed to heighten anxiety. It worked. No concern reached her conscious mind about the cameras. Being watched, scrutinized, now a given. Gift stared into the blackness of the vid screen as if she could *will* it to come to life and get this over with. An almost inaudible pitch of electronic components receiving weak current signaled the beginning of her latest ordeal. The faint reflection of herself on the black screen became shadows dissolved into shapes, into figures appearing from the silhouettes.

A lifeless voice came from the display. "Session twenty-seven point three commencing. The subject is identified as Gift Ojo. The time is nineteen fifty-eight. This session is being recorded."

Gift's mouth pushed a burst of air vibrating between her closed lips. *This session is being recorded. Like the others weren't.* To see seven people sitting in a row at a table, all facing her, added twisted cords around the knot sitting in her gut. In the center sat a distinguished woman. Aged but not old, she carried the look of experience. Her silver hair had a perfect line parting the middle and hung like a solid sheet down both sides of her face.

It ended flat and level. Gift marveled at it doing so, as if drawn in place more than styled.

"Miss Ojo, we represent the interests of this colony and have been assigned by direct appointment of the Board of Directors of New Europa. Before speaking with you, we reviewed all prior incidents, all interviews conducted with yourself, and all reports about such. We are here today regarding the incident in the Farm Dome, which occurred this afternoon and in which you played a key part."

Gift felt uneasy in her own skin, it no longer fit right over the muscle, cartilage, and bone. Used to this sort of thing but not comfortable, she wasn't sure her arms were right. Her reach to interlock her fingers reminded her of the limb lying in a sling.

"Miss Ojo, are you aware we have identified you as a person of interest in previous acts of sabotage enacted against this colony?"

"Well, the other day when—"

"Yes or no will do, Miss Ojo."

"Oh, sorry. Yes."

"As a person of interest in previous acts of sabotage, do you believe you should have been dispatched into the situation in the farm dome, which had the signs of being similar sabotage?"

"But I didn't do... I mean. I ran in there to help."

"As a *hypothetical*, do you feel sending a suspected saboteur into an active incident of similar sabotage is a wise course of action? *Yes* or *no*."

"Well... No? But—"

"Then Miss Ojo... How was it that you, a person of interest and suspected saboteur, came to be on point in today's incident?"

Gift's mind worked itself into hyperdrive as options flashed by her mental screen. The pain nudged her, reminding her of her fingers. What trouble could Gift bring upon Raff by admitting she'd sent her? *The logs. The cameras. They already know. They want to see how I'll answer.* A clarity came to her mind which her vision still lacked. Truth was on her side, she had to hope that would count for something.

"Raff received the alarm and started working on the incident. She gave me and Mike some hardware IDs to check. Then she and I agreed that we—Mike and me—we needed to go replace several pieces of faulty hardware."

"For the record, the person mentioned as Raff is identified as Raffaella Di Gaetano and Mike as Michael Russo. So, Miss Ojo, Miss Di Gaetano decided, along with *yourself,* you should be the one to go repair the systems. Units with faulty hardware likely placed by a saboteur. Equipment you would be the first one suspected of having sabotaged."

The callous woman presented that as a statement, yet her pause beckoned a reply. Fourteen eyes she couldn't see in focus but could sense crawling over her skin waited. The sustained silence was maddening.

"Yeah? I guess so."

"How many units failed today, causing the fires and damaging crops vital to our lives, our survival?"

"We think three."

"What do you mean, you think? How many?"

"Ma'am? The units are in clusters of four. Four are connected... physically. In all, twelve units caught fire. We believe... I mean, from what we saw, we believe only one unit in each cluster failed. So, three failed units. But we lost twelve. Twelve caught fire and burned, ma'am."

Gift watched the woman's mouth move without words, turned her head as someone else voicelessly spoke, then another. In a dream, Gift once taught herself to read lips. She found no understanding in the mouths moving on screen, so this must have been real. Unable to guess what their talking in secret meant, like the burns on her skin that started to itch, Gift knew it didn't promise anything good.

Silver Hair's voice returned. "Miss Ojo. We have images of the units before us and the parts you identified to be replaced. Please walk us through the repair process step by step."

Speaking to her technical knowledge helped calm her—she was more in her element. Her work was good. She'd saved most of those units and prevented more fires on the crops. Attempting to be clear and articulate, Gift outlined each step. To be given the opportunity to explain herself touched close to something right. Any reasonable person would see her as the protagonist in this story her life had become, not the saboteur.

"What we see clearly, Miss Ojo, is this: *You* knew which parts had been replaced with defective ones. *You* also knew the specific order each part needed to come off and go on those units. And *you* knew exactly how damaging this sabotage would be."

"*What*?" Gift hoped she'd only bounced the word around her head, but it passed her lips with outrage and contempt. They were single-minded in faulting her for this. Why?

"Excuse me, Miss Ojo. What did you say?"

"No, I? I'm just. I don't get it... I mean, I know *now*. Because I diagnose problems. It's my job. I had to learn those things, run diagnostics... Mike and I found the problem, and we, we figured it out. Crazy high up on a bouncing scary walkway over the open flames of a raging fire. We applied that knowledge to fix the rest. I called for help." Raising her right arm from its cradled position in the sling, she showed her bandaged fingers. "I almost lost three fingers. And... and we nearly died. We almost didn't make it to the hatch before suffocating in the failsafe."

Expecting the wetness of expressed tears, Gift put her face in her palm. There were none, not this time. They stirred up different emotions with no weakness in them, only found strength that emboldened her to go on. She hadn't planned to rise to her feet, but found herself standing, nonetheless.

"Let me add, in each of the incidents where I'm a person of interest? It was me. *Me*! I stopped it. I *risked my life,* more than once, to save and protect this colony. And, and you dare question my loyalty? If I was the only one who knew how to stop this? How... how... to fix it? Then you should all be thankful that I'm *that* good at my job and I was the one there today. So yes. *Yes.* It *absolutely* was the right decision to send me in there today."

Shocked by her monologue of righteous indignation, Gift's body swayed slowly like a young tree under an air vent. Someone should have patted her on the back. Where was the adulation she deserved?

'I see,' was not the response she'd hoped to elicit from Silver Hair. They muted again, talking among themselves. Deflated as much by the unimpressed response as by the expenditure of air her words required, Gift sat back down.

"Tell us how many people you can identify with the skills to write and deploy malicious software code that crippled the fire suppression system in the farm dome."

"Not many that I know of."

"Who, Miss Ojo?"

The *Miss Ojo* got under her skin. In this setting, she believed it better not to mention it. "Of course, Raff. So, be glad she's helping you. And Claudia. She, she could do it. Maybe this new guy Hans Fuchs—only from what Raff told me. But our guess, Raff and me, is Claudia, for sure. But you already know that, and took her right from her bench."

"Let the record show that the person mentioned as Claudia is identified as Claudia Giuntoni. Tell us about Miss Giuntoni."

"Tell you what? I didn't know her, really."

"*Didn't* know? Why did you use the past tense?"

Because you probably have her in a coma, which is as good as dead. Best to keep that thinking to herself. "I only saw her at work, and she doesn't work with us anymore."

Unnerving quietness filled the room. Gift saw—even in the cloudy vision of one eye—what looked like heated discussion across the table in whatever corner of the colony they were. Gift suffered the pressure of urine ready to leave her without regard for time or place. She raised her hand, which was ignored. "Hello? I guess you people can hear me? I really need to pee." No one paid her any mind. Overwhelmed by the feeling she couldn't restrain herself, she stood, rocking. Her thighs tensed, and her volume increased. "I'm about to pee myself."

The warm sensation spread more down her left thigh than her right. She stood stiff, facing the camera with arms crossed over her chest, waiting, fuming.

"Miss Ojo, we have—"

"Miss Ojo? You call me Miss Ojo? Say things like *please*. You call yourselves civilized people. Look at me!" She pointed her left hand at the darker fabric from her groin down her thighs. "I've been screaming at you, or a guard here—if there is one—I had to use the toilet. You left me here to pee myself. A grown woman soaked in her own urine."

Silence came again until Silver Hair broke it. "I apologize. We are deeply regretful we didn't respond to your request. Now please sit so we can continue."

We're sorry. Now sit in your pee and shut up. Gift hoped for a gram of compassion and found none. At least she understood her inquisitors more clearly, but that changed nothing. She sat down.

"Alright, Miss Ojo. You are a person of interest in at least three known acts of sabotage against this colony and you maintain your innocence. Having firsthand experience examining and being the one that corrected the incidents, please present us your theory."

"My what? What theory?"

"If we *took* Miss Giuntoni, as you say, how could she have carried out today's attacks?"

"Sleeper code."

"Care to elaborate?"

"Raff came up with this idea… It's plausible Claudia sent the code out before the failures. Even the last one, the water re—hydroponics regulator. She could have pushed her software to the suppression system days, even weeks ago. It learns a unit it's on… before it corrupts it."

"Very interesting hypothesis…" Gift took the opportunity for a smug smile, then pulled on the fabric over her left knee to adjust the soaked material. Her urine began to stink, and the wet coverall held tightly on the skin, pulling it taut. "However, I am afraid the facts don't support it."

"What do you mean? What facts?"

Minutes fell into the past before Silver Hair continued. "Miss Ojo, given the escalation of the situation and risks posed to the safety of this colony, we have upgraded your status from person of interest to suspect. You are hereby placed under Level One surveillance and assigned a constant guard escort. You may go to your home and your work assignment, nowhere else. Do you understand these restrictions as I have explained them to you? Yes or no answer, please."

"Yes."

"Due to your unfortunate… accident, you may have a shower here before you are taken home."

The screen blackened, leaving her in silence in the little gray room. The fabric of her wet garment had stiffened. Person of interest, suspect, whatever label they gave it, they treated her like a contemptible criminal. *How did this happen? Why?* The door slid open to Guard One. "I peed myself." Gift felt no shame, not her fault. "I sat on the chair, now it needs to be cleaned. If you have a cleaning wipe, I—"

The raised hand of the guard stopped the phrase from reaching its conclusion. "It will be taken care of."

"So... you're my escort now? For how long?"

"My shift ends at midnight. Let's get you home."

"Um, excuse me. The lady said I can have a shower."

"Right, I'll take you there first. Sorry, ma'am."

"No worries. And please, don't call me ma'am."

The shower was better than decent, the suds warm and lush. The surprise of its full-flow water invigorated Gift's flesh. Her hair and skin dried completely, something never accomplished by her habitat block's showers. It was, at least, a small reward for the horrendous treatment she endured.

27 | Day Twenty

As she considered her breakfast more than consumed it, Gift checked her fitness program and remembered Level One would keep her home until time for work. *My new status, they called it.* After a light in-Box workout, she needed to get her coveralls from Laundry Service. "Who do we have this morning?"

When her door did not open on her command, she knocked from inside her room—a profound wrongness in the act. A man stood before her with wide shoulders and a head a bit too small for his body, supported on a neck that appeared long for a human. "Morning, ma'am."

"Buongiorno. Please call me Gift, or we won't get along. And never call me ma'am again. Okay? I need the toilet first, then hit the laundry service. Um... may I?"

"Of course."

"First, your name."

"Tom."

"Shall we?"

Only two ahead in the toilet queue wasn't bad. The guard—Tom he was called—stood two meters away while his eyes stayed with her. Gift imagined two elongated cartoon eyes perched on her shoulder, seeing all she did. The eyes blinked rapidly, making a *bink-bink* sound, bringing a smile to her lips.

***

At the workbench, Tom stood two meters behind Gift with hands connected behind his back, at attention. A guard followed Raff into the work area, then Mike came in with his. "How's your hand?"

She raised it to show Mike the printed bandages. "Fine. Well, will be fine."

"Good, I was worried. I fought the guards to stay until I could see you were okay but..." He looked at his guard with contempt.

"I know. When did you get home?"

"Maybe nineteen thirty-*ish*. Tried to reach you."

"Me too. No comm—"

"You too? You tried to vidChat yourself?"

"What? Don't be a stupid idiot... Did you get the panel of seven?"

"Yep. Bunch of arrogant jerks."

"*Mike.*"

"Sorry, but for the second time we risked our necks to save this colony, and look how they treat us for it."

"Let's just do our work. Play one of your terrible songs while I knock out a few tasks."

Precisely at 12:00, the changing of the guards took place. When her new one took her post, Tom stepped to walk away. "Ciao Tom, thanks." He waved goodbye.

"*Ciao Tom? Thanks*?" Mike's mock impression of her voice missed, more whiney than Gift thought hers to be. "What the heck, Gift? These people are *not* our friends."

"*These people* are just doing their jobs. Don't take it out on them because they're the ones in front of us. That's not fair." Gift turned to smile at her new guard. "Ciao, I'm Gift. What's your name?"

"Sandra."

Gift assessed her in half a second. Young, likely younger than herself. The long straight hair distinguished her. Gift considered hers to be average at just off the shoulder—much longer if she ever straightened it. She never did. Sandra's reached three centimeters down her back. Straight, jet-black, and shiny, pulled tight into a ponytail. It reminded Gift of Sakura's, but they had no other traits in common.

"Sir, I'm to escort you to lunch now."

Mike turned to the voice behind him. "*Lunch*? At twelve-fifteen? We take lunch at thirteen hundred."

"Sorry, sir. Under your new status, you have staggered lunch breaks. Please, come with me."

Mike flapped his arms in the manner of something called a chicken and submitted. Level One. They didn't define it with any specificity.

At Raff's bench, Gift's attempted hug was thwarted.

"I heard about your hand. Let me see." Gift held up her fingers as a badge of honor. "Oh mamma, does it hurt?"

"Nope. Sakura patched me up. Medicated bandages quell the pain and rebuild my fingers or something. May as well have been you talking your data, way over my head." They shared a short but needed laugh.

"Ma'am, I must ask you to return to your workbench."

As they walked, Gift asked, "What happened to Sal, from the farm?"

"I'm not at liberty to say, ma'am."

Gift considered her facial expression. So empty. Just a guard with a name, but not yet with personality. *Still a caterpillar.* "Sandra, I really need you to call me Gift."

28 | Week Four

Carrying on this way for days, Gift missed her friends. She hadn't seen anyone. With no way to contact them, Gift could only guess what they had heard or imagined happened to her. Sara escorted her from work to Pronto Soccorso. She would finally see someone. Sakura could tell Charlie and Tina, get a message to Mom and Aimée. Optimism lifted her heart, floating it in her chest.

Gift's heart sank into her gut when met in the lobby by a different medic and told that Sakura wasn't available. "Miss Ojo, I'm afraid your test results are inconclusive. Negative for Early Chemical Imbalance Disorder in your bloodwork, but your interview results are marked 'suspect.' Your urine sample, however, does show trace elements related to E.CID, so we'll need to run more tests. Given your status, we'll schedule that for your next Medical Day. When is that?"

"Saturday morning."

"Okay, thank you. We've noted that in your file. That's all, Miss Ojo." He walked away without a greeting or giving his name. Had he never learned bedside manners, or was it merely his reaction to her *status?*

Plan A having failed, Gift decided to ask Sara for a favor. "It's the third day of this. I have no contact with my mom or my friends. They must be so worried. Is it possible... a message? Could you? I mean, just to let them know I'm alright."

"I wish I could." Gift heard genuine remorse in Sara's tone. "But I can tell you, we've apprised your mother of your status and that you are currently under investigation and not allowed communication."

"Thanks. But I wish…" The words ended while the thought carried on without them. How would her mom take that? 'Your daughter is under investigation. You can't contact her.'

Not bothering to change from her shower robe, Gift prepared a simple mushroom risotto. With nowhere to go, changing clothes seemed pointless. An episode of Banzai played while her risotto cooled to a temperature sure to leave the roof of her mouth unscathed. During the opening credits, she took her first spoonful, humming along to the catchy theme song she heard open the show thousands of times.

Frustration came when the subtitles switched on, the text nonsensical. Stranger still, they were familiar, but not from the show. 'Sonia makes good tacos' appeared over an external shot of the Banzai taking an orbit around Cestus Seven. Next, when Captain Arcadia said his famous catchphrase, 'Let's see what's out there,' the text read, 'Hardware grunts always blame the coders.'

"Raff."

Raff had broken through the communication lockdown. Little messages sneaked in subtitles told Gift it was her but said nothing beyond that. Subtitles kept coming, cleverly hidden among dialog and gibberish. Gift kept reading, completely disregarding the show behind them. 'Level 1 you.' That did not match the scene. *It must mean me on Level One surveillance,* Gift reasonably concluded.

'Eye in every box.' Could those guards have installed a camera? *In every Box. Where is there a camera in every Box?* If feeling stupid were a drug, Gift would have been higher than the farm dome ceiling. Every Box had a vid screen, and every screen had a camera for vidChat and video messages. It was pathetically obvious, conceivably made less so only by the presumption of privacy.

'Get those shields up.' Still wearing her shower robe, Gift considered the hook where it dries, too far to the side. She removed the robe with regard for the camera that could have been sending her live image to someone. That idea rattled her shoulders. As she slipped on her clothes, the corner of her eye noticed Nonna's giraffe carving on the shelf.

Anticipation mounted, wonderful and miserable. More out-of-place text appeared. Reading 'Nice view outside' turned her head toward the faux window beside her door. Simply a smaller vid screen, it did nothing but display pictures of outdoor vistas not yet existent at the current stage of terraforming. It stood in for a window, giving the place a homier feel. It did nothing but that—and one additional mundane function that just became the most important thing in the whole of her reality. It had a touchscreen interface for home automation features, though most everyone always used voice command.

Gift looked with intense focus, willing something to appear on the display. Its light pushed back an image of a wide-based tree with a low branch from which hung a rope swing with a small wooden seat. Over the grass lay leaves of assorted colors, from dull brown to vibrant reds, oranges, and yellows. That vista, called Autumn Swing, was her favorite. It looked almost real. Pondering the nothingness happening on the display gave her another powerful *Gift, you idiot* moment.

When her finger contacted the display, the image faded to reveal a menu. A new icon, a square of pleasing soft orange, had *Hi* in its center. Raff had worked her data-operator-magic to add an app to her system. A tap on it opened a rectangular window about twice as wide as it was high, horizontally split in half, its upper solid black, the lower half a full, although tiny, qwerty keyboard. Gift's vision had improved significantly in the days since the fires, yet the letters in the app needed effort to come into focus. They were literally a sight for her sore eyes.

> - R: Ciao bella.
>
> - G: Ciao cara.
>
> - R: Should be safe ma use sparingly.
>
> - G: Okay come stai?
>
> - R: Bene. We need a plan.
>
> - G: For what? What cab we do?
>
> - R: One of us needs to find way to sneak out.
>
> - G: How? Guard outside.
>
> - R: Don't see way. Think.
>
> - G: No idea. Were go if out?
>
> - R: Where? The All Lies group.
>
> - G: Can meet them?
>
> - R: If one of us gets out. Need your brain. Think.

Think Gift did, long and hard. On her walk back from work, could she break off? *Sneak out,* Raff said. Can't open her door, a guard stands—sits sometimes, there's a chair in the corridor—directly on the other side of her door even if it opened for her. To her dismay, Gift concluded she'd not be able to get out of her Box. "Ah ha." There was no way out of *her* Box, so she'd get out of Marco's.

> - G: Need contact Marco Fu,agalli. Box 36 beside me.
>
> - R: Marco Fumagalli? Why?
>
> - G: He get me in hos box.
>
> - G: his
>
> - R: You trust him?
>
> - G: Enough yes.
>
> - R: See what I can do. Try for tomorrow.
>
> - G: Can open this any time?
>
> - R: If window changes to Milano Rain is me.
>
> - G: Ottimo. This is great.
>
> - R: Si. Buonasera cara.
>
> - G: Buomasera.

Having a plan was exhilarating—details cloudier than the keys on the qwerty keyboard had been, but a plan just the same. Time enough to work out the trifles and wait for Raff to find a means to contact Marco and hope he was up for a little adventure.

Eating her cooled risotto was a mindless physical action of spoon to bowl, then to mouth. Chew, swallow. When the Banzai episode resumed, the subtitles were gone. Raff was gone. Knowing they were going to chat again was a salve that removed the pain from the idea and let the now cold risotto settle in her stomach without disturbance.

29

Tom had been her morning escort to work every day and took her to the toilet, third in the queue.

"Gift." Marco approached from behind.

Guards hadn't forbidden all contact, only sucked it of its joy, stopping it when it got anywhere beyond mundane pleasantries, the sort shared between acquaintances.

"Ciao, Marco."

"What's going on? What now?"

Tom cleared his throat, being kind to permit the conversation to go on under established boundaries while clearly conveying his readiness to shut it down if it strayed the course. *Message received.*

"Same old. How are you?"

"Me? *You.* How are you? They wouldn't let me check on you. Not even tell me if you were alright."

A nameless neighbor exited the toilet box and Gift took a step forward as the queue advanced.

"*Va bene.* My new normal these days. Hey, watching Banzai without me?"

"Huh?"

"MSS Banzai." She imagined his struggle to understand such an everyday topic chosen over the elephant in the room—or corridor, in this case.

Gift never understood that expression. Why would anyone have a gigantic elephant in a room? She'd seen them in historical nature vids from Earth—massive and never indoors. One of many idioms she figured people used because they did, perhaps for nostalgia's sake. Another neighbor exited and Gift moved forward, first in the queue.

"Let's watch together from our own vid screens later. We can make comments to our empty Boxes and maybe... it won't feel like we're alone. I'll start at nineteen-thirty, *Fractured Through Time*—one of my favorite episodes."

"Um... *sure*?"

"Great, nineteen-thirty. Don't forget."

Gift's steps felt lighter. She imagined the feeling her *First Ones* experienced walking in the lesser gravity for the first time, comparing it against memories of Earth's pull on their bones. It had been generations since anyone knew the difference. If only a state of mind, she figured it a close facsimile.

A painfully slow Wednesday morning with so few items in their queues allotted them downtime they were too afraid to use. When Mike took his isolated lunch, Gift shifted over to having a *meaningless* discussion with Raff.

"Ciao. You and Hans Fuchs found anything yet?"

"No. Keeping at it. *Come stai*?"

"Fine. I greeted Marco in the corridor this morning. He's the first *real person* I saw in days." An over-the-shoulder smirk told Sandra she joked about her guards not being *real people*.

"How is he? What's he up to?"

"He wasn't happy not being allowed to see me. I told him we can watch Banzai together at nineteen-thirty this evening."

Sandra leaned over Gift's shoulder, laying hot breath on her neck. "Excuse me. You told him what?"

Addressing Raff, Gift continued, "I'll be in my Box, he in his, at nineteen-thirty. We'll both watch *Fractured Through Time* and add commentary, joke about the silly stuff. Maybe it'll feel like we're watching it together even though we're not."

Sandra settled.

***

Sara the Guard followed Gift to grab some food, she wasn't in the mood to cook. When she stopped to use the toilet, Sara thoughtfully held her bag of noodles. As Sara's behavioral biometrics hid the door inside the wall, curiosity got the better of Gift. "When do *you* pee?

"Me? When I need to… like anyone."

"It's just none of you ever seem to go."

"One of many reasons our shifts are six hours, not eight."

"Fair enough. If I don't see you… Buonasera."

"You as well."

Gift ate her noodles alone and the heat of her first bite diminished her tongue's ability to distinguish the umami flavors, but not enough to ruin the bites that followed. Enjoyment purloined more from anticipation—eating while waiting for Raff to connect Marco to her. Sat cross-legged on her floor and tapping pages in her e-book one to the next, if anyone asked what she had read, she'd have had no clue.

At 19:30, Gift called up the episode of MSS Banzai. Half expecting subtitles, which Raff no longer needed for her, she turned them on herself. 'Mara, I'm your captain. You can't be kissing me while we're fighting the Gorlinack.' Captain Arcadia's audio and subtitles hid no messages. Magically, the faux window scene changed from Autumn Swing to Milano Rain. In the chat app, Gift found a new message.

- M: Ciao. This is genius.

Must be Marco, she did it.

- G: She the best.

- M: How are you really?

- G: Okay now especiallu.

- G: y

- M: Because the guards and all.

- R: How can we get G out M's box?

- G: Was thinking the bed wall.

- M: Yes. Can open wall between beds like dbl box.

- R: She's in your box. Guard outside. How get out?

- M: I distract.

- R: Risky.

- G: I can disguise myself some.

- R: Can we go tomorrow or need more time?

- M: Can be ready tomorrow. Time?

- G: 19:00?

- M: Take maybe 30 min. Start 19:00 out at 19:30. Good?

- R: Perfetto.

- G: Can't believe we're doing thid.

- This.

Assuming the guards knew everything about her life, Gift let the Banzai episode play to its finish. A mind too wired and active, she couldn't read her book, or even start the next Banzai. How she yearned for human contact, interaction, and conversation.

As she knocked on her own door from the inside, the unnaturalness of it felt like a t-shirt on backwards, pulling on the front of the neck where the fit should be loose. Gift allowed herself the fleeting joy of expectation. The only person she could speak to stood just on the other side of the door. For sure it was a reach, but it was worth a shot. When the door opened, Sara swung her arm in a way that said, *after you*, assuming Gift needed the toilet.

"Ciao Sara. Actually... I don't have to pee. Not now. I mean, later, sure. At least before bed, like usual." Gift became aware of the clumsiness of her tongue.

"You have little else. Home and using the toilet is it. You know that."

"Yeah. I know. It's just... I thought..." Gift ended it there, not sure what she thought.

"Miss Ojo, you understand I'm not here as your friend."

Setback. Sara reverted to using *Miss Ojo*—a bad sign. "I get exactly why you're here and what you're doing. It's just that I'm going a little crazy in here alone. I haven't seen or chatted with my friends for days. My mom."

"You understand your status and why they've imposed it. This is how it is now."

A thought so powerful and weighty, Gift felt the gravitational pull on her bones more heavily. *'This is how it is now'* became an idea in her mind, much stronger than a thought. It held no hope, no sign of returning to normal. "I mean, yeah... I get what they suspect me of. Am I *guilty* as a suspect? Would I be going to work and staying in my home if they *knew* I was guilty of something?"

"Not my place to say."

Considering that a copout, and for reasons that would never make sense to her, Gift was disappointed in Sara. "Look, I don't need a friend. I have those... If I ever get to see them again. I'm desperate just not to sit alone. I mean, even prisoners talk with their jailers. Would you consider coming in to watch over your assigned suspect... with a cup of tea?"

Gift prepared tea, a bioengineered substance to color and flavor the hot water, imagining that the aroma was reasonably close to tea leaves steeping. She brought her cup to the table and sat to drink it, alone. *Maybe it's a good thing,* she thought as she blew across the surface of the scalding beverage. *Now I won't have to feel bad about sneaking out on your watch, Sara the Guard.* Gift would have, and that didn't change.

30 | Day Twenty-four

As Tom walked her to work, Gift allowed optimism and hope to fill her lungs with her deep breaths. The air flowing in the corridors smelled fresher. Raff's chat and Marco's willingness to help gave Gift that. It would be a good day, a day to learn more about what was going on. For unknowable reasons, Raff was still permitted on the data stream—she could do something. Her success could eventually exonerate them. Now Gift had an opportunity to contribute toward that goal. Contemplative excitement nearly overpowered negative thoughts. But not all of them.

'It is easier to destroy than to build.' Gift's brain hurt trying to remember which of her tutors drilled that into it. She feared life might reteach that lesson in vivid detail if she failed.

Further workload reductions left Gift and Mike stuck in moments that should have been delightful. Cautiousness over comments, expressions, words, even looks, withdrew them into themselves rather than each other. Gift's mind reminisced about Mike's early days on the bench when the silence between them came from a hugely different awkwardness. Years spent building a rapport between them, which Gift cherished, were gone in an instant.

Hopefully not destroyed.

It caught Gift by surprise when Sara arrived and volunteered, "I just peed." She dared a smile and the two shared an unexpected chuckle, but nothing had changed. The Silence trailed two meters behind as Gift walked home with her mind wandering in a daydream, playing scenarios of her great escape as watching someone in a spy-thriller vid.

At 18:39, her door slid closed, again transforming her home into her prison cell. Marco would begin his work of opening the divider wall between their beds, converting the two into a joined Union bed. The idea of her bed joining Marco's in Union sent shivers down her spine. Her shoulders shook front to back to rid her of it.

"Time to don my disguise."

Gift watched as her Autumn Swing faux window scene became Milano Rain. With eager expectation, she opened the chat app, which looked different this time. The same qwerty keyboard filled the bottom half, but the top was now split vertically into two.

- R: Okay all here. Ready?

- M: Yes. Starting now

- G: Ready. Tell me what to do.

- M: Doing most my side.

- G: Okay.

That text appeared on the right. The next messages on the left.

- R: Gift, we chat private. Include M when needed.

- G: Okay. Why?

- R: He's great to help. Want keep him out of trouble. Didn't tell him my name.

- G: Good thinking.

- R: Piazza San Marco 20:00.

- G: Got it. How I find them?

- R: They will know you.

- G: Shiny. Also creepy.

- R: Need know all members.

- G: Right. What elsw?

- G: Else.

- R: Ask red who could code what we saw.

- G: Red?

- R: Red hair. Coder. Ask if know Claudia. Trying to get Red on chat. Need her handheld id.

- G: Will do.

- R: Tell them everything.

- G: Everything?

- R: Need work together.

- G: Wait. If can't chat how set meeting?

- R: Sneaked single text in app.

- G: Sure they be there?

- R: Si. Implicated too. Disguise?

- G: Red dress. Teased hair = HUGE.

- R: Must look like diff person.

- G: That the idea.

The private conversation ended as Marco returned to the chat.

- M: G need you. Ready?

- G: Yes.

- M: Can't open your side for security.

- G: Is good thing.

- M: Sure. You need open bed. 2 latches top corners. Release them. Go.

Ignoring the warning that only maintenance persons were permitted to use them, Gift found the latches and released both. After she heard a click from inside the divider, she told Marco she'd done it, and he instructed her to give them a second firm pull. They released fully when Gift gave them a yank. With a faint pop the wall beside her bed pulled away, tilting downward to reveal Marco's smiling face. He'd done it. Gift lifted her knee to climb when Marco raised a palm to stop her, then pointed to the touch display with Raff's chat app open. Gift tapped a palm to her forehead before she returned to the screen.

> - G: He's done it. Wish me luck.
>
> - R: In bocca al lupo Cara. Be careful.
>
> - G: I will.
>
> - R: Remember cameras.
>
> - G: Right. Chat after?
>
> - R: 23:30. Now be careful. Love you.

Marco grabbed her arm to assist her climb into his Box. "Nice disguise." The boy looked a bit too long at the red dress.

"You like the hair?"

"Didn't realize there was so much."

"*Right?* Hopefully makes me look like a different person."

"Think so. Now let's plan this. Distracting the guard to get you out should be easy. It's the back in that concerns me."

"Oh mamma, I hadn't considered that. I figured another distraction and I slip back in. But how do we know when?"

"I'm free. Sorry, you know what I mean." Gift smiled. "Tell me where and when to meet you. I'll distract the guard again while you sneak back in."

"I can't thank you enough for this. You're a lifesaver, maybe literally. I owe you huge."

"It's the least I can do. Well... I guess not *the least*. But I hate what's happened to you. I hope whatever you're doing this evening helps. Now, where and when for later?"

"Twenty-two hundred. Just outside our corridor."

"I'll be there."

Gift's lips reddened the boy's cheek. "Thank you."

"When I say I'm going to file a complaint, that means she's not looking, and you go. Ready?"

She nodded. "Ready."

Marco set his door not to shut. Stepping out, he started his diatribe against the home imprisonment of his neighbor. As Gift listened for her cue, she wondered if he'd rehearsed it. He was doing so well. "That's it! I'm going to file a formal complaint. What's your name?"

Her cue. A peek out found Sara standing between herself and Marco, with her back to Marco's door. Gingerly, shoes in hand, Gift stepped out and away from them toward the junction with the toilets, shower box, and stairs. A rush of epinephrine fluttered through her, elevating her senses—a sensation she very much enjoyed as she flew down the stairs.

She'd made it with plenty of time to reach Piazza San Marco for the meeting she hoped with all her might would take place. Lack of confirmation created doubts she had to wrestle with along the way. *Head down for cameras. Act natural*, she told herself, hopeful she pulled it off.

31

Stood in the center of Piazza San Marco, the fluttering in her stomach intensified and reached her heart. The fist-sized muscle slammed into her ribcage with every beat. A hand clutched her elbow, followed by, "Walk," whispered in her ear. In the alleyway, Gift froze as four nameless faces stood before her with invasive looks.

No, three nameless people and...

"*Marco?*" In complete shock, Gift barely managed the one-word question.

"Ciao, Gift. Didn't realize *this* was why you needed to get out. Thought you didn't trust us."

"What? How...? *What?*"

A gray-headed man spoke in a grumpy voice. "Don't worry about him. Why are you here? Where is Raffaella?"

"Um, sorry. I'm... Raff is under guard, full surveillance. Same as me."

"What the—" Her tall, plump guide wore a straggly beard that reminded Gift of Mike's before it had filled in. "You came to us under full surveillance? Are you crazy?"

"Yeah. I mean, no... not crazy. Hope not. I snuck away."

"She's right." Marco's words brought a hard look from the old man. "I helped her get out. The guard's still outside her Box."

A redheaded woman tilted her head toward the old guy. "Okay. We *are here* because we've found a little blind spot in the cameras. If she got here clean, let's find out why Raff sent her to us."

Gift settled into herself, instantly trusting the one Raff called Red. The deepness of her green eyes pulled her into them. It occurred to Gift she may have projected Raff onto the pink-skinned lady for no other reason than the color of her irises. Looking back at Marco, Gift puzzled to organize her thoughts to fit him into this group.

"Did Marco call you Gift?" She nodded to Red. "Cool code name. Why did Raff send you to us? What do you want?"

"Everything." The only word Gift recalled from Raff's coaching.

"Care to elaborate?" the gray-headed man said.

"Raff told me to tell you everything we've got in the hope we can work together to figure out what's been going on and how to stop it."

Red forced a mock chuckle. "*Ha*. Raff has quite an ego. And she's grossly overestimated our role in... *anything*."

"No, that's not it. Look... Me, Raff, another guy called Mike. All of us are the same, suspects in three sabotage events. An air handler, a water recycler, most recently, the most damaging, fires in the farm dome."

The guide's chin lifted. "I knew it. I knew it was worse than they told us. Too many witnesses to the fire. I told you it's much worse than they said."

"Sorry, what have they said about the fires?"

"Seriously?" a surprised Red asked.

"She's on a comms lockdown." Marco knew that well.

"Right. So, they reported that a malfunction caused a hydroponics garden to catch fire. Said the suppression systems handled it. Nonsense. Can't believe a word."

"That part's true, Red." Red smirked at the nickname. "But that was only the first one, there were more. Crops burned, and after the first fire, the suppression systems failed."

The bearded guy slapped his chest. "I knew it. I told you all, didn't I?"

"Wait, you were there, in the dome? Saw the fires?"

Gift raised her hand to show Red her fingers.

The older guy listened more than he spoke. "What did you mean when you said you came to us for *everything*?"

Following Raff's instructions, Gift related everything happening in the colony, starting with the frizzy-haired girl. "We assumed she was part of your group."

"She is. Was. Is, I guess." Marco looked at the floor.

Continuing, Gift left no detail unrecounted, from the original find of the sabotage code through its escalations. To have the full attention of all eight ears fixed on her felt empowering. She was an important cog in a machine to save the colony—grandiose in her head, if less so in reality. Then she remembered Raff's interest in Claudia. "Was Claudia Giuntoni also part of your group?"

"Not for some time," the gray-headed fellow said.

"I saw her get taken away by admin guards. Haven't seen her since. Raff's pretty sure it's her code doing the sabotage and all. And she said your group talked about doing... well, the things that happened. So, we thought for a while—"

"*No*. We don't do that." Red looked over her group, back to Gift. "We're truth seekers, nothing more. It's why Claudia split—we wouldn't entertain *her* ideas."

"But Raff...? When did Claudia leave the group? Raff said your group mentioned sabotage. Air handlers, and the like. Raff didn't think you could write it. No offense, she said your chat code's amazing. She borrowed it, in fact. It's how we chat and, and how we planned my escape for this meeting."

"She split six months ago." Gift barely heard the guide as Red spoke over him.

"Wait. What do you mean, Raff *borrowed* my code so you can chat? What sort of lockdown and surveillance do they have on you? And how'd she get my chat code to work?"

"They call it Level One surveillance. Scant detail what that means. We have guard escorts everywhere and can't leave our Boxes alone. We get no chat or messaging and no contact. Even... Raff figured, anyway... they may be using our vid screen cameras to watch us."

"Oh, that's super creepy. With no handhelds, how are you using my chat code?"

"Raff's a genius. She added a chat app to our fake window and home control touch screens." Red's only reply was a look of awe. "As I said, she's the best. Where was I? Claudia."

"She left six months ago," the bearded guy repeated.

To work out a timeline in her head, Gift pulled up her mental display. *Where did Claudia fit into the group? Was anyone else helping her? Someone in this group talked of sabotage.* "The talk of sabotage was recent, not from Claudia."

The group's elderly leader pointed to the pudgy guy who led Gift to the meeting. "Just him blowing off steam."

"*What*? I agreed with her to an *extent*. Not these extremes. What I meant was a brief *pause* on systems to make a statement, not what's been happening. This is our whole group, and none of us condoned that."

"Good to know." Gift appreciated the candidness of the guy's answer. "So that leaves us with what to do next."

They floated several ideas, most of them bad, the rest worse. Tired of anonymity Gift made a plea for its end. "Before we continue, I'm Gift and he's Marco. Can I get the rest of your names so we can talk more openly, civilized?"

"Keep calling her Red. He's Scabs—don't ask. You know Marco, but we call him Kid. They call me Boss. Not using names is safer. We'll keep calling you Gift and don't need your real name."

She decided to let that slide. If they thought *Gift* to be her covert name, that was fine. Having her own spy-name added to the thrill—even if it was her real name.

"Now, all the ideas I've heard so far suck. Really. They were all terrible. Let's outline our objectives and consider how to reach them." It became obvious Boss' position wasn't based solely on age as he outlined a logical approach, seeking order from chaos. "Objectives. One: we need to find any of Claudia's code and eradicate it before it causes more damage. None of us can feel safe 'til that's done. Gift and company keep their status and we remain in the shadows, peeing ourselves."

Gift didn't volunteer that she'd already done that.

"Claudia was the only one who could do it. I don't have the access needed to get anywhere close on the data stream."

"Raff's on it, Red. Searching for it is her primary task."

"How are they letting her do that, a suspect?"

"Hans Fuchs is on her like tomato sauce on pasta."

Boss said, "Okay. Raff stays on that."

Gift scrunched her shoulders. "Excuse me. Raff is trying to reach Red. If she had your handheld terminal ID... she could do it. I think she can work with you on this."

"It's crazy long. Can't write it. If they found it on you?"

Marco, he was called Kid, took a half-step forward. "I can get it to Raff. When she chats us later, I'll give her the terminal ID. No one watching me."

"Done. Objective two: we need to know exactly what happened to Claudia and if anyone is collaborating with her. Gift said someone physically replaced lots of parts up in the catwalks of the farm dome. We're looking for someone with access. Any thoughts on reaching that objective?"

"Let me start at Resident Services. I can access those systems and may be able to find Claudia's records. Her current location. Raff can help me once we get chatting."

"Good, Red. But what about who may be working with her? Access to the farm dome is key. So, Scabs?"

"What? I don't have access to the farm dome."

"And that's why you're still here and not booted like Claudia. You two talked about doing something like this. Did you talk to anyone else? Anyone agree with her radical suggestions? Go find out. Also, use your friendships with cultivation workers. We need you to be a detective."

"Okay Boss. I can do that."

"Gift, can you help on objectives one or two?"

"I don't see how, Boss. I'm totally cut off from anything. *Ma*, wait." Gift paused to check her mental display. "I can access my logs, the item numbers from Raff. I can try to find who took the parts used in the farm... Maybe even get names."

"Excellent, so that's covered." Boss made good progress. Logic from the madness soothed that dull pain she hadn't realized was there for the bulk of the meeting. "Objective three: find the connection, if there is one, to the medical condition. That... what did you call it, dear?"

"Early Chemical Imbalance Disorder. E.CID."

"We need to know if there's any connection to Pinch—that's what we call the frizzy-haired girl. Administration seems to be trying to link it. We need to know why. Do we know anyone in medical?"

The four looked at each other, shaking heads until Gift raised her hand. "I do. My friend who told me about it."

"And one of, let's see... *everybody* you can't contact?" Scabs' words snapped off his tongue.

"I can get Raff to connect her in chat."

Red's glower objected ahead of her mouth. "You need to be sparing with it. If it gets heavy usage, it will become more likely to be discovered. And not a good idea to bring someone new in. Don't use my chat."

Kid straightened. "I can help. I'll check the maintenance database records. It has every resident's home allocation and work assignment. I can make contact if Gift tells me who."

"Good. Three primary objectives and plans to reach them. Now, objective four, our founding purpose can't be forgotten. I'm still going to utilize my connections in the Admin building to uncover the secrets and lies underlining everything else we've discussed. Question their *methods*, the saboteurs' motive is the same as ours. It's connected to one or more dark secrets being kept from us."

"Hold on a second. Boss... you work in Administration?" Gift considered letting it go but couldn't.

"Yes. That's how I can get what we need. How I came to learn of the existence of these conspiracies."

"Sorry, does that not bother anyone?"

"Gift. I trusted you, and I was right. Trust me on this, he's on our side. He *made* our side. We all trust him, you can too."

"Okay Mar—Kid."

"Thanks. We need to think about getting you back."

"Right, but I have an objective we haven't mentioned."

Eight eyes fell on her. "What would that be?" Boss asked.

"Clearing us. Me, Raff, and Mike. I mean... how do we get our lives back?"

Taking a soft posture for the first time, the gruff older man took Gift's arms and looked at her with the first emotion he showed besides bother. "Dear girl, if we reach our three principal objectives, we will have reached yours. And maybe we get Pinch back too. These are *secondary goals* we hope to reach."

"Thank you."

"Reconvene here Monday, same time. Be careful."

Boss walked away on his last words. It disappointed Gift he hadn't said 'meeting adjourned.' Red and Scabs did their best nonchalant walk as they left the alley while Marco escorted Gift in haste to their corridor. *Head down,* Gift reminded herself. Traversing the Piazza, she nearly missed spotting her morning guard—barely recognizable out of uniform. An image of a fate worse than her *how it is now* motivated her arms.

In a purely impetuous survival instinct, Gift pulled her boy neighbor's head and started *sucking his face.* Locked in what she hoped bore a reasonable resemblance to a passionate kiss, she held the pose until Tom passed, completely unaware. Marco hadn't been privy to significant context for what transpired. His jaw hung open and his eyes managed a state of half-open delirium while being bright with shock and awe.

"What... happened?"

"Tom was coming."

"Okay?"

"My morning Guard. You've seen him. I almost didn't recognize him without the uniform. If he'd seen me..."

"Oh... right. Got it."

"Yeah, sorry about that. I panicked a little."

"No, no. It's... alright. Really." A broad smile hinted that Marco found enjoyment in her clever little charade. *Va bene. He's been so helpful.*

They had an idea more than a plan to get into Marco's Box unseen. The more she contemplated it, the stronger Gift felt fooling Sara twice with the same play was a sure fail. They'd need to use Plan B. They didn't have a Plan B. Hunched below the top step peeping over the concrete floor at Sara, they bounced ideas off each other, but none stuck.

"Your rant, good as it was, used up all reasonable complaints. Anyone would be suspicious if you started again."

"Are we sure? What would she be suspicious of?"

"But... she's sharp. Observant. She'll smell something's off."

"What if I pretend—"

"Shh." Sara walked toward them, causing shivers to roll over the fabric of Gift's red dress. "Get down, she's coming this way." Laid flat, pressing themselves onto the hard stairs, they assumed invisibility.

"You think she saw us?"

"She'd be running over if she saw me. Shh, she's almost here. Get up. She can see *you*. Signal if I need to run or if I'm safe."

Marco stood and climbed the last few steps. Gift had no idea what signal he'd devise telling her to run besides yelling 'run,' or how to signal if she was safe. Fortunately, they didn't have to sort that out as Sara entered the toilet box, proving to Gift that guards urinated.

"Okay, hurry."

The absconders ran and stepped inside Marco's Box as swiftly as possible. They made it. Both laughed through the exhalation of air as they caught their breath, giddy over their success. Gift hurried Marco to open her passage home. Crawling through, she contemplated the open divider. "Hey, we can use this for more than the next meeting sneak-out. If you want to hang out, maybe watch a vid. I just need to be careful and remember to block the camera."

"Camera?"

"In case they're spying on me, yeah."

"Right, you said. More than a little disturbing."

"Whatever. I've come to accept it. I mean, who knows? Perhaps they've been doing it all along."

"Would they? Creepy."

"Anyway, thanks so much again. Really, I'm so grateful. You remember the name I gave you, right?"

"Yep. I'll start tomorrow."

32

Sara the Guard stunned Gift by staying behind her in the shower queue, abandoning the two-meter position. Entering the shower box with her guard stiffened her muscles, and having nine people at eight booths made an off-balanced configuration. With Sara on her back at the frosted glass door waiting for the sanitization cycle, Gift's mind raced over every conceivable *why*.

Sara announced, "No talking."

For no reason she would let her mind entertain, Gift wondered if Shower Group Sara would tell Max about her humiliation. The booth door took longer than usual to close. No relaxation came from a shower with a guard on the other side of the frosted glass.

After a silent walk to Gift's Box, Sara followed Gift into her home. "Um, can I help you?" The sarcasm left a bitter taste on her tongue.

"New orders."

"I see... Actually, I don't. *New orders*? I'm not allowed the privacy of my home? You realize I need to change."

"You can dress if you like. Just continue as normal, like I'm not here."

"Seriously? Would you be able to *continue as normal...*" Gift put Sara's words in air quotes. "...with a stranger staring at you. Invading your home?"

Sara frowned. "Invasion? That's a harsh word. I've been right outside your door. The only change is I'm on this side."

"Pretty tremendous change."

With no choice, Gift tried to make the best of the situation, at least she had company. Sara even agreed to play a card game, Whist, German rules. Several hands into the game, Milano Rain appeared behind Sara's head, bringing a dryness to Gift's mouth. Sara became the reason Gift couldn't join the chat and the tone of the enjoyable game shifted into a competition. To beat Sara wasn't enough—she needed to destroy her.

It turned out Sara was good at Whist while Gift was bad at losing for the first time she could recall. Nostalgic sadness replaced the anger of defeat when Gift replayed a moment from the last game she'd lost. Ping-pong with Mike. She had played her best and found enjoyment in Mike's victory. Sara's victory left a foul aftertaste. Gift rubbed the tip of her tongue over her upper front teeth to chase it away, but it soured.

Gift read until she became drowsy. Sara sat in silence.

"So, are you leaving, so I can go to bed?"

"Soon. Harold will come in today to relieve me."

"*But...?*"

"He won't be in here while you're sleeping. He'll be outside, same as always. Tom and Harold will need to enter at O-six hundred for the change of duty shift."

"But... I wake at seven." The whiny inflection of her words reminded Gift of being a child complaining about her mom's bedtime rule.

"Sorry Gift. Now you wake at six."

***

The sound of masculine voices speaking split the middle part of a dream that had no beginning or context. Mike spoke with Max about Tina and

Sara, but Max lost interest in those women and declared his love for Gift. He called out to her, *Gift. Gift.*

"Gift? Gift?" Tom's voice called to her. *Why did it sound like Max? When did Tom enter the dream?* As her eyelids separated, slowed by the sleepiness still holding onto them, she understood Tom was not in her dream but in her home. The door opening hadn't woken her. The voices of him and Harold projected into her dream as Mike and Max. Two men stood in her Box, seeing her in bed. The sleep faded from her head and then the rest of her body, allowing Gift to sit up and adjust the nightshirt hours in bed had pulled and twisted.

"Tom?"

"Morning Gift. I'm with Harold for the change-over."

Her shoulders twitched at the idea of eyes observing her asleep, tossing and turning in bed in only a t-shirt and underwear. Waves of embarrassment came and quickly mutated into annoyance. If Raff was right, and the camera on the vid screen was active as part of their Level One surveillance, it would have been happening every night.

"I've got it from here, Harold."

"Acknowledged." Harold left.

"Don't tell me, I get it. You gotta stay in here with me."

When Tom's head lowered Gift saw shame. "Sorry. You may have six hours alone, no more."

Gift changed to Tom's back, did her fitness routine, then changed into shorts and a tee. Done and ready to go to her 07:30 medical visit by 06:38, she sat cross-legged on the floor. "Can we talk?"

"Depends on the topic."

"That reply must be in your guidebook. You all say the same thing. How about this: who is Tom the Guard when not a guard?"

"Same Tom. This is just my work assignment."

Gift snickered. "Copout."

"Not really. Who is Gift when not at her bench?" He must have thought it a clever comeback, hit her with her own illogic. He was wrong.

"See, now *that's* a brilliant question. At my bench I'm serious, focused, and have tons of tasks. Parts I diagnose and repair. Important work for the colony—parts for the most critical systems, life-sustaining systems. Well, not recently. No idea who's getting those now that me and Mike aren't. Anyway, that's Bench Gift. After-work Gift is fun-loving and social. I like to go to *La Musica* for karaoke or to hear Raff sing. We do weekly group dinners. I visit my mom often. My favorite food is her Jollof rice. Our group loves tacos and I'm getting to know Sonia, the taco lady. I've made a new friend, someone I thought was too young, just a foolish kid, but turned out to be a real sweetheart. To this day, I'm super close with my childhood best friend. Shall I go on?"

Tom raised his hands in surrender.

"Your turn. Who is the human under that uniform?"

"You know I can't answer that. You and I have... this relationship—"

"I know, I know. You're Tom the Guard, and I'm the subject. Your assignment."

"Sorry Gift, that's what this has to be."

"But to talk... like real people. Why's that so wrong for all of you? Why can't I know who Tom the human is? Where's the harm in that? I don't get it. I just don't."

Tom exhaled deeply. "We're real people. Maybe the protocol keeps us from becoming sympathetic to you—to our assignments, I mean. Like dropping our guard, relaxing the rules for misplaced friendship or senti-mentality. Look the other way when I shouldn't. If I saw you do something or be somewhere you couldn't be, and I said nothing?"

Did he see me in the piazza? Was he not fooled by my kissing Marco? The dress and hair not a good enough disguise? Not figuring him for someone who would shirk his responsibilities for her, Gift dismissed the idea. She also couldn't think her feminine charms so powerful; she didn't even know how to use them.

With her leash a little tighter, Gift walked to Medical for her weekly visit—irritated further when Tom entered with her and stood against the wall as she had her initial exams. She assumed everyone was aware of her status, as no one dared question Tom's presence. When Maria entered for the next exam, she ran Gift through a few extra tests for E.CID.

Her guard followed as the rest of the exams continued. Holly from Pronto Soccorso entered with a white box on a wheeled pole and scanned her fingers. Progress looked good and another week in bandages should have them completely healed.

What would Tom think of the next bit? Would James Müller's attitude of the prior week resurface? Would there be a second examiner to uncover more symptoms of E.CID?

Waiting for James Müller, Tom stood beside Gift as she lay on the soft gel-foam of the exam sofa. It stung Gift's eardrums when his handheld sounded repeatedly. The high-pitched noise did its job of ensuring it would be heard under any circumstance. Tom gave it his attention, eyes roving over the tiny display, draining what little color his face had and making it appear smaller than it was.

"What's happened?" Imagining the answer, another attack, Gift soaked herself in dread.

"It's a top priority request with administrative security override... for *you*."

"For me? What the—"

Tom handed the device to Gift, who had stood up beside him. Its screen switched to a vidChat.

"Raff?"

"*Gift*. We found more active code. I need you. Now."

33 | Day Twenty-seven

Standing straight, shoulders back, Gift ripped the handheld from Tom's grasp. It received logs behind Raff's face—a sharp and focused face, reflecting its fright. Tom had an off-putting uncertainty about himself. His authority had been expropriated. Given the security override, he offered time to the situation along with warm breath on Gift's neck.

"Raff? Raff? What's happened?"

"Happening. Happening right now. Hans and I—" She trailed off.

Before Raff could return to the vidChat a siren sounded throughout the colony, roiling in from the corridors and spilling into the medical office. Of the three unpleasantries Raff yelled in Italian, Gift understood only one. Even in the recent high-tension incidents, she'd never seen Raff so unnerved. It emerged as fright fueling anger, which Gift pulled into herself and made her own. An intoxication swept over her as the adrenaline started pumping.

"Raff, what's that alarm?"

In a trembling voice, Tom replied, "An airlock override."

"A *what*?"

"No one's heard it in a couple hundred years. They taught us all the alarm sounds in our training. Protocols for each. This siren? This is bad. *Really* bad."

"How bad? What happens when an airlock opens?" Shoving her own answer to that question to the ground, Gift stomped it into dust.

"Airlocks opening are fine. They're designed to be fine. They open safely, keeping the air in the colony protected."

Her answer reassembled itself and stood on its feet. "I'm getting that this is not that. This is something worse."

"No." A preadolescent squawk cracked his voice. "This is an airlock *override*, meaning when it opens it won't be sealed inside. It will evacuate the air in the colony."

"Oh mamma. What can we do? What can we do?"

"Someone's got to physically get to the controls to reroute the circuits in the command system, then bypass the safeties to manually counteract the overrides and all their redundancies."

"That's Bench Gift. I mean... I can do it."

"Tell Raff we need to know precisely which airlock is going to cycle and we need to move. *Now*." Mid-sentence, Tom grabbed Gift by the arm and pulled her out of the room and through the corridor, exiting the Medical Center into the passageway. She hadn't the time nor mental awareness to grab her shoes.

"Which way?" Gift felt herself fill with frenzied anxiety.

"That's just it. You need to get Raff to tell us. We need to know which one, and fast. Entire sections of this colony are about to start sealing themselves and we won't be able to reach the airlock. *Now*, Gift."

"Raff. Raff. We need to know which airlock." Gift fiercely shook the handheld to elicit a reply.

The face on the display paled more than it had already been. "Airlock? What airlock?"

"The siren is for an airlock override. One of the airlocks is going to cycle open with no safeties and our air's gonna be sucked out. We need you to find which one. Which one is it, Raff?"

"What? How do you—Hans, you know what she's talking about?" Hans Fuchs' muffled voice hid under the blare of the screaming siren. "Hans and I are on it."

Tom leaned over the device still permitted in Gift's hand. "Need info as you get it, hatches and seals are going to start closing. We need to move. Give us a general location. The code you found—which dome? Soon as you get it, we have little time to do this."

"We need to know which way to go before we can't move. And send Mike with a full field kit to meet us."

"Gift. Hans Fuchs' here. Start toward dome one. Mike's on his way."

Leading her guard, Gift ran flat out through her spoke toward Dome Two. The corridor archways were shrinking, the walls extending themselves, sides meeting like closing vertical mouths in a bizarre and wondrous dream. "Safety protocols are already active. Hatches being sealed throughout the colony. Hurry." Tom's pulling on her arm couldn't make Gift's legs move more swiftly. Yelling *Hurry* didn't help. Her sense of urgency had heightened, she pushed as fast as her muscles and adrenal glands made possible.

"I am," she said between panted breaths. "I'm trying."

Passing through Dome Two, Gift noticed each building and shop entrance with no secondary door closing, no protection for anyone inside a dome. *How many people will be in Dome One when the airlock opens? How many will suffocate and die?* As if he'd heard, Tom tried to assure her. "All those people will be safe, the domes each seal themselves. We need to worry about Dome One." Gift interpreted the words to say, *if we fail, at least* everyone *won't die.*

Running through Passageway One-Two, every hatch over the corridors had already been sealed, saving the people in the habitat blocks. Few were in their Boxes. Most were in their work assignments, many of those in peril. Between breaths consumed by the run, Gift sought to learn the stakes.

"The people in Dome One... The open areas... work assignments that don't... have hatches?" Gift pushed the question through a throat made arid by dread over an answer she wasn't ready to accept. The back of Tom's head shook. Message received.

"Hurry Gift. We've got to hurry. It's closing."

Ahead, Gift saw the steel door ascending the archway connecting the passageway to the dome. They didn't make it in time. "Raff, help. The door... it's closing."

"What door?"

"Hatch... Spoke One-Two... to Dome One... It's huge... And it's almost up.... We didn't make it... Any way... to get us through...? We need to... get through."

Tom pointed ahead as they approached the rising bulkhead. "Should be a small access hatch."

"Get that Raff...? Can you find it...? Get into system... and open it?" Panic filled Gift's voice, knowing she could stop the airlock if she reached it—a hope that dimmed in the shadow of the rising bulkhead.

"Hang on, we're getting Mike through a hatch now. He cut through the farm to get past the doors. He's almost in Dome One."

Out of breath and doubled-over, Gift reached the access hatch in the wall that was an open archway moments ago. Tom stood straight, taking deep breaths but nowhere near the level of exhaustion of Gift—an unfair byproduct of genetics in her mind.

"How do we get through?"

"Ordinarily, a hatch can be opened by manual override. In this lockdown, with all the safeties and the potential evacuation of all the air on the other side of this? No idea."

"I can do it. With Raff, I can." Eyes roved over the hatch for an identification marker, found on a small plate above the tumble seal. "Raff. We got the hatch ID. I need you."

"I'm here."

"H-T-H, one-dash-two, A-zero-one." A service schematic for modules in the hatch controller unit had the information she needed, and Gift began scanning over it.

"Got it. Let me see... Found it... No Hans, I don't think so... Yes, let's try that. Okay, Gift? We're going to attempt to bypass the override from here, it may not work. I've got Mike on the other side, opening the panel there. Can you open your side?"

Tom reached into one of the many pockets on his cool guard pants and retrieved an all-in-one utility tool.

"We're trying now." Tom took the panel off and tossed it aside in no time. "We'll have to get this hatch closed again. In case..." Unwilling to legitimize the possible outcome with words, Gift didn't elaborate.

"Right, try not to break it then," Tom said with a smirk.

"Raff, we're in the panel."

"Patching Mike in now."

The screen split, Mike's face beside Raff's. "Gift. I'm here. What do I do?"

"Anyone got any idea how much time we have? Do we know when that thing's gonna open and kill everyone?"

"Hans? Hans was looking at that. Hang on... Overrides are hardcoded in emergency evacuation mode. It'll take time to cycle air in and out of the two lock chambers between the dome and... outside."

"How much time?"

"Hans? Hans says... under twelve minutes."

"*Crap*. Mike, if we don't get this thing open in the next two minutes, you need to go stop that airlock."

"Not sure I can do that. Let's just get you through. I have the panel open on my side."

"Mine too. Raff we're ready, can you override the lockout on this hatch? Please tell me you can."

"Not exactly. They designed this thing not to do what we're trying to do under any circumstances. Ready Hans? Okay, we have a workaround. I'm about to attach a corrupt data packet to a standard log check reply sent to that hatch. It should screw up its primary redundancy circuit protocol—for a few seconds at best. Can you do something with that?"

"*Oh yes.* Mike, when she says go, I need you to pull two crystal conductors, two hands, at the same time. Sending you the parts on the schematic now."

"Got it."

"I need three hands." Tom leaned in and extended his hand toward the exposed panel. "See this primary control regulator? It may be a little hot. When Raff gives the word, yank it."

"Got it."

Gift found the two redundant circuit regulators she'd have to bypass to ensure that the control OS on the main board Mike was about to vandalize wouldn't fall back to either of the two redundancies. She freed the connectors and readied herself to cross them. If successful, she would be able to bypass the safety protocol and manually open the hatch that didn't want to open. "Raff, we're in place. Give the word."

"On three. Three, two, one. *Go.*"

The pop propelled Gift backward into Tom with such force it knocked him flat on his back with the back of Gift's head hitting what she assumed to be the concrete floor.

When they stood up, Tom's lips were reddened with blood, which he transferred to his sleeve. She reached into the open panel, ready to manually bypass a control circuit just long enough for Tom to open the door, setting it back fast enough not to overload the module. To seal the door again once they were through, for a *just-in-case* she couldn't consider, she had to prevent an overload.

"Okay Tom, open it." Gift felt the tingle of electricity, not from the circuit, from her giving orders to her guard. The role reversal felt empowering. Tom twisted the recessed handle which fought back with the rusty rigidity of two centuries of disuse. The handle gave, the tumbler locks released, and Tom pulled the door open to a joyous Mike. Gift looked Tom in the face. "Can we get them all out?"

A somber shake of his head said, *Not even close.*

"Okay. Then get that sealed again."

The bench-mates ran off to find the airlock with Mike's morning guard following. They soon learned Dome One had four external evacuation airlocks. "Raff, we're in. Which one's cycling?"

"A L dash One C."

They raced to the dome's outer wall, passed buildings, shops, and workspaces, teaming with people. Their lives were in her hands. *This is who Gift Ojo is,* she said to herself. *The best electronics engineer in the colony.* This was no time for humility. "Found it. Raff? Raff?"

Having correctly guessed Gift's question, Hans Fuchs replied, "Seven minutes, fifteen seconds. Nothing more we can do on our end. We've stopped the code from replicating, but that's it. We can't stop what it's begun."

"*What*? Raff? What's he saying?"

"We've tried everything. Sorry, it's all hardware now. You have this."

"I... I..." Gift took a deep breath, pointed to a panel nearly one meter tall by less than a half meter wide. "Let's do this. Mike, get this panel open."

While he did, Gift perused the airlock maintenance manual in haste. From the less than ample documentation, she learned the engineers designed the evacuation mode to fill the outer chamber with external atmosphere first, check the oxygen and carbon levels, and scan for contaminants.

If it returned all greens, the inner chamber blended internal and external air, equalized, and opened the airlock hatches.

Fear widened her eyes while reading, '...when an emergency evacuation with overrides is engaged, this verification process is omitted.' Gift shouted into the handheld, "Guys? Did you account for the air quality checks in your estimate of the time it will take this airlock to cycle and open?"

"Hans...? Yes. Factoring that in gave us an extra ninety seconds."

"*No*. How much time's left?"

"Just past the six-minute mark.... Now."

"Reset to four minutes twenty. Mark."

"Done. *Ma*, why?"

Gift pulled out the module from the open panel. In the lower half of the opening, she found direct access to a small maintenance duct and the words to reply. "Skipping that air check. Four minutes to go. Mike, I need you to do like we did on those regulators in the farm. Only these parts are good, and live."

Pointing to a redundancy fail-over control crystal, a relay for the main circuit to the airlock hatch control, and the secondary flow regulator, she said, "Remove this, this, and this on all three boards. Then yank these wires clean off and reset this crystal here."

"Got it. And you?"

After grabbing the toolkit from Mike's field bag and placing the handheld in her pocket, Gift bent on all fours and crawled headfirst into the shaft. Beyond the inner chamber she reached the second airlock hatch controller. The space she'd hoped to have to work freely wasn't there. "Va bene." Hunched over with her back pressed into the ceiling panel, she made it onto her knees and opened the toolkit in front of them. The sonic-power screwdriver to pop open the panel and narrow-end pliers should be all she'd need.

Deep breath in, released. "Objective one: stop the inner hatch from preventing manual override." Raff's call of Gift's name was ignored. "Mike is on that now. Objective two: getting the second airlock hatch to refuse the command to open when the chamber is filled. Status, ninety-one percent. Need to move fast. I'm on it."

Fingers slowed by bandages began adjusting the circuit bypass on the main board. The five data flow-control crystals easily popped off and she reset their configuration. "Objective three: reverse the chamber cycle. I'll do that next. Objective four: prevent the override from starting the cycle all over again. That's last."

Gift removed the last redundancy control module from the main board and snipped the wires to the secondary. Contemporary designs were more robust, not dependent on wires that could be frayed, melted, or, as in this case, easily cut. It delighted Gift as the old technology made this part easier. Crossing the wires and threading them carefully together took mere seconds. "Objective Two done. Time?"

"Two minutes, seven seconds." Raff's words escaped the device's tiny speaker with anxious dread.

"Mike. Status?"

"Almost there, last one. Wires... Got it. I'm setting the crystal electrodes now."

"Great work. I'm about to reverse the cycle to purge the air from the outer chamber. I'm hopeful that will stop the outer door opening. It's at, no, it's at ninety-nine point eight... Point nine... Hundred percent. Okay, I'm turning the manual hatch override now. With the computerized controls disabled... It's... Wait. Wait... Wait..."

"Where is she?" Tom caught up to them after sealing the hatch. *At least everyone* won't die today.

"There. The secondary hatch is holding. It's staying closed. Oh mamma."

An echo of Raff's voice cried out, "What Gift? What's happened?"

Manual override levers were purposely designed not to be engaged and left in their override positions. Forgetting to reset one to default would invite future catastrophe. While Gift appreciated that forethought in its design, she cursed it in her present circumstance. Releasing it with the outer chamber fully pressurized would flood the inner chamber and signal the inner door to open. The handheld needed to be connected as a terminal interface to reverse the cycle of the outer chamber. She had to do that while not letting go of the lever.

In her toolkit lay the cable needed for the task. Mere centimeters from her knees and a few millimeters from her fingertips, it could have been kilometers away. Her stretch to grab the lever pulled her just far enough not to manage it. *Why doesn't this have a near-fi port?* "Time?"

"One minute twenty-three."

Gift lifted her backside up farther from the ground to raise her knee, bending tight and pressing her back firmly into the metal ceiling of the low crawlspace. Contorting herself to extend a leg in front, she got her bare foot out, wrapping the toes around the lip of the toolkit.

"Gift? Status?" Raff's voice offered no calming assurance.

"Almost... there." Having pulled the toolkit, she reached the cable and placed it in her mouth. Pulling the handheld from her pocket, she raised it into the open panel, just getting enough grip to hold it from falling while keeping her all-important grasp on the lever. Retrieving the cable from her third hand, she connected one end to the device, the other to a data port on the control board. "Done."

"What's done? Gift?"

"Raff, I need you. Time?"

"Fifty-two. What do you need?"

"Tom's handheld. It's on the control board. Can you use it to reverse the cycle and purge the outer chamber?"

"On it."

Sounds of frantic fingers banging away carried over the vidChat. Gift watched the pressure monitor drop from one hundred to ninety-nine. Ninety-eight. "It's working. It's dropping. Time?"

"Thirteen seconds. You did it Gift. You did it." Raff's joy bled through the sound waves and wrapped Gift in a hug.

"*We* did it. But we have another objective. Forty-six percent and falling fast. I need to reset the circuit that will start the process again once it reaches zero. It's still set to evacuation mode, so it'll start again."

"What can I do?"

"I'll need to make two configuration changes to the crystal junction rectifier on the main board here, and then I'll need you to push an updated command code. Do you have the manual?"

"Got it."

"Page forty-one, find the command code to reset it."

Gift emerged from the maintenance vent to a cheering Mike and Tom. Mike enveloped her in a hug. The immediate ache in her foot caused a gasp, alerting Mike to remove the pressing weight of his shoe. With his arms around her, he raised Gift and spun three times before she became too heavy for him. Reminded of the device in her pocket still on vidChat, Gift heard Raff celebrating and Hans offering his congratulations. Another win for the team and save for the colony. Patterns holding true, it wouldn't exonerate them.

"*Ma* why? What is this ab—" Raff's vidChat closed abruptly. In Gift's hand the device displayed the New Europa logo, a dark blue background with the red planet in the center orbited by the circle of stars of the former European Union logo. When it reset to the ready screen, Gift's biometrics wouldn't unlock it. When Tom grabbed it, it immediately chirped a single offensive beep.

"Gift. Mike. Please come with us to the Administration building."

34

In the same room where they endured their first interrogation, Mike and Gift sat with their guards against the wall behind them. Gift considered Tom, how quickly he'd reverted to Tom the Guard after showing signs of being a person through the shared ordeal. Raff and her guard entered soon after.

"*Cara*. You okay?"

Gift wondered if she was. In the lifeless room, she sat in shorts and a t-shirt with bare feet on the cool tile floor. "We did it, Raff. Saved thousands of people."

"And here we are again." Mike dropped the negativity hard. "They'll thank us with more inhumane treatment, insults, and ridiculous accusations, no doubt. What's more than Level One surveillance?" He waved his hand at the guards. "Any of you know?"

"Raff, how'd it happen? I thought you and Hans Fuchs were tracking the code and removing it?"

"We *have* found a few traces and developed a means to eradicate it, but we're checking thousands of systems. We detected a data burst from activated code but hadn't tracked the source until you said, 'airlock.' We hadn't even considered the airlocks. Who could have imagined they'd have gone this far? This was attempted mass murder."

"Escalation. We need to stop whatever's next. What will be worse than today?"

"They kill us just to prove a point." No one contradicted Mike's conclusion.

One by one they entered with the silver-haired woman of the infamous panel of seven leading the procession. Then Jean and Fred. A slender man of stately elegance in a black suit that announced authority entered ahead of a shorter, rounder woman with a complexion not unlike Gift's. Gift considered her skin creamier and assumed traces of Sri Lankan genes in her mix.

Silver Hair retained her role, taking the middle seat, and adjusted the jacket of her suit—its color almost an exact match to her hair. She looked up at Raff in the seat directly across from her.

"Good, we are all here. Miss Di Gaetano, let's start with you. Tell us about when you first noticed an issue with the airlock today?"

"Allora... I noticed—actually *we* did, Hans and I—an issue. We saw that the code we've been hunting became active, but we had not found the location when the alarm went off."

Curiously, Silver Hair didn't clarify Hans Fuchs' full name.

"You found an issue but didn't know its source. How is that possible?"

"We have continuous scans running on thousands of systems connected to the data stream throughout the colony. Hans and I found instances of malicious programs on a few units. We've gotten pretty good at eradicating it on those devices, but we haven't found a way to eliminate it everywhere. We don't know if someone embedded it into the firmware of each device, or if it's self-replicating and propagating autonomously."

"Sounds to us like you don't know more than you do."

"It is sophisticated code, to be sure. And what we have found has locked us out of its source, the base code. We have yet to learn how it was programmed. We've only been able to find ways to spot certain activity in the data stream from an infected unit, trace it back to that unit, and hopefully stop it before it does any damage. Thus far, we've done that three times."

Silver Hair leaned forward. "And what happens when you don't stop it?"

"*Today*... That's what happens. It breaks systems where it executes and we start damage control, get the hardware people involved."

The woman sent a cold glance to Gift then to Mike. "These two '*hardware people*', the electronics engineers. Why them, specifically?"

Raff looked at Gift to find a blank expression. "Well, they're my team, my colleagues. Plus, Gift is the most talented and capable electronics engineer in the colony. Her record—"

"We are quite aware of her record, and Mister Russo's." The distinguished woman brought her hands together to interlock her fingers, setting them on the table. "Let's put a timeline on this, shall we? Miss Ojo was first to find an issue that you helped her diagnose as potential sabotage. It was a basic version of the software and didn't affect a functioning system. Next, the system dispatched Miss Ojo and Mister Russo to a malfunctioning air handler which you, Miss Di Gaetano, could not access remotely. That critical unit was offline for over an hour."

"Yes, but—" The woman's razor-sharp tongue cut Gift's thought.

"*Then*... a hydroponics regulator was destroyed. We tasked Mister Russo with examining key parts and his findings were sabotage by the same malicious software code. That brings us to the fires in the farm dome."

"Fires you tried to minimize."

Silver Hair replied with a harsh look that sank Mike into his chair. That this didn't feel more unnatural became a bothersome thought to Gift. Dressing to a guard's back, accusations and interrogations, and loss of freedom, were becoming normal. It brought a sensation so far from her life she feared it unrecoverable.

The panel chairperson in the hair and suit of matching silver raised her head. "Today. The timeline brings us to today. We have placed you three on Level One surveillance since the last incident involving the farm on Sunday. Miss Ojo had her home inspected last week and has just had her surveillance increased to limit alone time to the hours of midnight to O-six hundred."

Raff and Mike looked at her in shock. It seemed the eyes-on monitoring only applied to Gift.

"You are all persons of interest, suspects in each case of malicious sabotage and wanton vandalism against this colony and its residents. Today is no exception."

As the image of Mike standing and firing back occupied her mind, Gift rose to her feet. Her arm extended itself with her bandaged fingers pointed at the silver hair and the lady beneath it.

"How are we doing *this* again? Seriously. Each time... we are the ones that stop it. Today? How many today? How many were in Dome One? Huh? How, how many lives did we save? *Your lives.* When will you people see... we're the ones *fighting* this, not causing it?"

"Sit down, Miss Ojo." Tom loomed as a blur in her periphery, having stepped closer, ready to restrain her if needed.

Seated, Gift pointed her thumb over her shoulder at Tom. "Him. He was there, saw what we did. Ask, ask him. He saw us risk our lives, going *into* the dome... We were safe, we went in. Stopped the airlock opening, saved your lives. Go on, ask him."

Used strategically, silence was a powerful weapon of interrogation. Gift's mom used the technique on her as a child whenever she disobeyed and thought she'd gotten away with it. *'Eyes in the back of my head,'* she would say. The visual of it intrigued young Gift so much that one night while Mom slept, she painstakingly pulled back the hair on her head. Mom would ask what happened and Gift replied with a pout, or she'd say something children thought to be clever such as, *'I don't know.'* Mom sat there, silent as the night and scarier than the worst nightmare it could bring. Her eyes burned holes into Gift's young soul and each time Gift could remember, it had the same outcome—her volunteering every detail of the wrong in an unfiltered confession. Anything to break the silence. She recognized the panel's manipulation.

Disregarding Gift's concerns, Silver Hair shifted tactics. "Mister Russo, you are the history buff of the group?" He nodded and shrugged his shoulders in a way that made him look unsure his answer was correct. "Do you know of a previous incident of sabotage in New Europa?" Another nod, surer this time. "Please share with us what you know of that."

"Right." His voice calmed. "About sixty-three years ago a water reclamation unit malfunctioned, letting wastewater flood into the passageway. Three-Four, I think it was. That caused significant tightening in rations, reduced everyone to one shower a week. It was bad."

"Mister Russo, who found the issue and repaired it?"

"An environmental systems maintenance tech found it, swapped out parts, and reconfigured the main board. He practically rebuilt the whole unit. Saved the colony's water supply."

"Excellent memory. The technician was Mister Arthur Tedeschi, hero of the colony. His own logs supported his findings. Now Mister Russo, please tell us what happened when Administration completed its investigation?"

Scratching at his beard, Mike's face went pensive. "That tech, Tedeschi, *he* was the one that sabotaged the unit. Did it so he could play the hero and get special treatment. *Oh*. Wait... No. You can't think... You don't think we're doing this to make ourselves heroes..."

Seeing that they employed silence yet again, Gift broke it immediately. "You must also think we're the stupidest people alive. Your theory is that we're the ones causing these problems so we can... can swoop in and save the day. To be treated like heroes. Then? Each time, we get treated like... like criminals. Our privacy and freedom stripped from us." Waving her hand at them, the room, the guards, life, Gift continued, "Subjected to...*this*. And we do it again, and again?" Looking to Raff and Mike she said, "I really don't know what's more insulting, calling us saboteurs or, or... or thinking us stupid idiots."

"Are you quite finished, Miss Ojo?" The calm, stern tone said the answer to the question could only be *yes* and didn't need to be spoken. "Good. You three are among an exceedingly small number of people with the skills needed to enact these failures, as you have been told. The three of you are the only ones who keep finding the issues you subsequently repair, and you have also been the ones logging your own findings. We now add that each of you have been directly implicated in said acts of sabotage."

Gift sat up straight, eyes wide. "Implicated?"

"She means someone has accused us of these things."

"Yeah, Raff, we know that. They've been accusing us since the start."

"No, Gift. They mean someone else. If I follow, a witness has accused us."

An idea so devastating, it ripped Gift's heart from her chest, slammed it on the floor, and stomped it to a mushy lump. She had accepted the accusations, trumped-up charges, and the consequences those brought. That *someone* accused them, her, engulfed her in feelings of betrayal and doubt.

"Claudia. You have her in custody. She won't confess and you can't find evidence against her. She's trying to accuse us to save herself."

In retrospect, Gift found Raff's conclusion obvious.

"You do not have the right to know your accuser until you have been formally charged with the crime. When you stand trial, you have the right to face the witness."

"When? You are saying '*when*' like it's an inevitable fact. Are we being officially charged?"

"Not at this exact moment, Mister Russo."

Gift's mind sorted through the meaning behind the words. *The lady didn't say no. Not even, not today. Very deliberately, she said 'not at this exact moment.'* Sadness gave way to dread.

"Miss Di Gaetano, where you aware of the restrictions of the Level One surveillance not only on yourself but upon Miss Ojo and Mister Russo?"

"Yes."

"And are you aware that they aren't permitted to work on modules for any critical systems?"

"I wasn't told specifically tha—"

"Were you aware of this, Miss Di Gaetano?"

"Yes, ma'am."

"Then why is it that when a critical life support system alert activated, you, without authorization, dispatched those same two?"

"They're the best we have. And, *ciao*, I didn't know at first which system was affected."

Silver Hair crunched her face, shrinking her eyes and tightening her lips. "Has this malicious code targeted a *non*-critical unit? Was there any reason to conclude this software would be active today on a *non*-critical system?"

For the first time in this weeks-long ordeal, Gift saw Raff shrink back and disappear into herself like the turtle Mike had tried to be. Not pleasant on Mike, seeing Raff turtling that way frightened Gift to her bones until they felt frigid at the marrow.

"No, ma'am."

"Then we have the matter of *how* you did that, Miss Di Gaetano, on a communication lockdown. You impersonated the security system of this office and changed the clearance level of Miss Ojo and Mister Russo to allow them not only to be dispatched, but to be given unrestricted handhelds with full data stream access. You also subjugated our guards to their assigned subjects, and sent our prime suspects into a critical circumstance. How do you justify these violations of our security protocols?" Raff's blank stare and uncharacteristic loss for words sent a chill crawling down Gift's spine. "Miss Di Gaetano... answer please?"

After a deep breath, Raff stood, tugged her coverall at the waist, and folded her hands together. "As I said, Gift and Mike are the best, and there's no one I would trust more to handle a critical situation. Your protocols were meaningless. We had an emergency, and I sent the most qualified people to solve it. I think my point is proven by how excellently they performed today in stopping that airlock before all the air in Dome One, *this* dome, was evacuated, killing each and every one... of you."

"And tell us the how."

"Two days ago, I distracted Hans enough for me to send an unnoticeable bit of code to his terminal. It captured his passcode and behavioral biometrics print, and I used those today to commandeer the guards' handhelds and dispatch Gift and Mike."

"Fascinating..." The woman was the most pensive she'd been by far. "You have just confessed to crimes against this colony. Stealing security access codes, impersonating an agent of this office, falsifying security clearances, and dispatching suspected terrorists into an active situation of terrorism."

"Yes, ma'am." No excuses. No justification. These were found in the outcome, even if they were unwilling to accept it.

Still seated, the silver-haired lady looked up to address the guards. "Mister Mills, Miss Clemente, please escort Miss Ojo and Mister Russo to their homes. Their Level One surveillance status remains in effect, including the added monitoring on Miss Ojo. Check your devices for updated orders. Miss Wagner, please take Miss Di Gaetano to holding room two."

35 | WEEK FIVE

Adult life in New Europa began at sixteen with everything about a person—their home, friends, daily routine, and hygiene habits—created anew. The transformation made less dramatic by the lack of raging hormones of adolescence. Childhood friendships were augmented—weaker ones replaced—by work colleagues and new neighbors. However, the transformation into *adulthood* came closer to the age of thirty as mild changes in attitude, maturity, and emotional disposition.

Raffaella Di Gaetano was the first real friend Gift had in her adult life. Twelve years her senior, it surprised Gift to be taken into close companionship. The most sophisticated and elegant woman Gift had ever seen, she tried to emulate her new mature friend by wearing a dress to dinner. As feminine and glamorous as it made her feel, she was a little girl playing dress-up in her mom's clothes, not ready for the leap to womanhood. Now in her mid-twenties, the years have strengthened their friendship, bringing Gift closer to a peer, while holding Raff to her *big sister* mentor role.

All Gift could do was worry as she was led back to her Box. Never thinking more of the word than a description of the four-by-one-and-a-half-meter rectangular habitat, standard home for fifty thousand residents, double Boxes for Unions. 'Box' now became a word shaped in vastly different significance and understood and experienced in an altered context. Gift was being taken to her jail cell, a prison, her life reduced to confinement in a box.

"Tom, they *really* said I can't leave my Box now? What about work?"

"New orders just came. Box, toilet, shower."

"Were you not allowed to speak up? In our defense, I mean. You were there, you saw what we did. What I did. Risking my life going into the dome that was about to lose all its air. Why didn't you say anything?"

"Nothing I could have said would've changed anything. And you must remember, today hasn't changed this." Tom waved his hand between them. "I'm still your guard, and you are still a person of interest and a suspect in serious crimes against this colony."

"You really think I could be guilty of those things? Even after today?" Gift's head dropped.

"Not my call to make, just need to do my job."

"Would you at least put in a good word for me? Tell them I'm behaving? At least give me my evenings?" Gift's whiny tone sounded to her as desperate as a begging child asking for sweets she'd already been denied.

A surprise yank on her arm pulled the rest of Gift into the entry of a small dress shop. One clerk sat in the back at the till with no one shopping. Tom brought his face uncomfortably close to hers and crossed a finger over her lips, stiffening her. The tightness of the theoretical space pressed in on her from all sides.

"Let's say that there is someone in this colony that looks a lot like you, but has some differences, say, in hair... or clothes. No one here has siblings. But say there was someone like that, a decent enough match for you. And suppose one of your guards saw that person some place where there was no way *you* could be. That guard may be extra cautious. *That guard* might even suggest increasing the coverage on you, watching you a little more closely... Hypothetically."

Gift swallowed hard, choking on his words to force them down. The tremendous emotional discomfort manifested in physical cramping, lifting her nose in a desperate gasp for air. *Tom saw me but didn't turn me in?* Silence joined the rest of the walk until they reached Gift's Box.

"You staying here? What time even is it?" Delirious, Gift forgot about her vid screen. It displayed the time, 13:56.

"Sandra isn't coming. I'm here until Sara relieves me and Sandra is taking the night shift from now on... Oh."

"What's oh? What now?"

"You're on twenty-four-hour eyes-on monitoring."

"Meaning?"

"Meaning Sandra is replacing Harold because she'll be in the Box with you overnight. You are allowed zero alone time by administrative orders."

"I see." Standing in the middle of her Box, Gift didn't know whether to sit, stand, or scream. After an extended silence an urge rushed into her. "Lunch?"

"Says here your meals are being provided and they've frozen your rations. Lunch should be here any minute."

"Prison then. *Va bene.* I've seen them on historical vids. Funny, many prison cells were about this size." She waved her hand around the tiny room, sat on the floor, and leaned back into a sprawled-out lie-down and drifted into sleep.

Her hazel eyes popped with joy when they opened to find Raff sitting where Tom had been. Gift jumped out of bed, and they embraced as the minutes flowed by them. Pushing back from the hug, Tom's face looked back at her. His smile deepened his dimples.

"Thanks. Been waiting for that." Lines blurred between reality and imagination. Had desperation caused her to see Raff, offering her joy and love to Tom instead?

"Sorry. I... I'm not sure what happened."

He replied, "You've been wanting to do that since you saw me. It's the cool pants."

A snort plucked her abruptly from her slumber. Propping her elbows into a recline, she yawned. "I dozed off." For the first time Gift wondered if she snored but dared not ask. "Did they bring me any food? Kind of starved. Saving the colony does that to me."

"On the counter."

Dragging herself off the floor, Gift stood and opened the small bag. *What's with these people and sandwiches?* When she turned, Tom was unfolding her chair and table.

"Thank you, Tom."

"Welcome. Enjoy."

"Not likely. No idea where they get these sandwiches. It should be considered cruel and inhuman treatment."

Tom chuckled. "Truly. They gave me one. Wasn't the best."

To eat in silence while not alone became her normal, even at home. She watched Tom viewing his handheld. Was it an entertainment vid or vid message? With his earpiece in, no way to know. He smiled often and offered a breathed-out half chuckle twice. Gift wondered if he had a family, how old he was—she was so awful at guessing age. Having guessed Raff to be twenty-two when they met, she missed by six years.

Examining his features, Gift found Tom had less of his first-impression awkwardness. His face and head were not as disproportionate to his body as her initial assessment made them. Had her view of him been altered now that she'd seen evidence of personality? Or had her resentment at having the guards where she previously enjoyed freedom skewed her first optics? "Tom? I'm not in much of a position to make requests... but I *really* need to know about Raff. Can't you just tell me if she's been arrested, charged, sent home... anything?"

"You know I can't. You're on full comms lockdown."

"What if you go… I don't know? Go over there to wash your hands. Leave the handheld on the chair, open to Raff's status, where I just happen to see it. Then you wouldn't have told me anything."

"A half hour until Sara. Let's not have any more of this."

***

Sunday passed in the same boring fashion. Gift got Tom to play cards and was delighted Lisa shared her love for Banzai. In common, too, was the same slight crush on Captain Arcadia. Gift carefully considered the walls each of her guards constructed between themselves and her—their subject, their assignment. Finding the weak points in those walls became her pastime and breaking through them became her mission. Even if she failed, it gave her mind something to do.

Monday crept sluggishly along at a snail's pace until Sara arrived and presented Gift with a Margherita pizza. They knew every minute detail of her life but still didn't get her a pizza with salame picante.

"Home this evening." Sara's tone suggested a deeper meaning which floated over Gift's head.

"Yeah, like every evening."

Sara's mouth moved, but nothing came out. Gift looked more closely when it did it a second time. *Waffle yeller?* Gift mouthed back with a shrug. Sara's brow pitched and her mouth tried again, more deliberately. *Raf fa el la*. Gift mouthed back *Oh*.

"Yep, home this evening."

With glossy eyes, Gift mouthed, *Thank you. Thank you.*

The joy of the news faded to the thought that it was Monday, the day for the next group meeting, but there'd be no escape for her. It was up to Marco to report on his own to Boss, Red, and Scabs. Gift's mind raced through several plausible scenarios that ended in someone having such a nickname. *Prone to cutting himself? Was he one of those weirdos who enjoyed picking at scabs on his flesh, or on others?* Her skin crawled over the muscle, tingling in disgust.

As days passed, Gift's Whist game improved, narrowing the gap on trick points but still losing to Sara. She could beat Tom, but he bested her in Rummy. Lisa was quiet at first but started joining Gift in adding humorous commentary to Banzai episodes they watched together each afternoon. Walls slowly crumbled, one stone at a time. No connections were formed with Sandra, thankfully she had the night shift. She'd been a stern, no talking sort of guard at the lunch table, so being asleep for her entire shift worked well for both.

As far as Gift could tell, there hadn't been any further attacks. She knew if the tighter restrictions coincided with no other sabotage, those investigators were mounting even more reason to blame them for everything that had happened. Given the potential for far worse conditions than being confined to her Box, Gift managed a brief encounter with gratitude.

36 | Day Thirty-two

Friday's shower time came and again Marco stood at his door—the only time to find Gift. His obvious concern for her meant he was no longer there for the view. He said, '*Ciao,*' and tried to ask how she was, only to be shut down by Sara. Preciously brief, her shower relaxed away just a bit of the stress and worry.

With Sara standing on the other side of the frosted glass, Gift's mind gave itself exclusively to one topic brought into her mental spotlight on seeing Marco. *What happened on Monday? Did the group meet? Had they made progress on their goals?* Questions without answers unsettled her mind and the dull pain persisted.

A bloodcurdling pitch shouted from her pocket as Sara opened Gift's door, signaling receipt of an urgent alert now familiar to Gift's ear. Something new, something terrible, was happening. A new lump formed in Gift's throat around the persistent one, making her swallow her saliva forcibly, feeling its tension slide down her esophagus until it landed in her gut like a sucker punch. Seconds froze as they entered Gift's Box in slowed time, every sound sharp and crisp, every sight vivid and clear.

"What is it? What's happened?"

Sara offered a hard look at her device's display with a troubled brow and gaping mouth. "Come on. We need to go, now." She pulled Gift by the arm and dragged her out of her home. The commotion opened Marco's door.

"Go where? What's happened?"

"Fire in the secondary farm, I'm ordered to bring you." The shrillness of Sara's voice brought a chill over Gift.

"Secondary farm?" Marco stared with a blank face.

"*Now* Gift. We need to move now." Gift hadn't seen such frenzy on the woman.

"*In my robe?*"

"Hurry, throw on your coverall. *Hurry* Gift."

When Sara kept the door open, Gift didn't notice or didn't care, she ripped off her robe and pulled her coverall from the bin. Stepping into it took a second, maybe two. Gift rushed her feet into her work shoes and stepped back into the corridor raising the zipper. At full sprint following Sara, distracted ears heard Marco shouting something behind her. An over-the-shoulder glance found the boy running with them. Once again, Gift ran with her guard into the fire to help the colony that continued to criminalize her.

"What secondary farm?"

Gift had no clue to offer Marco in response. All anyone knew was the massive Farm Dome. That a secondary farm existed was as new to her as the fire raging in it.

Pacing Sara proved to be exceedingly easier than it had been with Tom, and Gift found an odd familiarity in racing with her guard-become-team-member into danger for the good of the colony. The irony of being called to action when the same call for the airlock landed Raff in custody hit her like a wall. Then she hit Sara like a wall, knocking them both to the ungiving ground. The handheld freed itself from its grip and slid across the floor. Marco scooped it up and helped Gift to her feet. Sara managed on her own.

"Why'd we stop?" The whack she'd taken on the floor echoed from the back of Gift's skull.

"Because I have no idea where this farm is."

"Didn't know we had one."

Sara looked up to notice Marco. "Me either, that's why I need directions." After ripping the device from his hand, she thumbed over the display. "This way, let's go."

The three ran hard into Dome Four. Toward the dome wall they passed airlock AL-4A to find a small building protruding from the perimeter. Its front wall extended up to the ceiling, making it appear larger than it was.

No windows broke the walls, just a double-sized door. That it sat off-centered unsettled Gift. The sign above the entrance read: Cultivation Supplies Storage.

The guard's biometrics failed to open it, so she banged on the door, which swung inward on the third thump of her fist, revealing the nameless man that had opened it. "Are you Gift?" he asked Sara.

"That's me."

"All of you, come." He turned and hurried them into the building, passing shelves stocked with farm and gardening supplies, bags of soil, and various tools. Gift suspected something different, the sign on the building a misdirect. At the back wall, they stopped at a large double door made of thick metal. That it was centered reduced the chaos rambling through her mind, if only slightly.

The hurried nameless man's biometrics unhid a farm, smaller and not under a dome. A rectangle of about one hundred meters left to right, and Gift estimated at least three hundred meters to the back. Flames toward the rear reached the ceiling thirty meters high. Gift noted the man's care to resealing the door, more of a thick hatch or bulkhead, before leading them into the farm.

A thud brought her shoulder a blunt pain as a group of six surpassed them in the narrow channel between crop beds. A man—not the one who slammed into her—turned to say sorry. The face of Matteo fell upon her as a stranger. He led a team into the fire, same as he'd done in the dome. A response from Gift's pores covered her in salty moisture from a fear for him so powerful she lost the same for herself.

They pressed on until the lead man halted their sprint as a rectangular railed platform descended toward them. Defying gravity? No. It was supported by an expandable arm off a small square machine, like a cart, but thicker and solid, with four rubber wheels half Gift's height. Three people floated on it.

When it rested millimeters from the ground a man in a cultivation coverall and a woman cloaked in an engineer's stepped off. They aided a third, an older balding man—conscious but not moving of his own strength.

As they staggered by, Gift saw blackened red covering over half the older guy's face and large lumps of swollen flesh around his eye. Bright red blisters decorated both hands of the tall female technician, who made them stop when she noticed Gift.

"Gift?" Her voice came out growly and she dry-coughed repeatedly.

"Yeah. What's happened?"

"We thought, same as that last time. Regulators going, starting fires. We were your secondary team in the Farm Dome. Followed your protocol same as then—" more coughs paused her speech "—swapping out parts as we did in the dome." A deeper cough came out dry and raspy, causing abdominal convulsions that pulled her shoulders forward. "When we did, the unit exploded in his face. This is something... something different. We laid the parts by each unit. Good luck."

They continued their retreat, leaving Gift to ponder what could be so different to cause the unit to explode. "C'mon Gift. Get on." The nameless guide stood on the platform with Sara and Marco waving her on. Full of trepidation, she climbed on. Its rising shook her knees as the ceiling lowered. A cloud of thick smoke so gray it looked black came over them. They had no fire gear, no tool kits. What could Gift do up there? Only when the smoke cleared did she detect their motion shift from upward to backward.

The ceiling coming into focus looked like a Box's door. Only these were massive, meter-wide glass panels, frosted a dull white. Speculative wonder filled her at the idea of them letting in light as her door did in the daytime. *Do they ever become transparent to whatever the sky is above?* The platform came to a stop with jerky motions which tightened Gift's already white-knuckle grip.

"It's a short hop Gift. You won't fall," Marco said from the catwalk. Her viselike grasp refused to release. With one leg extended from a suspended walkway he reached for her. "Your hand Gift. Give me your hand."

Courage had nothing to do with it. She stood on the catwalk before realizing what had happened. Sara had pulled her over in one quick motion. Gift's hand clamped the rail on the catwalk while the other squeezed Sara's so tight the guard had to pry it away.

Deep breaths can calm the nerves, clear the mind, and lead to rational action. It only made Gift gag and cough. The smoke, not as noticeable around them as the cloud they had penetrated, saturated the air they breathed. Their nameless guide pulled two handkerchiefs from his pocket and handed one to Gift, the other to Marco. "Tie these around your head, cover your nose and mouth. It'll help."

Sara had withdrawn something similar from one of the many pockets of her cool pants. The guide secured his and led them forward, toward the fire, its heat meeting them long before its flames.

"These units are not the same as in the dome, they're an older model. The fire suppression system's basically the same, also older. Offline for who-knows-why. We don't have a failsafe as such, but we can manually get the same result by opening an airlock. We're reasonably sure we can handle the existing fire, but if any others start, we're cooked. Sorry for the pun."

With remarkable calmness, Sara asked, "What about the fire suppression? Anyone working on that?"

"I'm told someone's coming."

"Objective one: stop any units up here from starting more fires. How many are we looking at?" Gift learned from Boss' methods and relished the order it brought, the clarity in it.

"Ten pairs. That one..." A finger pointed to one above the raging fire. "The one they blew." He motioned into a cloud of smoke. "And three more already in flames."

"Five more." Gift coughed twice into her improvised mask. "Take me to the closest one."

The four moved as one to the unit and Gift assessed it visually for lack of any diagnostic tools. An older model, but one she'd seen before, a half-meter dark gray 'egg' with a flat bottom joined by a rounded column to its paired unit. Instantly the other team's mistake became apparent. Going off her method from a wholly different unit, they pulled the wrong part, which generated a massive overload in the main transformer.

"Your all-in-one tool." Sara handed it to Gift from her pocket. "Marco, you help me." Pointing to a lever atop the device, she said, "Turn that one-quarter left and lift." As he did, the top half of the egg came loose.

"I've got it."

With the all-in-one set into a plier tool, Gift removed two small crystal diodes from an exposed circuit board. Next, she removed a secondary coprocessor chipset and handed it to Sara. "Don't lose that. I need that." If Sara nodded, it was behind Gift's head. "Sara?"

"I got it."

The engineer skillfully removed the modulator and main flow regulator and replaced them with parts the other team had left, then asked the chip back from Sara. Using the pliers, she rearranged three of the seven crystal cores on the bottom of the chip. Delicately, she reached into the device and reattached it. As the last step to complete the repair, Gift terminated a blue connector of a triad of clustered cables coupled to the main board. A green light shone on the outer panel.

"Marco, gently lower that back in place." He did. "Turn a quarter to the right until you feel it click to lock." When he did that a second green light appeared beside the first. "Two green, we're good. Next." Crouched in a squat, Gift waddled around the device to the other side to repeat the method.

"How are we not overtaken by smoke? This whole place should be filled by now," Sara said.

"Great exhaust system. The only thing keeping the fire under control." Pointing over the rail, the guard directed Sara's eyes to the fire's base. "That and Amanda's team. They've already soaked the surrounding crop beds. I see them trying to douse the base of the fire. I think we got this if we don't let more start."

"Don't speak too soon, you know what they—"

Vibration rippled through the platform beneath their feet as the echoing boom pushed Sara's words back in her mouth. Squeals of aged metal shifting and twisting passed through Gift's knees collapsing her to her bum. The next unit from them disappeared behind flames, sparks shooting out in every direction, the crop bed beneath it smoldering, trying to work itself into a flame. Gift looked for Matteo in Amanda's team as they shifted toward the new target, but the green coveralls were indistinguishable.

"How long?" Gift instinctively shouted at the nameless guy, but he didn't answer. "You, what's your name?"

"Bronson."

"Bronson, how long between blasts? I'm thinking a bit of delay. From the first to the fifth, how long's it been?"

He pulled out a handheld. "Not counting the one they blew, four units in forty-eight minutes. That first team came in after the second went. The third blew as they got on the walkway. Almost knocked the old guy off. Would have been quite a fall." An ear-piercing whistle underscored the point.

"Okay. When we got here, four had gone, plus the one they popped. Looks like they're going in order, look." Gift pointed from the fire's origin to the last one blown. "From there, each in a row, about twelve minutes between pops. It means we can stay ahead of it if we go in order. We've gotta keep moving."

"But that last one sparked another fire, look." Bronson pointed to the flames that had taken hold of a crop bed. "We may no longer be able to stop these. Might have to purge the air."

"What will that do, besides stop the fires? What did it do in the farm dome?"

"We lost a bunch of crops, as much as the fire took. Why it's a last resort."

"Someone's coming for the suppression system. Where are we on that?" Sara asked. After checking his device, Bronson shrugged. "I'm not much use here, I'll go check to see how much time we have." Departing, Sara left Gift unguarded for the first time in weeks.

"Okay. Let's go in order until we're done."

One by one, their same methodical approach prevented additional overloads. While sure to maintain focus on the task at hand, Gift used the opening to get an update. "Tell me Marco, Monday? Did you meet?"

"Yeah, we did. Sorry you couldn't come. This guard in your home stuff, what the heck is that? Anyway, we *are* making progress. Raff got Red going before she got cut off and we have a list of people that may be with Claudia. Scabs has a list of suspects with access to the farm."

"That's great. What about Sakura, did you find her?" Gift reset the crystal cores as Marco replied.

"Yes. Told her about you, what's happened. She says, hi. I asked about Pinch. You were right, placed in coma after not responding to treatment.

But Gift? Your friend didn't agree. She said they diagnosed others with E C whatever and put'em in comas for no reason."

"Poor Frizzy. We'll do something about that when it's all over." Gift waved her hand around the farm, the fire, everything. "Green. Lower the cover, please. Claudia? Did you find where she is?"

"We think so." A twist of the egg's top to lock it in place brought two green lights. "Red's pretty sure she's being held in the administration building. Seems they have rooms, cells I guess, for that."

They moved on to the second to last unit. "Two more to go." To ease her leg muscles, cramped from squatting, Gift raised her knees to her chest one after the other. Then with feet flat she bent to touch her toes. "Bronson. How's the fires looking?"

"Not great. Slowed them spreading, but not out yet. Without that suppression system, they're gonna evacuate the air."

"Need to know when."

Marco said, "And is that lift here? We're gonna need to get down quick."

Bronson nodded to his point and started tapping his device. "On it."

Back on task, Marco asked, "What about you? Those parts? Were you able to find anything... before?"

"Yeah. I passed it to Mike. No idea what happened next, but he didn't have the added babysitting. He and Raff could still chat, at least I think so. Hope they found something."

As they started their last pair, Bronson announced that their time was spent. Gift and Marco began the repair despite the warning. "*Now* guys. The fire is spreading again and they're cycling the airlock. It's nearly there, we need to go."

"I've almost got this, two minutes."

"Doubt you have that. We still gotta get down the—" Piercingly loud whistling saturated the surrounding air, an almost metallic noise.

"What's that?" Marco's shout to Bronson was barely audible.

"Suppression system. They got it going, it's working! Stage one of the suppression, inert gas."

"Yes. Yes. Marco, let's finish this before we lose the last one." Gift returned to task, and he joined her to settle the top back in place when she finished. Moved to the second unit of the pair—their final unit—he lifted its top open for Gift to access the board and her hand acted on the circuit as soon as it became accessible.

"What's stage two?" Before Bronson could reply, they felt stage two falling on them like the mist of the shower booth.

"Clean liquid compound."

Gift signaled Marco to lower the lid. Done. They stood under the rain of the liquid. Not water, thicker. "I got some in my eyes." When the rain ceased, Gift removed the handkerchief and wiped her face. "I hope the clean part means we're safe in here with it all over us?" The fabric of her doused coverall clung uncomfortably to her flesh. With the fires below extinguished, the completion of the last unit pair ensured no new fires. Job well done, again. Bronson gave attention to his handheld and stepped away from them farther along the catwalk.

Calmed, Gift's eyes spotted a manual control override for the frosted ceiling panel above her. Likely a backup for an automation that kept harmful radiation out and let sunlight nurture the crops. She'd never seen outside the colony. Never seen the sky above her or had a basis on which to imagine it. The skies she'd seen had been in vids and pictures of the heavens of Earth before they had been ruined. An irresistible temptation overpowered her.

Wonder bubbled up and lifted her to her toes, tingling her skin. Without permission or care for it, her finger pressed the button. Devoid of consideration for the terror that should have filled her as she stood on the lower railing, shins pressed against the upper for support, Gift teetered a sliver from tipping the balance and tumbling to her death. Eyes wide and round watched the frosted soft white become lighter and lighter versions of itself, then dissolve into stark darkness.

This black ran deep, dense, never ending. Yet it was broken, speckled. Gift saw what the twinkling lights on the dome ceilings tried to mimic in evening mode. Thousands of them. Distant, tiny shimmering sparkles too small to be lights. Illuminated pinheads scattered across the blackness—a night sky full of stars. Until that moment, her eyes had only seen finite spaces with an end to their vision wherever she gazed. The sheer magnificence of looking into infinity was mesmerizing. Mouth hung open in awe, Gift stared in wondrous amazement.

A delightful variety of tear dribbled over her cheek as she contemplated her existence and the vastness of the universe. Her life was reduced to insignificance, yet brilliant and vital. Feelings of belonging filled her, being part of something far grander than herself. There was nothing in the universe except her and the limitlessness of space reaching beyond the night. No colony, no sabotage, no fires, no tasks. She lost herself absolutely in that moment, wishing the euphoria to persist in her, to become part of her.

It was gone.

37

The frosted soft white returned to the glass panel and Gift didn't ask why, how, or who. A view not meant for her eyes, she saw it, experienced something wonderful. Marco stood beside her, his head by her shoulder, his face a mirror of her own down to the tear evaporating off the skin of his cheek. The tautness around her waist made known to her conscious mind the grip Marco had on her coverall, alerting her to her precarious posture on the railing.

The distance between herself and the ground decreased as she leaned forward, like waking too soon from a dream by the sensation of falling. Bronson took Gift by the arms, pulling her back onto his chest to gently reintroduce her feet to the walkway, then escorted her and Marco to the elevation platform. The realization of death's inescapable pursuit was a sucker punch, considering how her last gasp of air would have whispered out the airlock as her limp body fell on the walkway. They reached the ground, still alive and breathing oxygen.

Hans Fuchs and another guy were in the small office, a double box with two desks. Hans Fuchs the spy. He had defeated the rebel code in the suppression system and got it working, saving the farm no one knew was a farm just ninety minutes earlier. He smiled at someone on his handheld. Without a greeting he turned his device to face Gift.

"Gift. You did it. Brava."

Gift's eyes welled up, blurring Raff's exquisite face. She hadn't seen her in a week.

"Yes. But… why are you on Hans Fuchs' handheld?"

"Hans got there right away and managed to convince those… *people*, that he needed my help. Corinna gave me her handheld and I worked with Hans on the suppression systems. Can you believe there's a second farm?"

"*Right*? How'd you do it?"

"A simple solution, really."

"No. It was sheer elegance in its simplicity. Raff…" Hans Fuchs rambled on for a while about how he couldn't fix it, so Raff wrote a new controller Operating System. "…and forced an override in the firmware bootloader. Her OS has a simple menu, two options: Suppression On, Suppression Off. I clicked On and it worked."

"Gotta go." A refreshing lightness revisited Raff's voice. "Looks like we're going back to the interrogation room. I'll see you there."

As they made their way out, Gift looked over the various crop beds and noticed groupings of cultivation coveralls moving about. Some hauled away burned stalks while others rolled in wheelbarrows overflowing with soil. The restoration of the mystery farm had already gotten underway moments after the fires had been subdued. She tried to spot Matteo in one of the green coveralls without success. Observing the restoration teams approaching a woman in the cleanest coverall presently in the farm, Gift presumed a measure of authority on her. The lady with serious hair, that of a supervisor, considered Gift's coverall saturated with clean compound. "You were up there?" She pointed up, but at nothing.

"Both of us." Gift pointed to Marco beside her. "But I need to find Matteo. He was fighting the fires."

"Everyone has been sent to Pronto Soccorso. You two breathed the smoke, then that gas and the clean goo stuff. Better go too, get checked out."

Sara was nowhere to be found. For the first time in weeks, Gift walked her colony's corridors unconstrained by a guard's leash.

***

"*No.* First, I need to see him." Gift argued with the woman at reception who kept insisting that she go with Marco for a health checkup. "At least tell me if Matteo Leitner is here? Is he okay? He was in the fire, and they said they brought him here."

"Everyone from the fire is here. That's all I know. Now you need to go."

Left with no choice, Gift acquiesced, going with Marco to the make-shift triage station to be checked for smoke inhalation or other health concerns from the fire, inert gas, or the clean compound. Both were given injections to heal their lungs and told to be in good health. Gift looked over the other patients, Matteo not one of over a dozen, all in cultivation green coveralls. No, one had the recognizable cool pants and vest, the black uniform of an admin guard. "Sara?"

Slowly approaching the med cot, Gift hesitated with wild images flashing before her of Sara's probable state. The texture of her hair on one side reminded Gift of steel wool. She had never seen blisters like those masking half her face. Sara's hand was shriveled and charred. One eyelid had swollen, burned to a scarlet and black mess. Gift examined her other eye, hoping it conveyed life. Open a sliver it saw nothing. *She's dead,* Gift feared. Knew. A swell of relief came when she saw Sara's chest nearly imperceptibly rise and deflate as a medic came to check the IV drip in her arm.

"What happened? Is she going to...?" Gift dry-gulped. "Will she be, okay?"

"She'll make it. Friend of yours?"

"Well... she... Yeah. She is. Please, what happened?"

"As I heard it, she pulled three out of the fire before she collapsed."

"And her burns? Will they... heal?"

"Our restoration treatments are top notch. She'll need time, but she'll get there."

"Thank you so much. Take care of her, please."

With a clean bill of health, Gift marched back to reception, having lost track of Marco.

"Okay. I've had my checkup. Matteo Leitner, where is he?" Gift didn't like her tone, the frustration in it, the hardness. "Sorry. I'm sorry. *Please*, may I know where Matteo Leitner is?"

The desk attendant's mood sweetened with Gift's. "Yes, of course. He's being treated for burns and smoke inhalation. Through those doors, first room on the left."

"Thank you. Sorry for my tone, I was worried. It's no excuse. Sorry. Thank you."

Gift entered the corridor and found her little brother. "Matteo." More than a greeting, it was a request for his health status, assurance of her own, an expression of joy at seeing him alive, all rolled into a single word, his name. After a quick update and expressions of their concern for each other, Gift promised a vid night in her trailing words while being ushered out by a medic.

"Paging Miss Gift Ojo. Miss Gift Ojo to the reception desk please."

The voice came over an unseen speaker summoning her to the nice woman that gave her Matteo.

"Yes, I'm Gift Ojo. Someone paged me?"

"Miss Ojo, you are requested to go to the Admin Center building. Do you know where it is?"

"You mean the next building over? Yeah... All too familiar with it, actually."

When Marco was nowhere to be found, she walked to the admin building where the crackled voice on the main door panel allowed her into the laughably small lobby. Through the corridor she found Raff in the same room as the first time with Marco beside her in Mike's place. Both wearing smiles—an unfamiliar countenance in the dreary gray space Gift entered for the third time.

The silver-haired lady, Fred, and Jean were in the room with them. No panel of seven or even five, and of note, no guards. Gift's curiosity rose as she took a seat beside Raff after leaning into a long, firm embrace. Empty food containers sat in front of Raff and Marco, a third unopened.

"Mister Fumagalli," Silver Hair said. "You may go. Thank you for coming."

As he stood, he looked at Gift and said, "Magnificent work today. See you later."

"Miss Ojo, thank you for coming."

"Kinda figured I had no choice. Surprised someone didn't escort me."

"Yes, that's one reason you are here." For the first time since being introduced to Silver Hair, someone other than her was permitted to speak.

"Hello, Jean."

"We wish to thank you for your service today. After everything you, both of you... You came when we needed you and performed admirably, and we thank you for that. You helped save an extremely important part of our colony, a critical part of our lives here."

"*Okay*?" Skeptical, Gift didn't know what to make of being thanked for what they'd been condemned for previously.

"Miss Ojo, I am Margaret Heller." *Silver Hair has a name. That changes things. Does it change things?* "We have reduced you from suspect back to person of interest, reevaluated your status, and adjusted it to Level Two."

"Thank you. May I ask? After all of this… an incident that started with us all in custody. We again saved part of the colony, and we're *still not* exonerated?"

"I'm afraid not. Our investigation is ongoing. We have evidence pointing heavily toward our primary suspect, whom we do not believe is collaborating with you. Until we can completely close this case, you will remain persons of interest and have escorts. As of tomorrow, besides your work assignment, showers, and toilet, you have one hour in the evening to go to dinner. However, no association is permitted with anyone not involved in recent happenings."

"So that's it?" A disdainful bite lined Gift's tone.

"There is one more thing, Miss Ojo. You must accept a nondisclosure and information security agreement. You will not discuss the acts of sabotage, nor the existence of the ancillary farm via any means to other residents of New Europa. You are not to contradict the newsfeeds or make comments, even in the guise of humor or sarcasm, which suggest anything other than our official reports. Biometric confirmation is required and legally binding. Once you sign it, you may have limited communications. No vidChats, but you may send and receive video messages which will be screened before being delivered. Questions?"

Gift pushed the boundaries of her new status. "One. There's a cultivation worker, Matteo Leitner. He was in the fire today and fought the one in the Farm Dome, so he's… involved. I mean, he knows what's been going on. We have this tradition, once a year, sometimes more, we watch vids together in his Box until he leaves for work."

"Are you asking permission to spend an evening with this Matteo Leitner?"

"Well… yes. He got hurt, and… like I said, he knows, is involved. Fought the fires, twice."

"We shall leave that to the discretion of your guard team."

"Thank you."

"Anything else?" A head shake reply. "Very well. Since you were in the smoke and got covered in the suppression liquid, you may use the shower here and take a disposable coverall. First eat, it's well past dinner time."

***

Marco leaned against his door waiting for her when Gift reached her Box in her disposable coverall. Permitted the words, he greeted Gift. "Everything okay?"

"Improved at least. You know, *removing dividers* for conversation is always welcome." Eyes bouncing back and forth from her door to his believed he caught their meaning. In her Box, Gift closed her eyes, raised her chin, and breathed deeply. The same air flowed everywhere, but *her* air and the freedom in its scent tasted sweeter and fresher. Her Box was her home once more.

Marco gladly climbed through the divider wall onto her bed where they sat in total satisfaction that they'd joined Boxes again. Conversation lasted just longer than an hour in hushed voices, reviewing their progress and goals. To play the lead role in a mystery detective vid exhilarated Gift, immersing her in the story, investigative juices flowing. "Even if Claudia placed the code earlier, someone got in the Farm Dome—the most limited access in the colony."

"That should narrow it down," Marco said excitedly.

"And the secret farm. Access to that's gotta be super limited. Someone got in *there*."

"There can't be that many who could."

"So... someone with access *and* the technical skills *and* who is in Claudia's circle..."

"Now *that* will really narrow our list down."

"Can I tell you a secret?" Gift rose to her feet.

"Um, sure." Marco's face went flush with wonder.

"I really have to pee."

38 | Day Thirty-three

Tom escorted Gift to her Medical Day visit and waited in the lobby. An excellent report from Pronto Soccorso said her fingers healed nicely. With bandages removed, they gave Gift a topical cream to apply twice daily for a week.

With no work for the afternoon, Gift used her new freedom to meet Raff for an espresso. They chatted over Gift's half-eaten croissant with Raff pecking at a muffin. Speaking in code allowed spies to communicate freely in spy-thriller vids, so Gift decided to give it a try. "Sometimes I like to look at my faux window scene. The other day I switched to Milano Rain. Something different to look at in solitude, deep in thought. You know?"

"*Certo*. I love Milano Rain, too. I'll probably look at it later."

Tickled by how she and Raff managed less-than-clever spy talk, Gift smiled widely. Oblivious to their subterfuge, Tom and Sonya chitchatted until Sonya checked the time. "Your hour is just about up."

"But Miss Heller said we get an hour each *evening*."

"That's the new arrangement," Tom confirmed.

Sonya faced him with a piercing gaze. "Not exactly. They've had an hour already today."

"No. If this coffee was a mistake, that's on you. Miss Heller said we had an hour every *evening* for dinner. We have that hour this evening."

"Right." Tom's smirk suggested he replied before Sonya could object.

***

No vidChats permitted, but they said messages were allowed. Gift had so many to send. She started with Mom, as she must have been worried sick. After a quick check of her appearance in the mirror, a near-giddy Gift faced the vid screen, and an alert greeted her on the display. "Play message."

Mike's face filled the large display screen. Gift ran her fingers over his beard, the sensation of flat smooth glass a poor stand-in for the abrasive whiskers. He blabbered on about the reduced restrictions and suggested tacos for dinner. Of course. Gift replied to Mike before sending a reassuring message to her mom. Next, Aimée, Charlie, and Tina, then she waited, bored out of her mind, for anyone to reply. An evening of solace, cherished a few weeks back, now stabbed at her like torture. Laid on her back, Gift examined the ceiling for nothing more than something to occupy her mind.

After a knock on her door jolted her awake, it opened to Sandra. "Ciao Sandra. You back to the afternoon shift?"

"We get eight hours now, me and Tom. He's got O-seven to fifteen hundred, then you've got me till twenty-three hundred hours."

"Then? Harold back on the night shift?"

"Nope. You're on your own through the night."

Gift rubbed her eyes to get the rest of her nap out of them. "But I... I can't open my door. What if I need to go pee or... something?"

"The door will open. If you made a run, they'd be on you before you got out of your corridor. So don't." Sandra's tone sounded surprisingly sociable. Conceivably, she adjusted it to the corresponding status level. Level One meant cold and quiet, Level Two softer, leaning toward but not touching friendly. At Level Three, Sandra might even have been decent company, a butterfly freed of her chrysalis.

When her eye caught Milano Rain on the faux window, Gift excused herself to close the door and giddily opened the secret chat app.

- R: Finally.

- G: Sorry, fell asleep. Meet mike and me at tacos 19:00?

- R: Certo!

- G: Oh. Red and Scabs have list of Claudia's contracts.

- R: Contracts? Scabs?

- G: Contacts. Scabs is the pudgy one. You know red. The old guy called Boss and Marco is Kid. They think Gift is my spy codename.

- R: Can't believe Marco's the kid in group.

- G: Right?

- R: Claudia's contacts. Good.

- G: The lies, the group. Some is true. Secret farm? Stories on newsfeeds lies. Esic issie"

- G: ECID ISSUE. This tiny keyboard!!

- R: Think there's more. Red found update on atmosphere. Things may not be good outside.

- G: Wow.

> - R: Let's close. Too much risk if stay too long. Many monitors on the data stream. See you at 19:00.
>
> - G: Okay. Ciao for now.

Reaching to knock on her own door, something clicked. A properly timed toilet run could encounter Marco in the corridor to hint at him to open the wall. They'd have time to talk, to plan, and strategize. A guess for sure, as so many variables could alter Marco's arrival time by seconds or many minutes. When she stepped out, he wasn't there.

"So, Sandra..." Gift tried to find creative ways to stall. "How are you?"

"I've been standing here since I saw you ten minutes ago. Not much has changed since then."

"I..., how is Sara? She got burned pretty bad and I've been worried about her."

"Worried? *Really*?" Sandra looked intrigued that Gift would have compassionate concern for one of her guards.

"Yeah. Did they tell you she saved three people's lives? She's a real hero. Ran into the fire four times. She was in terrible shape when I saw her."

"You saw her? How? I couldn't get in to see her."

"I was looking for my friend, also hurt in the fire. Sara's medic said she'll be okay. They said the re-gen treatments would get her fixed-up."

The corner of Gift's eye registered the approaching blur of Marco. She had forgotten the conversation with Sandra was a stall tactic until the reason for it manifested. Checking on Sara was genuine.

"Ciao, Gift."

"Ciao, Marco. Going to the toilet, then they'll put me back in my Box, *alone*." With Sandra's eyes only seeing the back of her head, Gift gave him the secret spy-wink that anyone could easily have caught.

"I'm beat, may just hit the bed for a while. Ciao." He got the message, easy as it was, and she was proud of him and herself for it. Spy talk was fun.

Having laid it all out the previous night didn't stop them rehashing it. Both were drunk with excitement at getting away with being together. The energy it infused into Gift was electric, euphoric. They spent the rest of the time discussing the wonder of the night sky they'd shared and how they imagined it might look during the day.

39

Always meticulously groomed, Gift had never seen Mike's hair messy or disheveled in public. She thought it looked rather good on him, a pleasing contrast to the neatly primed beard. He could have painstakingly sculpted it to show just the right look of, *I don't care about such superfluous things*, or he may have excitedly run out and forgotten to comb it. She settled on the latter.

Not much time, one hour, so they got straight in the taco queue. Only one ahead of them, not bad. When Gift greeted Sonia to order her *one-of-each*, they exchanged their usual pleasantries. The taco lady looked hard at the guards beside her customers. Their existence puzzled everyone.

"So," she said as she piled the protein crumble into the taco shell. "Been a while. I wondered what happened to you."

Gift rolled her eyes in the general direction of Sandra and the other guards. "Some... *interesting* developments. *Ma*, it's all good. Tutto bene."

"Glad for that, sweetheart. I gave you extra hot sauce. I know you like it spicy. And if you need anything, I'll be right here."

"Where will you be *if we don't* need anything?" Mike's joke only landed with Gift, and only because he had explained it to her the last time he used it. It left a puzzled look in Sonia's eye.

With their subjects permitted conversation, the three babysitters allowed their standard two-meter positioning some freedom. Reduced attentiveness shifted them to being engulfed in their own discussion, and Gift ached with curiosity to hear them revealing their human alter egos when the *guard mode* switched off. With time preciously limited, she switched *them* off, leaned over her tacos and whispered, "Twenty-two hundred, check the view." An ardent wink ensured they got the hidden meaning.

"Yes, good. So... what the heck happened?" Mike stuttered, then added, "Oh, you got some hot sauce on your shirt."

A comical look of disgust blanketed Mike's face when Gift scraped the thick red glob onto her fingertip then sucked it dry. He could never tolerate that sauce's heat, especially not straight. He returned to rambling out his thoughts. "... and now an hour out. What's this all about?"

Gift outlined her experience in the ancillary farm and their meeting with the silver-haired woman.

"I guess it went well then? I mean, I know you did an excellent job, as usual. But how did *this* get them to finally reduce our status?"

"*Boh?*" Gift's shoulders nearly touched her ears in her emphatic *I don't know* shrug. "Who can say? Maybe that we were on such tight lockdown they figured no way we could've done it? And... they only called me after the first team failed, like they knew they had no choice."

"Plus, we had no knowledge of this farm. How would I send code, and how could Gift sabotage what we didn't know existed? On some level they can be reasonable."

After an exhaustive exposition dump, Gift said, "Mike, you have those names from the parts numbers? We'll need those later." She took the last bite of her veggie taco.

"I have names on several parts orders, but I can't tell which went to the farm. There are literally hundreds of repairs with these parts, common in so many units. Not sure it can help."

Gift rushed her swallow. "We have a way to narrow it down. Comparing your names with who we suspect to have connections to Claudia and access to both farms."

"The second farm's the key." Raff took a sip of water. "The Farm Dome has limited access, ma *ciao!* Thousands of cultivators work there, but our list will shrink once we eliminate those who can't get into the other farm."

"Right. Even Sara, my guard? Her biometrics didn't open the secret farm door. Not even the storage building. Guards can't access the secret farm, so they're out."

"Brava, Gift."

"What have I been telling you? My conspiracy theories? Not only true… but look how exciting. We're detectives on a case, investigators in our own film noir story vid."

"Mike?" Gift smiled impishly. "Shut up and eat." The three shared a chuckle.

When told it was time to go, Gift pushed in her last lukewarm protein taco bite. With no physical contact permitted, she bent toward Raff, then Mike—something she'd seen Sakura do—thinking a wave would be goofy. In retrospect, the bow looked just as silly, if not more.

***

"Sandra, Miss Heller said I may visit Matteo… in his Box one evening. He's in cultivation and knows about the fires so he's okay, for me, I mean. His Box, it's in Three-Four, in the cultivators' block. We have this tradition… We watch vids in his Box, and I stay the night there, not to get caught after Lights-Out when he leaves for his shift at O-three hundred, leaves me sleeping. I go to work from there the next day. It's nice. Started just before

I left Mom's for my life. He's a few years younger, like I imagine a little brother, if I had one."

"Well Gift? That was a lot of detail I didn't need."

"*Huh*? They said—"

"Actually, my summary order notes said they left it to my discretion."

"Matteo fought the fires. Sara pulled him out, saved his life. I need to see him tomorrow evening. *Please*."

"I couldn't care less where you sleep, so long as you're locked in."

"Oh, thank you. So, tomorrow then? Thanks so much. Thank you. Goodnight."

Giddiness sent tickles through Gift's stomach at her new status allowing her an evening with Matteo. When she turned to her vid screen to send him the good news, several vid messages greeted her. Mom, Aimée, Tina, Charlie. Practically her entire world. Gift played them one by one, Mom's first. Contagious tears in her eyes filled Gift's before the words came, words filled with worry for her precious daughter mixed with relief at finally receiving a vid message. Gift didn't remember ever receiving a vid message as long, not from anyone.

Aimée left a shorter message full of *I love you*'s and *I miss you*'s with a few *can't wait to see you*'s tossed in for good measure. Tina's said the least, not much more than a thank you for the update and see you soon. Charlie spoke ambiguously, leaving Gift unsure if he laced it with an attempt at spy talk. He mentioned how Sakura missed Gift and wanted to see her. As friendship had only started to bloom with his partner, perhaps he meant Sakura *needed* to see her.

After Gift returned the messages, it neared 22:00. A vid message to Matteo ended hastily when Milano Rain beckoned her on the faux window display, and she jumped over to that screen. Touching it with her finger didn't activate the interface, smearing a line of the second application of the medical cream over the icons. A quick wipe with the end of her t-shirt took care of that. Mike and Raff had exchanged pleasantries and paused their text messages when Raff typed *Gift...?*

To her dismay, the chat was brief. The word *sparingly* drew itself up from Gift's memory. Raff's concern that too much use may compromise the secrecy of it was sensible. The stance Red took amplified the caution. If the code writer thought it was discoverable—Raff *had* discovered it—they should be discreet. This couldn't become a social hangout, as much as she craved it to be. Their secret chat app served an important function. Gift would sneak out again on Monday to join the group meeting with Marco. They'd have Mike's long list of names once Raff sent it to Red. Feelings of hope ran through Gift, the powerful and euphoric drug of optimism. She had one more thing to tell her friends.

- G: Won't be online tomorrow.

- M: Why not?

- R: Dinner?

- G: Can't.

- M: ???

- R: Can't see anyone else. Why no dinner?

- M: May need to chat B4 Monday. Need you.

- G: Cant. Won't be in box.

- R: Where can you go?

- G: Letting me see Matteo. Hurt in fire in secret farn.

- G: farm.

- M: Maybe better wait. We need you.

- R: No Cara, go. We'll chat before you go on Monday.

- G: Grazie. Love you both. See you at work.

40 | Day Thirty-four

He'd been annoying, sure, when their childhood group was more impacted by the differences in age. Their four-year gap felt wider when Gift approached sixteen as Matteo crept up to twelve. When Aimée left her childhood behind, the remaining bonds were too weak for the group to survive, and Gift retracted from the juvenile boys. Little Matteo came around often just to be together, play games, and watch Banzai. Besides Mom and the tutors, he was her only companionship in the months before she left for her own adulthood.

Gift found humor in that she still thought of him as *little Matteo* and sometimes still called him that. He was easily seven or eight centimeters over her, wider and thicker as well. Yet he would always be her *little Matteo*, her little brother—however they could imagine such a relationship.

Traditions often started by happenstance, coincidence, or dumb luck, as Gift supposed. What became a treasured yearly occurrence just happened. Only days before Gift left home, they had spent one last evening together cuddled on a sofa chair made for one. Mom's late evening out ended in finding them both asleep, Gift's arms embracing the youngster. Too few minutes to Lights-Out meant the boy would not make it home.

Annual reunions recreated the moment in Matteo's Box. They never felt any shame in it until that question: *Did she and Matteo ever have any intimate physical relations*? Sakura asked if they ever had sex. Both were pre-G.M., and before learning of E.CID, that had been enough.

When Sandra entered his Box with Gift, Matteo looked puzzled. "Sorry," Gift said apologetically. "To get the privilege of a visit with me, there are... *things* that come with it."

"No worries, you're worth it." She smiled, his nearly as wide.

"They need to be sure you don't have any contraband. Nothing to give me I could use as a weapon, or to make unauthorized communication."

"Like this." Sandra raised a handheld, shaking it in her hand. "You can't have this while Miss Ojo is here."

Matteo mouthed *Miss Ojo?* to Gift and put on a smirk—a countenance that took her back to the mental image of an eleven-year-old excitedly saying he was twelve.

Chatting after dinner, more than an hour had passed, leaving them deep in conversation long overdue. Gift had filled Matteo in on the events of the last weeks but then indulged her curiosities of the secret farm.

"What's it for? You must know what grows there."

"Crops, plants. Like the Farm Dome."

That reply felt incomplete. "They told us it was vital for the life of the colony." Gift considered the power in the word *they*, being ambiguous yet explicitly identifying the subject. "Got the feeling it was more than just a farm. What's in there?" Sad, soulful eyes looked upon him. It always worked on Matteo.

"You're right. All I can say... it's a *specialty* farm. Vital crops for making medicines only grow there. It's why we fought so hard to contain the fires and were about to open that airlock. And Gift, they weren't going to wait for us."

"I know. We barely made it out of the Farm Dome before the failsafe."

"We *would not* have made it out of there."

"Oh."

"Something they were worried about? That farm has live insects and worms in the soil. They couldn't afford to lose those, it's difficult to impossible raising certain crops without them."

"*What*? I thought none of those made it here."

"Some did. There's even a smaller dome off Citadome Five that has bees. Live bees, with the most amazing flowers. And honey. I tasted it once. Oh Gift, I hope you get to try it. It's the most amazing... sweet and delicious. You'd love it."

"This makes my head spin... All these secrets."

Before starting Banzai, Gift said, "I'm afraid I need to borrow a tee shirt." Pulling the fabric on her coverall, she added, "Can't sleep in this. They didn't let me take anything. Not even the sonic for my teeth."

"No worries. I'm pretty sure I've got one I haven't worn." Stepping past her, he opened the bin and pulled out a shirt. Holding it to his nose soured his expression. "I wore this once." A folded bright white V-neck came out next. "This is clean." Playfully, he tossed it in her face.

"*Brat*. Thanks. Now turn around. No peeking like that first time." The words came from a big smile. Matteo's connected two blushing red cheeks before he gave her his back to change.

It was another life when that curious boy—pretending to be asleep on the tiny sofa chair in her mom's Box—watched Gift from behind as she cleaned herself with a body wipe on their last vid night before adult life began. They were different people then, kids.

***

When she woke at 07:00, she didn't find Matteo asleep on the floor, he'd gone to work, the blankets he'd fashioned into a bed cushion tossed in a pile. As Gift climbed out of bed, her knee catching on the loose material of the size L shirt caused a tumble, landing her on the floor. Reactive laughter came as an exuberant gust of air vibrating through closed lips and spraying spit.

"It's Monday," Gift said to the empty Box. It meant another sneak-out to meet with the secret group, so she needed to get the day going and done. Only when Gift slipped into the coverall did it dawn on her she had forgotten to sonic clean it in Matteo's sink. Being in yesterday's underwear presented more of a concern to her, but as Mike would say, *what can you do?*

41 | Day Thirty-five

Suspicion cemented itself in her mind as fact, Tom had seen her when she snuck out. Gift's disguise needed an upgrade. "Black dress." Held up over her, she checked the result in the mirror and confirmed her choice. The dress wore like a long V-neck tee shirt, being the same fabric but with a form-fitting tailored cut and only the suggestion of sleeves over the shoulders. Now for the hair—it needed to be unique. It couldn't be her usual tight curls, nor the super-frizzy-out-past-her-shoulders coiffure Tom may have seen through. Using two knives heated over the hob, she'd hide herself in plain sight.

Answering the call of Milano Rain, Gift joined the chat. Raff confirmed she sent Mike's list of the parts orders to Red. A quick review of the objectives followed, and Raff mentioned the need for what she called transparency, which Gift understood by context to mean leaving nothing hidden. It thrilled her when Raff said she would be present at the meeting via chat. Marco opened the bed wall and when Gift climbed through, he studied her new look.

"Can't remember the last time I wore this dress. Not sure why. It's sorta just a long tee. I actually like it a lot."

"Me too." His smirk returned. Gift preferred his smile.

"And the hair? Do you like it like this? I've never done it this way before."

"It's... different."

"*Different*? Like, in a bad way?"

"Just different. You look amazing though, really. How'd you get it so... straight?"

"Not easy, see..." Lifting the hair from her forehead revealed a burn at the hairline. "Heated two knives to make a kinda hair straightener. I got a little too close and burned myself. Hope it's worth it."

"*It is.*"

"I mean for the disguise, silly boy. In case Tom *did* see me, I wanted to look even more different from last time." As the back of her hand playfully tapped his chest, she said, "Don't think you're getting another kiss. Now, how will we distract Sandra?"

Marco pointed behind her. His warmer and hob were on the floor with the recycler bin next to them with empty space consuming most of his cabinet.

"We go that way." Gift smelled pride in his perspiration.

"We do what?"

"I figure they know that I'm at least aware of some of what happened. If I go making a hoopla for Sandra the way I did for Sara, I think she'd be on to me. Plus, the way back. We got ridiculously lucky last time when Sara went into the toilet. Can't really use it as a plan."

"True. I'm sorry.... did you say *hoopla*?" After a smile, she considered the gaping hole. "We're supposed to crawl in there? Where does that go?"

"Between one block and the next is a maintenance tunnel. Been in them lots of times for repairs. Just not... *designed* for what we're doing. I improvised."

"I can see that. So... you first or me?"

"You'd better follow me. It's tight in there."

On all fours, Marco inched through the opening and disappeared. From a distant voice, he called her to come through. With a shrug offered to the room, she clambered into his cabinet. The dim blue hue of the overhead light caught her eye as her head hit the opposite wall. Marco hadn't exaggerated its narrowness.

"You have to twist your way up, not much room." Marco took her hands and helped her contort herself to get sideways, sliding her bum out of the hole and into the cramped passageway. Then onto her knees and up to her feet. No need for grace, only practicality.

"Lovely." She rolled her eyes, patting the dust from her dress. "Had I been told this part of the plan… shorts and a tee would have been a much better choice. Now?"

"This way. We can make it a good way toward Dome Three before we pop out into public."

Gift's chuckle escaped as a snort as she repeated, *"Pop out."*

When a T-junction greeted them, Gift followed Marco to the left. With much larger conduits and pipes radiating heat, her dress clung to her moistened skin.

"Everything in and out of the Boxes." Marco excitedly acted as a tour guide. "Your power, air supply and return, shower drain, and recyclers. Data lines in there, climate regulators too—why it's so hot in here."

Not paying attention, Gift's head slammed into Marco's shoulder blade. "Sorry. Why are we stopping?"

"Because I'd rather not fall to my death. Like if a certain someone pushed me forward over this big hole here." His tone was playfully serious. He pointed to the ground in front of him, but only when Gift pushed her face between his arm and the wall did she see that millimeters from his feet there was no ground.

"Sorry. Didn't mean to almost kill you."

"It's a ladder to the floor level." Gift appreciated the lamps lining the shaft for seeing the rungs. As he began his descent Marco cautioned, "Don't look down."

Once Gift mounted the ladder, she became mindful of her dress. Partly in jest, she said, "Don't look up."

"Too late." The slightest boyish giggle trailed his words.

Popped out of the access hatch into Passageway Two-Three, they blended in with the passersby and entered Dome Three. No need to wait in the piazza for the elbow grab, she knew where to go and was already with Marco, whom she started calling Kid. Gift continued brushing the dust from her dress long after every speck had been removed—she *felt* it there.

Twisting and tugging at it, she adjusted the taut fabric, pulling it lower over her thighs. She still liked the dress, though not the ideal choice for maintenance shaft shenanigans. When they entered the alleyway, Boss, Red, and Scabs were there. Gift started offering greetings, but Boss cut her off, right to business.

"Good, we have Gift back. We have Raff online?" Red nodded to confirm. "Where are we on objective one, the code?"

"Progress." She read from her device. "Raff says with the last two incidents she and Hans were able to see activity in the data stream moments before it went active. They're watching for more of that activity. Should give us a heads up, make it a tad faster for a response at least."

Boss almost cracked a smile. "Good. Tell Raff we need to find it and stop it. Can we make that happen?"

Red's thumbs bounced frantically over the handheld in a back-and-forth messaging frenzy with Raff. "Yes. We're pretty sure we can. But Raff and Hans agree they won't be able to until they catch one more burst in the data stream. Then they'll be able to find the rest of it. But that means one more attack."

"Oh mamma." Gift failed to contain the outburst.

"Moving on to objective two. Red, any update on Claudia, who she's working with?"

Red bounced twice on her toes. "She's somewhere called level minus one. She's their prime suspect and believed to have accomplices. Gift and Raff are still persons of interest but flagged as not likely collaborators."

"What about Mike Russo? He's a person of interest too." Gift's intrusion brought a stern glare from Red.

"Don't know Mike, so don't care. Anyway, Boss, it's not likely we can get to Claudia."

"Don't be too sure."

"*O... kay.* And I got the list of everyone who had access to the parts put on the faulted units. It's long, but we have Scabs' contacts to cross-reference, hopefully that shrinks it."

"Yeah. I removed more than half that list at first go. Most of those can't get into the Farm Dome. And Kid told us about the second farm. There's a secret farm, *crazy.*" Scabs shook his head. "So... we reduced the list even more. I flagged those likely to know Claudia—that's where we need Kid and Red to work together."

"What do you have in mind?" Boss let his people offer ideas. Gift thought it a mark of good leadership.

"Red accesses Resident Services systems to add bogus maintenance requests, and we get Kid to go do them. Then we get intel on these people."

"How *exactly* do we get this intel?"

"Cameras, bugs. Then we watch them." Scabs looked proud of his own idea; one Gift found off-putting and wrong.

"Gift, can you get us some small cameras and mics?"

Discontented with this part of the plan, Gift shrugged at Boss. "My guards have loosened the leash a little. Not sure it's enough."

"I can get them," Marco, Kid, said. "We have lots of old equipment from replacements no one would notice gone missing. I'm sure I can scavenge some working cameras and mics."

"Objective two is coming together."

"So... we're *spying* on people now?" To Gift's disappointment, no one reacted. "Actually... can I see the short list? Those with access to the Farm Dome and the secret farm?" Handed Scabs' handheld, Gift promptly scrolled over the thirteen names to find Matteo's. "We can take this one off, he's not involved."

"How can you be sure?" Scabs' breath felt hot and damp on Gift's neck and his gaze called up memories of Luca and Max. Did the handheld hold his attention or had his eyes settled into her plunging neckline.

"He helped fight the fires, both times. Got burned on Friday. We spent the night together and talked about it."

"Really?" Gift was disagreeable to Red's innuendo.

"Not like that. And he's not involved. But... he can help us find who of these other twelve it could be."

Boss said, "Careful. We don't trust someone just because you do. Go ahead, probe this guy for information, but don't give any. And don't mention us."

"You got it."

"Now objective three, this medical business. Where are we?"

"I contacted Gift's friend in Medical. She'll give us a security code. Maybe Red and Raff can work with that?" The boy called Kid seemed to soak in the smile from Boss like shower foam.

Red tapped more intently on the handheld and read long replies from Raff. "Raff has something, says much of what we need will be in Resident Services. Easier to get into than medical, she's done it before. Hold on... she's telling me I should work with someone called, *Amy*? It's spelled weird."

"She means my friend Aimée... Runs Resident Services in her spoke. Raff helped her jump into my spoke's office."

Boss deliberately cleared his throat. "Again, we must be careful. Why are we bringing so many people in now? It's dangerous."

"Aimée's my best friend… She helped me break into my medical records. I'm sure she can help us."

"I repeat the need for caution." Raising a finger to Gift's face, he stiffened. "And no one mentions even the *idea* of us. As far as this Amy or Matteo know, you are working alone. Clear?"

"Crystal, sir."

Meeting adjourned—though Boss once again refrained from uttering the words—Gift and Marco made their way back to the maintenance hatch for their hidden passage back to his Box. No signs of Tom. Snuck successfully back into the access tunnel on the floor level, they reached the ladder and Gift stepped behind the young man.

"You go first, and I'll watch *your* butt this time."

"But *you* can't see *my* underwear." Marco giggled as he climbed.

Gift smacked him playfully but firmly on his buttock and pondered over how suddenly their relationship changed, grew into a friendship. Eating together, playing games, watching Banzai. Now sneaking out to attend secret meetings of suspected criminals to form a make-shift detective squad. *Normal friend stuff*, she laughed to herself.

42 | Week Six

The next few days had the sensation of normalcy, yet they were anything but. Gift felt as if she were walking through someone else's experiences, living their days, a spectator to another life in a fictional reality. All the newsfeeds were quiet. Not much news ever happened before, so that felt normal. Colonial updates had been about social activities such as which films filled the screens in the six piazzas on a Saturday evening, weekly lunch menus, or which fruit was in season in a sealed bubble without seasons.

Life before had been trivial, ordinary, blissful.

Did the masses believe the story of the airlock incident being a long overdue test of an emergency system? A plausible enough offering to have a ring of truth, if at a low timbre. Gift assumed she would have accepted the explanation had she not been involved in the *'everything'* of it all. Perhaps for most, things *were* normal.

Guard presence imperceptibly became routine. Gift's pondering led her to the illuminating conclusion that, in time, any change in the pattern of life would eventually come to be ordinary. Contemplating her personal *normal* found it had shifted, morphed so many times over the last few weeks, she nearly lost sight of herself. It was the *feeling* of it that bothered her, shook her to the core. Now her normal was about to change—again.

The group met on Thursday, a brief update via chat. Marco had met with Sakura and received the security code she promised. Red tried to work with it, but needed Raff's help. She had contacted Aimée—at least in chat no one mispronounced her name. With her help, they found a list of the patients flagged for E.CID, though not a full medical report. The staggering total had thirty-seven identified as suspect with only two actively mingling in society, the rest in comas. Out of nowhere, Boss dropped a bomb that blew everyone's minds.

- B: Saw Claudia. She looks ill. Not tell me if any working with her. No surprise. Did tell we soon see something. Made sound like something big coming. Arrogant about it. Said not even raff stop it.

- G: So confession. Raff not working with her.

- B: No dear. My conversation never happened, not recorded.

Gift wondered about the man and his connection to the Admins. True, he'd been helping—their group's leader. It wasn't enough to untie the knot her stomach had been in since learning where the guy worked.

- Ra: Haven't seen any activity in data stream.

- B: What did we find on collaborators?

- S: Short list getting shorter. Asking around. Have two marked. All need surveillance.

- G: Send me names, will chck with Matteo.

- S: Sandy Myers and William Zymler are most likely.

- G: Got it. Thanks.

- Re: Like to bring amie in. Think she can get me to physical location to tap into medical uplink.

- Ra: Could work. I can help with access.

- B: Anything else? Need to keep brief.

Boss' information bomb lost all significance when Raff dropped one of her own. It reassembled the blown minds, glued them together, then shattered them into dust.

- Ra: One more. Important. Going to tell Hans what we are doing. Need Admin to know.

- G: What? Raff no.

- S: Foolish. Crazy.

- B: Don't like this. Why? What goal?

- Ra: He works for admin. He is a good guy and been helpful. I think we need his help and we need them to know what we know. Show we're on the same side.

- B: Too big a risk. I wouldn't.

- Ra: Can't wait. Next event any day. I will speak for me, gift, mike. And not mention any of you.

- Re: That's on you then. Keep me out of it.

- S: Me too. Not a word about our group. It's crazy.

- G: Not sure about thid.

- Ra: Dai. We are losing. Made little progress but losing. If we find a person changed parts, work with Claudia, what do we do? Have to turn them in. We need the ones with the training for this. Only way to win this. No time.

- B: Don't agree. Can't stop you. Keep us out of it. Next meeting Monday in person. If Raf and company not arrested. Limit this chat.

- S: Still say it's crazy. Nice knowing you Raff and Gift.

Raff would entrust Hans Fuchs with their fates, maybe the fate of all New Europa. 'She's an excellent judge of character,' Gift recently said. Convincing herself proved exponentially easier than convincing Mike this was the right move. In a private chat with the three of them, Mike typed a message against the idea so lengthy Gift scrolled her screen three times to find its end. She tried the trust angle: 'I trust Raff and I'm asking you to trust me.' Mike agreed.

Friday morning would change their lives. They planned to tell a version omitting the existence of the group. Act of desperation? Possibly. Fundamentally, Gift agreed with Raff. If they had even a ghost of a chance to work together, they would take it.

Tossing and turning got annoying. Sitting in her bed in total darkness, Gift couldn't make her mind stop. *What may the new normal become tomorrow?* She tried to recount each of the changes to her routine, pre-fixing new, new, new, new onto *normal* in a string that pulled on her heart until it beat on the outside of her chest. In the dark quiet of her home, she listened to its rhythm.

***

Tom's face outside her door in the morning became routine, same as the walk to the toilet and later to work. If he were the morning escort for the rest of her days, it would become the new standard. But would it ever *feel* normal?

Hours took agonizingly long to pass that morning. Still made of sixty minutes each, each of those using sixty seconds, they flowed more slowly over her as she did next to nothing on her bench between trivial tasks. After a brief conversation with Hans Fuchs, Raff had been gone for the better part of the morning. Gift's perspiration had nothing to do with her always suffering those two degrees too warm. It was the powerlessness of it. Nothing to do but to wait for the call to the admin building. Another minute. An hour.

***

Walking to Dome One, Gift saw the passersby as if in a dream. At that hour, few moved about; cleaning personnel, guards on now-regular patrols, shop keepers, baristas, and maintenance workers. Feelings of normalcy crept up from the floor with each step. It brought a surreal anxiety that rattled her heart like a prisoner desperately tugging at the cell bars.

Tom ushered Gift into the room where she peed herself so long ago. *Where was Mike?* Hesitation to sit came in a memory of the chair being saturated in her liquid waste. Her logical brain telling her it had been cleaned and sanitized was not the one in control of the moment. When the vid screen switched on, Tom exited the room and the door slid closed, leaving her alone once again.

The silver-haired lady returned to the wall-mounted screen, seated in the center chair. Miss Heller. The name made her a little more human. Of the three on each side, she only recognized Fred and Jean. As usual, Heller took the lead. "Please sit Miss Ojo. You are here as our guest."

"Okay. Why am I a guest now?"

"Corroboration Miss Ojo. Please tell us everything you know about Miss Giuntoni and her associates, probable coconspirators, and what you and your friends have been up to in trying to find out."

"I see." Pensively, Gift paused to review what she had mentally rehearsed all morning.

In what she may have thought to be thirty breathless seconds but likely lasted several minutes, she told them everything she knew about the sabotaged units, the likely collaborators in the farm fires, how she learned of the ominous warning Raff gave that they'd only be able to stop this after one more attack. Carefully sidestepping mention of the group, Gift took all tasks and findings on herself, Mike, and Raff. She thought she had managed it, done well, told them *'everything'* without the bits she couldn't. Was it enough to convince them to work together? She couldn't be sure. Her mind considered it while the panel talked among themselves, leaving her again in *mal'd* silence.

She couldn't rule out the possibility they'd classify her as E.CID and rid themselves of a persistent nuisance.

A break in the silence. Heller said, "Please come to us."

Gift had never been in a lift. Her experience on the secret farm's rising platform approximated one, or so she imagined at the time. Prior to recent events, the highest elevation she had ever been took her to the first floor of her housing block—one flight up from ground level.

With walls instead of handrails, a proper lift gave an impression of safety. A closed box rather than an open platform hid the height and the fears it stirred within her. Immersed in such a fascinating experience, Gift barely felt the motion of it rising. Neither pleasant nor irritating, the lift dinged a neutral sound to tell the passengers they'd arrived at their destination. *BR* glowed white on a small screen above a series of buttons as the doors split open down the center and pulled apart, swallowed by the walls on either side.

The brightly lit expanse those doors revealed squinted Gift's eyes, pupils rapidly adjusting from the soft illumination in the lift. Around the fading gray spots, a new world emerged with soft white walls framed around large glass panels offering an overhead view of Citadome One. Luxurious chairs filled a tile floor so well-polished it glimmered like crystal. A room within a room, three glass walls outlined a long rectangular table of a material Gift didn't recognize. Soft brown laced with streaks of various shades of deeper browns. Its smooth, glossy surface reflected a glare from overhead lights, overlaying it with an elegant finish. Like teeth on a gear, twelve high-backed black chairs formed the massive table's perimeter. The hub of the *machine* running the entire colony.

Miniature trees reaching upward from round planters recessed into the buffed marble floor seemed to support the ceiling. Almost a park, it appeared to the engineer brain as half constructed, half grown. By far the most welcoming part of the admin building Gift had yet experienced. Miss Heller approached her with an extended hand. While not a common greeting, Gift understood and gently shook it. The gesture seemed hollow and strange. "Nice to properly meet you, Miss Ojo. Thank you for coming. Do you like the space?"

"It's beautiful, really. Is this the Boardroom?"

"Yes, Miss Ojo. We receive so few guests here."

"And you are... you are on the Board?"

"The panel of seven, the ones you know as Jean and Fred, James Müller, and two others. We are the Board of Directors of New Europa."

"And I'm here because...?" The words shaped themselves into a question and her shoulders withdrew, putting her insecurities on display.

"Please relax, Miss Ojo. We have had an extensive debriefing with Miss Di Gaetano. In a moment, the Board will enter and would very much like to discuss how we move forward together to end this threat on our way of life."

"So now we're... working together?" Following a glance over her shoulder to see Tom standing two meters behind her, Gift said, "At this moment I'm still being escorted by a guard anywhere I go. Still a person of interest. You said that to me just recently."

"All that is about to change."

As if on cue, the now familiar ding of the lift turned Gift around in expectation of who'd join them. When the metal doors pulled apart, Raff appeared, followed by Mike. They came up unescorted. Raff grabbed Gift, pulling her into a tight hug and rocking. "I told you to trust me."

"Ciao, Mike." It had been too long since Gift saw him smile.

"This is it. We're getting in on the ground floor."

Puzzled, Gift replied, "Pretty sure we're on the top floor."

43

In the bright space at the top of the Administration building, she stood peering over the rooftops below—the shops, parks, piazza, and people in Citadome One—serenity shrouding her. Inexplicably calm and untroubled, Gift waited. She hadn't yet known what might conceivably result from their proposed partnership with the admins and the Board. Had Raff convinced them working together was the best way forward? How did they react to what Gift and her friends had been doing in the shadows, the spotlight now on, their intentions and actions openly exposed?

Gift hadn't noticed Tom's activity until she spotted him placing a third chair on the end of the unusual Boardroom table that was longer than her entire Box.

"Please…" Miss Heller waved a hand over those chairs.

How much Gift wanted to sit in one of those black high-back chairs for the feeling of being important enough to merit such an honor. She placed a hand on one, smoothing her palm over the plush cushion. "Could I? Just for a second?"

"Go ahead. For a second."

Gift sank blissfully into the luxurious chair. Its gel-foam responded to her body, giving firm support where it felt right, and soft gel to let parts of her drift into a peaceful state. Instantly she understood why they had these chairs as she became both relaxed and equally alert sitting in one.

The three guests took their seats in the regular chairs, alert, but not relaxed. Practiced or learned behavior, they took their stations with Raff in the center, Gift to her left, and Mike on the far right. Miss Heller took the first black chair adjacent to Gift as heel taps crept up from behind, clacking on the tile.

One by one, the Board members passed to take their places. Fred and Jean with nameless members of the panel of seven filled in along with James Müller and... *Boss*? The man Gift was told to call Boss was on the Board. That same guy who started the group that wrote those ridiculous and now forgotten 'All Lies' messages. He claimed his connections in Administration could get him to Claudia, and they did. Raff said it was time to work with the Board, and now Gift wondered if they'd been doing so all along.

One open seat remained. One mountainous surprise more than sufficient, Gift expected another nameless person to complete the Board's membership. The lift's ding lacked the attraction to turn her head. Mike looked to be trying to get his brain to believe his eyes.

Starting from the base of her neck and shooting down her spine into her tailbone, chills came with a hand resting on her shoulder. *They know me,* Gift realized. The unmistakable, "Yeah, hi," that skimmed over her ear fell from Charlie's lips and he plopped into the last open chair, purposefully left beside Miss Heller.

"*Charlie?*" Gift shouted before she realized she would.

"Yeah, we aren't supposed to tell anyone. Sorry."

"Sorry? This is awesome." Mike leaned over the table. "Wait... you knew all the crap they put us through? The interrogations, surveillance. And you did nothing?"

With a hand raised, Miss Heller requested silence. "Mister Atkinson is correct. Board members' identities are not public knowledge. A few of our partners do not know that we serve as such, not at first. And Mister Russo, the complete Board did not act in harmony against current threats."

"Sakura doesn't know yet," Charlie said.

Miss Heller elucidated, "Earth's governments failed, allowing catastrophic and irreversible damage to every part of the environment. Economic failure happened years before what we call the global financial collapse. Politics stalled the colonization programs as nations fought over sovereign space, Earth's moon, and land on Mars. The only genuine progress in space travel and planned colonization happened in the private sector, the wealthiest leading the way." The Founders. Gift wondered who those heroes had been. No names preserved in history books; their faceless statues offered no clues. "...dwindling governments and unions proved unable to supply basic human needs, police their citizens, and fund the floundering colonization projects. Then, a corporate structure took hold."

While she knew this history, same as everyone, Gift perceived Miss Heller spoke from a deeper well of knowledge.

"The same structure that oversaw humanity's survival into the colonies became the functional management structure of the colonies themselves. Divisions of wealth and poverty disappeared as money became devoid of all meaning and value. We simply became *people*, equal." Recent weeks had robbed Gift of the feeling of equality, but she followed Heller's point. "...founding tenets of New Europa's colonial framework instituted an anonymous Board of Directors chosen from all classes in the colony. Today you see that legacy. We are from every working class and group, and each of us does their work assignment, like everyone. We come together here as needed—more often recently, obviously."

"And now?" Raff asked rhetorically. "There's a threat, and you had no idea how to respond. Overseeing everyday life was easy, with barely any management needed. Maybe your first real problem was the medical issues with chemical imbalance patients. The induced comas speak to you not knowing how to address that. Now terrorism? You detained, questioned, and harassed anyone close to the issue with no idea how to investigate or who to trust."

Blank faces and cleared throats fluttered over the table in reply, everyone looking to Miss Heller, the obvious Chairperson. She permitted Raff's words to reach their conclusion. "And that's why we're here. It's clear you need us. And as much as I hate to admit, we need you. We've gone as far as we can fighting this. We don't stop it unless we work together."

"Thank you, Miss Di Gaetano." Heller panned the room. "Miss Di Gaetano is correct. But she is missing pieces that make it urgent that we cooperate and be transparent. Mister Bauer, please explain to the Board your recent activities with the small group of protesters."

Explosions went off in Gift's mind like tiny pins touching a hundred points on her scalp at once. Boss was on the Board and working undercover the entire time. Heller said, 'explain to the Board.' They didn't know what he was doing. *No wonder*, she supposed, *that these conspiracy theories took root and grew.*

"A little over six months ago, I learned of gatherings of small groups discussing alleged conspiracies at all levels of colony administration. One by one, I investigated these. One group stood out, calling for a voice and speaking of sabotage. Margaret and I agreed I would join them before their chaos erupted. Soon after they made me their leader, Miss Giuntoni was removed. She was the one we were watching. I tasked Mister Fuchs with monitoring her activities remotely and, ironically, Miss Di Gaetano's work afforded Miss Giuntoni her measure of success."

"What?" Puzzled eyebrows climbed up Raff's forehead. "How do you mean?"

"You, along with Miss Ojo, found her first code. It was sloppy and ineffective. She watched you, learned from how you dealt with and disabled her software, and improved it. We believe this is when she recruited help with the physical sabotage. I was about to use my remaining group members to do unofficial investigating while our office did its official one. Then you three got in the mix, and you *just kept getting involved*. A nuisance at first. Raff finding us was unexpected, but something I wanted to exploit. To her credit, she hesitated. We couldn't know if any of you had been working with Miss Giuntoni or not."

"And now?"

"We have Miss Giuntoni in custody. This wasn't shared with the Board. My... *conversation* with her led us to believe she's the sole coder and has someone colluding with her on the hardware damage—which we now know is not Miss Ojo. Honestly, the work you three have done narrowing down the suspects has been a tremendous help. We've taken the first two, Miss Myers and Mister Zymler, into custody. We hope their interrogations will yield results."

"How do we go forward?" The calm returned to Raff's voice helped Gift's mind come down. "We still have a lot to do, and we need to know the next target. Hans and I will be able to track and kill all the remaining code, *ma*, only after the software executes again, after the next attack."

"Do you remember our objectives from those group meetings? Those are the goals of this Board. You and Hans stay on the code, monitoring and hopefully eradicating it, all day, every day, until it's resolved. Gift, you will work with Marco Fumagalli surveilling the remaining suspects. The only change is, *we* will supply the equipment and receive the feeds." Gift nodded, accepting the task. In retrospect, she came to realize she hadn't been asked but assigned.

Miss Heller resumed point. "And the... *work,* you were going to do with the one called Red and Aimée Toussaint? Proceed. But again, we will supply the equipment and receive its feed."

She was careful not to mention details about the hack and its target. It became apparent this Board of Directors lacked trust among themselves and had members acting independently. Gift wondered how things hadn't yet fully imploded.

"Miss Ojo, we also need you to use your contact with Mister Leitner. He is temporarily kept off the suspect list by your word. We may need his aid in naming anyone with physical access to the ancillary farm."

"No problem."

Uncharacteristically quiet to this point, Mike scratched at his beard and said, "I haven't heard my name. I mean, usually that's a good thing when dealing with you people. But I don't seem to have a role."

"Oh, but you do, Mister Russo. You are the point man on hardware for Miss Di Gaetano and Mister Fuchs. As they search for malicious code, you will lead a small team to physically inspect the hardware on the most critical systems—two teams of two persons each. We have taken the liberty of assigning two of our best environmental engineers from the terraforming division. Do you have a suggestion for a fourth teammate?"

Mike looked more to Gift than Miss Heller. "Of course, I'd choose Gift. But if she's on other things... Could I have Tina? Tina Keller? She's in Systems Assembly and Repair and could be extremely helpful on larger units."

"Very well. But I remind you all that information is strictly *need-to-know*. Are we clear on that?"

The three nodded. "Clear."

Gift raised her hand and waited until Miss Heller gave a nod before speaking. "What about our status? Guards? Contacting friends and family? Is that... I mean, are we back to normal?"

"Yes Miss Ojo, your guards will be reassigned."

"Thank you. So, I can visit my mother? Aimée? We can have our lunches back?"

"Yes Miss Ojo, back to normal."

"Finally," Mike blurted.

"However, you must prioritize your time to *this* cause. It will leave little time for fraternization."

"Another question, if I may?" Another nod. "Sorry if we said this, sometimes slow to process. Raff can stop this code, but only *after* another attack. The incidents have a pattern, progressively escalating in their size, scope, and danger to the colony. Everything we're doing now, all the tasks? They'll take time."

Mister Bauer smiled at Gift. "Valid point. We have limited time, but we've also noted one more part of the pattern."

"Time between incidents."

"Exactly. And from what Miss Giuntoni divulged about the learning curve on the A.I. module of her software, we believe we have at least several days before the next one. That's a best guess, and we need to plan for the worst. So, get going."

"We will give each of you a secure handheld device connected to this office, and you will each be assigned a guard." When Gift pouted at the notion, Miss Heller clarified, "If you need access to a secured area, or you find a suspect that needs to be subdued, you will have a guard *as an assistant.* Do any of you have a preference from those you have met? They have not yet been reassigned."

"Tom." Gift questioned her expressed enthusiasm. "He was with me at the airlock, helped me. I like him... I mean, I *would like* him. Please."

"Very well. Anyone else?"

A thought popped into Gift's mind when scrolling her guards across her mental display. "Sorry. Sara, my guard. She got hurt pulling people from the secret farm fire. Please, may I know how she's doing?"

"Very thoughtful Miss Ojo. She is recovering well. We have her on desk duties but expect a full recovery."

"Thank you. I've been so worried."

"You're welcome. Miss Di Gaetano? Mister Russo?"

"Corinna for me, please," Raff asked and was granted.

"I don't know the difference from mine." Mike's matter-of-fact reply said he still hadn't bothered to learn their names and didn't care to.

"We'll assign Michele then as he has experience in repair and may be useful to you in that way."

Charlie raised his hand.

"Mister Atkinson?"

"Guys, Gift. Please understand how much I wanted to tell you... but couldn't. You know, it's one of our tenets here, anonymity. Mostly, like Raff correctly surmised, we don't have to do much. Met a few times a year to review reports. Yeah, this? This is all new."

"Charlie, you don't have to, we get it."

Less understanding than Gift, Mike didn't let him off so easily. "Let him speak. He's been lying to us for months, or years. How long have you been with these people?"

"Yeah, been years, actually. Gift, you remember Luca, your dodgy bench-mate?" How could she have forgotten? Connections formed, pieces creating a picture. Charlie had taken care of it, but Gift couldn't understand how. "My first act as Board member, that. When I brought it up, we got him reassigned with strong disciplinary action. Not likely he's done that to anyone since. Until recently, yeah, that had been my biggest issue on this Board."

Raff looked him in the eye. "Sakura? Those E.CID cases? Is your relationship an... *assignment?* It's the first real issue, the only problem before this sabotage. It's been going on now for... *Ciao.* Charlie?"

Pulling his eyes from Raff, Charlie lowered his head and said nothing. Miss Heller stood, but before she spoke, he whispered, "I do love her."

"I think we end it here. We have precious little time, so your assignments start now. Miss Di Gaetano, Miss Ojo, Mister Russo, please retrieve your equipment downstairs. We want the data tap monitoring done yesterday.

Miss Ojo, we need that monitoring on all suspects sooner than possible." The three agreed with firm head nods. "Meeting adjourned."

There it was. An official meeting. Gift felt a part of something genuine—no longer needing to hide in the shadows, no back-alley meetings. Did Red, Scabs, or Kid have any idea Boss was on The Board? A Board unsure of itself. They left the rogue group to its work. Gift figured the more working on it the better, use every available resource. Murky, but it made sense to her. More concerning was the disunity of this Board keeping secrets from itself, it made her question the validity of the word 'Directors' in its descriptive title. The instability of it brought no clear direction, no order, only chaos, and now everyone in New Europa could pay a high price for their lack of accord.

44

Clouded eyes distorted the vision of the table and its lunchtime diners. Gift let the moment consume her, it had been so long since the group shared a table. Those awkward meals in silence, an audience of one watching her eat, was the old normal, and the older one was new again.

"Missed you guys." Proud of herself, Gift suppressed annoyance at Tina speaking around the pasta mush in her mouth. "Where've you been? What's going on?"

Only the highlights. There was so much to tell, time would come for that. Mike did most of the talking. "We've been working against the sabotage, yes. Gift, she saved the farms and a bunch of crops, an air handler, and stopped an airlock opening. She's a real hero."

"Wow, way to go Gift."

"But... we were suspects in the same," he added.

"What? How does that... What sense does that make?"

"None at all. Now though, it seems they finally have us on their side, and they assigned me to do hardware reconnaissance. I asked if I could have you on my team... if you're willing."

"Any extra rations in it?" Tina showed her teeth in a wide smile.

"Um, we didn't ask. It's kinda more about saving the colony, all our lives."

"Joking Mikey, settle down. Of course, count me in."

Not having been on restrictions, Tina and Charlie shared their observations on the normalcy of things, news reports of minor maintenance issues accepted with no reason not. Tina even bought into the whole emergency-system-test excuse as she had no other theories to float over it and found alternate speculations laughable.

"Heard some crazy ideas, in the shadows. Mikey, you'd have fit right in. I'd've thought you'd be the one telling. Massive conspiracy theories. One said we were attacked by one of the other colonies. New Republic of China was most favored as the one—may have been some wagers on it. This one bag of nuts said it was aliens, maybe ancient Martians awoken by the terraforming. That one got a little traction, too. But mostly, people carried on as usual, you know? Like nothing happened because that's what we'd been told."

"*Exactly.*" Mike heaped layers of self-exoneration on the word.

Tina squinted. "Sorry, Chuckles? I don't see your role in this. You helping the cause here or just being your usual sorry self?"

"I am yeah... No. I mean, I'm not... that. I *am* helping... with the medical bits of this. Sakura's been working on the E.CID thing for some time now. I'm going to get with her, see what's going on and how, or if, it connects to this rise in destructive behavior."

Gift didn't love how Charlie put himself with Sakura on the medical issue. Thoughts grew into ideas that his Union was a sham, poor Sakura duped. She didn't think Charlie could recover from the loss of respect that brought.

Tina leaned her round face forward. "So, your role is to get your partner to do it. Typical. Why am I even pursuing a man at this point? Look at the lot of you."

Pausing for reflection grounded ideas, reducing them to thoughts to restrain the tongue. Too bad Gift forgot that. This moment didn't leave room for pause and her tongue flew on its own. "About that, Tina. About Max, I mean."

"Massimo."

"Right. Sorry. See… I met a guy. Max, he called himself, so I didn't make the connection until Mike learned your Massimo's name… called him Max. I was wondering if he, maybe, is the same guy?"

"Only Massimo, or Max, I know is my guy. How do you know yours?"

"*Mine*?" Gift blushed and wished she hadn't as she felt her blood's warmth fill her cheeks. "No, just a guy I met. But here's the thing, he's… well, he's…"

"With someone else?"

Gift felt her eyes attempting to pop from their sockets. "Maybe. Wait… *you knew*?"

"Suspected." Tina's blank face morphed into a scowl. "He's always been illusive about why he's not free, where he goes and who with. I'm not an engineer like you, but give me a couple of twos and I can make a decent four of 'em."

"Tina, I'm so sorry."

"No need. It's one reason I've been cautious, haven't brought him around. That and, well, you guys being locked up kinda didn't help." Everyone chuckled. "So… what do *you* know about him?"

"Does he have blond hair, short on the sides, puffed a bit on top? Chiseled jaw and blue eyes?"

"Sounds like him alright."

"He's… *with* Sara, in my block, and…"

"And what? Go on."

"He's… sorta… come on to me. *Twice*. Once in front of Sara. So creepy."

"Men! Raff, you're the smart one." As if on cue, Hans Fuchs approached the table. "Well, you *were* anyway." Tina tossed the dig at Raff with a wink and said, "Good luck."

Hans Fuchs' face showed indifference to the laughter—intense and focused, it implied theirs should be the same. Its strength changed the collective countenance to one matching his. Power in the idea, implied in a single look from a man hardly known to them. And he was right. They had much to do, little time, and a next attack that could come in days or as they sat there enjoying their lunch. They needed to get to work.

Gift told Raff she would tell her best friend about the new plans and raced off with her bag of spy gadgets, which were nothing more than mics and cameras so tiny they'd be hard to spot left in the open. She and Marco were to hide these in people's homes, shedding their privacy.

***

Her ribs ached. She wouldn't have guessed Aimée's strength as expressed in her hug—such a tiny frame. In her light-yellow office accented in shades of orange, Gift stared into a canvas oil painting hung above Aimée's sofa showing a field laced with flowers of greenish-brown circles with bright yellow petals held on long green stems. They faced the same direction, looking at something in the distance, and Gift considered it one of the most beautiful pictures she had ever seen.

Gift gave her trusted companion the abridged version of an information dump of what had happened since their act of espionage into her medical records. Then came the reason for the visit—besides needing to see Aimée—she needed her help yet again. The *for the good of the colony* mantra never truer than now, all Gift had to say was, *I need your help,* to get Aimée on board, excited for another hack.

***

The idea hit Gift hard. She wished more than anything she could be on the hardware team. Her connection to Marco? Is that why they gave her this task of robbing people of their privacy, taking away their dignity? She saw herself becoming what she resented so powerfully when someone else did it to her—a spy.

In a moment of clarity, Gift reflected on her stance with Max, guilty-until-proven-so, while resenting the admins for doing the same to her. Ironic how different a thing can feel depending on which side of it you stood. Still, with Max she'd been right. Did the end justify the means? Would the surveillance prove the same? To execute her role in the plan, it had to be that way, so it was.

"Tom." His name came out too enthusiastically when Gift called him on her handheld. "I need your help. At my disposal, remember?"

"Of course. What do you need?"

"Meet me at the main residential maintenance office in Dome Two please. I'm headed there now."

"You got it."

A vidChat to Marco called him to join them. Tom arrived first, greeting Gift in the friendliest voice she'd heard his larynx make. She hoped he could be Tom the Human and not hide behind the guard persona. The thought made her question within herself why she chose him, and why she thought of the reasons only now. Best to keep those musings private. When Marco arrived, Tom's existence appeared to puzzle him.

"He's mine now... I mean... he's at my disposal. My assistant. He's here to help me. *Us*. He's helping *us*."

"Helping us do what?"

"The plan. The suspects with farm access." Marco's eyes popped at Gift discussing the secret plans of the group in front of an adversary. "It's okay. You remember we were going to talk to the admins? We did. We're working together, it's all good."

"But us? Remember what we agreed?"

"*Ciao*, they already knew about you. And Red and Boss. That we were working together. Everything."

"Oh."

"It'll make sense as we go. We're on the same mission, officially. Our new work assignments. Check your tasks for the rest of the afternoon."

The boy's confusion blended with satisfaction as his device showed his former tasks reassigned and suspected collaborators' homes filling his updated list of *repairs*—narrowed down from twelve to seven. Standing in Dome Two, the first one wouldn't be in a Box, and Gift tingled with excitement at going into a Flat. They set off on their adventure racing against the clock—a clock that was a ticking time bomb.

Spy thriller vid scenes panned across her mind's eye, but one story set on replay. Captain Arcadia found an explosive device in the engineering section with seconds counting down until the MSS Banzai got blown to bits. Of course, had that happened the series would have ended, so he would stop it somehow. Still, Gift remembered being literally on the edge of her seat on the first watch, sweating in suspense. This felt the same, yet completely different. The present reality lacked the confidence she had that Arcadia would stop it just as the clock ticked from one to zero so the show could continue. This was real in stakes as well as in its uncertainty.

Might this be her final episode?

45

To have a friend, you must be a friend. How often Gift recalled the lesson when considering her companions. Friendships took time and investment to grow, flourish, and endure. Could her best friend from childhood be considered a *chosen* friendship? The only two girls in the colony of the same age, brought together by their parents, timing, and genetics. Yet Gift couldn't imagine anyone else she would have picked as a lifelong friend. The choice, her choice, was in keeping the friendship and nurturing it through the passing years.

In her adult life, were the foundations of her friendships any different? Called colleagues and neighbors, Gift had been placed in unfamiliar groups of nameless people, some remained acquaintances while others ascended to the level of friends. It was in which of the two a person became that presented choice.

With Gen-Maturity expected around the age of thirty—even if initial stirrings of the next stage had begun—Gift's emotional character needed to mature. She thought of her Colonial Family playset and the perception of life as a colony resident as seen through the one-sided eyes of a child. What formed the concepts of friendship and family, elevating them into constructs of life?

Love?

As a child, she felt the effects of love more deeply than she could understand. Appreciation for it came long after its expression through the unyielding, unconditional love from her mother. How did love between a man and a woman differ? Her mother didn't have it, and Gift still wrestled to understand it. Having assumed it to be what she recognized in Charlie and Sakura, she had to wonder, to doubt.

That Charlie had lied to them for years didn't bother Gift. Every resident needed to put the good of the colony first. Charlie did that, serving on the Board. With what reward? He worked a full shift and lived in a standard Union Box. That struck Gift as odd, having assumed all Board members would get flats. Speculative as they were, Raff's words fostered an idea so powerful Gift couldn't circumvent it. Her mind refused to let it out of focus, making it real whether it was or not. Charlie's Union was nothing but an assignment, the same as her to her guards. Not the result of love, affection, or choice. Profound sadness came over her, not only for Sakura, but also for Charlie.

How would sweet Sakura take the news? Devastated, used, an object of interest instead of affection. Thoughts chased ideas for form and substance. Clouded by such, Gift couldn't be sure how long ago she'd seen the alert first appear on her handheld: Message from Charles Atkinson.

"Play."

"Yeah Gift. Hi." He casually spoke, as if everything were normal, as if he were still just Charlie. "I'm with Sakura here in her office. We need you to come by if you can. Something important. When you can."

"VidChat Sakura Tanaka." Better to try her than her fake partner, who may or may not still have been Gift's friend. Way too much was happening to make the final call, but it didn't look good. The swirling blue faded into Charlie's face.

"Hey Gift. Yeah, I answered Sakura's. I'm here with her. I guess you got my message. Can you come over here, to her office?"

"I'm about to knock out the first um... *task*. Can't come. Put Sakura on; I called *her*." Unsure Charlie deserved any positivity of emotion, she replied curtly.

"Hi Gift. How are you, sweetie?"

"You know, same old. But I'm real busy now. Charlie said you had something important for me, said 'when I can.' Sounded like he meant now. Can't come now, in the middle of stuff."

"Oh, okay. Can we talk later, then? Perhaps you could come to ours after shift?"

"Not on my normal shift. Not sure when I'll finish."

"Whenever is fine. Please come."

"Look. You're being kind, I get it. But I think I know what this is about and it's fine. Really. I've already accepted it. You need to tell me I have Early CID. It's fine. But I need to finish what I'm doing, so please, just hold whatever needs to come next 'til I'm done. A few days is all I'm asking."

"Oh, no, that is not it, not exactly."

"Then just tell me, please. I really need to go."

"I would rather not tell you here, not like this. It is not bad news, so please, do not worry. You do not have Chemical Imbalance Disorder. It is about that other thing... But not over vidChat. Later, please."

"I don't have E.CID? Shiny. Should've led with that."

"You are right. Please, come see me later."

"Okay. Gotta go... End."

"What was all that?" Marco's question reminded her of his existence.

"*Huh*? Oh, nothing. Just some medical tests I had done. *Good news*, I'm fine. Now let's get going."

When Tom reached for her arm, Gift shrugged his hand away. "I heard the E.CID part. They tested you for that?"

"Yeah, but that's none of your business, *Guard*." Hitting that word hard put him in his place, setting up the relationship as he and each of the guards had done with her. It felt fantastically empowering for a second, horrible in the seconds that followed.

"Sorry, but I think we need to talk about this. Not you. The Early CID stuff, I mean."

"Not me? What are you on about? We have a lot to do."

"I brought a few residents to Pronto Soccorso that were quickly diagnosed with E.CID. They were doing things like vandalizing kiosks with that *All Lies* message. Others were in intense arguments with their colleagues or supervisor. One with her own mother. That almost became violent. As I understand it, there's a significant increase, like from few ever to dozens now."

"Yeah, we know all that."

"But that woman you were talking with, that medic? She's the one who made the fast diagnoses, each time I was involved. She'd ask them a few questions, push for answers, wave a handheld scanner over them, stick them with a hypo, and shuffle them off to what she called C.I.D. Critical Treatment."

"*What*? No. You're wrong."

"I wondered what critical treatment was, so I sneaked by and followed one of them to what looked more like a lab than an exam room. Gift, they put them in this... *box* thing, medical chamber of some kind, then hooked an IV to it. I heard a tech say they were inducing a coma. This girl—young, pretty, whole life ahead of her—was put in a coma just like that." It stung her ear when his fingers snapped louder than Gift had ever heard anyone snap.

"Frizzy hair?" Marco had the same notion as Gift.

"Straight. But I'm telling you, she wasn't even twenty."

"You saw wrong. It's not her." Despair bled into Gift's words as the possibility solidified. "I mean, it wasn't Sakura, couldn't be. The other stuff... we, we suspected. But *her*? She's the one who told us. She said... No, she didn't agree with the stuff they were doing… the comas. You must've seen someone else. It wasn't her. I mean it, not her."

"I was there *five times*." He lifted a hand with fingers splayed. "They took a suspect to admin, a woman maybe in her thirties or forties with darker skin, taken from her work assignment for no specified reason. But the other four, all four? It was her, Sakura, who did the fast track to coma. It was her every time, Gift. I'm sorry, it was her."

Stepping back didn't conceal her glossy eyes. An arm came over her shoulder. Marco said nothing, he was being sweet. Gift swatted his hand away. Sufficient time allowed conscious thought to return and with it came clarity. If Charlie's Union was only an assignment, could this be why? Was Sakura involved in something underhanded? What could her role in all this possibly be? Did it connect to the sabotage?

It was obviously Claudia, taken by the admins. Her CID diagnosis didn't lead her into a coma. *Critical Treatment.* Good thing Gift hadn't made her final verdict on Charlie. It seemed she needed more to complete this picture, pieces fallen to the floor, hiding under the bed, making the scene impossible to complete. She'd need those pieces. When Gift hit Sara's back in a full-out run it felt like a wall. Now, standing still, she was hit by a wall. If Sakura was in some way involved with the medical conspiracy, acting independently from the Board, why would she offer a security code to tap into the feeds that could expose and condemn her? She wouldn't.

"I need Raff."

46

Adventure vids had the power to take Gift to another world, one of fantasy, becoming absorbed in the story of other people's lives, no longer in her own. Having full surveillance, casting her as the lead role in a twenty-four-hour, seven-day-per-week story of her life gifted her the opposite of escapism, trapping and suffocating her. Now she had to do it to someone else, *seven* someone's. Only worse, they'd have no idea. Would that be worse?

Outside the housing building of their first intrusion, Gift paused. "Vid-Chat Raffaella Di Gaetano."

"Ciao, *Cara.*"

"Yeah, ciao. Slight problem. Big, actually. Maybe huge."

"*Che cosa*? What problem?"

"That security code we got for Aimée and Red's little project? It's no good."

"What? How do you mean? We got it from Sakura, no?"

"That's the problem. It seems, well… it seems she might be involved, could be, in the very conspiracy we're trying to find. The medical one, not the others. Maybe, I guess."

"Gift, *Cara*. Relax. Tell me."

Gift took a deep breath, then another when one didn't settle her mind and allow it to string words into sentences. "It seems Sakura was… she was the one... quickly diagnosing the patients, sending them into comas. Need to verify, of course. *Ma*, we can't trust her code. I mean, she knew we were looking for the people doing what *she's* apparently doing—might be, probably is. Why would she help us? I have a bad feeling about this. Just... don't use that security clearance code."

"*What?* You must be wrong, I can't believe... *Dai*, we'll handle that later. *Ma*, this sets us back. I'll have to work with Red to get a way around it. Access to those systems without a security code. Oh mamma."

"What about Aimée? Can't you use her access?"

"Not without getting her caught... *Oh*. Yes, we can do that. We're working on the inside. I'll tell Miss Heller and we'll use Aimée's access. Good shout Gift."

"Shiny. Gotta run, I'm at the first stop now."

"In bocca al lupo."

"Ciao... End."

The first time in a housing building, not a habitat block of Boxes, she let her imagination run over expectations. A small but tasteful lobby greeted them, and Gift recognized the lift by the shiny doors and call button. Rising in it, Marco described how buildings in domes were all small because, of course, they needed to be for the limited space. Each dome had only one housing building, each of those with six flats, two per floor.

Red had assigned Marco a bogus maintenance task for a safety check on a faulty line coupling found in another flat. If the occupants had no maintenance background, it wouldn't raise suspicions. That a request existed allowed his biometrics to open the door. Stood before it as it slid open, Gift's stomach fluttered with anticipation at seeing her first flat. Like letting air out of a balloon then pinching it closed half released, some anticipation seeped out, but it didn't completely deflate.

Nothing fancy or ornate, just bigger. So much space with room enough to dance or just to pace nervously without needing to turn as often. Gift pondered for a passing second why those were the pictures her brain made of herself in the room. She settled on anxiety being a near constant in her current normal leading to pacing. So why would she be dancing?

A proper kitchen, or at least more storage space and a food chiller, not just a bin. "Life changing," she said as she opened it to find cold water, fresh vegetables, and leftover pasta with sauce. The dining area left her dumbfounded, with a table and four chairs that didn't need to be folded into the wall. The bed had its own room, laid open with space around it to walk and reach bins in the walls—so many bins. Stepping in the ensuite, drool dribbled over Gift's bottom lip at seeing the shower and toilet. At that point the flat could have been exactly the size of her Box, the space became unimportant. But an ensuite would be life-changing indeed. To permit her imagination to run wild, she stepped in the shower, closed her eyes, and imagined the burst of warm suds on her skin.

"Gift?" Snapping her out of her trance, Marco called her back to the main room. "We need to plant the devices. One camera in here. What do you think? Up there in the air return? Better idea?"

"That should work, full view."

"What about the bedroom?"

"I really don't like this." Gift's face soured as it did when her last sip of cold espresso bittered. "I should be on the hardware. Why the heck did I get this *mal'd* job?"

"The breaks. I guess they trust you."

"Whatever. So, the bedroom? No camera, just a mic."

"Yes. One camera here and a mic, a second mic in the bedroom. Go do that one, I'll get these in here. Hurry, we didn't get these folks' agenda, don't want any surprises."

"But you're supposed to be here, the maintenance request." Gift needed to shout from the bedroom.

"But a guard out in the corridor? And you in here with me? A bit suspicious."

Timing is everything, Gift had heard. As the conclusion of Marco's words reached her, a noise in the hall entered the flat and the woman who made it followed it in. "*Oh.*"

"Sorry, ma'am. They should've notified you of my visit to check a coupling that gave us problems in other flats."

"Yes, my partner mentioned. I didn't realize it was today."

As she stepped toward the bedroom, Marco cleared his throat and took his distraction talents out for another go. "Have you been in this flat for long?"

"Sorry? I'm quite busy. In and out." She seemed wholly uninterested in small talk, so Gift stepped out from the bedroom with her coverall unzipped to her navel and her hair disheveled. She came face to face with the nameless woman, middle-aged or closer to senior, but well maintained. Her elegant trouser suit said she had an office work assignment.

"Oh sorry, didn't think anyone would be here. It's just..." Gift offered a nervous laugh she believed made her more convincing. "I never saw a flat before, so when my guy said he was coming here... I begged him to let me see." Deliberately, she pulled the zipper up.

"Looks like *he* begged to see something too." Looking Gift up and down, her condescension morphed into a wide smile as she said, "Youth."

"Sorry... ma'am." The young maintenance tech's nerves stuttered the words. "We're all done, ma'am. Have a lovely day, ma'am."

When the door closed behind them, they shared quiet giggles. Gift couldn't hold hers back. Air vibrating through closed lips made a joyous noise as drops of saliva sprayed into the corridor. She looked at the short vacant space for Tom, nowhere to be found until a panel opened beside the lift doors, a narrow opening from which Tom emerged.

"Where'd you go? What's in there?" Gift had understood it to be a solid wall.

"In case of power failure or fire, every housing building has emergency stairs."

"Clever." Gift questioned the smile she threw Tom, and her low pitch reminded her of Max's flirtation. It fit just as wrong on her, though not as creepy. In the lift, Gift felt it safe to ask Marco about the bug. "That woman's partner works in the secret farm?"

"Her. Well, she works in life sciences. Her specialty is in crop development and soil nutritional enhancement. She has access to both farms and crossed paths with Claudia several times in recent months."

"Whoa." Tom looked impressed. "You guys did a ton of cross-referencing."

Marco said, "Needed to narrow the list down."

"Yeah. Access to the secret—I mean, *ancillary* farm, was a huge key. Cut the list a lot. So, six more then?"

Before answering Gift, Tom looked at his handheld. "We have a detour, one other Box they want us to do right now, before we continue the list. It's in Five-Six."

Fluttering returned, not in a good way, not anticipation of another new and exciting experience. This was dread—all too familiar now, easily recognized. It filled Gift as they entered the corridor that led to Charlie's block. With four blocks full of Boxes, it didn't mean they were going to his, but of course it did. Tom must have reported his discovery about Sakura.

The thing about doing Charlie's Box, it made the ones after easier. Well, she'd say not as guilt-ridden, anyway. Gift didn't like herself any better for doing it, even less for not feeling as awful about it as she thought she should have. By 18:27, they had managed to have seven bugged suspects dispossessed of privacy. Same for Charlie and Sakura—her friends she only believed she knew. Now their once personal lives came under constant and tedious scrutiny by the very ones Charlie trusted, his secret or ancillary group, the Board of Directors.

She had to hurry to make her shower slot.

Gift couldn't stop her mind flipping through its photo album. One by one, names, pictures, and memories of the most precious people in her life scrolled over the mental display—all flagged as 'suspect.' What didn't she know about Raff? Tina? Was there some dark alter ego she'd never seen in Aimée? Mike? Did she really know anyone? Was it possible to truly know anyone at all? And what had she become, who was Gift Ojo now? How would Charlie react when he learned she bugged his home?

Sara seemed unusually cheerful in the shower queue. When she saw Gift, she couldn't contain herself and didn't even notice the coverall. "Hi, Gift. Guess what...? We got promised, Max and me. We'll be joined in Union in a couple of months. Can you believe it?"

"Oh. Sure... nice."

"Gee, thanks. Why do you have to be such a downer? I get it, he thinks you're pretty. I mean, who could blame him? C'mon, look at you... *Coveralls...*? Anyway, I get it. He made your inners tingle, got you all warm and such. But he's with me. You could at least try to act happy for me."

"Look, Sara. If you're okay with him flirting or spending time with other women? I mean, if that makes you happy, then great. Happy for you."

"What do you mean, flirting and spending time with women? He looked at you, smiled at you, said you were gorgeous. I said the same thing. That's nothing. He's not like that."

"You do what you want. But maybe, just to know what kind of man he really is, ask him about Tina. Ask him, when you see him, how he broke his nose."

Joy drained from Sara's face. Gift pondered over how much people didn't know about each other in contrast to what they believed they did.

How Tina and Sara hadn't *known* Max. Her recent revelations about Charlie, then Sakura, shattered the foundations of all relationships.

Were any of them real?

47

One of her tutors, the one with the stutter he had mostly overcome, Mister Wagner, liked to drop an ancient wise saying, profound quotation, or proverb in every lesson. Until now, the understanding of the African proverb he often recited evaded Gift.

'If you want to know the end, look at the beginning.'

It made sense now that it had context. To see how this sabotage would end, Gift needed to look to its beginning. Where did the rebellion, dissatisfaction in colonial life, and the conspiracy theories start? What drove Claudia and however many people working with her to this point?

For the first group dinner in ages, Gift slipped into her black dress, making the evening special. Raff also wore her black dress, but the style differed from Gift's with a variant shade, so it was fine. The group felt incomplete without Charlie and Sakura and dinner had to be hurried, cut short for important business. Later they met with Red, Marco, Scabs and Aimée, but not in secret, no longer the need.

Somber faces adorned each of them, setting the tone for the importance of the task at hand: stop the sabotage and save the colony. Flaunting her independence, Aimée didn't follow the crowd—not then, not ever. A wide smile glowed as she rocked back and forth with excitement. The group sat in a circle in the little secluded patch of green grass in Dome Three. Aimée leaned back and propped herself into a recline on her elbows. "Nice location Gift. Some wonderful memories here." Smiling with her friend, Gift removed the melancholy from her face and tossed the mask aside. It didn't fit quite right on her.

Leading in Boss' absence, Raff said, "Thank you for coming. Until, well, until this is over, we'll meet nightly for updates. We need to stay ahead of this."

"Where's Boss?" Scabs asked.

"Allora. There have been some recent... developments. He's working his angles at the admin building. *We* are the group that will beat this thing. Now, not all of you know each other so... Red, junior data operator. Aimée runs one of the Resident Services offices. We have Mike and Tina on hardware, already found and repaired one sabotaged unit today before it malfunctioned. Splendid work, you two." They nodded in gratitude. "Scabs is our man on the ground, has contacts and helped us get a list of suspected collaborators. I believe everyone knows Gift, and that's Marco in maintenance, those two are on surveillance."

Raff called Gift to report her activity before Mike outlined what they found and how he and Tina fixed it. Hating labels, Gift never used words like mentor or mentee, but she absorbed the pride of a master whose apprentice performed well. For the next days, for as long as it took, everyone in the group would work twelve-hour shifts. The unknowable approaching next attack pushing them into overtime loomed over them, casting a shadow of dread.

To lay out the goals, Raff said, "We need to make headway on the coconspirators. Surveillance may help or may give us nothing. Narrowing down the seven is a priority but we shouldn't drop anyone with access to either farm. Highly likely we're dealing with more than one person here."

Scabs raised his hand but didn't wait. "I'm on that. Been getting the buzz in the colony and I think there may be many, many more, actually. And something worse."

Impatient fear flooded into Gift. "Worse? What, what could be worse?"

"Lots of people talking. They're not buying the cover stories. I think… it seems anyway, that Claudia continued our campaign of getting people riled up about lies, but way more than we did with our cryptic kiosk messages. She's got an underground movement of followers, sympathizers to real nut job conspiracy theorists. They *are* riled up. Don't have any detail, but I'll keep trying."

"Oh mamma. That *is* worse."

"Stay on that Scabs, top priority." With a nod he accepted Raff as the pack's new alpha. "Meantime, we're trying to find any connections to the medical, especially E.CID. They blame it for some of this, but I keep thinking it's somehow related to the bigger picture. We had a setback and couldn't use the security code from Pronto Soccorso. Red's working on Plan B."

"Right, Plan B. We got the hardware from admin—so strange working with them now, but okay. They gave us two, like, data… *interceptors*." Red spoke with less eloquence of tongue. "We needed physical contact, had to attach the thing to live conduits patched into the data stream segment we wanted to capture, outside Amy's office." After spending the day together, Red still mispronounced her name. "Raff already figured how to bounce into all the Resident Services offices, so with one tap into the medical uplink, we got access to data from all six. Pretty sweet hack, actually."

The recognizable grimace warned Gift of Mike's objection. "Sorry, the real data on the Chemical Imbalance Disorder is in Pronto Soccorso. I mean, how is capturing data from a bunch of Resident Services offices doing us any good?"

"Really good question. That's why we have two routers, those data interceptor gizmos. Getting the data from those offices, sure, it's good data. Got us the first list on those diagnosed. But more important, we used the first hack to identify the location of the next primary conduit to tap into, where it uplinks to Medical. That gets us the data we really need. Been logging tons since it went active this morning."

Scabs raised his hand and kept it raised. "If we're working with the Board, I don't get why we're tapping into *their* network and hijacking *their* data."

"They don't trust their own," Raff explained. "We're operating like this to keep some of what we're doing hidden from individual Board members. Left hand not knowing what the right is doing situation."

"That makes sense." The face Scabs wore disagreed with his words.

"I don't trust their transparency. They insisted our data capture be routed to their secure server, *ma,* I hacked the routing process and have the data streaming to us and to them. That's how we're able to process it."

Scabs pointed to Aimée and returned her smile. "Why is she here? Is she actually *doing* anything on this?"

"I'm your good luck charm." Aimée winked as she sat with her legs stretched inward toward the center of the human circle, ankles crossed with her top foot rocking. Gift saw her as that confident and free-spirited sixteen-year-old.

"I can live with that. Cute one too." The smile Scabs gave her smacked of Luca and Max, but with an innocence those of the other two creeps lacked.

Raff added, "We are using her access codes, and we need her biometrics for access again tomorrow, so she'll be hands on, literally."

"Got it. Welcome to the team, Amy."

"Merci." When his face crinkled in confusion, she added, "Thank you."

They had made tremendous progress on their first half-day of collaborative effort with Administration. Everyone knew their assignments for the next day. With any luck, they hoped to uncover more detail on the disturbing additional aspect, an underground movement. It was getting late, and Gift had a stop to make before going to her Box to melt into sound sleep.

48

When the door opened, Gift saw Charlie's arm around Sakura's shoulder as they welcomed her. Any time before that very day she'd have seen it as an adorable sight, evidence of their love. In this instance, she had no idea what it meant—unsure she knew what anything meant. In the double Box she entered just hours earlier to rip away the couple's privacy, she knew they were being watched, her included, in their unknown new reality she helped create.

"Ciao. I'm super tired, but you made it sound like it was important, so here I am." Her opening lacked any evidence of friendship, and she thought it too harsh. Sakura more than made up for her friendliness deficiency with a warm, enduring embrace. It felt genuine enough, lending doubt to Gift's making her into a horrible monster casting her prey into a comatose state, staving off the inevitable conclusion and consuming their lives. Such a lovely hug.

"Yeah." Charlie spoke dryly, as he always did. "It's important. I think it is, pretty much, yeah. Better you came right away, not over vidChat either. Private is better."

Hastily, Gift called her eyes back when they moved toward the camera she had placed in the nightlight on the wall. Plaguing thoughts overcame her. *Private is better, but it's not here, maybe not actually real. We find such comfort in a concept. Perhaps that's all privacy was to anyone.* Packing those thoughts away in the darkest corners of her mind, Gift said, "Okay, so I figured Sakura wasn't truthful earlier, didn't want to say it, so said the opposite. I get nervous like that a lot. Just tell me I have E.CID. It's okay, really. But please, I need a few days before…"

"No, Gift, you do not have Early CID, truthfully. Your detailed blood-work, scans, and the extra tests, all showed negative results. You do not have it."

"*Okay*? So then… I've got something else? Something bad?"

"No, not exactly. Can we sit? And maybe Charlie, would you please give us this time alone?"

After putting a hand and soulful eyes on Gift's shoulder, Charlie left the Box as requested.

They sat facing each other, knees practically touching. Sakura grabbed Gift's hands, considering the lack of bandages on her fingers, and raised Gift's right hand for closer inspection. "Healed very well."

"Good as new. But that's not why you asked me here."

"No. You are right. Gift, this is about that categorization in your medical file, EXP One forty-two. You do not know what that means, do you?"

"No idea. As I told you, it means they do bloodwork and extra tests every single week since I turned twenty-six. Oh, and I'm somehow… *special*."

"You did tell me that, and I started digging. Also, your first results, when we tested your blood and urine? They were inconclusive, which is not common. In fact, I have never seen that before. Positive or negative, every time."

"Like I said, special, me."

"The symptoms that you have manifested looked like Early Chemical Imbalance Disorder. It is why we flagged you from your chat with Mister Müller and the interview I did with you. The conflicting results from your blood and urine confused the whole thing. Then the confirmed result from last week was negative. It did not add up."

"So, this EXP one-four-two? It somehow explains this?"

"It does." Sakura paused, straightened her back while keeping hold of Gift's hands, and took a deep breath before continuing. "What do you know about childbirth in the colony?"

"*Huh*...? You mean, like, where babies come from?"

"Like in your case. Do you know how your mother came to have you?"

"She applied, like everyone. Was accepted."

"And it is more than rare for a solo to be accepted. You do know that, right? It does *not* happen, ever. It violates one of the core tenets. They *invited* your mother to apply because she had certain... very favorable characteristics in her genes. Her DNA showed traces of a retro genome code strand not common in the colony. Her being a solo meant no partner for male DNA and the genome-sciences team could select from tens of thousands of male specimens to be your father, well, your gene source."

Leapt onto her feet, Gift shook her arms then walked in a tight circle with both hands interlocked, holding the back of her head where the dull pain came. "You make me sound like, like, some kind of... of... science experiment."

"In a way Gift, you were. Sorry, no, not an experiment... More like carefully selected, genetically, to give you the best chances of what they hoped they might see in your physical development. And they have been watching you closely for it since you turned sixteen, then from twenty-six, the weekly DNA tests and bloodwork. It has all been to confirm, track, monitor, and protect, their success in you."

"Their *success* in me? What does that even mean? Am I some kinda freak?"

"Not at all. In an exceptionally beautiful and wonderful way, you are the most human of us, of the entire colony."

"I'm what... *most human*... in what...?" Tears gathered in her eyes, and she blinked them away, hopeful that clear vision would somehow clear her mind.

"You can have a child Gift, the natural way. You are the first woman in over two hundred years or much more... who can produce a child."

Gift tried to process it, to call up her display and scroll over the data, but nothing came. Her mind had no notion of what to do with the information it had just received. For the first time in an exceedingly long time, she was blank—blank in her brain activity and equally in her lack of emotional response. It felt like dying. Sakura told her to breathe normally.

"But I mean... women have babies all the time, don't they? Not *all the time*, I mean... You know what I mean. Look how many of us were born in the last century. All fifty-something thousand. Women have babies. What makes me different, exactly? The *natural* way?"

"Yes Gift, the natural way. Everyone donates their eggs and sperm for possible Union and childbearing approval. Of course, not every Union applies, and many are not approved. When childbearing is granted, if the female egg is healthy and the male sperm in the bank is also, we do in vitro fertilization. Once confirmed viable for life—and the success rate is not high—we implant the embryo in the womb. In your mother's case, they selected the sperm by careful research in the medical database for certain genetic markers and other factors believed to be the best match to give you the greatest chance of success. And, well... they achieved it."

Foggy thoughts prevented Gift's brain from making the connections that became obvious only later, out of the moment, with its emotional weight eliminated. "So... I'm a lab rat, then."

"No, sweetie. In most ways, your birth was like anyone else in the colony. Normal. You are just like everyone else, only... special." When Sakura waved her hand for Gift to sit, she folded herself into the chair with every gram of strength drained from her. "Remember when I asked about your spending the night with your friend?"

"Matteo... Yeah."

"A valid E.CID exam question, true. But in your case, they also needed to know because... the natural way. You can be impregnated from having intercourse. You are the only one, Gift. The natural way of fertilization in your ovary from sperm introduced during coitus. And not only become pregnant, but you could also have a *healthy* baby. That makes you incredibly special."

Under a shadow not made by light—no light shone on this—Gift sat in silence, unsure what any of it could possibly mean or if it meant anything. Not in G.M. yet, she had no desire to rush it. But biologically, she could have a child? She wasn't even old enough for Union. The pieces didn't fit. It hurt her head to have such chaos of thought, a voice of an idea that was barely a whisper yet shouting like a klaxon. All Gift wanted to do was lose herself in sleep.

Sakura offered to have Charlie walk her home.

49

When she had learned the Italian word *famiglia*—with its silent *g* and the *ia* forming a *ya* sound—Gift heard the link to the word familiar. She wondered if one could be an adjective of the other, as each carried similar sentiments. Did something familiar engender the comfort of family? Or did family and friends bring the warmth and security they did because they were familiar?

Passageways, shops, buildings, people, even guards, were familiar sights passing her by as they walked. Charlie strolled beside her, keeping his long stride bridled not to rush Gift's pace. She found no comfort in the familiarity—the friendship now a chasm she wasn't sure could be bridged, or if she wished it to be.

Who was Charlie? Who was Sakura? Could either of them truly answer that question about the other?

"So, Sakura has no idea you are on the Board?"

"Not allowed to tell her, yeah. Hate keeping that secret. Soon, I think, I can say."

"I've gotta ask. Was she... an *assignment?* I mean, your Union?"

"Oh no. Not like that. I met her, yeah, that bit is true, actually. I met her because I was looking into her work for the Board. But no, Gift, they didn't ask me to seduce her or join in Union. No."

"So, you investigated her work… and decided she's the one. All based on, on a lie?"

"No. It wasn't… not like that." Gift could almost see the sadness envelope him like the thick smoke in the farm. "I love her. I did check into her work, when we caught that little note about an increase in Early CID cases. Yeah. We looked more closely and found out about the comas."

"So… you found out Sakura was rush-diagnosing this awful thing, and sentencing those poor people to coma… And what? You fell in love with her, after learning *that*?"

Clearly shaken, Charlie grabbed Gift's arm at the elbow and pulled her over to a closed espresso stand away from the main path of passersby. Her face showed a dazed and startled pallor. It wasn't fear, she'd felt that enough to recognize, but it was close. "What do you know about that?" A trepidatious voice from Charlie, a first in Gift's experience.

"I know she made several hasty diagnoses of E.CID and sent patients off to be put in coma with no chance of being set free. Disappeared. Condemned to a… life-sentence in an unconscious prison. That's what I know about it."

"No, Gift, actually, you *don't* know." His eyes rolled up while he sucked a deep breath and paused. Seconds felt like forever until he exhaled and released his irises. "She's been *saving* those people."

"*Huh*? How? Someone has seen them getting put into boxes, in comas. Seen *her* do it."

"Exactly, they do get put in boxes, comas induced. Those boxes? They're the hibernation chambers we used to get here during the migration—as close to cryo-freeze as we get. They're put in storage, basically, where they hardly need to be checked. And Sakura's the one that checks them." He looked around anxiously. "Let's take this chat to your Box."

Words were there, strung into coherent sentences, yet devoid of sense. Charlie agreed Sakura had fast-diagnosed E.CID and sent people into comas. But he said doing so somehow saved them? Eyes bounced side to side as Gift sorted the information in columns on her mental display and tried to find the logic, to see rationality in what Charlie said. Then it clicked, the last piece of this little puzzle snapped in place. Silence stayed in the corridor, not permitted into her Box.

"Where are those people? Are they still in comas?"

"Some are still there, yeah, really in awful shape, no cure. Sakura had orders to either place them in comas or else they were arrested and detained indefinitely. It was her idea to set them free. Now most, yeah, just about most of them are free. Woke and set free."

Pensive, Gift hesitated around a significant flaw in the underlying rationale. "Hold on. The system, their records, show them in a coma, under medical care. They can't be going to their Boxes, their work assignments, spending rations."

"Yeah, that's the tricky bit for us. We get them set up in sort of like, a *refugee* area. They work the farms on the third shift, live in the storage compartments in the ancillary farm warehouse. They eat off the farm mostly, no rations. A few of them set up the underground markets, barter and trade."

"You said, us. You and Sakura both help these people?"

"Yeah." He relaxed into a smile. "Part of my role on the Board is oversight of cultivation workers and their support services, including storage areas of the farm warehouse."

"Wait." Rapid head-shaking made Gift dizzy. "I'm getting lost. I... You said she doesn't know... about you being on the Board?"

"Thinks I'm working through a friend on the Board."

"Oh. It's all... just... too much. A couple weeks ago, none of this existed. I mean, I didn't know it, so it just... just didn't exist. You know? Now we've got people trying to expose secrets, crazier ones trying to kill us by attacking our vital systems. These poor sick people with this horrible disorder. Lives ruined. And now, we have... *refugees* living in the farm? And—" Clarity came to her mind like her Box door switching from nighttime blackout to one-way transparency. It was right on the other side of the door. It just needed that one setting flipped to see it, plain as the nose on Charlie's face. "—and the refugees? They're setup in *both* farms?"

"In the ancillary farm warehouse. They're much less noticeable there. That's where they live and sleep."

"Charlie?" Hopeful eyes said she had his attention. "I misjudged you. You *are* a good guy. I mean, I thought you were. But... when I saw you on that Board? You lied to Sakura. I started... You weren't such a good guy anymore, you know?" His head dipped. "You're a good guy and I love you. Again, I mean. I do. *Ma*, you're an idiot. Oblivious. An oblivious idiot." His face screamed with confusion. "You *do* realize we've built our list of suspects for the physical sabotage from people with access to the farm, and narrowed it even more to those who could access the secret farm, *right*?"

"Yeah. Decent work on that. Narrowed it down a good—" His own raised hands stopped Charlie mid-thought and Gift smiled at him for catching up. "So, any of these E.CID refugees could also be involved in it. Your list of possible coconspirators just grew exponentially."

"*There* it is. Could you get us a list of all the ones who have access to the secret farm, please?"

"Ancillary. And sure. Not in any organized data file, but I have the names, marked in their medical histories. Well, Sakura did that, but I can get them... Yeah, search the keywords on my handheld, send them to you."

Charlie pulled the device from his pocket and found the records. A swipe sent the data to Gift's handheld, growing their list of seven to twenty-three with the flick of a finger over the smooth glass. No Boxes to bug, and no way to watch them without exposing them—as well as Charlie and Sakura—to the admins. Gift would need Matteo's help.

"Oh mamma. If people's emotions are all... out of whack and twisted up? And so many of them are out there, roaming free?"

"Oh. Could be what we've done... We may have helped their cause by setting them free. Made this a lot worse."

"What was the plan? I mean, these people live their days, years, as refugees hiding in the farm. What happens to them? Tell me you had a plan for them."

"Yeah. The idea was that once she found a cure, or something Sakura could treat them with, she'd log that it had cured them. They get released and get to go back to their Boxes, jobs... live their lives. Figured it may take some months, but she thinks she'll get there."

Too physically and emotionally drained to stand, Gift sat on the floor. Considering her black dress, she bent onto her knees and sat seiza-style. Folding her neck to look at Charlie, he became a giant looming over her, hanging from the ceiling by his hair. A tired hand patted the floor, inviting him to sit. When he did, Gift leaned forward and, stretching her neck, lent his cheek a gentle peck.

"What's that for?"

"Because I'm sorry I doubted you. Glad I was wrong."

"I still lied, or at least didn't tell the truth. You can be mad if you need."

All Gift could do was smile in return. She couldn't be mad at him now if she tried. It came so easily in the moments just before this one. Gone now, replaced by the familiar, the comfort of friends and family brought the sensation of a warm hug when she sorely needed one.

"Gift?" He wrapped her name in gentleness. "Are you okay... with what Sakura told you earlier? It was heavy. Have you had time to process it yet?"

"That I don't have Chemical Imbalance Disorder? Yeah, I'm good with that." She deflected the words like lasers fired at the Banzai, but her shields were weakening.

"No, seriously. I mean the other. Perhaps I'm not the one to be asking, talking about something like this. But... how you handling that?"

The question straightened her back and Gift rubbed her open palms down and back up her thighs, staring at the ceiling. Staring at nothing, up into her mind to find which of the thousands of thoughts running across it she wanted to form into words and string into sentences. "I..." After an exhale she leveled her head. "I don't know what to make of it, really. I haven't thought about Union... much less applying for a child. I mean, why would I? Too young still, not even allowed. So now I'm told I can have one, a *baby*... the natural way? Does that even change anything? It's... well, it's just that I wonder if... maybe the G.M.? I wonder if maybe it *is* early... for me."

"You don't have Early CID."

"I mean regular G.M., healthy Gen-Maturity. It comes earlier for some. And I don't know, maybe my... *condition*. Could it be that? I might want to ask Sakura about that. If maybe I... I'm already there. It'd explain a lot, actually. All these crazy feelings. And the *anger*. I've gotten real angry, even at Raff. And for nothing."

Leaning in to embrace Gift, Charlie squeezed her in a tight hug expressing a torrent of thoughts and emotions through its power. *You'll be fine. Sakura will help you. I'm here for you. Don't worry.* All the things he didn't say brought her mind down and enveloped her in warm waves of comforting friendship and support—welcome, needed, familiar.

"Can I ask you something?" she softly whispered as he pulled away.

"Shoot."

"With you being on the Board and all, why don't you guys have a flat?" Their laughter surrounded them, filling the tiny space.

"Anonymity. Plus, Board members don't automatically get a flat. Actually, it's Sakura's work that got us added to the waiting list. If we get one, we'll have a group dinner at ours for sure."

"Can't wait. But be ready, I'll be over *a lot*... Oh. Lights-Out. You'll get a Tardy."

"Now *that's* one of the perks of being on the Board. I have some leeway."

50 | DAY FORTY

outine carried in it a stability that felt like security and safety—a reliability in events happening as expected and people being who and what they were supposed to be. For Gift, that was an especially vital element of life in the colony. Her life. Her routine had always carried comfort in the absence of chaos. Its predictability provided the symmetry she desperately needed, sending the dull pain away.

Every day forward would be unexpected. The dull pain escalated, now a constant companion. She had to push its acknowledgement to the side and soldier-on for the good of the colony. For the first time in over ten years, she skipped her Saturday medical day visit. No time. Less than the day before for its relentless passage, exacerbated by the plethora of new names added to her list of suspects.

Gift called an emergency breakfast meeting with Raff, Charlie, Marco, and Scabs. Unable to conceive any reason for the need in her past life—a life she hadn't yet understood ended weeks ago—she pondered the weight of this new life of hers as a person who called emergency breakfast meetings.

The reveal of refugee patients added to their list melted the expressions from everyone's faces. The plan needed adjustment and Gift's only suggestion was talking to Matteo sooner than possible. It wouldn't be enough, but it was what she had. Speaking calmly, Raff summarized each of their group members' tasks for the day. Gift sipped her espresso but hadn't touched her brioche.

"If our plan to stop it has any chance of success, we need to catch the next activation immediately—why I'm leaving the medical stuff to Red and Aimée. Now this recent problem." When she paused, Raff seemed to be looking for suggestions.

"We need to divide." Not having anything close to a solution, Gift offered what she could. "I've gotta see Matteo now, get his input on these new names, everyone with access to the secret farm, and hopefully narrow this list down. I'll call Tom to go with me. Charlie, please show Marco where these refugees sleep. Marco, add surveillance there. We need to know if they're part of this and what they're planning. Raff, make sure those streams come only to us. We can't risk exposing these people, or Charlie and Sakura." Raff nodded acceptance as Gift downed her last sip of espresso, passed lukewarm and on to cool.

Once Charlie and Marco left, Gift turned to Scabs. "We need your contacts again—need more intel. Talk to your friends, associates, informants, anyone. I think... I believe something bigger is about to happen, more than sabotage and units going bad."

"How do you mean?"

"That stuff you said about an underground movement. Claudia's group is much larger than anything we thought, more than a couple of hardware grunts. I think, I'm afraid, there will be... human action with the next attack."

From under a troubled eyebrow, Raff asked, "Why'd you say that?"

"Remember what Boss got from Claudia? She smugly implied something big was coming, said you couldn't stop it. If this was a long play on her code, she'd be crapping her pants thinking you'd stop it. Right? Of all people, she knows how good you are. I'd think so, anyway. The next move is her endgame."

"I see that. *Ma*, human action? Gift... What do you think will happen?"

"What we've seen so far, even what we've imagined is coming? Could've been her and, like, maybe *two* hardware jockeys. But this massive underground movement... *Why*? I think we're going to see, and soon, there's gonna be human action, violence... I think, they're planning an uprising, like a sorta revolution."

"And you want me to stop that?" Scabs squawked.

"We need you to find what you can. You sympathized with Claudia. Maybe... you could work your way into this movement, gain their confidence and learn what they're about to do."

"I can try."

As he scurried off, Gift tried to read Raff's expression, harder to interpret than usual. Gift saw the uncertainty—not common on Raff even in the predicaments of late—in how the ends of her mouth sunk into her face, outlining her cheeks in greater definition.

"Gift... If you're right... we won't, we won't be able to stop it. We're counting on that one next incident, as serious as it may be. Ma, *one isolated* incident we could deal with. Then Hans and I would get what we need to track the rest of the code and kill it all off for good. If the next act is her finale... we... we can't stop it."

"I know." Gift felt calmer than she'd expected, the way she was trying to be strong but crumbling inside. "I think you and Hans Fuchs will be doing damage control... real soon."

"*Cara*, I think you may be right."

"But for now, there's one more piece I placed on the puzzle, and the picture it made was the Boardroom. Oh, that long brown table? Charlie told me it's made from this hardwood tree from Earth called African mahogany." She blinked hard twice to snap herself back. "Focus... Okay. So, someone on the Board must be in on this, working with Claudia—has to be. Pushing the medical agenda. I think Boss was actually looking for a conspirator on the Board. I mean, they keep secrets from each other. Claudia knows who it is, and I think it's tied into everything else."

"Their version of full transparency." Raff cut her words with the blade of sarcasm. "The Board didn't even know Frank was Boss and working with the protester group."

"Raff, you trust Hans Fuchs? I mean, *really* trust him?"

"*Certo*. And I was right, he *did* allow me to steal his code and use his biometrics... to help me, *us*, as I suspected. I trust him."

"And I trust you. If you trust him, that's enough for me. We're gonna need his help on a new project."

"*Infatti*. We need him to shift to trying to see who on the Board may be working with Claudia. Need to find out what they're planning and with whom." Gift nodded. "I'll get him on that first thing this morning. Boss placed him with me, so I guess he's his, well, boss. Hans can work with him."

Not having realized that she'd already exhausted its contents, Gift raised her espresso cup to her lips and sucked in the last drip of cold, black liquid. The bitterness pinched the tip of her tongue. Rubbing it between her lips didn't remove the unpleasantness but turned it into a sour aftertaste. She thought it a decent metaphor for the day she was about to have.

Particularly tight and enduring, Raff's parting hug felt to Gift more of a departure, an *addio* rather than an *arrivederci*. Her chest tightened into a knot around her heart, making every beat a thump she could feel slamming against bone and flesh in a desperate attempt to burst the chest cavity open and escape, to cling to Raff. Forcing a swallow, Gift held back the tears—proud of herself for it.

Left alone, Gift withdrew her handheld from her pocket to summon Matteo, only to find an alert of an incoming vidChat from Aimée. Disheveled never described her childhood friend's appearance. It fit now. She wore the same clothes as the day prior. Guilt swept over Gift for keeping her up on their late-night vidChat, but she just had to talk to her about the enormity of the revelation Sakura had laid upon her.

"Morning, Love. We're getting meaningful data already from the medical tap." A wide yawn distorted the last words.

"Shiny. That was super-fast. Whatcha got?"

"Red, she's great. Wrote an app to sort the data... Gift, Love? It's sort of... about... *you.*"

"What? *Me*? How do you mean?"

"It's all connected. Your... *special* condition? The E.CID? All of it's connected."

"I'm lost. Sakura just confirmed that I wasn't sick. Any symptoms I've had were because of..." She couldn't say it because words brought realism. "Not from E.CID."

"Yes, right. That's what we found too. Not sure, but this came from high up—Board of Directors high. Someone's been running a project for years, Love. *Years*. And what you told me last night? They've been looking to duplicate your condition, replicate it in others. Trying to manipulate other women genetically to get them to, well... to have the same possibility to... you know... that you have."

"Oh... *Oh*. And, you're saying *that's* connected to the rise in Early CID cases?"

"Causing it. These tests, the experiments they're doing on people? It's what's causing the early chemical imbalance. They've been messing with their DNA. Gift, they used yours, made a compound from your blood, from your genetic code."

"My blood? My blood's been making these people ill?"

"No, not exactly. But... yes, a chemical compound they made from it. Misguided narcissists. That's what's caused the illness, they've been experimenting on these women."

"Now what? What... happens to those poor people? Twenty-three of them."

"More now. Red's on it, she's working her way through the data. Perhaps the good news is, if they did this, maybe it can be reversed or something. We'll keep at it."

"Okay."

"Keep you posted, Love. Be safe."

Suspended in place as if shot by one of those stun guns on Banzai, Gift fought to keep her pause brief, necessary from the most recent of the overwhelming revelations, but brief. Much needed to be done with little to no time to do it. Gift called Matteo to meet her outside the storage building that was the secret entrance to the secret farm. When he confirmed, she requested Tom's presence as well, unsure why she felt the pull to have him with her. Sure of violence in the escalation, she'd want a guard—she'd want Tom nearby.

The hairs on the back of her neck stood to accentuate the dull pain hammering loudly in her brain, screaming of the next attack's imminence. Nothing to do now but hurry to execute their modified plan. It was a good plan. If they'd have the time to run it through its course, they could stop the sabotage. She didn't know they would, couldn't bring herself to fully believe it nor to be incredulous about it. Only knowing they will succeed would allow them to succeed. *We'll have enough time because we need to have enough time*, she tried to convince herself.

Straight as a board, Tom stood as a guard at attention, hands behind his back, waiting for Gift. She assumed the stance his default. His masculinity held a handsomeness Gift had seen prior, but only now allowed to the more frontal parts of her consciousness. But that couldn't be why she chose him as her personal attaché or called him to be by her side. If it was, she couldn't deal with that right now, so it wasn't. How his smile at seeing her melted her more than she cared to admit made for a strong counter-argument. The corner of her eye caught Matteo approaching.

"Hi Gift." Tom's cheeriness pleased her.

"Ciao Tom. Thanks for coming."

His 'My assignment' reply disappointed her, he should have been delighted to see her. Gift convinced herself he was, but the moment demanded Tom the Guard, so he wore that persona.

A grin on Matteo hid nothing. "Ciao Gift. Seeing a lot of you these days. I guess this is business, my supervisor excused me immediately when you called. No fire alerts in the farm today."

"Not *yet*. Any day... Look, I know about the refugees." Matteo's eyes told her he knew and felt sorry for keeping it from her. "It's fine. I need to know whatever I can about these people, the ones with access to this farm. Marco's in there with Charlie now." She pointed to the storage building but meant the ancillary farm behind it. "I've got names, files on all of them. You need to help me."

"Of course. How do you know about—"

"Not important. That they exist is, and that they have access to *this* farm." Gift stabbed her finger repeatedly as if impatiently pressing a button until it did what she wanted. "We need to narrow the search. Do you know these people?" Her voice carried undeniable desperation.

"I do," Matteo said apologetically. "Let me see the list." Handed her device with the list pulled up, he started sliding a finger over the glass and bookmarked the ones he thought might be at least sympathetic. "She speaks against administration... This one simpers when the attacks are mentioned... She excused herself before the last fire or she'd have been in the ancillary farm... This one's got a hardware background."

The helpfulness deflated Gift's hopes, with many more being retained on the list than removed. Her optimism refused to die and attached itself to

Marco's bugs in the refugees' makeshift quarters and to Hans Fuchs' efforts to find the mole on the Board. She thought of what—

Everything was gone.

51

Voices shouted, muffled and distant, yet enveloping her. Through a foggy haze Gift didn't know what she saw, and the ringing in her ears was deafening, its pitch and frequency sending shivers over her neck and shooting down her spine.

Off balanced, the space tilted. Was she on the MSS Banzai when something hit and inertial dampeners went offline? It hurt. The pain in her back pulled tight and hot—Gift hadn't known pain to feel hot. Then wet, as if her scalp sweat profusely. The hand she sent to wipe her forehead returned dripping a warm crimson fluid.

Am I bleeding? Why am I bleeding? Gift failed to surface an answer. The only responsive cognitive reaction, she called up confusion, raw and powerful. "What, what's happened?" she screamed, not knowing to whom.

Sudden tightness around her arms startled her, hands clutching her—powerful hands. A muffled voice of someone calling her name from across the dome, loud and firm, yet not there. *Gift. Gift.* She thought she heard her name. It had the sound of her name. Deep fear hid inside the voice, utter panic seeping through in the tone. Masculine, but shaky.

"Gift?" a voice behind her said. When she turned, its closeness surprised her, it had sounded so distant, from behind a door.

"Tom?" She looked upon him with disbelief, not fully understanding what she couldn't believe. "What's happening?"

"An explosion... *Huge*... In there."

Looking at his hand, she saw one finger extended. What did that mean? She should have known what that meant. Unsure, Gift allowed her eyes to follow it, to see where it would reach if it stretched longer and longer. The secret farm. "How'd we get in the farm?" Gift didn't remember the travel. *Am I dreaming? Yes, that must be it.* In dreams she never knew how she got somewhere, simply finding herself there. Or a memory? A horrible replay of past events, the farm in flames.

"We're not in the farm, Gift." Tom layered a calm in the words over the panic still present. Even in the race to stop the airlock, she'd never heard such dread in his voice.

Gift told him with a look, unspoken words written on her face, *I don't understand. How can we not be in the farm? I see it there, burning.* She thought she said it.

"The explosion."

A delirious Gift felt weirdly detached from herself and moving, but not moving. Being moved violently back and forth, shaken. "Gift, you're in shock. Look at me."

Confused eyes tried to see his face, looking for the reassurance it might bring. The outline of a face could have belonged to anyone. Her eyes clamped shut—they were being useless anyway. A deep breath. Another. "Okay, okay... I'm here. Tell me what's happened."

"The *explosion*. It took out half the storage building and blew a hole in the wall to the ancillary farm. Started a fire in there."

"I see," she heard someone say. An unfamiliar voice, or someone known to her. Soft, feminine—*her* voice.

"Open your eyes. *Gift.* Open your eyes. I need to see you're okay."

Reluctantly, her eyelids pulled apart like they had just remembered how to do that. "I think... I'm bleeding." The outline formed a face that bore a resemblance to Tom.

"Yes, you hit your head. The blast threw us."

Hazily, she searched over the surrounding rubble and debris, small stones, twisted metal she thought may have been a door a minute ago. Nothing came into sharp focus. Larger chunks of wall that would likely have crushed the life out of her had one hit. Farm tools were broken and warped into shrapnel strewn about. Total chaos.

"Matteo. Where is he?" Utter panic and anxious dread drowned her words when Gift's eyes couldn't find Matteo anywhere.

Pointing into the fire, Tom anxiously shouted from a closer yet distant echo, "He ran in there."

"*What*?" Gift yelled, partly of fear and partly because she couldn't hear well for the ringing in her ears. Turning swiftly, she determined—without doing the mental work of considering it—to run through the half building and the massive hole in the wall and into the fire. Tom's reflexes brought his hand to her arm with a grip strong enough to tell her to stop and forcibly compel her to obey. In a futile attempt to release herself she twisted and bent her torso. Her free hand slapped his face so hard she heard the pop of it like a second explosion and he grabbed her wrist to subdue her.

"You can't go in there. He's doing his job. You can't—"

"Let *me* go. Let *go* of me! I have *to*." Desperately she continued her futile attempts to squirm free.

Pulling Gift into himself, Tom wrapped his arms around her. "I've got you. He'll be fine. I've got you."

Mental images of Matteo engulfed in flames—his boiling skin peeling, charred and blistered—contrasted what Tom said, sending Gift's mind into an inferno as real as the flames in the farm. *He'll be fine? How could Tom know that?* How often attempts to comfort were nothing more than wishful thinking, fanciful outcomes that couldn't be predicted, not with any accuracy. Yet the words combined with feeling the brawny arms enveloping her brought her mind down and lessened her anxiety. Not calmed, not completely comforted, but she became hopeful when a split-second prior Matteo being burned alive had been a forgone conclusion.

He's doing his job. Time to do mine. What's mine?

Rumblings thundered and roiled in, echoing through the dome to scream at them. Another explosion. Fear solidified into the reality of what Gift had predicted as the endgame.

Plans abandoned them, leaving only time for action, but time ceased to exist, nothing existed but now. To find clarity, Gift thought of Boss, back when he was only Boss and not Mister what's-his-name on the Board of Directors. Objectives, a logical outline of the goals at hand, is what she needed.

Objective one: assessment. What's happened? What is happening, may happen? Objective two: the team, my friends. Are they okay? What are they doing? What do they need to do? Objective three: human action.

Knowing nothing about how that might manifest, her speculations could only be vague and that wasn't in the now. Perhaps time would return for that.

52

As a child, Gift couldn't see the value in history lessons with her tutors. Life was now. Yesterday and tomorrow didn't exist, only *today*. In the *now* of this moment, history became relevant. Some saw that history in a different light, which shaped their view of *today* in alternate realities from her own. It dawned on Gift not everyone saw life in the colony as she did, and more profoundly, maybe not everyone should.

Realization that many of her nameless neighbors—the ones she'd pass on her way to work, a few she worked with, others she would greet in her own corridor—had a radically different worldview and were willing to kill for it devastated her. New Europa provided a good life. That fact lost its certitude. Conspiracy theories ran over her invisible display, sorted by likelihood when weeks ago they would have been tossed in the bin.

What she found most off-putting as her world burned and crumbled around her was how the conspiracy at the center of thought was the medical one. Once beyond far-fetched, the seed of a thought germinated and grew into an idea. Those last few generations living under the harsh conditions of the ruined Earth and the manipulated gene-therapy to control GnRH-M made everyone sterile. Science replaced nature, taking upon itself the job of producing children. *What had humanity become?*

Gift was an anomaly. Special.

Undeniable logic brought one idea—not a thought, but something stronger—to the spotlight of her mind's stage. What fueled the radicals was born of a belief so strong its sheer power willed its adherents to acts that threatened the very existence of the colony. They had been lied to about the terraforming project. 'It's safe to go outside.' 'They're controlling us.' With conviction leaving no room for error or even misunderstanding, they risked the lives of everyone on their faith. Gift couldn't comprehend the hubris. Yet, it was happening.

It became her *now*.

The glass device trembled in her hand as she raised it. "VidChat Raffaella Di Gaetano." The near-instantaneous connection took much too long.

"Gift. Grazie a Dio, you're alright. It's the endgame, you were right. Is that blood on your head? Are you okay?"

"Fine. Nothing. What's the status? What are you seeing out there?"

Raff's pause pulled Gift into the security offered in her eyes, beckoning her to stay there until the nightmare ended. "Seven explosions so far. The farm where you are, one in the main farm, an air handler, no two. The other three seem random. I don't see..."

"I need locations. They *must* be strategic targets."

"Okay, found them. You should have them now."

"What about our teams? Our friends?"

"Mike and Tina were almost at the air handler when it exploded. A few more seconds, they'd be gone. They ran to the next on the list and disarmed an explosive device."

"Wait, device? These are like, *bombs*? Not bad parts or Claudia's code?"

"That's what we're seeing. So far, no trace of the code, nothing we can capture and use to stop the rest. *And*? A unit Mike and Tina had cleared yesterday exploded today. Whoever did this, they did it today."

"Charlie and Marco." Worry for them shuddered Gift's shoulders. "They went into the storage area in the secret farm. Any word?"

"No idea. I need to focus on this. Go find them."

"I will. But Raff? She's saving the one last deployment of her code. It'll be big. I think she'll try an all-out assault on our environmental support systems."

"I'm searching. All we can do from here."

"*Oh*. The fire in the secret farm, it looks like it's gone out." Gift saw it through the hollow that used to be a wall hiding behind what was a building—now blown to bits.

"Suppression system's working manually since we fixed it. I was able to turn it on. In the main farm dome as well. Took a little time, but they've gone out."

"Your on-off switch. *Some* good news."

"Hans needs me, he's been on the admin conspirators. Check-in soon."

When Raff's face faded, the screen crowded with notes and location data on the three random explosions Gift knew were not in any way random. Another clarity came: with the fire going out she could go find Matteo, and Charlie and Marco. Tom didn't stop her this time but ran with her—not two meters behind, that was Guard and Subject posture.

Chaos flooded the farm, overlaid with crews already in repair mode and moving so frantically they were stepping into each other. No. A closer look saw fighting. Green coveralls attacking more green coveralls, thrashing one another ruthlessly. Claudia's underground network actively engaged in trying to stop the repair work. E.CID refugees. Conclusion drawn, infallible in her mind, the imbalance in the patients left them susceptible to propaganda. They had become radicalized, mobilized, and stirred to action. But there were more, many more. Men and women on both sides. With no way to find Matteo, she shifted to Charlie and Marco.

"Tom, we need to get to the warehouse for this farm." Gift figured his height gave him a better view.

Tom pulled her as they ran past three men exchanging blows, two on one. The one burly fellow held his own but took repeated hits to the abdomen before one landed square on his jaw with a pop. With no way to know which side he was on, Gift couldn't know to be glad or feel sorry for the guy.

Cutting through a narrow path between crop beds, their run halted abruptly by a brawl between five cultivators. Two women and three men knew which side they were on despite being clad in the same green coveralls. The petite woman looked practiced in hand-to-hand fighting; landing fists punctuated with kicks on a man Gift assessed at nearly twice her body mass. After a fast jab to his mouth, he casually wiped the blood dripping from his lip like pasta sauce.

The nimble lady's skill lacked the power to overtake the man's bulk as his sheer strength and weight fell over her, pushing her to the ground. A knee resting on the small of her back kept her pinned for as long as the big guy wished. Without knowing which team she fought for, Gift felt sympathetic to the girl—a prejudice for nothing more than sharing the same set of chromosomes.

When a second woman with deep wrinkles leathering her face—*too old to be in this fight*—jumped on the back of a small but vigorous man, he tried to fling her off in a hurried spin. Shock followed by writhing pain doubled Gift over before she knew what happened. The girl's boot heel had planted itself firmly into Gift's kidney.

Giving her his attention, Tom hunched to steady Gift and took a fist to the face that painted an opaque red over his front teeth. The last of the coverall men must have figured him for the other side, whichever that was. Tom countered with a fist squared on the man's jaw, knocking him back, then landed a boot in his gut, pushing him off balance to dissolve into a field of tall viny crops at his back.

Grabbing Gift's wrist, Tom pulled her up and into a full run, forgetting how her legs lacked the length and muscle bulk to keep his pace. She screamed in agony at the pop from Tom yanking her arm from its socket. Without a word, he moved behind her, raised the arm and bent it at the elbow, bringing her forearm behind her head. Placing his other hand on the front of her shoulder, he pulled back in a quick jerk, setting the joint back into place. Gift bellowed one last roar of pain and fought the tears with moderate success.

Continuing at Gift's best run-speed, they reached the warehouse. The force of an explosion had blown the doors outward. An explosion in the storage facility where Charlie and Marco had been working. Her heart stopped for a moment, and she thought she felt the blood in her arteries pause their flow. When it beat again, the muscle could have shot out of her chest.

A chirp from her handheld signaled they had arrived at one of the three mystery explosion locations, identified as the Ancillary Farm Storage Warehouse. Without pause to evaluate her judgment, Gift ran in screaming the names Charlie and Marco on a loop, as loud as she could. Tom's voice joined hers. Hopefully Charlie and Marco weren't there. She had to believe it. Storage shelves that towered ten meters high now showed as mangled twisted remains, scrap metal at best, their contents reduced to pieces of worthless debris or disintegrated into dust.

The space, still engulfed in an aftermath of hazy smoke, carried the distasteful odor of burnt hair, familiar to her from the hot-knife-jerry-rigged hair straightener. The massive area was a good place to hide over a dozen refugees. Charlie had chosen well.

No dead bodies.

Figuring the shelter would be in a rear corner where makeshift housing would be less likely to be discovered, Gift led the way, stepping around or climbing over the piles of rubble, unhindered by tiny lacerations they lent to her hands. The pain in her shin was intense, but brief. She hadn't noticed whacking it as she traversed a mound of broken concrete and twisted steel. Tom followed as she pressed on.

Hopefulness elevated as they neared the rear, seeing the damage hadn't touched that far. Charlie and Marco weren't in the blast. When Marco finally replied to the echoed calls of his and Charlie's names, they followed the voice. He was on his knees when they found him, hovered over Charlie, who was sat on the ground, leaned back against a storage crate with his legs straight out in front of him. Marco had one hand over the other, pressed in on Charlie's gut.

It was everywhere. There was so much.

Gift told herself he'd be okay, but with that much blood on and around him it was a hard sell. Charlie's face dripped sweat. Marco's was as white as a frosted door panel and full of gloom, as if it had already happened. Having raced over, Gift fell to her knees beside Charlie, putting her palms to his cheeks. Tears had to wait; their time would come. Gift tried not to focus on the blood's increasing volume under Marco's hands, the gray coverall painted deep red.

He has to be okay. He'll be okay.

"Charlie? Charlie." Listlessly he moved his head toward her soft shout, tender yet urgent in tone. His eyes stayed closed, and he offered no reply. "Call for medics."

"I did. Right away," a frantic Marco blurted.

"What happened?" Dread cracked Gift's voice.

"We were back here when the... the... whatever that was, happened. We were safe, away from the blast. Then these three big guys came running in from... somewhere. Didn't say anything... just started attacking us. One of 'em knocked me to the floor. I tried to get up, took a swing, but he kicked me hard in the stomach, winded me." Marco sucked in a massive breath to stifle his hysterics. "Charlie threw a few punches but... one... one of them...

he... locked onto him. When he pulled away, there... there was um, um, *blood*... dripping from his hand and the sonic trowel. Charlie went down... right here. The guys opened a crate and grabbed a bunch of tools and ran off. I'm... I'm sorry. I'm so, so sorry."

A bucket of tears overtook Marco's face.

One hand cradling her dear friend's cheek, Gift moved the other over his head stroking his thinning hair gently as she leaned in closer. "Charlie... I'm here. It's me, Gift. I'm here. *Charlie*?"

When his eyes opened, they had no luster in them. The irises had dulled and gave no impression they could find focus until they met hers. "Gift?" Charlie breathed out a rattled exhale and faintly whispered, "Hey..."

"Hey," she squeaked in reply. Tears piled from her lower eyelids, clouding her vision. "I'm here. Help is coming... Medics." To keep the mucus from dripping from her nose, Gift sniffled hard and ran the back of her hand under her nostrils. "They're on their way. Hold on for me... *Please* Charlie. You gotta hold on... They're coming."

"Sakura." He pushed the word out, struggling to have the air for it. "Tell her why. Tell her... I love her... I'm sorry." He gargled the last word as blood followed it over his bottom lip onto his chin.

"You'll tell her yourself." She sniffled hard again but kept both hands on his cheeks, letting the warm mucus onto her upper lip. "You'll tell her yourself." Gift leaned over him to press her lips to his forehead.

"You'll tell her yourself."

His eyes found a brief spark of light. "Gift... Thank you."

Charlie Atkinson tilted his head to the side, exhaled, and closed his eyes.

53

Life. A delicate and wondrous thing, a precious gift to be treasured, guarded, and protected. It was meant to be full, enjoyed, productive, impactful, lived.

Never had Gift pondered death, not in a philosophical way. So young when her grandmother turned ninety-eight and departed. Being older when she had Gift's mom—Mom in her mid-forties when she had Gift—meant Nonna had precious few years with her darling Gift. Limited as the time was, if measured only by its impact on Gift, it was a life lived to the full, meaningful, valuable, and lasting. It extinguished as the normal passage she'd prepared Gift for it to be. '*Ninety-eight is what we get*,' she would say. '*Nothing to mourn, but to celebrate*.' That view of departure needed no further contemplation.

Drowned in unstoppable tears, Gift stayed hunched over Charlie until the medics arrived, one attempting to pull her away until Tom took the reins. He held her arms from behind as she watched the medics check Charlie for a pulse, lift his eyelids and let them close again. He looked at peace. She bawled out a deep, open howl that ended in a gasp for air as they lifted the lifeless body of one of her dearest friends onto a stretcher.

So far from ninety-eight, with so much more life he was supposed to live—with Sakura, now a widow, only she didn't know it yet. The picture of her reaction submerged Gift in a fresh round of sobs and thickened the lump so deep in her throat she felt it in her chest. As the gurney rolled away her stomach went with him, leaving a gaping hole in her gut. She turned into Tom's arms and buried her face in the vest, soaking it with tears and the mucus flowing from her nose. His arms held her tight, doing their best to offer consolation. Nothing could possibly be adequate.

Unaware of time's passage, her head raised instantly at the chirp of her handheld. She considered the mess of body fluids she left on Tom's vest and said, "Sorry." He shrugged. Pulling herself from his arms, Gift addressed her device. A vid message from Mike. "Play." Mike's face appeared, and for reasons deep inside a sentiment she was even then burying to continue the day, his face contained unspeakable beauty—precious and full of life.

"Gift," he began then paused when Tina's voice uttered indiscernible words. "We think the explosions are over. Grabbed anyone we could trust and raced through all the remaining critical systems and even the ones we checked yesterday. We pulled two more explosive devices before they blew. Tina had to rip apart this one water recycler to get into the primary wastewater flow regulator. She was great, you should have seen her. Smells like dirty underwear now, but what can you do?"

A hint of a smile moved Gift's lips when she saw Tina's fist enter the frame and land on Mike's upper arm, scrunching his face. "It's getting violent out here. If they find us working against the sabotage, they try to stop us. Tina knocked these two guys flat on their butts when they tried to block our way to finding the last explosives. So, if you got anything else for us let us know, otherwise we're going back and rechecking to be sure we haven't missed any."

The message ended, back to the screen listing the three unidentified explosion locations. Two. The one in the farm warehouse was a tactical placement to keep the farm workers from repairing the damage. Only it wasn't enough, and the radicals who started the fights to slow the work had killed Charlie. Those last two explosions; Gift knew they had to play a key role in the endgame, but she couldn't place the pieces she didn't have. She knew every bit of equipment in the colony, so why didn't she know these two?

An alert, incoming vidChat from Raff. Gift checked her reflection in the display that she didn't appear a complete slobbering mess. She would hold the news of Charlie for when this ended—keep everyone focused and grieve later. "Accept."

"Gift, anything on those last three explosions?"

"Not yet. Looking into it. How's things, the violence? Mike said they were attacked. Are we in full insurrection?"

"Seems so. Seeing reports of fighting all over, especially around the sites of the explosions. It's anarchy out there. And Gift, the Board has no idea how to deal with this. There must be hundreds of them. All the guards are out trying to control the situation, *ma*, I don't think they're doing so well."

"What about admin? Has Hans Fuchs found a name? Who on the Board is collaborating on this? There has to be, it's too well coordinated... Someone, someone let this happen." Tears tried to come, held to a gloss enough to distort Raff's face, nothing more. Gift wiped her nose away from the camera's view.

"He's close, cross-referencing data from Red and Aimée. He's confident he can find the conspirator or at least narrow the choices."

"Good. And the code, any malicious activity yet?"

"Niente. I won't see it until it starts. Oh, did you find Charlie and Mar—"

Gift hit *End* before her face fell apart over the vidChat. She stood there, in the place where Charlie died, with Marco and Tom. Her vomit came suddenly and ended quickly. Mindlessly, she wiped her mouth with the back of her hand. Where she needed to go and what she had to do still escaped her. What was it about those last two explosion locations? If two heads were better than one, and a second set of eyes could help see what she missed… She had three heads and two extra sets of eyes. A shared display with Marco and Tom invited them to speculate as to why those targets were selected.

Tom spotted a connection. "These are both related to that emergency atmo-seal we saw when the airlock in Dome One cycled the emergency e-vac."

"*Atmo-seal*? In English?"

"*Atmo* as in atmospheric seal. All those bulkheads you didn't know existed, that prevented loss of environment in one area from killing the whole colony."

"Oh mamma. Only reason to attack that system would be… *Open an airlock*." Tom said the last words with her. "That's the finale of her endgame. With all this chaos, guards on crowd control breaking up fights and human violence all over, all of us in reactive mode. It'll be another airlock, with no bulkheads. The *whole* colony."

"Six domes, four airlocks in each." Tom stared deeply at nothing. "If we go the wrong way? We may not make it to the right one. The time for the cycles isn't enough if we're on the opposite side of the colony."

"Let me see those locations again." Pulling Gift's hand brought the device closer to Marco's face.

"Those locations are *not at* airlocks, they're the master controllers."

"Yeah, Tom, but… control units have naming markers linked to the physical locations of whatever it is they're controlling. Gift, let me have it. I might be able to get a location, at least which dome we're looking at."

The young maintenance tech looked carefully at the location descriptors of each controller an explosion had targeted. One near the master had a physically separated redundancy which was still running. He urged Gift to have someone check it for explosives as the master could take them all off the data stream and they'd have no way to know which started cycling. Gift grabbed the handheld and dispatched Mike and Tina in haste. Device back in hand, Marco found the location of the last explosion by the controller for the emergency evacuation system for Domes Three and Four. It damaged the systems that controlled airlocks and hatches in Dome Four, so he said one of *its* airlocks must be the target. The three stood in Dome Four.

With the men closely following, Gift sprinted out of the ancillary farm's inner warehouse, relieved the fighting had stopped. The guards' presence in the farm was now a welcome sight. Making their way through the rubble that had been half of the outer storage building, they ran over to airlock AL-4A. Raff found no code starting up or running, and with no way to know if it had been embedded, they couldn't leave it to chance. As it hadn't activated, Gift easily disabled it and Raff pushed an overwrite of the control OS, preventing Claudia's software from being able to load.

"One and done."

They went in search of airlock AL-4B and came to AL-4D. Where other domes had additional airlocks, the massive farm and supply building claimed the space from the outer wall. Gift and Raff repeated their process to disable the airlock. Two done and safe. *It was too easy,* Gift thought, as anxious fear crawled its way up her spine. *Nothing about this has been easy thus far.*

"You think we should do the same on all the airlocks, just in case?" Tom's tone hinted at a suggestion more than a question, to which Marco gave a stern look.

"But no other controllers were targeted."

"Yeah, but maybe Raff and I do'em just to be safe. That last time… the airlock almost opened, an, and it had nothing to do with those controllers."

"Guys, the target was a *Dome Four airlock*," Marco said emphatically.

Tom disagreed with the youngster's input. "And we shut those down."

"There are four airlocks in *every* dome. Two in this one." Gift spoke aloud, but to herself. To coax an idea from it into conscious thought, she tapped her handheld on the side of her forehead. "Two in this—" Perhaps the head tapping helped. To fight the fire in the secret farm they were going to open an airlock. "It's in the secret farm... The blown storage building. *That's* why... The farm is, it's *open* to the dome. No seal. That airlock... When it opens, all the oxygen... Oh mamma. The whole colony." Gift and the guys headed once again through the half-building and into the ancillary farm. In a hurried jog to the rear of the rectangular space nearly three hundred meters deep, Gift called up Raff in a vidChat.

"Gift, good. We're making good progress. Hans has two strong possibilities. He's working fast, he's—"

"Yeah, fine. *Listen*... We believe... I—there's gonna be... another airlock breach attempt." The jog chopped Gift's words as Raff bounced in her hand. "Narrowed it down... to one in secret farm... headed there now... Go ahead... and start... watching it and... get ready to jump in ... on the controller."

"Okay. I see A L four A and D on either side of the farm, *ma*... there's no B or C."

"No," Marco said. "Look for... airlock A L dash A F."

"Found it. Okay, I'll be ready."

Aside from the black of burned stalks spotting two crop beds, the farm looked in good condition—including men and women laying on the ground in zip-tie restraints. The damage seemed a small-scale setback compared to the raging fires of the prior attack. While Gift panned the expansive space of the farm hoping to find Matteo, her mind raced back over her friends, her team, her loved ones. Was Mom safe? Did Aimée and Red have violence around them? Mike and Tina had been assaulted, but they were safe, she had to think that. They were all safe, except of course for Charlie. New tears had to wait as Gift needed unclouded vision.

"*No.* You've gotta be kidding me." Gift's spirits deflated when airlock AL-AF came into clear sight. "What the heck is this?"

Marco asked, "Problem? I mean, besides... *everything*."

The handheld seized Gift's full attention, so Tom answered. "This one's different from the others, not the same as the airlock Gift stopped."

"Oh, so not good."

"Read me the identification number." Gift didn't care who replied—she just needed the number.

"Gift, problem. That airlock? It's not the same." Gift said the last four words with Raff.

"Number?"

"A L A F, zero, zero, one, dash seven," one of the men said.

"You get that Raff? I need you to find the schematic for that one. And the maintenance plans. I can't find it on this stupid thing." In frustration she banged the side of the little device with her palm. It didn't help.

"On it... Found them. Sending to you."

"Have you been able to access the bulkhead controls? Can we close everything off... in case we can't—"

Stunned by the sound of it, Gift stopped. Everything went still as a photo. Another explosion? It could have been that, but it wasn't. A clang followed by a loud pop akin to the thud of the dome light circuits shutting down for Lights-Out had come from *in front* of her.

The airlock started its cycle, and she hadn't begun to understand how it differed from the others. An image of the older man's burnt face returned to plague her. He made the critical mistake of applying a protocol from one unit on a vastly different one, and it quite literally blew up in his face. Not about to make the same blunder, she couldn't stop this one the way she stopped the last.

A small display screen beside the inner hatch told Gift one key difference. This one would open much more quickly. No safety checks, no time taken to completely fill the outer chamber before opening it to flood the inner one. Designed with a two-fold purpose as the failsafe for the farm, they meant it to open with minimal delay.

She had less than two minutes to work.

The outer chamber had already filled with air, or gases, or whatever the state of the outer atmosphere was. The pop of the outer seal's release had been sudden, violent, and its ringing played on a repeated loop in Gift's ear like a hammer pounding her skull.

"Raff. Can you close the bulkheads? Protect everyone else?" Gift couldn't say, *Can we save anyone, or will I fail, letting fifty thousand perish in the whiff of a final stale breath?*

"No. Those systems and redundancies weren't hacked, tampered with, or corrupted. They're just... *gone*. They need to be rebuilt."

"I see." Astonished by her calmness, Gift channeled her inner Boss to organize the chaos riddling her mind to find clarity.

Ninety-three seconds.

"That panel. Take that panel off." Commanding either of the men she pointed to a small panel at eye level beside the hatch. When Marco started on it, Gift slammed the back of her hand into Tom's chest. "You, take that one off, I think it's the crawlspace." Starting at once, he had it off in two seconds. Glancing over the mess of wires and circuit boards in the smaller panel Marco had opened, Gift studied her device screen, poring over the maintenance notes.

"Marco, I need you to rip this board out then turn this one-quarter from here to here." As he reached his hand in to do as he'd been instructed, Gift's extended palm stopped him. "No. When I say."

Without further word or hesitation, she dropped on all fours and crawled into the tiny opening beside the sealed hatch. It offered no room greater than enough space for a slender human body to slither through. "Time?" she yelled behind her as she flipped onto her side and faced the access panel for the middle hatch. The sound of her voice came back in on her from all directions off the metal walls encasing her. '*Sixty-nine*,' the distant reply echoed. "Oh mamma."

With nothing to work with but Tom's all-in-one tool, she opened the panel—the seconds it demanded coming at too high a cost. The opening, centimeters from Gift's face, housed a nest of mangled wires like spaghetti folded into its sauce—if spaghetti were blue, yellow, red, and green, in a sauce of melting casings. Mindfully she studied the configuration, mentally labeling the wires by color.

"Got it." Gift forgot about the vidChat until she heard Raff's voice. "Found the code's start sequence in a data burst when it activated on that airlock. We can stop it now from starting anywhere else."

What anywhere else? Gift thought as she snipped a green wire. Somewhere deep in the back of her mind a thought she couldn't face gradually surfaced, an idea so powerful she'd not be able to endure it and do what needed to be done. *We're all about to die. New Europa is going to die.*

Pulling one wire, snipping another, she carried on with fierce determination. Removing a crystal circuit inducer proved a failed attempt to short out a redundancy to the unseen second hatch she could feel beside her through the metal wall of the crawlspace in which she would die. *I'm about to die.*

A calm rushed in on her and she hoped that in his last seconds, Charlie felt the same peace—something she saw on his face, the countenance of a man comfortable in the acceptance of the inevitable. She sensed it, understood it in a way she couldn't have when she saw it earlier on her dear friend. Sweat moistening her skin saturated the back of her coverall. *How could I* feel *the hatch?*

Deafened by the pop, the moment froze and extended. The ringing intensified over the first as the metal of her coffin buckled in, then out, resonating from the sound waves that pounded it. She knew. The second hatch seals had released, the inner chamber compromised. *I'm about to die.*

"Raff, I love you. Grazie, for everything. I love you."

With closed eyes Gift readied herself to fall asleep into the void. Her departure, everyone's departure, came far too early. No ninety-eight years for her or anyone else. The calming sensation reminded her of sinking into her bed cushion and falling asleep. *Will it be just like sleep?*

"Gift. Gift?" *Am I sleeping? Do you dream after departure?* Someone called her name, muffled. Tom and Marco's voices surrounded her in a re-verberated echo. "Are you okay?" It came just before the jolt. The sensation of being dragged by the ankles, her wet back skidding over the smooth metal surface heated her skin. Light from the dome slammed into her eyes, prompting her forearm to cover them. She was alive, breathing. The seal had broken on the middle and the inner hatches. How could she be breathing? How could she be alive?

Tom and Marco each took a hand and helped hoist Gift to her feet. Faint and distant, Raff's voice reached her ears desperate for a reply. The echoing call emanated from the handheld dropped in the crawlspace when they yanked Gift out. "Tell her I'm alright."

Tom bent before the open shaft. "She's okay. We all are. Not sure how."

The high pitch of the hissing irritated the incessant ringing in Gift's ears. The seal of the inner hatch venting atmosphere. Gift held her hand over the edge of the hatch door and followed it along the side as it rounded the lower curve of its oval shape. "Not *venting*?" She felt it wafting against her palm as the steady push from an infuser. Air *entering* the dome rather than rushing out. Leaning into it, Gift let it meet her face, lifting and fluttering her hair the way the dry cycle did in the shower booth. A delicate floral scent stimulated her nose and filled her lungs.

How could air from outside carry such an alluring fragrance? And how could she be breathing it? Questions rambled over her conscious thought while her chin raised to allow every bit of skin on her face and neck to taste the rush of fresh air. Deep breaths puffed her chest. It was delightful. She wondered for a moment about the dream of departure, if Nonna had felt it. Charlie. Swiftly Gift returned to herself and settled into the moment's reality. She was alive.

"We... we were *right*?" Marco expressed ecstatic confusion. "The terraforming isn't way behind schedule, as we've been told. The air, out there... It's good."

Tom stood speechless. He reached for Gift as her hand pulled away to take hold of the circular latch-release on the inner airlock hatch. Bit by bit, it turned. Crackling rust and puffs of orange dust confirmed the hatch's age and lack of use in nearly two hundred years.

The thud of the release brought Gift stiff, motionless for a moment, but only that. A rush of adrenaline from euphoric anticipation empowered her to pull on the hatch door. Heavy and stiff, it moved with the shrill of metal rubbing over metal that hadn't been lubricated in decades, tightening the sternocleidomastoid muscle from Gift's ears to her collarbone. Without a hint of hesitation, she stepped through into the inner chamber.

Still breathing. Still alive.

Three deliberate steps brought her to confront the middle hatch leading to the outer chamber. Slowly she turned the lever and released the latch on the second portal, pulled, and stepped through.

Still breathing. Still alive.

The outer hatch. Its seals had popped what felt like hours prior and as if it had only just happened. The wheel rotated tentatively, Gift's fingers tingling with excitement. Anticipation manifested in deep breaths drawn, followed by slow exhalation. Then the thud of the lock release came, rattling her bones deep into the marrow. All she had to do was pull, and she would be outside the colony for the first time.

Outside the colony.

The weight of that idea overwhelmed her. Powerful and frightful, it drowned Gift in joyous wonder. A glance found Tom's usually blank face full of wondrous curiosity. Marco's had the same look of majestic awe from their shared gaze into the night sky. The fluttering inside her bubbled and tingled like epinephrine on full release.

She pulled.

54 | Colony's Dawn

A crayon. That's what sparked Gift's very first memory of Aimée. Her own forced cry overshadowed by her friend's rolling laughter. Each had been drawing a picture—what they thought of as art at the time—of an outdoor vista. Were they replicating scenes of an Earth long in the past, never to be viewed? Or was it speculative hopefulness of a future Mars landscape, one they might even see before their departures? One of many details lost to the memory, yet that one broken crayon became part of an indelible image burned in her mind.

Blue.

Both girls wanted a blue crayon, needed blue, because that's what color the sky should be. Every sky they'd ever seen in an old photo or in vids from Earth—be it history or entertainment—the sky was always blue. Pre-terraform images of a lilac shade of Mars' unseen skyscape didn't have the same rightness. It wasn't blue. It wasn't sky.

The depth of it captivated her eyes, her mind, her total consciousness. Gift couldn't comprehend it, the vastness of it. The same as the darkness speckled with tiny glimmers of distant stars and nothing like it in ways. No dots of light, nothing to fracture the endless blue. Hues, variations, shades, diffused into each other. Lowering her gaze, the blue seemed to soften and get lighter where it neared the land of the distant horizon, yet she knew it extended beyond that and into infinity.

Deeper, darker blue infused the panorama as she followed it upward over her head, farther as she folded her neck back. Gift loosened her grip on equilibrium for a moment, and a sour taste hit the back of her throat. She suppressed a reflex to vomit, allowing nothing to spoil the moment she had completely surrendered to ecstasy. *How can it be this blue?* she thought. "How could it be so... endless?" she said. Gradually leveling her head, her eyes soaked in the landscape's vista. Deep greens with patches of brown flowed away from her, rising and sinking and rising again in gentle waves.

Gift had learned the word mountain to describe a mass of rock reaching skyward, seen pictures, of course. The one filling her eyes towered many kilometers into the blue. It seemed massive. She saw it in sharp clarity, yet the vast distance diffused its detail. The top of it shined white, the stark white of Pronto Soccorso, only purer, a purity Gift could *feel*. Below the white caps it took on shades of gray mixed with deeper blue—darker, but not quite black. Shadows of dark and speckles of light danced across it, revealing structure and texture as parts shone, leaving others hiding their detail. A second mountain reached down, no, the first one reflected from the ground as if it were a mirror. Then the mirror rippled. The water's magnificence pulled at her.

To her right, Gift found a field covered in those unusual flowers—the ones in Aimée's office painting—stretching out to an open field. Their orange-brown circles had brilliant yellow corollas reaching out with heads that looked too big and heavy for their stalks, yet they stood upright. Gift noticed them looking at something, stretching toward it, as they had in the picture. Up and to the left they reached, practically glowing in the light. Natural sunlight, not the fabrication she had only known. Turning toward the light source caused Gift's eyes to squint shut at once—the brightness too intense.

The remembrance of the sparks of light that damaged her vision told her not to keep looking, to protect her retinas. Especially with so much to see, so much for her corneas to capture and transmit through the ocular nerves to the brain. New and spectacular memories in the making. The tears were different, full of ecstasy and awe at the spectacle before her. The majesty of it all flooded every pore, tingling every millimeter of skin, and tiny hairs too subtle to be seen or considered stood on end. She wished the moment to freeze her in time.

Tom held her hand in a gentle squeeze. Gift traced a tear rolling down his cheek. Her other hand came away to find Marco's hand. He clutched hers in his. She glanced to notice the tears welled up in his eyes, deeper too, for him, than the night sky they shared in an intoxicated dreamlike moment.

They stood on the planet's surface and the colony, meters from their backs, ceased to exist. Gift, Tom, and Marco shared this moment with everything else the universe laid before them. The wonder and the unknown, the joy and the fear. All the possibilities, as endless as the blue above their heads.

Normal ceased to exist as a concept or a feeling.

The idea of her past life faded, as ideas did. A life that ended in that crawlspace as she had prepared herself to accept it would. Is that why it felt so calm, so peaceful? Instead of an ending, a transition to something wonderful. Gift hoped beyond all hope that for Charlie, it was similar. Not an end for him, but another type of transition, something beyond the closing of his eyes that last time. The power of that idea brought with it profound comfort, and new tears she didn't mind shedding.

***

Childish astonishment filled them. Time enough for the new world before them but not anywhere near enough time. Not today, maybe not in their lifetimes. Gift and Raff were drawn to the sparkle of the water. So much water. Dreams taken form, the lakeside left them dumbstruck, holding hands in awe-inspired silence, a silence that honored their fallen friend.

Aimée announced her approach with an ear-piercing whistle, hailing the magnificent panorama. Knowing Gift would want to share the moment with her, Raff had called her to join them. Her tears welled up to fill her eyes. Gift couldn't recall ever seeing her best friend's eyes in such a state.

Contemplative, Gift stood with one hand in Raff's, the other held tight by Aimée, with shoes off and feet in the abundant water. Gift's thoughts focused on her tininess in the universe, of life, its meaning and purpose. A sudden rush of belonging swept over her, tingling as it caressed her skin and penetrated deep into her organs and bones. She had a place in the vastness. For that moment, she was the entire universe. Shivers came as much from the emotion of such revelations as the icy-cold water in which they stood.

***

Miss Heller walked through the hatch and called to Tom. She appeared less awestricken by the sight. Gift assumed some Board members knew of breathable atmosphere and must have been outside before this day. After ordering Tom to heard everyone else inside, Miss Heller stood before Raff and Gift, took Raff's hand, and shook it for what felt like hours. "You have done an outstanding job, both of you."

"Not really, not today," Raff replied.

"We sorta failed, hard. The airlock opened. If the lies, I mean... if it hadn't been true, the whole colony...." Gift ended it there, unable to consider the lives of every person in the colony ending because she failed.

Claudia had been right, that's what really burned. Arrogantly, she said Raff couldn't stop her. Violence and body count aside, the woman's plan was masterful, and it worked. Raff's former bench-mate had exposed the lies and ended the history of keeping secrets. Her willingness to pay such a high price was born of her own hubris and ambition. Had she imagined vindication? So distorted had her thinking become, it wouldn't have surprised Gift if Claudia expected a seat on the Board for her outstanding work. Then she remembered, there was a seat on the Board involved in this, someone who helped to coordinate it—maybe the grand orchestrator of the entire uprising.

"Ma'am," Raff said to Miss Heller. "We have sound reason to believe a member of the Board had been collaborating with Claudia on this plot. No way she did this alone, she needed help high up. Hans was working on that, and he has leads."

"Yes, Miss Di Gaetano, we have much to discuss. You and Miss Ojo go home, have a free bonus shower, and come to the Board room. You must have many questions, and I am prepared to answer them."

55 | Day One

When the lift doors separated, they revealed the long Boardroom table covered with food. Boss, Fred, and Jean stood with Miss Heller, looking ready to devour everything on the table. Edibles Gift had never seen sent aromas wafting from a feast so tantalizing her mouth flooded with saliva. Well into the afternoon, she was starved. Such an assortment of fresh fruits and vegetables. Something Raff kept calling protein, Fred called wild boar. It had a texture unlike any protein Gift had ever eaten. Its mouthfeel was smooth and soft, yet more fibrous than any protein she knew. Gift practically drank down spoonfuls of the golden thick liquid called honey. Mateo had told her bees made it. The mental construct of how bees made anything boggled her imagination.

Everyone departed but the two of them and Miss Heller. Pulling a drop of honey from her white blouse, Gift licked it off her fingertip. Miss Heller directed them to the soft, cushioned chairs that were little sofas in the lobby outside of the Boardroom. Miss Heller sat facing the two of them.

"We have much to discuss. Let me first say how sorry I am for your loss. Mister Atkinson was a good man, a friend and colleague. A trusted and valuable member of this Board of Directors."

"Thank you," Gift and Raff said in unison.

"Now for the formality. His passing leaves a place on the Board we need to fill. The Board itself will be radically different now, of course. So much will need to be done in the wake of the day's events. New regulations and amended charters. The future of New Europa will require much planning and administration."

"Everything's changed." As it slipped off her tongue, Gift realized what a profound understatement she had made.

"Miss Ojo. We would very much like you to take the vacant seat on the Board."

The color left Gift's face and Raff gave her some water. "*Me?*" Gift said, after gulping the water made her cough.

Miss Heller gave her a moment. "Yes, Miss Ojo. Your loyalty to the *for the good of the colony* ideology, and your experience with the events leading up to this new status, this new... life, into which we are about to embark. You are the perfect choice. Plus, you handled yourself remarkably well under pressure, and you have shown excellent problem-solving skills. Most of all, Miss Ojo, you care about people and our colony. That has always been the utmost priority for the selection of Board members. Will you join us?"

Raff cast a wide, warm smile at Gift.

"No. I mean, I appreciate your kind words. But I don't think... That's not me. I'm no leader. I just do my job... solve problems and do my tasks."

"Gift, *Cara*. You would be perfect. I completely agree with what Miss Heller just said. You should do it, for the good of the colony. *Dai*, do it."

"Please Gift, join us." A noted change, Heller used a first name.

"Raff... It should be Raff. She's a leader, a mentor. And she keeps much calmer under pressure than me. She led our team, not me. It should be Raff."

Heller smiled at Gift, then turned to Raff. "About that, Raffaella. I have Mister Fuchs' data, what he shared with you. It's why we are meeting alone. We have taken Mister Müller into custody. He was in direct collaboration with Miss Giuntoni. In fact, the evidence strongly suggests it was he who recruited her and started this whole thing."

"*Him?*" Gift's eyes widened. "James Müller's been my one-way friend for over ten years."

"*One-way* friend." Miss Heller smiled and breathed out what nearly became a laugh. "That is where it all began for him."

"Where it all began? How do you mean?" When Raff asked, Gift realized she hadn't the time to tell her about her *condition.*

"Gift's unique classification of EXP One forty-two. We know you understand what that means now, right Gift?"

"Yeah." Gift glanced at Raff, saw the confusion wrinkling her brow.

"He found out about your birth and classification from your adolescent medical history and arranged to be your examiner for your weekly psychophysical. He soon began collaborating with the same geneticists who started your... project. Then he arranged to have Miss Giuntoni assigned to Raffaella's bench. We believe he was waiting for you to mature, to confirm that, nearing G.M., you were able to conceive and bear children as they had hoped."

"I see."

As if the weight of her chin became insurmountable for her jaw muscles to raise, Raff's mouth hung wide open. She set a hand on Gift's knee. Miss Heller leaned forward and took Gift's hand. "For years, he had been collaborating with key persons in medical and nutritional sciences in hopes of replicating the effect in others. They even tried to use your DNA to create treatments and gave these to other young women, without success."

"Wait, this is a lot." Raff turned to Gift. "*Cara,* I... I don't know what to say." Looking back at Miss Heller she said, "So the sharp rise in E.CID cases, over thirty young women. Was that the result of his work?"

"Exactly."

"What about them now? All those poor young women in comas?" Gift asked.

"Now that we know the cause, Miss Tanaka will lead a medical team to find an effective treatment. She's done great work thus far while being in the dark as to the cause. Of course, we'll give her time to grieve Charlie. We're quite confident she'll find a way to help these poor women."

"That's wonderful. I'm sure Sakura will. Thank you."

"How does this connect to Claudia and the sabotage? To opening an airlock?" The confusion in the words matched Raff's squinted gaze.

"We believe Mister Müller concluded the current level of environmental sustainability, along with humanity, *you*, Gift, reverting to what we once were biologically, made this the perfect time to reunite us with the Earth outside. In fact, their success in you, Gift, accelerated his—"

"Wait," Raff interrupted. "What, *what* did you say?"

"Their success in Gift accelerated—"

"No. Did you say... did you say the *Earth* outside?"

Gift had no idea what to make of this shift in the conversation.

Heller sat back and crossed her legs. "You ladies didn't think we had the technology to terraform Mars into what you found outside, did you?" She paused to blank stares from Gift and Raff. "I'd have thought it became obvious once you stood out there. We never left Earth."

"*Huh*?" Gift tried to piece this together. "You're saying New Europa isn't on *Mars*. None of the colonies? We've been on *Earth* this whole time?"

"We have. Only the United Republic of Mars was built on Mars."

"Why the ruse?" Raff asked what Gift couldn't understand.

"All those years ago, some spoke out against the aggressive Mars migration project. It became evident early in the planning stages that it was not feasible to build five massive colonies and transport hundreds of thousands of people to another planet. The ruse, the lie about being on Mars, ensured that until the environment was ready for us, and we for it, no one would dare open an airlock, try to go outside, or disrupt the peaceful life of our colony."

Gift took it in, crowding her mental display with an overload of data. "So, the other colonies, they think they're on Mars too?"

"As far as we know." Heller uncrossed her legs and leaned forward. "Like us, they were to have a few Board members and environmental scientists hand the truth down from generation to generation."

"I see."

"The Earth has been healing itself, proving the Founders right. Staying here until the environment recovered *was* better than building off-world and waiting hundreds of years for terraforming, if it would even work. Now Earth is getting back to the job of supporting the circle of life upon it."

"Lies. Since the colony began." Raff seemed to catch up faster than Gift. "The conspiracy theorists had gotten most of it wrong, *ma*, they had a solid foundation. There *were* lies, full of shocking deceit about the fabric of what we all thought to be our unshakable reality, like which planet we were on."

Miss Heller nodded. "But conspiracies and corruption were not found in colonial leadership. We've been inept at times, perhaps. Covering up secrets, surely. But no malice was in it, I assure you. We did what was best, for the good of the colony. The Founders' legacy has lived on for over a century and a half after the last of them drew their final breaths."

Tiring of the conspiracy talk, Gift asked, "So, we can live outside now?"

"Not yet, no. You may have noticed some of those outside today got headaches. A few of the ancillary farm workers who stepped out before we guarded the airlock became sick, some vomited."

"I felt fine. I never wanted to come back inside."

"I know, Gift. It affects everyone differently. But no one can live out there, not yet. Humanity has changed, altered equally by what our irresponsible recklessness did to the Earth for its last generations, and by life in a sealed microenvironment for two centuries. Our nutrition programs, chemical supplements, artificial light, and recycled air. It makes you, Gift, a miracle. The first known in generations that can conceive and bear a child as humans had been doing for all time, since *before.*"

"This is a lot." Raff stood, paced in a circle, and stopped beside Gift's seat. "And now you want Gift on the Board to help regulate all… *this*? Dealing with the outside? So, you finally plan to tell everyone the truth?"

"Yes. No more secrets."

Looking down over Gift, Raff said, "Then you should take Charlie's place. There's no one I trust more to make sense of this and manage it properly."

"You. You take it. You're a leader, not me."

"I think you both missed an important implication. With Mister Müller gone, we have two places to fill on the Board. We wish to welcome both of you to the New Europa Board of Directors.

With much prodding from Raff, Gift reluctantly accepted. After biometrically signing a digital mountain of agreements and contracts, Heller brought the last one on centuries-old synthetic parchment. Once Gift and Raff signed it with an ink pen, Heller placed the official seal over the Foundation document, and they were certified Board members.

"Now that that is done, we have one more… *secret.* We can be sure it's about to become known." Heller handed a tablet to Raff with a transcribed message. Gift read over her shoulder.

> - Reply: No guard support needed. Situation managed.
>
> - Received: Copy. Supply transport loaded, eta 4.5 hours.
>
> - Reply: Much appreciated Russian Federation. New Europa out.

Gift consider this the first issue she and Raff would address on the Board, part of the recovery from a horrible chapter in their colony's history. She wondered what new chapters were to come.

Life as she knew it had ended for Gift in that metal coffin. New Europa now stood on the precipice of new possibilities for her and all residents. Hope filled Gift contemplating the new life of hers that emerged from that crawlspace, reaffirming a truth she had almost lost. They had a good life in New Europa.

And with the dawn of a new day, that life had changed.

| Epilogue |

Sakura's father delivered a touching memorial speech before those assembled around a small mound of packed fresh dirt. The spot chosen was just twenty or so meters from the airlock labeled AL-1A, behind Citadome One. The slightly elevated plot of land sat atop a hill in a superbly peaceful setting of tall green grass waving gently in the breeze beside a stately tree, tall and evergreen—symbolic of the eternal, of endurance, of life. Life continued even if altered in form or definition. Not the least of all potential definitions being how a life continued in its legacy, its memory, in the hearts of those it had touched in its years drawing breath as a fleshly organism in its own little place in the universe.

Now Charlie had his place to rest. A view over the rolling hills and distant mountain, capable of taking the breath away from those still drawing them who'd come to pay respects to their dearly departed.

Gift expected it to be harder—not that it wasn't hard enough—saying their goodbyes. She had no words for Charlie's parents, only a warm, tearful embrace. Being in such a setting, something unimaginable just days prior, offered surprising comfort and reassurance. It hosted a commemorative celebration of a beautiful life more than the mourning of one passing. Sakura acted strong and brave, sharing her tears equally for Charlie, for her own heartache, and for the grief of everyone else.

It was nothing akin to the remembrance of a life that made a departure ceremony—the departed and the ones closest to them fully prepared for it, expecting it, able to celebrate the full and well lived ninety-eight years every colony resident got to live. Thirty-two fell so short of that expectation that, for the first time, Gift saw departure age as more of a goal than the forgone conclusion it had been. Yet the richness of Charlie's life, brief as it was, it was. So, they commemorated it, honored it, and remembered him. It was as touching and uplifting as it was miserable and sorrowful.

Turning one last time as she walked away, Gift said, "Goodbye, dear Charlie. I love you."

Thank You!

I'm truly grateful you read my story and hope you enjoyed the journey with Gift and her friends. As their world expands, so do their adventures and challenges in Colony's Fall and Colony's End.

As an indie author, it means a great deal to me to have people find and enjoy my work. Beyond the joy of the creative process for myself, this is why I write, to share my stories. If you enjoyed Colony's Dawn, please tell a friend.

Stories by indie writers like me don't always find the audience that will enjoy them. It means so much to us, to me, to have reviews so others can find this exciting series. Please consider taking just a couple of minutes to review this book.

Follow my writing and engage with me in the Glass Panorama. As a 'thank you' for subscribing you will receive a free copy of 'All Lies', a New Europa short story exploring the beginning of Boss' misfit group of conspiracy theorists.

go.glassauthor.com/dawn

OTHER BOOKS IN THE NEW EUROPA SERIES

All Lies is a New Europa novella best read after *Colony's Dawn*. It tells the origin of the group Raffaela discovered and the role they came to play in the overarching conspiracy that rocked the foundations of Gift's happy colony. Your gift for joining my newsletter at go.glassauthor.com/dawn.

Book Two. In *Colony's Fall,* our characters' world expands into something they never could have imagined. Along with the marvels and wonder come new and horrific tests of their humanity, threatening their existence.

Book Three. In *Colony's End,* we follow Gift on her journey to grow into her own person to face all-out war. Will she have what it takes to stand against her people and find her choice, a solution to stop the endless cycle of humanity fighting and killing each other?

About the Author

Reading is a passion; writing is an obsession.

And *IT consulting is a job*. While N Joseph Glass enjoys the challenges of managing a virtual infrastructure, backups, email systems, and cloud environments, crafting stories is his cherished second job.

Born and raised in Brooklyn, NY, Glass lives and writes in Milan, Italy. A fan of science fiction and other genres, he loves to expound stories that are driven by relatable characters on meaningful journeys.

Drawing from personal experiences enriches the writing process and leaves readers feeling like they know the characters they spend time with in a story. That human connection between his characters, readers, and himself, fuels his drive as an author.

Optimistic views of the future through art always interest him, as Glass believes ours will be bright.

www.ingramcontent.com/pod-product-compliance
Lightning Source LLC
Chambersburg PA
CBHW062113290726
48975CB00001B/212